RANDOM
HOUSE

LARGE
PRINT

DJINN PATROL
ON THE PURPLE LINE

DJINN PATROL
ON THE PURPLE
LINE

a novel

DEEPA ANAPPARA

RANDOM HOUSE
LARGE PRINT

Copyright © 2020 by Deepa Anappara

All rights reserved.
Published in the United States of America by Random House Large Print, in association with Random House, an imprint and division of Penguin Random House LLC, New York.

Originally published in the United Kingdom by Chatto & Windus, an imprint of Penguin Random House UK, London, and simultaneously in Canada by McClelland & Stewart, a division of Penguin Random House Canada Limited, Toronto.

Cover design: Greg Mollica
Cover illustration: Mark Stutzman

The Library of Congress has established a Cataloging-in-Publication record for this title.

ISBN: 978-0-593-20706-2

www.penguinrandomhouse.com/large-print-format-books

FIRST LARGE PRINT EDITION

Printed in the United States of America

10 9 8 7 6 5 4 3 2 1

This Large Print edition published in accord with the standards of the N.A.V.H.

For
Divya Anappara
and
Param

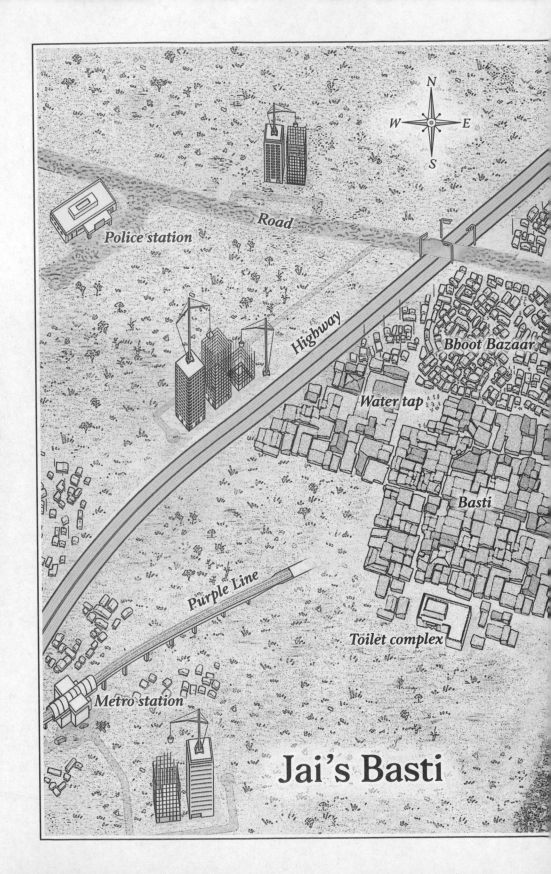

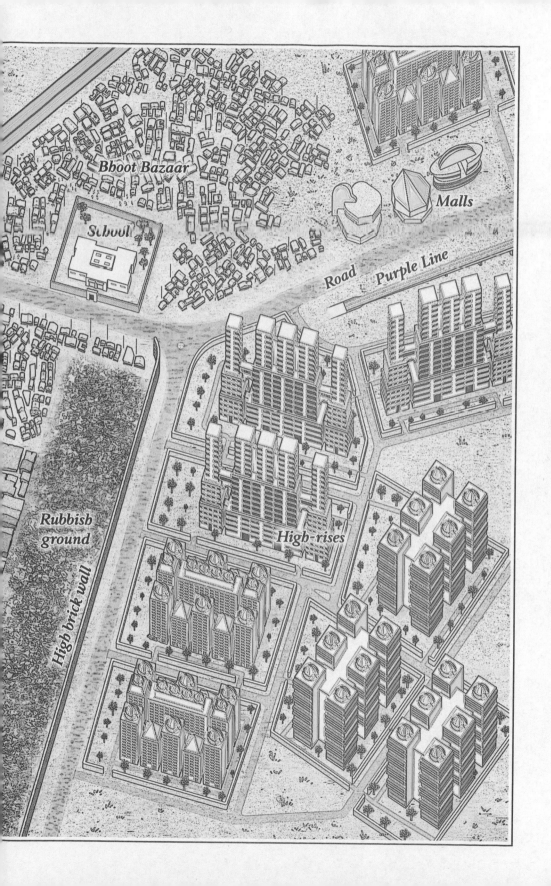

ONE

THIS STORY
WILL SAVE YOUR LIFE

When Mental was alive, he was a boss-man with eighteen or twenty children working for him, and he almost never raised his hand against any of them. Every week he gave them 5Stars to split between themselves, or packs of Gems, and he made them invisible to the police and the evangelist-types who wanted to salvage them from the streets, and the men who watched them with hungry eyes as the children hurtled down railway tracks, gathering up plastic water bottles before a train could ram into them.

Mental didn't mind if his rag-picker boys gave him five Bisleri bottles instead of fifty, or if he caught them outside the cinema when they should have been working, wearing their best clothes and standing in a queue for a First Day First Show ticket they couldn't even afford. But he turned on them the days they showed up with their noses red, their words mixing together like blood and water, their eyes swollen like full moons from sniffing whitener. Then Mental stubbed out his Gold Flake Kings on their wrists or shoulders, and he called it a waste of a good cigarette.

The pungent fumes of burnt flesh trailed his boys, and washed away the sweet, short thrills of Dendrite or Eraz-ex. He knocked some major sense into their heads, Mental did.

We never met him because he lived in this neighborhood long before our time. But the people who knew him, like the barber who has been shaving stubbly cheeks for decades, and the madman who smears ash across his chest and calls himself a saint, still talk about him. They say Mental's boys never picked fights about who got to board a running train first, or who could claim a stuffed toy or a bump-and-go racing car wedged into the gap behind a seat-berth. Mental taught his boys to be different. That's why, of all the children who worked at all the railway stations across the country, they lived the longest.

But Mental himself died one day. His boys knew he hadn't planned on it. He was young and healthy and had promised to hire a tempo and drive them to the Taj before the monsoon came to the city. They cried over him for days. Weeds flowered in the bald ground watered by their tears.

Then the boys had to work for men who were nothing like Mental. There were no chocolate bars or movies in their new lives, only hands scorched by railway lines gleaming like gold in the summer sun, the temperature forty-five degrees by eleven in the morning. In winter, it bellyflopped to one or two degrees and sometimes, when the mist was white and grainy like dust, the knife-edge of the icy tracks skinned their blistered fingers.

Every day after scavenging, the boys cleaned their faces with the water dribbling from a leaky pipe at the station and sent a collective prayer up to Mental to rescue them before a train's wheels ground their arms and legs to bone-dust, or a belt whistled through the air to snap their hunched spines into two and they never walked again.

In the months that followed Mental's death, two boys died chasing after trains. Kites circled their splintered corpses and flies kissed their blue-black lips. The men who employed them thought it a waste of money to have their bodies picked up and cremated. The trains didn't stop and the engines screamed late into the night.

One evening soon after the deaths, three of Mental's boys crossed the road that separated the railway station from the hotchpotch of shops and hotels whose terraces were packed with red-and-white mobile-phone towers and black Sintex tanks. Neon signs flashed PURE VEG FOODS and STATION VIEW and INCREDIBLE !NDIA and FAMILY COMFORT. The boys were visiting a place not far from here: a brick wall with iron railings on which Mental had dried his clothes, and below which he had slept at night with everything he owned tied up in a sack that he hugged tight as if it were his wife.

In the yellow-pink light of the letters that formed HOTEL ROYAL PINK, they saw the small clay gods that Mental had arranged in a niche in the wall, Lord Ganesh with his trunk curled up in his chest and Lord Hanuman lifting a mountain with one hand and Lord Krishna playing the flute, sun-dried marigolds pressed down with stones at their feet.

The boys knocked their foreheads against the wall and asked Mental why he had to die. One of them whispered Mental's real name into the wind, which was a secret known only to them, and a shadow stirred in the lane. The boys thought it was a cat or a flying fox, though there was a charge in the air, the metallic taste of electricity on their tongues, the flicker of a rainbow-colored bolt of light, gone so soon they could have only imagined it. They were worn out from hunting bottles and light-headed from hunger. But the next day, rooting through the trash on the floor of a train, each one of the three boys found a fifty-rupee note under different seat-berths.

They knew the money was a gift from Mental's ghost because the air around them rippled with the warm breath he exhaled, smelling of Gold Flake Kings. He had come to them because they had called him by his real name.

The boys started leaving cigarettes for Mental at his wall, and tinfoil bowls of spiced chickpeas tangy with lime juice and garnished with coriander leaves and slivers of red onions. They cracked rude jokes about the smells and sounds that Mental had produced the afternoon he ate a quarter-kilo of chickpeas in one sitting. His ghost didn't care for their wisecracks and afterward they found cigarette holes in their shirts.

Mental's boys are scattered across the city now, and we hear some of them are grown up and married with children of their own. But even today, a famished boy who falls asleep with Mental's true name on his cracked lips will wake up to find a white tourist buying him ice cream or a grandmother-type lady pressing a paratha into his hands. It's not much, but Mental wasn't a rich man, so he didn't become a rich ghost.

The funny thing about Mental is that his boys were the ones who gave him that name. When they first met him, they saw he was tough in many ways but his eyes turned soft if they showed him a missing toe or a scar thrashing like a dying fish on the back of their thighs where they had been whipped with red-hot iron chains. They decided that only a man who was **Mental** could be half-good in this crooked world. But first they called him **Brother** and the youngest boys called him **Uncle** and much later they started to say **Mental, look at how many bottles I found today,** and he didn't mind because he knew why they had settled on that name.

Months after he became Mental, on a spring night when he had drained several glasses of bhang, he bought the boys creamy phirni in clay cups and whispered to them the name his parents had given him. He told them he ran away from home when he was seven because his mother cuffed him for ditching school to hang about with the town's Roadside Romeos, who burst into shrill song each time a girl walked past them.

His first few weeks in the city, Mental lived in the railway station, wolfing down scraps from the half-eaten parcels of food that passengers threw out of train windows, and hiding from the police in the alcoves beneath footbridges. Every thumping step above him felt like a blow to his head. For a while he believed his parents would arrive by train to find him, scold him for frightening them and take him home. At night he slept fitfully, hearing his mother call his name, but it was only the wind, the rattle of a train, or the glassy voice of a woman announcing that the Northeast Express from Shillong was delayed by four hours. Mental thought of going back home but he didn't, because he was ashamed of himself, and because the city made men out of boys, and he was fed up of being a child and wanted to be a man.

Now that Mental is a ghost, he wishes he were seven again. We figure that's why he wants to hear his old name. It reminds him of his parents, and the boy he used to be before he hitched a ride on a train.

Mental's real name is a secret. His boys won't tell anyone. We think it must be a name so good, if Mental had gone to Mumbai instead of coming here, a film star would have flicked it from him.

There are many Mentals in this city. We shouldn't be afraid of them. Our gods are too busy to hear our prayers, but ghosts—ghosts have nothing to do but wait and wander, wander and wait, and they are always listening to our words because they are bored and that's one way to pass the time.

Remember, they don't work for free. They help us only if we offer them something in return. For Mental, it's a voice calling his true name, and for others it's a glass of hooch or a string of jasmine or a kebab from Ustad's. It's no different from what gods ask people to do for them, except most ghosts don't want us to fast or light lamps or write their names over and over again in a notebook.

The hardest part is finding the right ghost. Mental is for boys because he never hired girls, but there are woman ghosts and old woman ghosts and even baby girl ghosts who can guard girls. We need ghosts more than anyone else maybe, because we are railway-station boys without parents and homes. If we are still here, it's only because we know how to summon ghosts at will.

Some people think we believe in the supernatural because we inhale glue and snort heroin and drink desi daru that's strong enough to put a mustache on a baby. But these people, these people with marble floors and electric heaters, they weren't with Mental's boys on the winter night the police chased them out of the railway station.

That night, a bitter-cold wind blew across the city, scoring lines into stone. The boys didn't have twenty rupees between them to rent a quilt for eight hours, and the quilt-wallah swore at them when they asked if he could lend them one on credit. They sat shivering under a dark street lamp with a shattered glass cage, outside a shelter with no more beds free for the night. Spokes of pain turned in their hands and legs. When they couldn't bear it anymore, they called Mental.

We are sorry to disturb you again, they said. **But we are afraid we will die.**

The broken street lamp crackled and glowed. The boys looked up. Beams of light syrupy and yellow with warmth tumbled down.

"Wait," Mental's ghost said to them, "let me see what else I can do."

I LOOK AT OUR HOUSE WITH—

—upside-down eyes and count five holes in our tin roof. There might be more, but I can't see them because the black smog outside has wiped the stars off the sky. I picture a djinn crouching down on the roof, his eye turning like a key in a lock as he watches us through a hole, waiting for Ma and Papa and Runu-Didi to fall asleep so that he can draw out my soul. Djinns aren't real, but if they were, they would only steal children because we have the most delicious souls.

My elbows wobble on the bed, so I lean my legs against the wall. Runu-Didi stops counting the seconds I have been topsy-turvy and says, "Arrey,

Jai, I'm right here and still you're cheating-cheating. You have no shame, kya?" Her voice is high and jumpy because she's too happy that I can't stay upside down for as long as she can.

Didi and I are having a headstand contest but it's not a fair one. The yoga classes at our school are for students in Standard Six and above, and Runu-Didi is in Standard Seven, so she gets to learn from a real teacher. I'm in Standard Four, so I have to rely on Baba Devanand on TV, who says that if we do headstands, children like me will:

- never have to wear glasses our whole lives;
- never have white in our hair or black holes in our teeth;
- never have puddles in our brains or slowness in our arms and legs;
- always be No. 1 in School + College + Office + Home.

I like headstands a lot more than the huff-puff exercises Baba Devanand does with his legs crossed in the lotus position. But right now, if I stay upside down any longer, I'll break my neck, so I flump to the bed that smells of coriander powder and raw onions and Ma and bricks and cement and Papa.

"Baba Jai has been proved to be a conman," Runu-Didi shouts like the newspeople whose faces redden every night from the angry news they have to read out on TV. "Will our nation just stand and watch?"

"Uff, Runu, you're giving me a headache with your screaming," Ma says from the kitchen corner of our house. She's shaping rotis into perfect rounds with the same rolling pin that she uses to whack my backside when I shout bad words while Didi talks to Nana-Nani on Ma's mobile phone.

"I won I won I won," Didi sings now. She's louder than next-door's TV and next-to-next-door's howling baby and the neighbors who squabble every day about who stole water from whose water barrel.

I stick my fingers in my ears. Runu-Didi's lips move but it's as if she's speaking the bubble language of fish in a glass tank. I can't hear a word of her chik-chik. If I lived in a big house, I would take my shut-ears and run up the stairs two at a time and squash myself inside a cupboard. But we live in a basti, so our house has only one room. Papa likes to say that this room has everything we need for our happiness to grow. He means me and Didi and Ma, and not the TV, which is the best thing we own.

From where I'm lying on the bed, I can see the TV clearly. It looks down on me from a shelf that also holds steel plates and aluminum tins. Round letters on the TV screen say, **Dilli: Police Commissioner's Missing Cat Spotted**. Sometimes the Hindi news is written in letters that look like they are spurting blood, especially when the newspeople ask us tough questions we can't answer, like:

Does a Ghost Live in the Supreme Court?

or

Are Pigeons Terrorists Trained by Pakistan?

or

Is a Bull this Varanasi Sari Shop's Best Customer?

or

Did a Rasgulla Break Up Actress Veena's Marriage?

Ma likes such stories because she and Papa can argue about them for hours.

My favorite shows are ones that Ma says I'm not old enough to watch, like **Police Patrol** and **Live Crime**. Sometimes Ma switches off the TV right in the middle of a murder because she says it's too sick-making. But sometimes she leaves it on because she likes guessing who the evil people are and telling me how the policemen are sons-of-owls for never spotting criminals as fast as she can.

Runu-Didi has stopped talking to stretch her hands behind her back. She thinks she's Usain Bolt, but she's only on the school's relay team. Relay isn't a real sport. That's why Ma and Papa let her take part though some of the chachas and cha-chis in our basti say running brings dishonor to girls. Didi says basti-people will shut up once her team wins the inter-district tournament and also the state championships.

My fingers are going numb in my ears, so I pull them out and wipe them against my cargo pants that are already spattered with ink and mud and grease. All my clothes are dirty like these pants, my uniform too.

I have been asking Ma to let me wear the new uniform that I got free from school this winter, but Ma keeps it on top of a shelf where I can't reach it. She says only rich people throw clothes away when there's still life left in them. If I show her how my brown trousers end well above my ankles, Ma will say even film stars wear ill-fitting clothes because it's the latest fashion.

She's still making up things to trick me like she did when I was smaller than I'm now. She doesn't know that every morning, Pari and Faiz laugh when they see me and tell me I look like a joss stick but one that smells of fart.

"Ma, listen, my uniform—" I say and I stop

because there's a scream from outside so loud I think it will squish the walls of our house. Runu-Didi gasps and Ma's hand brushes against a hot pan by mistake and her face goes all sharp and jagged like bitter-gourd skin.

I think it's Papa trying to scare us. He's always singing old Hindi songs in his hairy voice that rolls down the alleys of our basti like an empty LPG cylinder, waking up stray dogs and babies and making them bawl. But then the scream punches our walls again, and Ma switches off the stove and we run out of the house.

The cold slithers up my bare feet. Shadows and voices judder across the alley. The smog combs my hair with fingers that are smoky but also damp at the same time. People shout, "What's happening? Has something happened? Who's screaming? Did someone scream?" Goats that their owners have dressed in old sweaters and shirts so they won't catch a chill hide under the charpais on both sides of the alley. The lights in the hi-fi buildings near our basti blink like fireflies and then disappear. The current's gone off.

I don't know where Ma and Runu-Didi are. Women wearing clinking glass bangles hold up mobile-phone torches and kerosene lanterns but their light is wishy-washy in the smog.

Everyone around me is taller than I am, and their worried hips and elbows knock into my face as they ask each other about the screams. We can tell by now that they are coming from Drunkard Laloo's house.

"Something bad is going on over there," a cha-cha who lives in our alley says. "Laloo's wife was running around the basti, asking if anyone had seen her son. She was even at the rubbish ground, calling his name."

"That Laloo too, na, all the time beating his wife, beating his children," a woman says. "Just you wait and see, one day his wife will also disappear. What will that useless fellow do for money then? From where will he get his hooch, haan?"

I wonder which one of Drunkard Laloo's sons is missing. The eldest, Bahadur, is a stutterer who is in my class.

The earth twitches as a metro train rumbles underground somewhere near us. It will worm out of a tunnel, zoom past half-finished buildings, and climb up a bridge to an above-ground station before returning to the city because this is where the Purple Line ends. The metro station is new, and Papa was one of the people who built its sparkly walls. Now he's making a tower so tall they have to put flashing red lights on top to warn pilots not to fly too low.

The screams have stopped. I'm cold and my teeth are talking among themselves. Then Runu-Didi's hand darts out of the darkness, snatches me, and drags me forward. She runs fast, as if she's competing in a relay race and I'm the baton she's about to pass to a teammate.

"Stop," I say, hitting the brakes. "Where are we going?"

"Didn't you hear what people were saying about Bahadur?"

"He's lost?"

"You don't want to find out more?"

Runu-Didi can't see my face in the smog but I nod. We follow a lantern swinging from someone's hands, but it's not bright enough to show us the puddles where washing-up water has collected and we keep stepping into them. The water is icky and I should turn around but I also want to know what happened to Bahadur. Teachers never ask him questions in class because of his stammer. When I was in Standard Two, I tried going ka-ka-ka too, but that only got me a rap on the knuckles with a wooden ruler. Ruler beatings hurt much worse than canings.

I almost trip over Fatima-ben's buffalo, who's lying in the middle of the alley, a giant black smudge that I can't tell apart from the smog. Ma says the buffalo is like a sage who has been meditating for hundreds and hundreds of years in the sun and the rain and the snow. Faiz and I once pretended to be lions and roared at Buffalo-Baba, and we pelted him with pebbles, but he didn't even roll his big buffalo eyes or shake his backward-curving horns at us.

All the lanterns and phone-torches have stopped outside Bahadur's house. We can't see anything because of the crowd. I tell Runu-Didi to wait and jostle past trouser-clad, sari-clad, dhoti-clad legs, and hands that smell of kerosene and sweat and food and metal. Bahadur's ma is sitting on the doorstep, crying, folded in half like a sheet of paper, with my ma on one side and our neighbor Shanti-Chachi on the other. Drunkard Laloo squats next to them, his head bobbling as his red-rivered eyes squint up at our faces.

I don't know how Ma got here before me. Shanti-Chachi smooths Bahadur's ma's hair, rubs her back, and says things like, "He's only a child, must be somewhere around here. Can't have gone that far."

Bahadur's ma doesn't stop sobbing, but the gaps between her sobs grow longer. That's because Shanti-Chachi has magic in her hands. Ma says chachi is the best midwife in the world. If a baby is blue and quiet when it's born, chachi can bring red to its cheeks and screams to its lips just by rubbing its feet.

Ma sees me in the crowd and asks, "Jai, was Bahadur at school today?"

"No," I say. Bahadur's ma looks so sad that I wish I could remember when I last saw him. Bahadur doesn't speak much, so no one notices if he's in the classroom or not. Then Pari sticks her head out of the sea of legs and says, "He hasn't been coming to school. We saw him last Thursday."

Today is Tuesday, so Bahadur has been gone for five days. Pari and Faiz mutter "side-side-side" as if they are waiters carrying wire racks of steaming chai glasses, and people make way for them to pass. Then they stand next to me. Both of them are still wearing our school uniform. Ma has told me to change into home clothes as soon as I enter the house so that my uniform won't get even more mucky. She's too strict.

"Where were you?" Pari asks. "We looked for you everywhere."

"Here only," I say.

Pari has pinned back her fringe at such a height that it looks like one-half of a mosque's onion dome. Before I can ask why no one realized Bahadur was missing until today, Pari and Faiz tell me why, because they are my friends and they can see the thoughts in my head.

"His mother, na, for a week or so she wasn't here," Faiz whispers. "And his father—"

"—is World-Best Bewda No. 1. If a bandicoot chews off his ears, he won't know because he's ful-too drunk all the time," Pari says loudly as if she wants Drunkard Laloo to hear her. "The chachis next door should have noticed that Bahadur is missing, don't you think?"

Pari is always quick to blame others because she thinks she's perfect.

"The chachis have been taking care of Bahadur's brother and sister," Faiz explains to me. "They thought Bahadur was staying with a friend."

I nudge Pari and zoom my eyes toward Omvir, who's hiding behind grown-ups and twisting a ring on his finger that glows white in the dark. He's Bahadur's only friend, though Omvir is in Standard Five and doesn't come to school often because he has to help his papa, a press-wallah who irons the creases out of hi-fi people's clothes.

"Listen, Omvir, you know where Bahadur is?" Pari asks.

Omvir hunches into his maroon sweater, but Bahadur's ma's ears have already picked up the question. "He doesn't know," she says. "He was the first person I asked."

Pari points her onion-fringe at Drunkard Laloo and says, "All this must be his fault."

Every day we see Drunkard Laloo stumbling around the basti, drool dripping from his mouth, doing nothing but eating air. He's a beggy-type fellow who sometimes asks even Pari and me if we have coins to spare so that he can buy a glass of kadak chai. It's Bahadur's ma who makes money by working as a nanny and maid for a family in one of the hi-fi buildings near our basti. Ma and lots of chachis in the basti also work for the hi-fi people who live up there.

I turn to look at the buildings that have fancy names like Palm Springs and Mayfair and Golden Gate and Athena. They are close to our basti but seem far because of the rubbish ground in between, and also a tall brick wall with barbed wire on top that Ma says is not tall enough to keep out the stink from the rubbish mounds. There are many grown-ups behind me but through the spaces between their monkey caps I can see that the hi-fi buildings have light now. It must be because they have diesel generators. Our basti is still dark.

"Why did I go?" Bahadur's ma asks Shanti-Chachi. "I should have never left them alone."

"The hi-fi family went to Neemrana, and they took Bahadur's ma with them. To look after their babies," Pari tells me.

"What's Neemrana?" I ask.

"It's a fort-palace in Rajasthan," Pari says. "On top of a hill."

"Bahadur could be with his nana-nani," someone tells Bahadur's ma. "Or one of his chacha-chachis."

"I called them," Bahadur's ma says. "He isn't with any of them."

Drunkard Laloo tries to stand, one hand pressing the ground. Someone helps him up and, swinging from side to side, he hobbles toward us.

"Where is Bahadur?" he asks. "You play with him, don't you?"

We step backward, bumping into people. Omvir and his maroon sweater vanish into the crowd. Drunkard Laloo kneels down in front of us, nearly toppling over, but he manages to level his old-man eyes with my child-eyes. Then he catches me by my shoulders and shakes me back and forth as if I'm a soda bottle and he wants to make me fizz. I try to wriggle out of his grip. Instead of saving me, Pari and Faiz scoot off.

"You know where my son is, don't you?" Drunkard Laloo asks.

I guess I could help him find Bahadur because I know loads about detecting, but his smelly breath is rushing into my face and all I want to do is run away.

"Leave that boy alone," someone shouts.

I don't think Drunkard Laloo will listen, but he ruffles my hair and mutters, "Okay, okay." Then he lets go of me.

———

Papa always leaves for work early, when I'm still sleeping, but the next morning I wake up to the smell of turpentine on his shirt, and his rough hands grazing my cheeks.

"Be careful. You walk with Runu to school and back, you hear me?" he says.

I scrunch up my nose. Papa treats me like a small child though I'm nine years old.

"After class, come straight home," he says. "No wandering around Bhoot Bazaar by yourself." He kisses me on the forehead, and says again, "You'll be careful?"

I wonder what he imagines has happened to Bahadur. Does he think a djinn snatched him? But Papa doesn't believe in djinns.

I go outside to say okay-tata-bye to him, then I brush my teeth. Men who are Papa's age soap their faces, and cough and spit as if they hope the insides of their throats will jump out of them into the ground. I want to see how far my frothy-white spit can go, so I let my mouth make boom-boom explosions.

"Stop that right now, Jai," I hear Ma say. She and Runu-Didi are carrying the pots and jerrycans of water they have collected from the one tap in our basti that works, but only between six and eight in the morning and sometimes for an hour in the evening. Didi opens the lids of the two water barrels standing on either side of our door, and Ma empties the pots and jerrycans into them, splashing water all over herself in her hurry.

I finish tooth-brushing. "Why are you still here?" Ma snaps at me. "You want to be late for school again?"

It's actually Ma who's late for work, so she runs

off while also fixing her hair, which has come loose from the knot at the back of her head. The hi-fi madam whose flat Ma cleans is a mean lady who has already put two strikes against Ma's name for being late. One night when I was pretending to sleep, Ma told Papa that the madam had threatened to chop her into tiny-tiny pieces and chuck slices of her over the balcony for the kites circling the building to catch.

Runu-Didi and I go to the toilet complex near the rubbish ground, carrying buckets into which we have thrown soaps, towels and mugs. The black smog is still sulking above us. It pricks my eyes and plashes tears onto my cheeks. Didi teases me by saying that I must be missing Bahadur.

"You're crying for your dost?" she asks, and I would tell her to shut up, but there are long queues for the toilets even though it costs two rupees to go, and I have to focus on shifting my weight from one leg to another so that my backside won't burst.

The caretaker, who sits behind a desk at the main entrance of the toilets where it divides into Ladies and Gents, is taking ages to collect the money and let people through. He's supposed to work from five in the morning till eleven in the night, but he locks up the complex whenever he wants and leaves. Then we have to go in the rubbish ground. It's free, but anyone can see our backsides there, our classmates and pigs and dogs and cows as old as Nana-Nani that will eat our clothes off us if they can.

Runu-Didi stands in the ladies' queue, I stand in the gents'. Didi says men keep trying to peep into the Ladies. Probably to see if their toilets and bathrooms are cleaner.

The people in my queue are chatting about Bahadur. "That boy must be hiding somewhere," a chacha says, "waiting for his mother to kick his father out." Everyone murmurs in agreement. They decide Bahadur will come home once he tires of brawling with stray dogs for an old roti in a pile of rubbish.

The men talk about how loudly Bahadur's ma screamed last night, loud enough to scare the ghosts that live in Bhoot Bazaar, and they joke with each other about how long it will take them to realize that one of their own children is missing. Hours-days-weeks-months?

A chacha says that even if he notices he won't bring it up. "I have eight children. What difference will one less or one more make?" he says, and every-one laughs. The smog is worrying their eyes too, so they are also crying at the same time.

I get to the front of the queue, pay the caretaker, and do my business quickly. I wonder if Bahadur has run off to some place with nice-clean toilets and bathrooms that smell of jasmine. If I had a bathroom like that, I would have taken bucket-baths every day.

———

Back at home, Didi gives me chai and rusk for breakfast. The rusk is hard and tastes of nothing, but I obediently chew it up. I won't get any other food till afternoon. Then I change into my uniform and we leave for school.

Though Papa told me not to, I plan to give Runu-Didi the slip as soon as I can. But there's a swarm of people around Buffalo-Baba, some standing on plastic chairs and charpais and craning their necks to get a good look. They are blocking our way. I hear a voice I recognize from last night. "Find my son, baba, find my son for me. I won't move from here until my Bahadur is found," Drunkard Laloo cries.

"Accha, now you can't live without your son?" a woman exclaims. "You didn't think of that when you were hitting him?"

"Only the police can help us," another woman says. "Six nights he hasn't been home. That's too long." I think that's Bahadur's ma talking.

"We're going to be so late," Runu-Didi says. She holds her school bag in front of her and uses it to slam into people so that they will move, and I do the same. By the time we are out of the crowd, our hair is messy and our uniforms crumply.

Runu-Didi straightens her kameez. Before she can stop me, I jump over a gutter, and sprint past cows and hens and dogs, and goats wearing better sweaters than I am, past a woman sweeping the alley while listening to loud music on her mobile with earphones, and a white-haired grandmother stringing beans. My school bag knocks into an old man sitting on a plastic chair, one of its legs shorter than the others, the difference in height made up with bricks. The chair topples over and the man lands on the ground with his backside in the mud. I rub my left knee, which hurts a bit, then I run off again and the man's curses chase me all the way to another alley that smells of chole-bhature.

Here Pari and Faiz are waiting for me, outside a store that sells Tau jee and Chulbule and other salty, masala-coated snacks. The bright reds and greens and blues of the namkeen wrappers look dreary in the smog today, and the husband and wife who run the shop are sitting behind the counter with mufflers wrapped over their faces. The smog doesn't bother me as much, probably because I'm strong.

"This Faiz, na," Pari says as soon as I join them, "is an idiot." Her minaret fringe looks like it will collapse any second.

"You're the idiot," Faiz says.

"You saw?" I ask. "Drunkard Laloo is praying to Buffalo-Baba, like baba is an actual god."

"Bahadur's ma was saying she'll go to the police," Pari says.

"She's ekdum-mad," Faiz says.

"The police will kick us out if we complain," I say. "They're always threatening to send bulldozers to demolish our basti."

"They can't do anything. We have got ration cards," Pari says. "Also, we pay them a hafta. If they throw us out, who will they extort money from?"

"Loads of people," I say. "India has more people than any other country in the world. Except China." There's rusk stuck between my teeth and I pry it out with my tongue.

"Faiz thinks Bahadur is dead," Pari says.

"Bahadur is our age. We aren't old enough to die."

"I didn't say he died," Faiz protests, and then he coughs. He hawks up spit and wipes his mouth with his hands.

"Maybe what's happened is that Bahadur's asthma went bad because of the smog, and he fell into a ditch and couldn't get out," Pari says. "Remember how he couldn't breathe this one time we were in Standard Two?"

"You cried," I say.

"I never cry," Pari says. "Ma does, but not me."

"If Bahadur fell into a ditch, someone would have pulled him out. Look at the number of people here," Faiz says.

I eye the people walking past us, to establish if they seem like the helpful-type. But their faces are half-hidden by handkerchiefs to keep the smog from getting inside their ears and noses and mouths. Some of the men and women bark into their mobiles through their make-do masks. There's a chole-bhature vendor on the roadside, and though his face isn't covered by a scarf, it's enveloped in a cloud of smoke rising from a vat of sizzling hot oil in which he's frying bhaturas. His customers are laborers on their way to factories and construction sites, sweepers and carpenters, mechanics and security guards at malls returning home after a night shift. The men scoop up the chole with steel spoons and munch, their kerchiefs pulled down to their chins. Their eyes are fixed on their plates of hot food. If a demon were to stomp toward them right now, they wouldn't notice.

"Listen," I say, "why don't we look for Bahadur? Either he's lying sick in a hospital—"

"His ma went to all the hospitals near our basti," Pari says. "The women at the toilet complex were talking about it."

"If he was snatched, we can solve a case of kidnapping also," I say. "**Police Patrol** tells you exactly how to find someone missing. First you—"

"Maybe a djinn took him," Faiz says, touching the gold-colored taweez that hangs from a frayed black string tied around his neck. The amulet keeps him safe from the evil eye and bad djinns.

"Even babies know better than to believe in djinns," Pari says.

Faiz furrows his forehead, and the groove of the white scar that runs across his left temple, just missing his eye, deepens as if something is pulling at his skin from the inside.

"Let's go," I say. Watching the two of them argue is the most boring thing in the world. "We'll be late for assembly."

Faiz fast-walks, even when we get to the lanes of Bhoot Bazaar, which are crammed with too many people and dogs and cycle-rickshaws and autorick-shaws and e-rickshaws. To keep pace with him, I can't do the things I usually do at the bazaar, like count the bloodied goat hooves on sale at Afsal-Chacha's shop or cadge a slice of melon off a fruit chaat vendor.

No one will believe me but I'm one hundred percent pakka that my nose grows longer when I'm in the bazaar because of its smells, of tea and raw meat and buns and kebabs and rotis. My ears get bigger too, because of the sounds, ladles scraping against pans, butchers' knives thwacking against chopping boards, rickshaws and scooters honking, and gunfire and bad words boom-booming out of video-game parlors hidden behind grimy curtains. But today my nose and ears stay the same size because Bahadur has vanished, my friends are sulking, and the smog is making everything blurry.

In front of us, sparks fall on the ground from a bird's nest of electric wires hanging over the bazaar.

"That's a warning," Faiz says. "Allah is telling us to be careful."

Pari looks at me, her eyebrows climbing up her forehead.

I peer into ditches for the rest of our walk to school, just in case Bahadur has fallen into one of them. All I see are empty wrappers and holey plastic bags and eggshells and dead rats and dead cats and chicken and mutton bones sucked clean by hungry mouths. No sign of djinns, no sign of Bahadur.

OUR SCHOOL IS LOCKED UP—

—behind a six-foot wall with barbed wire on top, and an iron gate that has a door painted purple. From the outside, it looks like the jails I have seen in movies. We even have a watchman, though he's never at the gate because he has to run errands for the headmaster: pick up Mrs. Headmaster's blouse from her tailor in Bhoot Bazaar or fill a tiffin box with gulab-jamuns for her and the headmaster's No. 1 and No. 2 sons.

Today too the watchman isn't around. Instead there's a queue starting at the gate-door, which is too narrow for all of us to go through at the same time. The headmaster won't open the main gate fully because he thinks strangers will run into the school along with us. He likes to tell us that 180 children go missing across India **every single day**. He says **Stranger is Danger**, which is a line he has stolen from a Hindi film song. But if he were really worried about strangers, he wouldn't keep sending the watchman away.

The headmaster must hate us. There's no other reason why he makes us wait outside the gate on smoggy winter mornings like today when the cold traces our breath in white. Even the pigeons with plumped-up feathers, sitting in a row on a droopy electric wire above us, haven't yet opened their eyes.

"Why can't these children make a proper queue?" Pari says, scowling at the many shorter lines that have branched out of the main one. "We're going to be standing here forever."

She says this every day.

The shortest queue totters forward as if to prove her wrong. I scuttle across to stand behind a boy who is in Runu-Didi's class. A comb the color of milky tea sticks out of the back pocket of his trousers. He removes the comb, sweeps it through his hair, plucks the strands caught between its close-packed teeth and pushes it back into his pocket. His face is spotty like a banana gone bad.

Pari and Faiz cut in line in front of me. "How dare you?" I say to them, but they grin because they know I'm joking and I grin back. I look around to see if Bahadur has turned up. Maybe he doesn't know that back in the basti his ma is about to call the police. But he isn't here and I don't want to talk about him because that will break up Pari's and Faiz's smiles. They have already forgotten they were squabbling a few minutes ago.

I spot Quarter reaching the school gate. He's in Standard Nine but he has failed the ninth standard two or three times. His father is the pradhan of our basti and a member of the Hindu Samaj, a shouty party that hates Muslims. We hardly ever see the pradhan anymore because he has bought a hi-fi flat and only meets hi-fi people. I don't know if that's true or just something Ma says when the basti-tap stays dry for days and everyone has to chip in for a water tanker.

Quarter is standing by the gate now, directing the movement of the queues like a traffic policeman on a busy road. He thrusts his long right hand in the air, with his palm facing forward, for our line to STOP. I obey at once and so does everyone else.

In our school Quarter runs a gang that beats up teachers and rents out fake parents to students when they get into trouble and the headmaster insists on meeting their ma-papas. Quarter doesn't work for free, and I don't know how students have the money to buy a papa or a ma. Faiz does loads of odd jobs, and he gives most of his money to his ammi and some money he sets aside to buy his favorite Purple Lotus and Cream Lux soaps and a bottle of Sunsilk Stunning Black Shine shampoo. Faiz says ma-papas cost more than a dozen soaps and shampoos.

Some boys are holding up the queue by making small talk with Quarter. They are always telling him about the one time they shouted at a teacher or a policeman to prove they can be rough-and-tough too. But there's no one like Quarter because:

- first of all, every day, he stops at a theka in Bhoot Bazaar to drink a quarter-peg of daru, which is how he got the name Quarter. His eyes are always red and puffy and he smells like daru too;
- second of all, he never wears the school uniform;
- third of all, he dresses only in black: black shirt, black trousers, and a black shawl wrapped around his shoulders if he's feeling cold;
- fourth of all, every morning, right after assembly, the headmaster throws Quarter out for not wearing the school uniform. The teachers keep threatening to strike him off the roll because he has zero attendance but they haven't done that so far.

Instead of attending classes, Quarter loiters around Bhoot Bazaar until it's time for the midday meal break. Then he swaggers back into school and stands under a neem tree in the playground, surrounded by students who want to join his gang or hire his gang-members, and idiot-senior girls who point finger guns at each other and call themselves Revolver Ranis. Most girls stay away from Quarter though because he's always making eyes at them.

Quarter is the only criminal-type I have seen up close. He has never been arrested by the police, maybe because his pradhan-papa bribes them. I wonder if somebody paid Quarter to make Bahadur disappear. But who would do such a thing?

Our queue shuffles forward.

I decide Quarter is my prime suspect. He and djinns, but I can't question djinns. They may not be real.

When we get to the gate, I make myself brave and tell Quarter, "A boy in our basti has gone missing." I have never talked to him before but now I stand straight as if I'm about to sing the national anthem at assembly. I watch Quarter's face to see if he looks caught out because good cops and detectives can tell from the way someone blinks their eyes or tightens their lips if they are lying.

Quarter smiles an oily smile at a senior girl standing behind me. He strokes the hair sprouting above his lips and on his cheeks, too sparse to be a real mustache and beard even though he must be very old, like seventeen or something. Then he says "Chalo-chalo-chalo," swatting me toward the gate.

"The missing boy, his name is Bahadur," I say.

Quarter snaps his fingers too close to my ears, making their tips burn. "Chal-hut," he growls.

I run into the school grounds.

"You mad or what?" Faiz asks. "Why were you talking to that fellow?"

"Quarter could have cut off your arm and thrown it into one of these bins," Pari says, pointing at a penguin bin next to us.

The penguin's yellow beak is open so wide that our heads can fit inside. Its white pot belly screams **USE ME USE ME**. Toffee wrappers sprinkle the ground around it because students toss stuff into the penguin's mouth from a long way away and keep missing.

"I was doing detective work," I tell Pari.

———

The next India-Pakistan war the news says will happen any time now has started in our classroom. It's about who should win **Sa Re Ga Ma Pa Li'l Champs**. The Indian side says the best singer in the competition is Ankit, a plump boy everyone calls Jalebi because his voice is sticky-sweet. The Pakistani side wants Saira, a hijab-wearing Muslim girl who must be a head shorter than me at least, to win, because she goes to school in the mornings and, in the afternoons, sings in the streets of

Mumbai for coins to feed her family. Pari and I try to tell everyone that Bahadur is missing. Half of my classmates know that already because they live in our basti. But they don't care about Bahadur, not right now in the middle of a war.

"Saira's people kill cows and they also kill Hindus," says Gaurav, whose mother fingerprints a red tilak on his forehead every morning as if he's going into battle.

Faiz will never kill me. He even forgets he is Muslim sometimes.

"Gaurav is a donkey," I whisper to Faiz.

Our class has nine or ten Muslim children, besides Faiz. They are sitting quietly, holding textbooks open in front of their faces.

Faiz and I take our places at a desk in the third row. Pari sits next to us. She shares her desk with Tanvi, who has a backpack shaped like a slice of watermelon, pink with black pips.

"What if Quarter really snatched Bahadur?" I ask Pari. "Maybe stealing children is his new business. Maybe he supplies fake kids to parents the same way he rents out fake parents to us."

"Quarter doesn't even know who Bahadur is, why would he?" Pari says.

"I have seen Quarter make fun of Bahadur," Tanvi announces, stroking her backpack as if it's a cat. "He calls him Ba-Ba-Ba-Bahadur."

Kirpal-Sir comes into our classroom. "Silence,

silence," he shouts as he turns to the blackboard, gripping a stub of chalk between the tips of his fingers. His hand is shaky because it was broken a year ago and hasn't mended right. He writes **MAPS** at the very top of the board and **INDIA** below it, then starts drawing a squiggly map of India.

"Bachao, bachao," I whisper to Pari. "I'm only a poor little chalk and this teacher is choking me to death."

Everyone else is whispering to each other too but Pari's face goes all frowny and she hisses, "Sshhhh, sshhhh."

I curve my right hand as if it's the head of a cobra and sink my fangs into her left shoulder.

"Sir, teacher-sir," Pari cries.

I slink down in my seat until most of me is under the desk. Kirpal-Sir can't see me now. The classroom is darker than usual because of the smog.

Pari stands up with her hand raised and shouts **teacher-sir** again.

"What is it?" he asks, sounding miffed, maybe because he hates drawing.

"Don't you think you should take our attendance first?" Pari asks.

Some students titter. Faiz sneezes without looking up from the swear word he's carving onto our desk with his compass.

"Sir," Pari says, "if you take roll call, then we'll know if everybody's here or not."

I sit up. Of course, Pari was never going to tell on me.

Kirpal-Sir puts the chalk down on the table, and it rolls toward the attendance register that he never opens. His nose twitches like it does just before he takes out his wooden ruler to beat the air.

"Sir, you remember Bahadur, he used to sit there," Pari says, spinning around to look at a seat in the last row behind her. "We found out yesterday that he hasn't been home in five days."

"What should I do? Go look for him in the market? His parents should file a complaint with the police."

"If a student doesn't turn up for two-three days, isn't the school supposed to tell the family?"

Pari has made her eyes as big as she can and is talking in a sing-song voice, but her acting isn't fooling Kirpal-Sir.

"O-ho," Faiz mutters, his compass still carving letters. "Pari is in trouble. Major trouble."

We know why Pari is asking Kirpal-Sir these questions. It shouldn't take us five days to realize someone is missing. But Kirpal-Sir's roll call can't help Bahadur now. It's too late.

I'm the only one who can do something about it. I can find Bahadur because I have seen many-hundred programs on TV and I know exactly how detectives like Byomkesh Bakshi catch the bad people who steal children and gold and wives and diamonds.

With his head bowed, Kirpal-Sir circles his table as if it's a temple and he's praying silently.

"If I take attendance every morning, who's going to do the teaching? You? You'll teach? You?" Kirpal-Sir aims his fingers at each one of the students in the front row, then rubs his right wrist.

Pari sticks her bottom lip out as if she's about to cry. Faiz returns his compass to his geometry box though he hasn't finished carving ha-ra-mi on the desk, with an arrow pointing to the boy to his left.

"How many of you are here? Forty, fifty?" Kirpal-Sir asks. "Do you know how much time I'll need to call out each one of your names?"

Pari sits down and prods her hair dome with a pencil. A few strands come loose. She's trying to hide her tears. This is new for her. She isn't used to getting shouted at like the rest of us.

"And your parents, they keep taking you out of school so that you can visit your native place, without saying a word to us," Kirpal-Sir says though Pari has never missed a day of school. "None of you will have a place here if I follow the government rules."

"Sir, we won't do anything to you if you mark us absent," I say. "We're only small."

"Arrey, paagal," Faiz says under his breath, "don't you know when to keep your mouth shut?"

The whole class goes quiet except for sniffles and coughs. I can hear teachers in other classrooms asking questions, and the shrieky voices of students answering together. Kirpal-Sir's eyebrows slant down to make a V. Then he picks up his powdery chalk and turns to the blackboard.

"Anyone else would have given you a good caning," Faiz whispers.

I don't think so. I didn't say anything wrong.

Last year, Quarter put a curse on sir and turned him into a mouse. It happened after sir crossed out the names of three senior students from the register because they didn't attend school for four months. A week later, when Kirpal-Sir was going home on his old Bajaj Chetak, Quarter's boys followed him and, as soon as he stopped at a red light, hit him on the head with iron rods. He was wearing a helmet, so I don't think they meant to kill him; it was a warning, like how Ma glares at me for a few seconds to see if I'll stop doing whatever I'm doing that's infuriating her before she has to start screaming at me.

Quarter's boys ended up breaking a bone in sir's right hand. We didn't have school for days afterward because the teachers went on strike, asking the government to protect them, but then they came back and so we had to come back too. The two boys the police finally arrested for the attack weren't from our school, so Quarter wasn't expelled. Kirpal-Sir stopped taking the roll call from that day onward, but he carries the register everywhere, tucked under his armpit. It's not a secret. Even the headmaster knows sir will never expel anyone again for missing school.

Kirpal-Sir's chalk is screeching again. Some of the boys in the front row crick their necks to look at me. I roll my upper lip and bare my front teeth. They snicker and turn away.

Pari scribbles on the newspaper that covers her Social Science textbook. Faiz has a sneezing fit. I shift to the side, so that his snot bullets won't hit me.

"Silence," Kirpal-Sir turns around and shouts. I think he says **silence** more often than any other word; he must yell it in his sleep. He lobs the chalk-stub in my direction. It misses me and falls between my desk and Pari's.

"But, sir," I say, "I didn't do anything."

He picks up the register with his left hand and flick-flicks the pages with his floppy right hand.

"Here you are," he says. He raises his eyebrows at me when he says **you**. Then he removes the pen clipped to his shirt pocket, writes something on the page, slams the register shut and drops it on the table. "There, it's done. Happy?"

I don't know why I should be happy.

"What are you still doing here?" Kirpal-Sir says. "Jai, come on, pack up your things. I have marked you absent for the day, just as you wanted. Huzoor, this means you're getting a day off"—now he sweeps both his hands toward the classroom door—"out you go."

"If just like that you're getting a chutti," Faiz says, "take it, yaar."

I don't want a day off. I don't want to miss the midday meal because then I'll have to go hungry until dinner, which is more hours away than I can count on my fingers.

"Out, now," Kirpal-Sir says. The whole class is silent. Everyone is shocked that sir is showing his anger instead of swallowing it whole like he usually does.

"Sir—"

"There are other students here who, unlike you, want to learn. They hope to become doctors and engineers and suchlike. But"—spit bubbles at the corners of his mouth—"your calling is to be a goonda. It's best you learn about that outside the school gate."

The anger in my stomach hops to my chest and my arms and legs. I wish Quarter's boys had killed Kirpal-Sir. He's a terrible teacher.

I push my things into my bag, go out into the corridor, and stand on the tips of my toes to peer outside the school wall. Maybe Quarter is there. I'll ask him if I can become a member of his gang.

Kirpal-Sir barges into the corridor, his face dotted with strange winter-sweat, and says, "Oye, loafer, didn't I tell you to leave? No free lunch for you today."

I have been sent out of the class before, because I forgot to do the homework or got into a scrap, but I have never been thrown out of the school. I walk toward the gate, stopping to kick the penguins, and don't look back even once. I'm going to leave school for good and take up a life of crime, just like Quarter. I'll be the scariest don in all of India and everyone will be frightened of me. My face will come on TV but I'll hide behind large, dark glasses and I'll look a bit like me but no one will be able to tell for sure, not even Ma or Papa or Runu-Didi.

I WALK AROUND BHOOT BAZAAR, IMAGINING MY LIFE—

—as a criminal. It won't be easy. I'll have to grow taller and heavier because only then will people take me seriously. Right now, even shop-keepers treat me like a scruffy dog. When I squash my nose against the glass cabinets in which they display their wares—orange rows of Karachi halwa and half-moons of gujiyas decorated with powdered green cardamom—they poke me on the head with broomsticks and threaten to douse me with mugs of cold water.

My feet slip through the holes in the pavement. "Beta, watch your step," says a chacha whose face is as wrinkled as my shirt. He's sipping chai in a tea shop that juts out into the lane. Playing on a radio at the shop is an old Hindi film song that's Papa's favorite. "This Journey, So Beautiful," the hero sings.

The men sitting next to the helpful chacha, on knee-high barrels and upturned plastic crates, don't see me. Their eyes are full of sadness at not being picked for a job today. All morning they must have waited at the junction near the highway for the contractors who arrive in jeeps and trucks to hire people for laying bricks or painting walls. There are too many men and too few contractors, so not everyone gets work.

Papa used to wait at the highway too until he got the good job at the Purple Line metro station and then the building site. He has told me about beastly contractors who steal money from workers and make men swing from tattered rope harnesses to clean hi-fi windows. Papa says he doesn't want that dangerous life for me, so I should study well and get an office job and be hi-fi myself.

My eyes sting when I think of how ashamed he'll be if I become a criminal. I decide I don't want to be Quarter 2 after all.

———

I turn into the alley that leads to our basti and cough with my hand covering my mouth. This way, if a lady from Ma's basti-ladies' network sees me and snitches to Ma about me cutting classes, she'll also have to say that I looked quite sick.

I realize that my cough is as loud as an airplane. Something is not right but I can't tell what. I stop and look around. Hold my breath and listen. My heart knocks against my ribs. I open my mouth wide and blow my breath out and catch it back like Baba Devanand does on TV. Slowly the knots in my stomach loosen. Then I see what's wrong.

The alley is quiet and empty. Everyone is missing, the grandpas reading newspapers, the jobless men playing rummy or bluff, the mothers soaking clothes in old paint tubs, and the little children waddling around with mud-caked knees. Dirty vessels, some of them half-washed, are scattered around the plastic water barrels that guard every door in the basti. Something rumbles behind the smog. Maybe it's a djinn. A bad feeling flickers through me. I want to pee.

A door to my left creaks open. I jump. I'm going to be snatched. But it's just a woman in a sari. She has vermillion paste in the parting of her hair, and it's smudged all over her face.

"Boy, don't you have a brain on you?" she bellows. "There are policemen everywhere in our basti. You want them to catch you?"

I shake my head, but I stop feeling like I have to go to the toilet. Policemen are scary but not as scary as djinns. I want to ask the woman why the cops are here and if they have brought bulldozers with them to frighten us and shouldn't someone start a bucket collection to pay them off, but instead I say, "You have got sindoor on your cheeks."

"What will your mother think?" the woman asks. "She's working so hard that she doesn't have any time to pray at the temple, and just look at you. Cutting classes and enjoying yourself, haan? Don't do this, boy. Don't disappoint your mother. Go back to school now. Otherwise you'll regret it one day. You understand what I'm saying?"

"Understood," I say. I don't think she and Ma are friends.

"Don't let me catch you again," she says and shuts the door in my face.

I can't believe Bahadur's ma got the police to come to our basti. That's why everyone's hiding. I should hide too, but I also want to find out what the policemen are doing. They are supposed to **Serve and Protect** us, but the cops I see around Bhoot Bazaar only ever do the opposite of that. They pester shopkeepers, fill their tummies with free food from the carts of vendors, and ask anyone late with a hafta payment to choose between a baton up their backside or a visit from the bull-dozer.

The smog proves useful for once because it gives me good cover. I stick to the sides of the lane, close to the water barrels, even though the ground is squishy there because of all the vessel-washing. I pass two pushcart vendors covering their vegetables and fruits with tarpaulin sheets. Three cobblers squat nearby, the black bristles of their shoeshine brushes poking out of the sacks slung over their shoulders. They are on their marks to get set, go at the first whiff of trouble.

I'm not scared like these men. I'm not spineless either, like Shanti-Chachi's second husband. Everyone says he does whatever chachi asks him to do: cooks for her, washes her underskirts, and hangs them out to dry even when the whole lane is watching him. As a midwife, chachi makes loads more money than her husband too, even though he has two jobs.

I see Buffalo-Baba in his usual spot in the middle of a lane, and a policeman in a khaki uniform. Watching the cop are Fatima-ben, worried perhaps that the policeman will do something bad to her buffalo, grandpas with their hands folded across their chests, mothers with babies on their hips, children who don't go to school so that they can do embroidery or snack-making work at home, and Bahadur's ma and Drunkard Laloo even though they don't live on this lane.

I edge closer, ducking under clotheslines heavy with wet shirts and saris, their hems brushing against my hair. Just two houses away from where everyone is standing is a black water barrel by a closed door. It's the perfect hiding place. I put my school bag down, crouch behind the barrel, and make my breathing shallow so that no one can hear me. Then I peek out with one eye.

The policeman prods Buffalo-Baba with his shoes and asks Drunkard Laloo, "So it's true? This animal never gets up? How does it eat?"

Maybe this policeman thinks Buffalo-Baba is hiding Bahadur under his dungy backside.

A second policeman steps out of a house. He's wearing a khaki shirt that has red arm-badges shaped like arrowheads pointing down.

Only senior constables wear such badges. I know because last month I saw a **Live Crime** episode about a crook who fooled people by putting on a senior constable's uniform. The fake cop even went to the police barracks in Jaipur to drink tea with the real cops there and left with their wallets.

"Making friendship with a buffalo? Good, good," the senior constable says to the policeman whose khaki uniform doesn't have any badges stitched to the sleeves, which means he's only a junior. Then the senior steps over Buffalo-Baba's tail to stand in front of Bahadur's ma.

"Your boy, he has a problem, is what I have come to understand," the senior says. "He's slow-brained, isn't he?"

"My son is a good student," Bahadur's ma says.

Her voice is raspy from crying and shouting but it's got a red glow to it because it's smoldering with anger. "You ask at his school, they'll tell you. He has a little problem speaking, but the teachers say he's getting better."

The senior constable purses his lips and breathes air into Bahadur's ma's face. She doesn't even wince.

"In my opinion," the junior constable says, "the best thing to do is wait for a few days. I have seen many such cases. These children run away because they want to be free, then they come running right back because they realize freedom doesn't fill their stomachs."

"Although," the senior says, "it appears your husband . . . now . . . how can I put it"—he glances at Drunkard Laloo, who hangs his head—"was violent with your son?"

A scratchy silence fills the lane, broken by the clucks of hens that have escaped from clumsily bolted wire cages and the bleats of a goat from inside a house.

No one in our basti wants Drunkard Laloo to end up in prison. But we shouldn't lie because the senior constable is smart. I can tell because he's young like a college student and already a senior, and he's asking questions exactly like the good-cop types on TV. He doesn't want our money. His only mission is to put bad guys behind bars.

"Saab, once or twice who doesn't beat their

children, haan, saab?" a man standing near Drunkard Laloo answers for him. "That doesn't mean they should run away. Our children are more intelligent than we are. They know we want the best for them."

The senior constable studies the man's face and the man laughs nervously and looks elsewhere, at the silvery insides of empty namkeen packets on the ground and the small children trying to shake off their mothers' hands holding them back.

Drunkard Laloo opens his mouth. No words come out. Then he shivers as if a current from the earth is shooting up through his legs and hands.

Pari and Faiz won't believe me when I tell them what I'm seeing now. The best thing is that my grey uniform is good camouflage in the smog.

"You," the senior constable shouts, pointing at me. "Come here right now."

My head slams against the barrel as I hunch down quickly but I know I haven't been quick enough. **He'll shove your shit up your mouth**, I think. It's something I once heard my Muslim-hater classmate Gaurav say; he was talking about what Quarter would do to anyone who crossed him.

"Where's he gone? Where's the boy?"

My eyes lock on the white plate of a dish antenna angled toward the sky, attached to the edge of a tin roof across the lane. If I look at it with both my eyes, really look at it, I won't be able to see anything else. Everyone will disappear, even the policeman.

But he's standing at my side with his fingers drumming the lid of the water barrel. He takes off his khaki cap. Its tight elastic band has left a blotchy red line in the middle of his forehead.

"Let's see if this fits you better," he says, smiling and waving the cap in my face.

I shrink back from the cap that smells like armpits, and jails maybe.

"Don't want?" he asks.

"No," I say, and my voice is so weak even I can't hear it.

The policeman places the cap back on his head but doesn't pull it down. Then he scrapes the mud off his black leather shoes against a brick. The sole of his left shoe falls slack-mouth open, and loose stitches tremble like threads of spit. His shoes are torn exactly like my old ones.

"No school today?" he asks.

I haven't been coughing, so I say, "Dysentery. The teacher sent me home."

"O-ho," the policeman says. "You ate something you shouldn't have, didn't you? Mummy's cooking not to your liking?"

"No, good, it's very good."

Everything is going wrong today and it's all because of Bahadur.

"This boy we're looking for," he says, "you know him? He's in your school?"

"Same class only."

"Did he say anything about running off?"

"Bahadur can't speak. Stutter he has, right? He can't make words like proper children."

"What about his father?" The senior constable lowers his voice. "The boy said anything about his father beating him up?"

"Could be, that's why Bahadur ran away. But Faiz thinks djinns took him."

"Djinns?"

"Faiz says Allah made djinns. There are good and bad djinns same as there are good and bad people. A bad djinn might have snatched Bahadur."

"Faiz is your friend?"

"Yes."

I feel a bit guilty about snitching to the senior constable but I'm helping him in his investigation. Something I say will turn out to be a big clue that will help him crack the case. Then a child actor will play me on a **Police Patrol** show. It will be called **The Mysterious Disappearance of an Innocent Slum Boy—Part 1** or **In Search of a Missing Stutterer: A Heartbreaking Saga of Life in a Slum**. Police Patrol episodes have brilliant names.

"We don't have enough space to hold people in our jails. Now if we start arresting djinns too, where will we put them?" the policeman asks.

He is making fun of me, but I don't mind. I just wish I knew what he's waiting for me to say so that

I can say it and he can find Bahadur. Also, my neck is hurting from looking up at him.

The policeman scratches his cheeks. My stomach growls. Faiz usually helps me shush it by giving me the sugar-coated saunf he carries in his pockets, stolen from the dhaba where he works on some Sundays as a waiter.

"Maybe Bahadur was bored here, you think?" the policeman asks.

My stomach rumbles again and I push it down with my hands so that it will stay quiet. "Did his ma say that?" I ask. "She called you, didn't she? We never go to the police."

I have said too much but the policeman's face is empty. He hitches his khaki trousers up, straightens his cap, and turns to leave.

"There's a cobbler two lanes away," I say after him.

He stops and looks at me as if he's only seeing me for the first time now.

"For your shoes," I say. "He's very good. His name is Sulaiman and after he stitches the shoes, they'll look like there are no stitches only and he—"

"Has the president awarded him a Padma Shri too for his service?" the policeman asks. I don't answer because it's a joke but not a funny one.

He struts back to where everyone is standing. He nods his head at the junior constable, three sharp nods that are part of a secret signal like the ones between bowlers and fielders on a cricket field. Pari, Faiz, and I should make up a secret signal too.

"Nothing to see here," the junior constable shouts. "All of you, and I mean all of you, go back to your homes."

The fathers and mothers and children run inside, but a brown goat, dressed in a spotted sweater that makes it look like it's part leopard, comes out of a house and butts its head against the junior constable's legs.

"Motherfucker," he says, and kicks the goat.

I laugh. It comes out more loudly than I wanted it to.

"What are you looking at?" the junior constable asks. "Taking a video of me on your mobile?"

"No phone," I shout before he can arrest me. I step away from my barrel-shield, slowly, like a hero in a film with a gun pulled on him, and I turn the pockets of my trousers inside out so that he can see all I have is a striker from the school carrom board that I forgot to return.

"Chokra has to do No. 2," the senior constable tells the junior. "Let him go."

I grab my school bag and dart around the corner of the house where I had taken shelter, into an alley that's so narrow only children and goats and dogs can fit inside. It's safe here even if the ground is coated with goat pellets.

My shoulders brush against the walls. The filth

gets on my uniform. Ma is going to be very upset with me today.

I creep closer to the opening, my ears turned up to full volume to catch any whispers, and look outside. The junior constable waves a stick he must have picked up from the ground. "Everyone, inside," he shouts at the people who are still standing in the alley. "You two, stay," he tells Bahadur's ma and Drunkard Laloo.

The senior constable moves closer to them and says something that I can't hear. Bahadur's ma twists the gold chain around her neck and tries to unhook its clasp. Drunkard Laloo reaches to help her but Bahadur's ma pushes him away. She loves her gold chain.

When word got around the basti a few months back that Bahadur's ma had a gold chain that was twenty-four-carat gold, not fake like the glittery necklaces sold in Bhoot Bazaar, Papa said Bahadur's ma must have stolen it from her hi-fi madam. But Bahadur's ma told everyone that her madam had gifted it to her.

Ma said Bahadur's ma was unlucky in marriage but was lucky in work, and that everyone had something going right and wrong in their lives—their good or bad children, kind or cruel neighbors, or an ache in the bones that a doctor could cure easily or not at all—and this was how you knew the gods at least tried to be fair. Ma told Papa she would rather have a husband who didn't beat her than a real gold chain. Papa looked a bit taller after that.

Now Bahadur's ma unhooks the chain, cups it in her palm and extends it toward the senior constable. He leaps backward as if she has asked him to hold fire. She turns to Drunkard Laloo but he starts shivering again. He's good for nothing. I bet she wishes her boss-lady was with her instead of her husband.

"How can I take a gift from a woman?" the senior constable says. "I can't do this, no." His voice is bright like the apples that vendors polish with wax in the mornings.

Bahadur's ma sucks in air through her clenched teeth, slaps Drunkard Laloo on the wrist, and hands him her gold chain. The senior constable looks around, maybe to make sure no one else is watching. There's only the junior who's drawing lines on the ground with his stick, and Buffalo-Baba, and me, but he doesn't see me.

"Bahadur ki Ma, are you sure?" Drunkard Laloo finally speaks, shaking his curled-up fist with the chain over her head.

"It's fine," she says. "It's nothing."

"You two want to argue, you do that inside your house," the senior tells them. "I'm not here to solve your miya-biwi problems. But what I can do, what I'll have to do, is arrest you for creating a public nuisance."

"Forgive us, saab," Drunkard Laloo says, and hands over the gold chain to the senior constable, who swiftly deposits it in his pocket.

The policemen on **Live Crime** never take bribes, not even from men. I feel like a bad detective because I didn't see the wickedness inside the senior constable.

"Your son," he says now, "give him a couple of weeks. If he doesn't return by then, let me know."

"Saab," Bahadur's ma says, "but you said you'll look for him right away?"

"Everything in its own time," the senior says. Then he tells the junior, "Those NCs aren't going to write themselves. Chalo, bhai, hurry up."

"You're troublemakers, the whole lot of you," the junior constable tells Drunkard Laloo, "stealing current from the main lines, making hooch at home, gambling away everything you own. You keep misbehaving like this, the municipality will send JCBs to raze your homes."

Fatima comes out of her house after the policemen leave, scratches Buffalo-Baba between his horns, and feeds him a handful of spinach.

I don't want our basti to be bulldozed. When I find Bahadur, I'll give him a tight slap for making trouble. He won't even stop me because in his heart he will know, that's exactly what he deserves.

BAHADUR

From a distance the boy watched three men swathed in blankets huddle by a fire. Ash-tipped flames rose from a large metal bowl once used to carry cement at a construction site. The men let their hands hover above the fire as if performing a solemn ritual. Yellow sparks leaped higher than their faces but their hands didn't return to the folds of their blankets.

There was a silent companionship between these men that made Bahadur wish he were older, so that he too could have sat with them. But he was only a boy hiding under a pushcart that smelled of guavas, a faint sweet note that trickled down to him through the charred winter air.

The cart's owner was sleeping on the footpath nearby, his body turned toward a shop's padlocked shutter, and covered like a corpse from head to toe with a sheet that wasn't thick enough to muffle his snores. Bahadur had searched, carefully, under the folded tarpaulin sheets and sacks on the cart for guavas and found none. The owner must have walked long and far to sell the fruit.

Bahadur wasn't sure how long he had been watching the men. It was well past midnight and he knew he should sleep, but it was cold, and he wanted to walk and warm the blood in his veins. He crawled out and turned to look at the men again. They were drinking from the same bottle, each man taking a sip, then wiping its lip against his sweater sleeve before passing it on. In another hour, they would be drowsing by the fire, with bricks for pillows, legs half-covered by blankets splayed out across the lane.

The alleys of Bhoot Bazaar stretched around Bahadur like the gaping mouths of demons. He wasn't scared. He used to be, when he first started sleeping outside on those nights his mother stayed back at the flat where she worked, to care for madam's feverish child, or to serve guests at a party that madam was hosting. Until then Bahadur had seen the bazaar only in the day, when it heaved with people and animals and vehicles and the gods invoked in the prayers drifting out of loudspeakers from a temple, a gurudwara, and a mosque. All these scents and sounds so thick they seeped into him as if he were made of gauze.

So, aged seven, when he first snuck away to the bazaar late at night to escape his father, its stillness spooked him. The sky roiled blackish-blue above tangled cables and dusty street lamps. The market was mostly empty but for the crumpled forms of sleeping men. Then his ears grew accustomed to the distant, steady thrum of the highway. His nose learned to catch the weakest of smells from hours before—marigold garlands, sliced papayas served with a pinch of chaat powder on top, puris fried in oil—to guide his steps to the right or left in dark corners. His eyes could tell the stray dogs in the alleys apart by the curves of their tails or the shapes of the white patches on their brown or black coats.

Now he was almost ten, old enough to be on his own though he would never say that to his mother. She didn't know that he came here. The world had long ago receded from his father's hooch-stained eyes such that he couldn't tell flesh from shadow.

On the nights his mother was away, his siblings cajoled the neighborhood aunties into taking them in. They thought a friend's family did the same for him. But Bahadur didn't want a corner of anyone's crowded floor. In every house—even his only friend

Omvir's—there was a chachi who clucked her tongue too often and asked the gods to lift the curse they had put on him, and children who sneered at the way letters stayed glued to his tongue no matter how much he tried to spit them loose. To them he was always That Idiot or Duffer or Ka-Ka-Ka-Ka or He-He-He-Ro-Ro. They called him Rat-eater and asked him if his mother cleaned the shit crusting the basti's toilets. There was none of that in the bazaar at night. He didn't have to talk to anyone. If he wanted, he could even pretend that he was a prince patrolling his kingdom disguised as a street child.

The downed shutters of shops were crinkled like waves. The cold caught up with him, no matter how fast he walked. He stopped near a cycle-rickshaw driver sleeping under a blanket on the passenger seat of his vehicle. Hanging from the handlebar was a white plastic bag that the man had used to pack his lunch or dinner, with something dark and thick pooled at the bottom. Bahadur untied the bag as quietly as he could, then ran ahead and inspected its contents. A ladle's worth of black dal, which he guzzled with his neck tilted toward the sky.

This was his third night wandering around the bazaar. His best chance for a proper meal would be when his mother returned home on Tuesday, but it was still Saturday and the hours stretched ahead as dark and boundless as the sky. He chucked the bag in his hand into a gutter, then kneeled down and sifted through a pile of trash heaped by the stalls where in the day vendors sold papdi chaat and aloo tikkis glazed with curd and tamarind chutney. But the animals of the bazaar had got to the food before him. He wiped his hands against the bottom of a discarded aluminum foil bowl and stood up.

A heaviness settled in his chest. The air was sharp with smoke and soon the tickle in his nostrils would turn into a cough that would leave him gasping for breath. He knew that it would pass, in a few minutes perhaps. It seemed unfair to him that he struggled with the things that came naturally to everyone else, things like talking and breathing. But he was done with cursing gods, done with trying to get them on his side with prayers.

He walked a little ahead to Hakim's Electronics and Electrical Repair Shop, which was his favorite place in the bazaar. Hakim-Chacha never expected him to talk and instead taught him about blown capacitors and loose cables and paid him for the work he did around the store though Bahadur would have done it for nothing. Bahadur's mother had once hired two boys to bring home a clattering refrigerator and a TV that a hi-fi madam had tossed into the rubbish ground near their basti. Bahadur had fixed them in no time, made them as good as new. Chacha said that Bahadur had a gift. That when he grew up he would be an engineer and live in a hi-fi flat.

Bahadur wished a man like chacha had been his father. The past two days, each time he visited the electronics shop, chacha had bought him newspaper cones filled with warm peanuts roasted in salt. He had done so without knowing Bahadur was hungry. Bahadur had stored a few peanuts in the pockets of his jeans for later, though they were all gone now. He checked again, without hope, pushing his hands deep into his pockets. When he brought them out, a few papery skins were stuck to the tips of his fingers. He licked them, tasting the salt, remembering too late that it would make him thirsty.

A smog was beginning to swill against the street lights. He swallowed the air in big gulps and curled up on a raised platform outside the repair shop, his hands around himself, his knees pulled up toward his chest. He was still cold. He got up and found two red crates caked with dirt stacked outside the shop next door, and balanced them on top of his legs, but they were uncomfortable and didn't lessen the chill. He pushed them aside and lay down again.

The smog looked like the devil's own breath. It hid the street lights and made the darkness darker. To calm himself Bahadur thought of all the things

he liked to do: pulling the orange ears of a blue
mother-elephant toy, an elephant baby the size of a
gol-gappa nestled in its trunk, bought on a whim
from a roadside vendor at Bhoot Bazaar; swinging
on rubber tires tied to the branches of toothbrush
trees; and holding a warm brick swaddled in rags
that his ma gave him on moon-cold nights. He
imagined her rubbing his chest with Vicks VapoRub
though he had only seen this on TV and they didn't
even have a tub of the ointment in their house.
But it soothed him, and he decided to hold on to
that picture until he fell asleep.

Then: a movement in the alley that he sensed
in the ground. He cocked his ears for footsteps, but
there was nothing.

Memories that he didn't care to remember rustled
in his head. On a summer night two years ago, a
man who smelled of cigarettes, with a mustache as
thick as a squirrel's tail, had pinioned him against a
wall with one hand and, with the other, loosened
the knot of his own salwar. Bahadur shook a little,
still feeling the pressure of the man's palm. A group
of laborers returning home had seen what was happening and chased the man, giving Bahadur enough
time to run away. He had stopped wandering in the
bazaar for months afterward until his fears dulled
and his father's temper flared again.

Bahadur wondered if he should pick another

spot to sleep. Outside the repair shop the alley was too empty. Any other night it would have been fine, but who knew what beast lurked in this smog, waiting to clamp its teeth on his legs? Where had this smog come from? He had never seen anything like it. Above him, on the roof overhang, pigeons grunted and shuffled. Then, as if nervous, they took off.

He sat up and stared into the darkness, his palms fixed to the floor, small stones stabbing his skin. A cat mewled and a dog barked as if to hush it. He thought of the ghosts after whom Bhoot Bazaar had been named, the friendly spirits of the people who had lived in these parts hundreds of years ago when the Mughals had been kings. "Allah ki kasam," Hakim-Chacha had told Bahadur once, "they'll never hurt us."

If a ghost from the bazaar was in fact approaching Bahadur, maybe it wanted to help him breathe or tell him it was foolish to sleep outside on a night like this. Maybe if he showed the ghost his face, the impress of his father's hand on his skin, the ghost would let him stay. Hakim-Chacha never said a word about his wounds or the Band-Aids his mother plastered over them. But only the day before, Bahadur had glimpsed his own reflection on the screen of an ancient TV at the repair shop, behind which he had hidden the precious things he couldn't keep at home, and the bruise around his eye had looked shiny and black like the river that divided his city in two.

Bahadur told himself he was being silly. Ghosts and monsters lived only in the stories people told each other. But the air pulsed with dread, palpable like static. He thought he could see phantom limbs outlined in white, mouths without lips drawn toward him by the clamor of his breathing.

Maybe he should get up and run home. Maybe tonight he should knock on Omvir's door. But the cold snagged his bones, which felt so brittle that he thought they would snap. He wished the blackness would part, the moon would shine, and the men he had seen by the fire would saunter down this alley. The smog tightened around his neck like a coil of coarse rope.

Now he could hear them: the pitter-patter of bandicoots hunting in packs for crumbs, a horse neighing somewhere, the clang of a metal bucket being overturned by a cat or a dog, and then, the slow footsteps of something or someone he was certain was coming toward him. He opened his mouth to scream but couldn't. The sound of it stayed pinned to the back of his throat like all the words he had never been able to say.

TONIGHT IS
OUR LAST NIGHT—

—in the basti, Ma says. No need for this drama-baazi, Papa says. What if we lose everything, Runu-Didi says.

I sit cross-legged on the bed and watch Ma make a clearing on the floor. She stacks against the wall our books, plastic footstools, and the pots she and Didi use to bring water from the tap. In the new empty space, she spreads out a pink bedsheet with black flowers, the colors wrung out to almost-grey by too many washings. Then she picks up the things we can't do without and heaps them on the sheet: our best clothes, including my plastic-wrapped uniform, her roti rolling pin and board, and a small statue of Lord Ganesh that Dada gave Papa years ago. The TV stays on the shelf. It's too heavy for us to carry around.

"When did our house become a set for a Hindi picture, haan, Jai?" Papa asks, sitting next to me with the TV remote in his hand. I straighten his crooked shirt collar. It's tattered where Runu-Didi or Ma scrubbed it too hard to get rid of dirt and paint stains.

Didi tries to help Ma but keeps getting in her way. Ma doesn't scold her. Instead she keeps muttering Bahadur's ma was wrong to go to the police.

"Her brain isn't working," Ma says. "All this running around hospitals, I suppose it can make anyone go mad. Arrey, she even asked Baba Bengali to tell her where her boy is. Paid him a fortune too. Everyone was talking about it when Runu and I went to the tap to get water in the evening."

Baba Bengali looks like he has just stepped out of a cave in the Himalayas, with his ropey hair and muddy feet, but he uses computers. Once I saw him outside Dev Cyber Print House in Bhoot Bazaar, holding a sheaf of posters that he then pasted around the bazaar. The posters claimed he had answers to grave problems such as cheating wives, cheating husbands, angry mothers-in-law, hungry ghosts, black magic, bad debt and bad health.

Ma walks around the room, deciding what else needs to go into her bedsheet. She picks up her alarm clock that never runs on time but puts it back on the shelf.

"What did Baba Bengali say?" I ask.

"He said Bahadur will never come back," Runu-Didi says.

"That baba is a fraud," Papa says. "He makes money out of people's misery."

"Ji, you don't believe in him, that's fine," Ma says. "But don't badmouth him like this. We don't want him cursing us."

Then she stands on a footstool and removes an old, blue plastic tub of Parachute 100% Pure Coconut Oil from the topmost shelf. The oil inside it is all gone. Instead, there are a few hundred-rupee notes that Ma stores in case "Something Happens," though she has never said what the Something is that might Happen. She puts the tub on top of her mango-powder tin, from where it's easier to grab if we have to run out of the house in the dark. The tub is like Ma's purse except I have never seen her open it.

"Listen," Papa tells Ma, "Madhu, meri jaan, the police won't do anything to us. Drunkard Laloo's wife has given them her gold chain. Nobody's bringing JCBs to crush our basti."

I look at Papa open-mouthed because he only

just came home but has already found out about the gold chain. What if he knows Kirpal-Sir kicked me out of school too?

So far no one has asked me why I got home early, not Shanti-Chachi who gave me a plate of the kadhi pakora and rice her husband had made for her, or Runu-Didi, whose No. 1 job Papa says is to keep a sharp eye on me. Ma didn't even notice the new dirt-stains on my uniform, probably because the basti was full of talk about Bahadur and the police, whispery-scary talk that made people forget me.

"What do we lose by being a little careful?" Ma says now. "Maybe there'll be bulldozers, maybe not. Who knows anything for sure?" She wraps two cotton dupattas around a framed certificate that Runu-Didi's team won for coming first in a state-level relay race, and places it gently on top of her pile. It slips down to the side and lies crooked above the rolling pin. Ma straightens the frame again, biting the inside of her cheeks and breathing heavily.

The dangly bulb above me hums with hot current, and its shadow swishes over the shelves, the cracks on the wall, and the watermarks from monsoon floods that I can see now because Ma has moved tins and plates around. Ma likes our house to be clean, and she scolds me if I don't put my school books and clothes where she has told me to put them, and now she's the one making a big mess.

Papa puts his arm around my shoulders and brings me close to his paint-and-smog smells. "Women, na," he says. "Getting worried over nothing."

"It's not nothing," I say.

"Jai, the police can't just start a demolition drive. They have to give us advance warning," Papa says. "They have to paste notices, talk to our pradhan. Our basti has been here for years. We have identity cards, we have rights. We're not Bangladeshis."

"What rights?" Ma asks. "These minister-people only remember us a week before the elections. And how can anyone trust that badmash pradhan? He doesn't even live here anymore."

"Is that really true?" I ask. It's hard to imagine Quarter in a hi-fi flat. He looks like he belongs in jail.

"Madhu, if the police demolish our basti, where will they get bribes from?" Papa says, which is what Pari had said too. "How will their fat wives eat chicken every day?"

Papa pretends his teeth are tearing the meat off a chicken leg. He makes slurpy-hungry noises and licks his fingers.

I laugh but Ma's lips are turned down and she keeps packing. When she finally finishes, she places the bundle by the door. She has to lift it with both hands because she has stuffed too many things inside. Only Papa will be able to run with it slung over his shoulder.

Afterward, we have dinner.

"If our basti is demolished," Runu-Didi says, "will you make us live with Dada-Dadi? I won't go there, okay, I'm telling you right now. I won't do all this purdah-vurdah nonsense. I'm going to win a medal for India one day."

"That day a donkey will sing like Geeta Dutt," I say.

Geeta Dutt is Papa's favorite singer. She sings in black and white.

"Children," Papa says, "the worst thing that's going to happen is that we won't be able to eat rotis until your very wise, very beautiful mother unpacks her rolling pin. That's all. Understand?"

He looks at Ma and smiles. Ma doesn't smile back.

Papa tucks my hair behind my ear with his left hand. "We have been paying the police hafta on time. And now they have got an extra gold chain. Like a second Diwali bonus. They won't bother us for a while."

When dinner is done and the washing-up is finished, Ma dries her hands on her sari and tells me I can sleep on the bed tonight. Papa looks startled.

"Why?" he asks. "What did I do?"

"My back's hurting," Ma says without looking at him. "Easier to sleep on the floor."

Didi drags out the mat she and I usually share

from under the bed. She does it so quickly that the bags Ma stores there spill out.

"Watch it," Papa says and angry lines crease his face.

I help Didi put everything back into the bags, a plastic gun and a wooden monkey that I haven't played with in ages, and the torn clothes Didi and I have outgrown. Together we spread the mat out on the floor. Its edges are permanently curled where they hit the legs of the bed.

Papa switches on the TV. The news doesn't have anything interesting today. It's all about politics. I stand at the door, listening to our neighbors argue about police and bribes and whether our basti will be demolished or not.

Once I find Bahadur, people won't have these silly discussions. Instead they'll talk about me, Jasoos Jai, the Greatest Detective on Earth.

Tomorrow I'll ask Faiz to be my assistant. We'll be like Byomkesh Bakshi and Ajit and we'll detect in the smog-dark lanes of Bhoot Bazaar. We'll even have our own secret signal, which will be much better than the one the police constables had.

Papa gets tired of the news and tells me to come to bed. I shut the door and switch off the light. Ma lies down on the mat next to Didi. Papa snores in no time, but I pinch myself so that I'll stay awake. What if Papa is wrong about JCBs? I draw a map

of the basti in my head and think of the quickest
escape route we can take.

I turn toward the posters of Lord Shiva and
Lord Krishna that Papa has taped to the wall. I
can't see them in the dark but I know they are
there. I ask them and all the other gods I can
name to help us. I decide to say the same prayer
nine times so that the gods know how badly I want
this. Ma says nine is the gods' favorite number.

Please God, don't send bulldozers to our basti.
Please God, don't send bulldozers to our basti.
Please God, don't send bulldozers to our basti.
When I find Bahadur, I'll shove his shit up his
mouth.

I slap myself on the forehead for thinking bad
thoughts while praying.

"Mosquitoes?" Ma asks.

"Haan."

I hear the jingle of Ma's glass bangles, and the
rustle of a blanket she has probably pulled up to
her nose.

Dear God, no bulldozers. **Please please please.**

———

The next morning, we are late for school, and we
have to run, so I don't get to talk to Faiz about my
detectiving idea. I'm tired and sleepy at assembly.
In the classroom too, my eyes keep shutting, so I

have to hold them open with my fingers. It's easier to stay awake if you're flying paper rockets or taking part in arm-wrestling contests like everybody else is doing now.

Kirpal-Sir doesn't try to stop us. He's pretending like all of yesterday didn't happen; like he didn't scold Pari or throw me out of school. I can pretend too. When I hear the loud phad-phad of a Bullet motorbike on the road outside, I drop a pencil and bend down to pick it up. With my head under the table, I imitate the bike, **taka-taka-taka-taka**. It's like a hundred firecrackers bursting in my mouth, filling it with sparks. It wakes me up proper. Others in the classroom laugh. Kirpal-Sir shouts **silence, silence**, but the laughter only gets louder.

Gaurav makes the Bullet noise along with me. Kirpal-Sir takes out his ruler and raps the table. Slowly the classroom falls quiet.

Sir teaches us Social Science for one hour, then Maths for another; he teaches us everything because they don't let him into the senior classes anymore. He stops talking only when the bell rings for the midday meal.

In the corridor, we sit cross-legged with our backs against the wall. I look for Omvir, so I can ask him about Bahadur, but I don't see him anywhere.

The midday-meal people put stainless steel plates in front of us.

"That India map Kirpal-Sir made, with the sun in the east?" I say. "How bad was that? His sun looked like a broken-shelled egg."

"I hope we get eggs today," Faiz says.

"When have we ever had an egg?" I ask. I'm annoyed he's not letting me finish what I want to say, but I wouldn't mind an egg either.

I sniff the air to detect what the midday-meal people have brought for us, but everywhere smells only of smog now.

"I want puri-subzi," Pari says. Then she chants **puri-subzi puri-subzi puri-subzi** and other students giggle and join in too until the midday-meal people slop vegetable daliya onto our plates. It's so watery we have to drink it holding the plates up to our mouths as if it's gruel. Our plates are empty soon but our tummies are still growly.

"These midday-meal people are making donkeys out of the government," Pari says. "They keep all the good food for their own children and give us this." She says this often but there's never a grain of rice left on her plate.

"Stop complaining, yaar," Faiz says. "At least it's not made with pesticide like in Bihar."

Pari can't argue with that because she was the one who told us about the children in Bihar who died after eating their midday meal. She knows so much because she reads everything, greasy news-papers wrapped around naans and pappads, the covers of magazines hanging outside stalls, and the books at the reading center near the mosque in Bhoot Bazaar where Faiz goes to pray.

The didi at the center once told Pari's ma that she should ask a private school to take Pari under their "poor quota," because Pari was too clever for a government school. Pari's ma said they had tried and it hadn't worked out. Pari claimed it doesn't matter where she studies. On the news, she had seen an interview with a boy from a basti like ours who had topped the civil services exam and was now a district collector. If he could do it, she could too, Pari said. I agreed with her but didn't say so aloud.

Now we grovel for more daliya but the midday-meal people have shut off their ears, so we wash our hands and troop down to the playground. Bhoot Bazaar sounds noisy from here, but we are even noisier.

Runu-Didi is standing in the corridor, talking to her friends. She doesn't look sleepy like me. She can snore even when the earth is quaking and breaking apart. But the good thing about her is that once we are inside the school, she acts as if she doesn't know me. I like it that way because she never rats on me either.

Four boys are looking at Runu-Didi's group with sly eyes and toothy smiles. One of them is the spotty boy who was in my school queue yesterday.

His friends laugh at something he says. Runu-Didi and the other girls glare at them.

Near the neem tree where Quarter is holding his afternoon court, I find a twig that I can chew to fool my tummy into thinking more food is on its way. A few boys are standing around Quarter, hands tucked into their armpits for warmth. Paresh, who's in Standard Six and from our basti, is telling Quarter about the police constables and Bahadur. But Paresh wasn't even there like I was when it happened.

"The constables asked every woman in the basti to give them whatever they could, gold or cash," he says. "The policemen hit Buffalo-Baba with batons too."

I want to put Paresh right but break will be over soon and I have an important task to do. I order Pari and Faiz to follow me to an empty space under an amaltas tree whose flowers paint the ground yellow in spring. Tanvi and her watermelon backpack that she carries everywhere try to join us, but I shoo-shoo them away.

"This whole poor-Bahadur-is-missing thing," I tell Pari and Faiz, "it's like a bad Hindi picture, it's been going on for too long."

I have to speak up because the small children playing kabbadi-kabbadi-kabbadi are squealing too loud, their fast-as-cheetahs feet kicking up dust from the ground in big, brown swirls.

"I'm going to be a detective, and I'm going to find Bahadur," I say, putting on my best grown-up voice. "And Faiz, you'll be my assistant. Every detective has one. Like Byomkesh has Ajit and Feluda has Topshe."

Pari and Faiz look at each other.

"Feluda is a detective and Topshe is his cousin," I explain. "They're Bengalis. The Bengali Sweets-wallah in Bhoot Bazaar, next to Afsal-Chacha's shop, you have seen him. The old man who shakes a broomstick at us if we go too close to his sweets? That guy. His son reads Feluda comics. He told me a Feluda story once."

"What kind of name is Feluda?" Faiz asks.

"How come you get to be the detective?" Pari asks.

"That's very true," Faiz says. "Why can't you be my assistant?"

"Arrey, what do you know about being a detective? You don't watch **Police Patrol**."

"I know about Sherlock and Watson," Pari says. "You two haven't even heard of them."

"What-son?" Faiz asks. "Is that also a Bengali name?"

"Leave it," Pari says.

"Just because you read books doesn't mean you know everything," Faiz tells her. "I work. Life's the best teacher. Everyone says so."

"Only people who can't read say such things," Pari says.

These two are always quarrelling like a husband and a wife who have been married for too long. But they can't even get married when we grow up because Faiz is a Muslim. It's too dangerous to marry a Muslim if you're a Hindu. On the TV news, I have seen blood-red photos of people who were murdered because they married someone from a different religion or caste. Also, Faiz is shorter than Pari, so they wouldn't make a good match anyway.

"This assistant job," Faiz says, "how much does it pay?"

"No one is paying us," I say. "Bahadur's ma is poor. She had a gold chain and now that's also gone."

"Why should I do this then?" Faiz asks.

"Bahadur's ma will keep going to the police and the police will get angry and demolish our basti," Pari explains **my thinking** to Faiz. "But we can stop her if we find him."

"I don't have time," Faiz says. "I have to work."

"So that your hair will be Silky Soft?" Pari asks. "Or Stunning Black?"

"So that I'll smell like Purple Lotus and Cream," Faiz says.

"There's no such thing. It's made up. Your life-teacher forgot to tell you that or what?" Pari sneers.

"Listen," I say, so they'll stop fighting. "I'll ask a

few questions. Whoever gets the most answers right can become my assistant."

They both groan loudly, as if they have stubbed their toes against a big stone.

"Jai, you na," Pari says.

"He's mad," Faiz agrees.

"Okay, first question. Are most children in India kidnapped by: (a) people they know, or (b) people they don't know?"

Pari doesn't answer. Faiz doesn't answer.

The bell rings.

"We can look for Bahadur together," Pari tells me, "but I won't be your assistant or anything. No way."

I'm sad Faiz won't be my assistant, but a girl can be a good assistant too. Maybe. Papa told me about a detective show called **Karamchand** that came on TV a long time ago. Karamchand had a woman-assistant named Kitty, but unfortunately Kitty wasn't smart and Karamchand had to spend the whole show telling her to shut up. It's the kind of story that would make Pari furious. If I tell Pari to shut up, she'll kick my shins.

"What should our secret signal be?" I ask Pari. "Detectives should have secret signals."

"That's the first order of business? A secret signal?" Pari asks. "Be serious."

"This is serious."

Pari rolls her eyes. We walk back to the class-room.

"If a child has been missing for more than twenty-four hours, the police have to file a case of kidnapping," I say.

"How do you know that?" Pari asks.

"TV," I say. "The police haven't done that for Bahadur."

"Didn't read about this police rule in your books?" Faiz asks Pari.

"Most children in India are kidnapped by strangers," I tell them. I don't know that for sure, but it sounds about right to me.

OUR FIRST JOB
AS DETECTIVES—

—is to interview Omvir. He will know more about Bahadur than anyone else. That's the rule; our friends know the things we hide from our parents. Ma has no idea that before Diwali, the headmaster boxed my ears when I sang "Twinkle Twinkle Little Star" instead of "Jana Gana Mana" at assembly. But Pari and Faiz do. They called me Twinkle for a few days and then forgot about it. Ma would never forget. This is why I can't tell her anything.

Faiz, who's not even part of our detective team, shoots down my interview-plan the second I suggest it.

"You should question Quarter first," he says as we head home from school. The smog sloshes in and out of his mouth, making him cough. "Quarter is your No. 1 suspect, right, Jai? That's why you talked to him yesterday."

"What do you know? You think a djinn took Bahadur."

I speak in a whisper. If djinns are real, I don't want them to hear me.

"We can interview everyone," Pari says. "Let's stop at the theka and ask people about Quarter. If they're drunk, they might tell us the truth."

"Accha, now you're an expert on drunkards also?" Faiz asks.

It's my job to decide what we should do, but before I can protest, Faiz punches the black air with his rolled-up fist and shouts, "Theka chalo."

He'll be late for his shift at a kirana store where he stocks shelves and bags rice and lentils, but he doesn't mind. He's hoping he'll run into his older brothers at the theka.

Muslims aren't supposed to drink, and Tariq-Bhai and Wajid-Bhai are good Muslims who pray five times a day, but they also sneak out sometimes to share a bottle of daru. If Faiz catches them, they'll pay him big money to keep it a secret from their ammi. Otherwise Faiz will ask their ammi to sniff his brothers' faces closely that night. "Something black in the dal, don't you think, Ammi?" Faiz will say pointedly.

He has done it before.

Faiz and Pari march into the lane that leads to the theka, not even waiting for me. My detectiving hasn't begun and it's already gone off track.

The lane is filled with suspicious people and smells. A nani-type lady with a marigold stuck behind her ear runs a beedi-paan stall, but when boys and men hand her money, she gives them plastic pouches packed with something dried and brown-green instead of cigarettes.

"Focus," Pari hisses into my ear and drags me away.

Drunkards squat or lie on the ground outside the theka, singing and speaking gibberish. The loud beats bouncing out of the theka make the air tremble.

"We can't talk to these idiots," Pari says.

Faiz points to a man selling eggs and bread from his cart. "Ask the anda-wallah. He's always here."

We stand to the side of the cart because the anda-wallah has stacked egg cartons to the front; we aren't tall enough for him to see us behind them.

"Quarter, you know him?" I ask. The anda-wallah is sharpening knives, and the clink-clank of it is louder than the music blaring out of the theka. He doesn't look up.

"Quarter only wears black. He's our pradhan's son," Pari says. Then she turns to Faiz and whispers, "What's his real name?"

Faiz shrugs. I don't know Quarter's name either.

"Make it fast-fast," a customer to the front of the cart says.

The anda-wallah puts his knives down and flings a slab of butter into the pan, then a fistful of chopped onions, tomatoes and green chillies. He coats them with salt and chili powder and garam masala. My mouth waters too much for me to ask questions. Just this afternoon we were talking about eating eggs, and now I'm at an egg stall. I wonder if Byomkesh Bakshi ever felt too hungry to investigate.

"Sir-ji," Faiz says, "we're looking for Quarter." Actually, Faiz's eyes are scanning the lane for his brothers, but his luck is bad today because they aren't here.

"He'll grace us with his presence in a while, no doubt," the anda-wallah says.

"Was he here"—Pari asks and pauses to count something on her fingers—"seven nights ago? Last Thursday?"

I hate that it's a good question; if Quarter was at the theka the night Bahadur disappeared, then he couldn't have snatched Bahadur.

"Probably," the anda-wallah says, breaking two

eggs at a time into the pan. "What do you care where he was?"

"We're looking for a friend of ours who has gone missing," Pari says. "He could have been with the pradhan's son. We're worried about him."

She looks worried too. Her eyes narrow, her lips wobble like she's about to cry.

The anda-wallah props his ladle against his shoulder. His shirt is yolk-stained yellow. "Quarter and his gang are usually here even when I leave at two or three in the morning. But I haven't seen a single child with them. They're too old to be friends with children."

"But Quarter was here last week, every night?" I ask.

"Of course he was here. He doesn't have to pay for daru. You get something for free, you'll take it too, won't you?"

I look at the eggs hopefully. The anda-wallah transfers the bhurji onto a paper plate, sticks a spoon on top of the egg mountain, and hands it to his impatient customer.

"Look who's here," Faiz whispers.

Quarter staggers past the cart as if he's already drunk, eyeing us curiously. We can't ask people about him when he's around, so we leave.

Faiz knows everything about Bhoot Bazaar because he spends more time here than Pari or me.
"The pradhan keeps the theka in business," he says
when we are at a safe distance from Quarter. "It's
illegal, but he has told the police not to touch it."

The pradhan's hand smudges every lane in our
basti. He has a network of informers who give him
the basti-news 24/7. Ma is contemptuous of these
men who watch us so that they can run to
the pradhan with stories of a shiny-new TV or
fridge in a basti-home or gossip about whose hi-fi
madam was generous with baksheesh during
Diwali. Ma says the pradhan sends policemen to
separate people from the little happiness they have.

Faiz leaves for the kirana shop. He has had a
bad day. No eggs, no bhai-sightings at the theka,
no more detective work with us.

"If Quarter spends every night at the theka,
does that mean he didn't snatch Bahadur?" I ask,
pulling Pari away from the path of an e-rick that
swerves and falters through the lane.

"The anda-wallah wasn't hundred-percent sure,"
Pari says. "He said **usually** Quarter's there at night.
Also, we don't know what time Bahadur disappeared. It could have been at four in the morning
even."

This is just how detectiving is; everything is
guesswork at first, even for Byomkesh Bakshi and
probably for Sherlock too.

We walk toward Omvir's house. A boy with a stray dog on a leash walks alongside us. His dog is a pretend-horse; he holds the leash like it's a rein, click-clicks his tongue and makes the clip-clop sounds of horses' hooves.

"We should get a dog too," I tell Pari. "It will lead us to criminals."

"Focus," Pari says. "Why would Quarter snatch Bahadur?"

"Maybe he wants a ransom."

"If someone had asked Bahadur's ma for a ransom, we would have heard of it by now."

"She mustn't have told anybody," I say.

———

We can't talk to Omvir because he isn't at home.

"Since that friend of his went missing, he's been dawdling around Bhoot Bazaar, hoping he'll run into Bahadur somewhere," Omvir's ma says. She's holding a small baby boy who keeps punching her face with his tiny fists.

Omvir's brother is susu-ing into the drain outside their house. Doing No. 1 and No. 2 right where you live can put long worms into your stomach, which is why Ma insists I use the toilet complex. Omvir's ma tires of her boxer-baby's punches and goes inside her house to put him to sleep, drawing their curtain-door shut behind her.

The boy, who's smaller than us, finishes peeing and zips up his jeans-pant.

"Does Omvir have a mobile?" Pari asks him. "We need to talk to him."

"Bhaiyya is with Papa. Papa has a mobile. You want his number?"

"No," I say. It will be tough to explain our detecting to a grown-up.

"Omvir doesn't come to school or what?" Pari asks.

"Bhaiyya is busy. He has to help Papa all day. He picks up clothes to be ironed from customers and, once it's done, he drops them back. If he has any free time, he spends it dancing, not studying."

"Dancing?" Pari asks.

"That's all he talks about. He thinks he's the new Hrithik."

The boy hums the notes of a Hrithik song, swings his hands, bobs his head, jiggles his legs. It takes me a while to figure out he's dancing.

"Why Am I Like This?" he wails, prancing around happily. "Why Am I Like This?"

Pari grins. She's enjoying the show.

"Our work's not over," I remind her.

———

The front door to Bahadur's house is open. When we peer inside, it's exactly like my home except there's more of everything: more clothes hanging from the clotheslines above us, more upturned pots and pans on a raised platform that's the kitchen corner, more framed photos of gods on the walls, the glass turning sooty because of the joss sticks thrust into the corners of the frames, a bigger TV, and even a fridge, which we don't have at all, so in the summer everything Ma makes we have to eat the same day. Bahadur's ma must get paid a lot more than my ma and papa.

Drunkard Laloo is sleeping on a bed that looks like a hi-fi bed. A blanket is pulled up to his shoulders. Bahadur's younger brother and sister are sitting on the floor, picking out stones from the grains of rice spread on a steel plate.

"Namaste," Pari says, standing at the doorstep. She never greets anyone that way. "Can you please come outside? We want to find out about Bahadur."

"Bhaiyya isn't here," Bahadur's sister says as she gets up obediently, gaping at us though Pari and I are wearing the same school uniform that she must have seen Bahadur wearing. Her brother comes out too.

"Do you know where Bahadur is?" Pari asks, which is a bad question. They would have told their ma if they had known.

"What's your name?" I ask the girl because good detectives become friends with everyone first so that they'll speak the truth. The girl wiggles. She's wearing boy's trousers several sizes too big for her, tightened at the waist with a long, fat safety pin.

"We're Bahadur's classmates," Pari says. "I'm Pari and this here is Jai. We're trying to find your brother. Was there some place he liked to go to after school?"

"Bhoot Bazaar," the boy says. He's wearing a girl's blouse with white ruffles and pink embroidery. Maybe he swapped clothes with his sister and his ma didn't notice.

"Where in the bazaar?" Pari asks.

"Bahadur-Bhaiyya worked at Hakim-Chacha's Electronics Shop. He fixed our TV and also our fridge and also that air cooler."

"Bahadur fixes things?" I ask. A cobwebbed pink cooler is plonked on top of bricks so that it faces a window-like gap in the wall, from where it can blast cold air into their house.

Pari shoots me a warning glance with her eyes as round as she can make them. If we had a secret signal, she would have used that right now to shut me up.

"We think Bhaiyya has run away," the boy says.

"To where?" I ask.

The girl presses the bridge of her nose with her hand, squashing it. "My name is Barkha," she says. Then she puts a finger inside her nose.

"Bhaiyya used to talk about running away to

Manali," the boy says. "With the press-wallah's son. Omvir."

"No Manali. Mumbai yes," the girl says.

"Is it Manali or is it Mumbai?" Pari asks.

The boy scratches his ear. The girl pulls her finger out of her nose and looks at her nails.

"Omvir wants to go to Mumbai to see Hrithik Roshan," the boy says. "But Bhaiyya wants to see the snow in Manali. Now it's winter, na, so there's lots of snow."

"Omvir is still here," I say.

"Haan, maybe Bhaiyya went to Manali by himself," the boy says. "He'll come back once he has played in the snow."

"At home everything has been okay?" Pari asks. "The last time I saw Bahadur at school he seemed a bit"—her face scrunches up as she tries to find the right word—"bruised?"

"Papa slaps us a lot," Bahadur's brother says, like it's nothing. "Bhaiyya would have run away a long time ago if that bothered him."

"Was anyone else troubling Bahadur?" Pari asks.

"Any enemies?" I finally manage to ask a question.

"Bhaiyya never gets into trouble," the boy says.

"Do you have a photo of him?" Pari asks.

I kick myself for not thinking of it first. Photos are the most important part of any investigation. Policemen are supposed to put up a missing-child's photo on their computer from where the Internet will carry it to other police stations the same way our veins carry blood to our arms and legs and brain.

The safety pin holding up the girl's trousers pops open. She starts crying. The boy grins. Three or four of his front teeth are missing.

Pari says "uff" like she has had enough, but she tells the girl, "Don't cry. I'll make it right in a minute. One minute only." She pins it back in two seconds.

"Papa will have a photo," the boy says, running his hand over his shirt-blouse ruffles.

We tiptoe into Bahadur's house. It smells sour like sickness and sweet like rotting fruit. Bahadur's brother and sister sit down on the floor, away from the bed. I want them to wake up Drunkard Laloo but their eyes are already on the rice, divided into two sections: one that has been cleared of stones, and the other yet to be inspected.

"You do it," Pari whispers to me.

Only Drunkard Laloo's face can be seen outside his blanket. His mouth is half-open and so are his eyes. It's like he's watching us in his sleep.

"Don't be a wet cat," Pari whispers.

Easy for her to say. She isn't standing as close to him as I am.

There's nothing else to do. I'm Byomkesh and

Feluda and Sherlock and Karamchand all at once. I shake Drunkard Laloo's blanket-covered right arm. It's rough and spiky. The blanket slips down and, when I touch his hand, it's too-warm, like he has a fever. He turns around and sleeps on his side.

I joggle Drunkard Laloo again, strongly this time.

Drunkard Laloo jumps up. "What's it?" he shouts, his scared eyes popping out of his sunken face. "Bahadur? You came back?"

"His classmate," I say. "You have a photo of him?"

"Who's this?" a woman's voice asks. It's Bahadur's ma, holding plastic bags in her hands that must be filled with the scrumptious food I have heard her nice hi-fi madam gives her every day. She switches on the light and Drunkard Laloo first blinks his eyes and then shades them with his hands as if the bulb's rays are spears poking him.

"We're Bahadur's friends," Pari says. "We were wondering if you have a photo of him. We're going to ask at the bazaar if anyone has seen him. If we have a photo, it will be easier."

Maybe Pari is so quick at coming up with lies because she has read many books and has all their stories in her head.

"I have already asked around at the bazaar," Bahadur's ma says. "He isn't there."

"What about the railway station?" Pari asks.

"Station?"

Bahadur's sister and brother look up at us with terror sizzling in their eyes. I guess they haven't told their ma about Bahadur's plans, maybe because they are scared she'll scold them for not ratting out Bahadur when he first stuttered about Mumbai-Manali.

"We'll check again," Pari says. "It's good if we check again, right?"

I think Bahadur's ma will chase us away, but she puts the plastic bags down, opens a cupboard, pulls a notebook out of its insides, and flips through the book until she finds a photo that she hands over to Pari. I move to the side to look at the photo. It's Bahadur in a red shirt, his oiled hair neatly parted in the middle. The shirt's red looks bright and happy against a dull cream background. He isn't smiling.

"You'll return it to me?" Bahadur's ma asks. "I don't have many photos of him."

"Of course," I say.

Pari touches a corner of Bahadur's photo and moves her finger back and forth as if she wants to get a paper cut.

"People think he has run away," Bahadur's ma says, "but my boy, he'll never give me a reason to worry. You know, he works at Hakim's and buys sweets for us with the money he makes. If I'm too tired to cook, he'll say, **Ma, wait**, and he'll run to the bazaar and come back with packets of chow mein for everyone. Heart of gold my son has."

"He's the best," Pari says, which is another lie.

"If he had run away, like those policemen said, wouldn't he have taken something with him, money, food? Nothing's gone from the house. His clothes are here, his school bag too. Why would he run off in his uniform?"

Bahadur's ma looks above us, at something on the wall maybe, a fixed point where her eyes focus before misting over. She rocks back and forth. I check the floor to see if it's moving. But under my feet the ground is solid and stock-still. Behind us, Drunkard Laloo burps.

"No one has asked you for anything, no, cha-chi?" Pari asks. "Like money to give Bahadur back?"

"You think someone has snatched him?" Bahadur's ma asks. "That baba, Baba Bengali, he said . . ."

"Chachi," Pari says, "even babas can be wrong sometimes. My ma says so."

"No one has called me for money," Bahadur's ma says.

"I'm sure Bahadur will come back," Pari says.

"Who knows if he has eaten anything?" Bahadur's ma says. "He must be hungry." Then she lurches toward the bed on which Drunkard Laloo is sitting. He shifts his legs to make space for her.

Pari opens her mouth to talk more but I shout, "Okay-tata-bye, we're going." Then I run out as fast as I can because inside that house sadness sticks to me like a shirt damp with sweat on a hot summer's day.

WE HAVE ENOUGH TIME
BEFORE—

—it gets too dark to go to Bhoot Bazaar and look for Hakim from Hakim's TV-repair shop. My legs don't want to walk with me anymore. I have to keep dragging them forward.

The bazaar seems to be growing bigger and bigger. I pass alleys I have never been to. Pari is tired too and our pace is tortoise-slow.

"When will we study?" she asks. Just like her to worry about silly things.

I prepare a list of questions in my head so that Pari can't pretend she's in charge again. But when we meet Hakim, the TV-repair chacha, he talks about Bahadur without any prompting from us.

"I saw him on Friday, maybe even on Saturday, but definitely I didn't see him on Sunday," he says, stroking his pointy beard that's henna-orange at the bottom and white at the top, just like his hair. "That was two whole days **after** his own brother and sister saw him, I found out later. He was wearing his uniform the whole time. I assumed he was avoiding school because of the bullies—you must have seen them teasing Bahadur? Poor child. Shall I get you a cup of tea? You're doing a good job, looking for him. You deserve a reward."

Before we can say yes or no, he calls for cardamom tea from a stall nearby, and it comes in tall glasses, frothy-bubbly at the top. It tastes expensive, this tea. Puffs of pricey steam warm our cheeks as we drink.

"Bahadur isn't here, at the basti or the bazaar," the TV-repair chacha tells us. "If he were, he would have come to see me by now."

I believe him because chacha is the nicest person I have ever met. He even takes our investigations seriously. He tells us that Bahadur:

- never got into a fight with anyone, even the children who made fun of his stutter;
- hasn't taken anything from the shop;
- had no plans to run off to Mumbai-Manali.

I ask the TV-repair chacha if Quarter was one of the people who bullied Bahadur, but the chacha doesn't know Quarter, only the pradhan. "That man," the chacha says, wrinkling his nose like something is stinking, "he'll do anything for money."

"Snatch children too?" I ask.

The chacha looks puzzled. Pari glares at me from behind the cardamom-scented steam.

"Could a djinn have taken Bahadur?" I ask.

"There are bad djinns," the chacha says, "who will possess your soul. Very rarely do they abduct children. You can't put it past them, certainly. Some djinns are big troublemakers."

Then a commotion in the alley distracts him. It's two beggars I have seen before, but they are special because one is in a wheelchair and the other is his bow-legged friend who shuffles behind, pushing the chair. The recorded voice of a woman jets out of a loudspeaker fitted to the back of the wheelchair. **We're both ill of leg,** she says. **Please help us by giving us money. We're both ill of leg,** she goes on. **Please . . .** She never gets tired.

"Here, here." Chacha gestures at them to come over, and he buys them tea as well.

"It must be getting late," Pari says when street lights turn patches of the black smog yellow.

We say goodbye to the chacha and walk home.

"My instinct tells me Bahadur ran away." Pari

speaks like a detective. "No one in our basti has any reason to snatch him. He must have made a lot of money working for the chacha, and now, he has gone off to join another TV-repair shop. One far away from here, and Drunkard Laloo."

"In Manali?"

"Why not? People in Manali watch TV too."

Boys and girls from our school, playing in the alley, wave at us. I don't wave back. I don't want to encourage them to join our detectiving team.

"Either we tell Bahadur's ma about his Manali plans," Pari says, "or we go to the main railway station, show his photo to people, and ask them if they have seen him."

"We can't tell Bahadur's ma and Drunkard Laloo. They will get angry with Bahadur's sister and brother, beat them up even."

"Then we have to go to the city station," Pari says. "Stop Bahadur before he gets on a train."

"Arrey, but what if he's already in Manali?"

"If we can find out for sure that he took a train to Manali, the police there will look for him. They can't be as bad as our basti-police, can they? Right now we don't know if Bahadur is here or where. What we need is one good clue, that's it."

I remember that the railway station will have CCTV cameras; **Police Patrol** cops often scour CCTV footage to catch criminals and runaway children. I don't tell Pari that. Instead I say, "You have forgotten or what, first of all, you have to get to the station, which is so far away in the city. Second of all, you have to take the Purple Line till there and you can't even get on a metro platform without a ticket. The metro is not like the Indian Railways."

"I know that."

"Is your father a crorepati that he can spare money for our tickets?"

"We can ask Faiz for money."

"Never."

"Didn't you say, after the first forty-eight hours, it becomes more and more difficult to find a missing child?"

I don't remember saying that, but it also sounds like the kind of thing I would say.

———

It's dark when I reach my house, but I'm lucky, Ma and Papa aren't home yet. Runu-Didi is talking to Shanti-Chachi, and stretching by standing crane-like on her right leg. Her left leg is folded at the knee.

"Shouldn't you be making dinner?" I ask Didi.

"Listen to how he speaks to me," she tells Shanti-Chachi. "He thinks he's a prince and I should wait on him hand and foot."

"When he grows up," chachi says, "with some luck, he'll get a wife like me who'll teach him that he can either cook himself or starve, it's his choice."

Maybe that's why Shanti-Chachi's first husband said okay-tata-bye to her, and why her three grown-up children never visit her. But I know better than to point that out.

"I'm never getting married," I tell Runu-Didi when we are in our house.

"Don't worry, any girl will smell you from a mile away and run off."

I sniff my armpits. I don't smell that bad.

Ma and Papa get back late, but together. They stand in the alley, talking to our neighbors. Their faces are too full of worry and crossness for me to ask them where they bumped into each other. Runu-Didi finishes making rice and dal, and calls Ma and Papa, but they tell her **not now, Runu**.

"Arrey, a man is dying of hunger here," I say, pressing my belly.

Runu-Didi troops outside. I march behind her, singing "Why Am I Like This?" Smoke crawls out of houses, heavy with the smell of dal and baingan-bharta.

Papa points at me and says, "If we don't watch this little shaitan, he'll be the next one to vanish."

"What?" I ask.

"The press-wallah's son has disappeared," Ma says. "We saw him just two days back, haan, Jai, you remember?" Then Ma turns to the others and says: "We asked that boy, **do you know where Bahadur is?** He said he didn't. How he could lie with a straight face, I'll never understand."

"Omvir is missing?" I ask.

"He and Bahadur must have planned it all along," Ma says.

"Such selfish children," a chachi says. "Didn't even stop to think how worried their parents would be. Now the police will get involved. They'll come here with their machines. All of us will lose our homes."

"Let's not get ahead of ourselves," Shanti-Chachi says.

"Yes, true," Ma agrees as if she hasn't packed our house into a bundle and left it by the door.

"Our people are looking for the children," Shanti-Chachi says. "They'll bring the boys home tonight, I'm sure."

"They might have gone to Mumbai," I say in a hushed voice. "Manali maybe."

I'm giving up my secret, but not all of it.

"What did you say?" Papa asks, hands on his hips.

"Can I go to Pari's?" I ask Ma. It's the wrong question for **right-now**, I realize as soon as I say it.

"Whatever work you have with her, it can wait till tomorrow," Ma says.

"You should buy me a mobile," I say, and turn to go back into the house.

"Not so fast," Papa says, his hand on my

shoulder. "Did Bahadur tell you he was going to Manali?"

"I have never talked to him," I say. This is the truth. I should ask Pari to teach me how to lie.

Papa's fingers dig into my bones. "Omvir isn't even in my class," I say.

"How will we find these children if they have gone that far?" a chachi says, eyes squeezed small, fingers pressing her forehead as if it's throbbing with pain.

"My son wants to see Dubai. Doesn't mean he's getting there any time soon," another chachi says.

"The boys must be hiding in a park near a hi-fi building," a chacha says. "Even the grass there is softer than our charpais."

"Homework," I mouth to Papa so that he'll stop interrogating me. He lets me go.

Inside our house, I stand in front of the kitchen shelf where Ma has put the Parachute tub. I can reach it easily now that Ma has changed its position. On its lid is a bindi shaped like a black teardrop that Ma must have stuck there, meaning to wear it again and forgetting. Before going to sleep or washing their faces, Ma and Runu-Didi take their bindis off their foreheads and stick them on whatever their hands can reach, the sides of the bed, the water barrel, the TV remote, my textbooks even.

I twist the lid open and fish out all the notes.

There's 450 rupees, the most money I have ever seen. I put fifty rupees back, screw the lid tight, and stand the tub back on the mango-powder tin. I hide the rest of the money in the pockets of my cargo pants.

My hands have gone clammy and my tongue is scalding-hot in my mouth. Stealing money makes you feel terrible. But having 400 rupees in your pocket feels excellent. I can eat anda-bhurji and bread-butter for a whole year with this money. Maybe not a whole year. Maybe a month.

I should put the money back. I feel a note in my pocket, crisp and smooth and full of hi-fi power. It sends a flash of current through my fingertips, makes me sway like Drunkard Laloo.

"When will this end?" Ma asks as she enters the house. "As if we don't have enough problems."

She looks at me. I'm her No. 1 problem.

"Come now, let's eat, beta," she says, smiling at me. "You must be hungry."

She tickles the back of my neck. I push her hand off.

I'm a detective and I have just committed a crime.

It's for a good cause though. If Pari and I bring Bahadur and Omvir back, we won't lose our homes. Our home is worth loads more than 400 rupees.

———

The next morning, we talk about Omvir as we make our way to school through the smog. He is still nowhere to be found. I tell Pari I borrowed money from Runu-Didi. "She won a race and got a cash prize," I lie.

"How much?" Pari asks.

"Enough for one Purple Line ticket," I say. I don't know what the fare is, but it can't be more than 400 rupees. I'm not sharing my money with anybody, not even Pari.

"Runu-Didi is so good," Pari says. "I wish I had a sister." Then she looks at Faiz. "You're lucky you have brothers and also a sister."

"They're okay," Faiz says, trying to get the hair standing up on his head to sit down. He hasn't washed today. He must have worked till late and turned around and kept sleeping in the morning after his ammi or his sister Farzana-Baji tried to shake him awake.

Pari believed my lie too easily. Maybe I'm a good liar. I just didn't know it. The part about Runu-Didi winning a race wasn't a lie though. Only, instead of money, she got the certificate that Ma has now put in the bundle by the door, and a gold-plated medal that Ma traded for a two-liter bottle of sunflower oil. Runu-Didi cried for many nights afterward about the medal, and that's why Ma got her certificate framed.

"Jai, listen," Pari says, "we should cut class today and take the Purple Line."

"What?" I say. "You want to cut class?" I don't think Pari has ever missed a day of school.

"A djinn has got into her, looks like," Faiz says.

"Shut up," Pari says, pinching Faiz's arm.

"What about your ticket money?" I ask Pari. I wonder if she has guessed the exact amount I stole.

"We have no time to lose," she says. "Maybe this was their plan all along—Bahadur goes to the city station first, then Omvir. By now Omvir must have got there too." She speaks hurriedly, swallowing a few letters so that her words can come out faster. "Maybe Drunkard Laloo beat Bahadur too much this time and Bahadur decided he couldn't stay in our basti for a day more."

"But the ticket—"

"Faiz is helping us investigate," Pari says.

Faiz frowns a big frown. "I'm not," he says.

"I saw Faiz at the toilet complex this morning," Pari says. "He said he'll give us the money for the metro tickets. You said that, didn't you, Faiz?"

"Maybe."

"What **maybe**, idiot?" She looks at me. "He came to the chole-bhature alley with 120 rupees in his pocket. That should be enough, no, for one person to get to the city railway station and back."

"That's a lot of money," I say.

"It's pricey because we live too far from the city. Also, we don't get a discount on the metro."

I know that already. Papa told me a long time ago that only those under three feet can travel free on the metro.

"I was thinking I'll go alone to the city station, but your didi has given you money, so we can both go," Pari says.

"Assistants can't do detective work on their own," I say.

"Stop fighting," Faiz says, leaping over a dog's No. 2 on the ground.

"Why are you giving away your money?" I ask him. "How will you buy your fancy shampoo and soap now?"

"I don't need it," Faiz says. "I have got a natural good smell, not like you. Want to check?"

"Never."

"I'll return the money to you," Pari tells Faiz.

"How?" I ask.

Pari has no answer.

Faiz is right, she's behaving strangely. She never breaks rules and always does whatever grown-ups ask her to do, even when it's something silly; like she pinches her nose for a minute at night because her ma wants her to. Her ma says Pari's nose is too big, and pinching will make it small and narrow. Pari says it's nonsense but does it anyway.

We reach the queues at the school gate. A man

wearing a crumpled white cotton shirt and an equally creased pair of khaki trousers stumbles up and down the lines, clutching a photo that he holds in front of each one of our faces. "Have you seen my son? Have you?" he asks, urgently, his voice hoarse as if he has been screaming for hours. "Omvir, you know him?"

It's the press-wallah.

I try to look at Omvir's photo but the press-wallah's hands are shaking, and I see only a splotch of blue and brown. Before I can ask him to hold it steady, he drifts away to speak to someone else.

"He's a goner," Faiz whispers. The press-wallah does seem to be shrinking with every step he takes.

"We have to do something to end this," Pari says. "Haan, Jai?"

"Let's talk to Omvir's classmates first," I say, mostly because I'm afraid to spend Ma's money. "Maybe he told them where he was going. That's the right way to do detective work."

I look at the press-wallah, I think about Ma's **what-if** rupees that I have rolled into my geometry box. There's a lump in my throat I can't shift by coughing.

————

Omvir's classmates don't see much of him because he's hardly ever at school. Pari brings out a notebook and writes down what they tell us. I steal a look at her case notes, which are full of question marks:

- dancer?
- Hrithik?
- Juhu? Mumbai?
- **Boogie-Woogie Kids?**

Boogie-Woogie Kids is a dance contest on TV, but Omvir doesn't have to go to Mumbai to audition for it. They hold auditions everywhere, even in the one-mall towns near Nana-Nani's village.

Omvir's classmates say his disappearance is the best thing ever.

"The next time we see him, he'll be on TV. Eight-thirty, Saturday night," a boy says breathlessly.

"He'll be wearing a silver shirt," another boy cuts in, "and gold-colored trousers."

They are older than us and also sillier. Faiz doesn't help us. He plays cricket in the corridor outside the classroom, bowling a make-believe cricket ball toward an invisible batsman.

At assembly, the headmaster warns us against running away. "An epidemic is spreading through our school," he thunders. "Children think they can enjoy a celebrity lifestyle if they take the train to Mumbai. It must seem like a holiday to you, a life with no studies, no exams, no teachers"—someone whoop-whoops and heads turn to pinpoint the source of the sound—"but you have no idea about the horrors that await you outside these walls."

I think about Pari's notebook. Maybe I should keep one too, but I hate writing and I get spellings wrong.

"The government has ordered the closure of all schools from today until Tuesday on account of the smog," the headmaster says. "This smog is killing us."

The students cheer. "Quiet," the headmaster says to even-louder cheers. This is why he didn't start his speech with the most important announcement.

When assembly is over, we walk to our classrooms in jumbly queues to collect our bags.

"Jai, we have to go to the city today," Pari says. "We'll get back before our parents are home. We won't get a chance like this again."

"Your ma will cry and scream if she finds you gone," I tell Pari. It's true. Pari's ma cries for everything: when someone is sad in a serial on TV; when Pari gets excellent marks; when Pari's papa has a cold; and when a chachi or chacha in our basti dies of TB or dengue or typhoid. Loads of diseases prowl around our basti, waiting to catch people and kill them.

"Ma won't find out," Pari says.

"Why don't you come with us?" I ask Faiz, though I don't want to pay for his tickets.

"I told you it's a djinn," Faiz says. "You won't catch it on the Purple Line."

"What will a djinn do with Bahadur and Omvir?" Pari asks.

"Djinns like dark places, so they'll drag children into an empty underground cave, bring out their long teeth and go chomp-chomp-chomp," Faiz says.

"This is too stupid, even for you," Pari tells Faiz, and turns to me. "Jai, you're getting a chance to do real detective work, and you're running scared."

"There's nothing in this world I'm afraid of," I say, which is another lie. I'm scared of JCBs, exams, djinns that are probably real and Ma's slaps.

OMVIR

Sometimes he forgot Maple Towers was a hi-fi building because of the way its insides were rotting. The lifts creaked, the walls cast off flakes of paint, and dirty nappies spilled out of the rubbish chutes into the edges of corridors. The staircase, which he used when his hands were unencumbered by bundles of wrinkled or ironed clothes, smelled of dead rat. Running down the stairs now, Omvir caught sight of the smog that made faces at him through the glass windows. Behind its dark coat, he couldn't tell if the world was alive or dead.

At the gates, a security guard halfheartedly patted him down to ascertain he hadn't stolen anything, a ritual left over from the time Maple Towers began its life as the first of the high-rises in this neighborhood, heady with fresh paint and the promise of wealth. Now its inhabitants were resentful young people with office jobs they probably thought didn't pay enough, and retired men and women whose children worked abroad and hired agency nurses to check on them each week.

Omvir had peered into the homes of both the young and the old and, while they weren't wealthy, they weren't poor either. They could be fleshy or thin, their fingers snapping with impatience or gripping a walking stick, their eyes cloudy-white with cataracts or blue from contact lenses, but most of them dismissed him briskly once he had picked up their creased clothes to be pressed or returned them still warm from the soleplate of his father's charcoal-iron. The few times they asked him to wait at the door, it was only so that they could inspect their trousers, shirts and blouses, and their underwear and vests, which some of them also wanted ironed for reasons Omvir hoped he would never have to discover. Once satisfied there were no cinder marks or ash stains on their clothes, they let him leave.

His father worried press-wallahs were going out of fashion in the manner of landlines and Doordarshan and tape-recorders, and told Omvir not to mind their eccentricities. From his rickety stall exposed to the elements, he was competing against the neatness of laundromats conveniently positioned inside all-in-one malls with cinemas and restaurants and shops, and Dhobi Ghats and Dhobi Haats mysteriously located on the Internet, offering round-the-clock washing and ironing services and neat packaging.

For safekeeping, his father wrapped ironed clothes in clean but worn bedsheets like the one Omvir had now tied around his shoulders to make a cape. Sometimes his father promised his customers hangers and biodegradable plastic sheet covers, promises Omvir knew he couldn't deliver. Always a melancholic man, his father, knee-deep in debt, waited for certain ruin with the patience of a heron standing still in murky water.

If he didn't get away, Omvir imagined he too would spend his life in the shadow of hi-fi buildings like Maple Towers. He felt the weight of his father's crushed hopes on his spindly, ten-year-old shoulders. He could understand why Bahadur had run off, if that was indeed what he had done.

Tucking his cape behind him, Omvir thought of how others considered Bahadur's stutter a weakness, something to be mercilessly mocked, a sign of sins committed in past lives. But Omvir himself had seen it as a source of strength, much like the two thumbs Hrithik Roshan had on his right hand. He believed the actor's rhythm, the deftness with which he could manipulate his legs and torso and hands to the beats of a song—as if he had no spine, no bones—came from the extra appendage that others thought freakish. What was God-given couldn't be a mere imperfection; it was a gift. Omvir wanted to believe there was a reason for everything. Otherwise, what was the point?

A pack of stray dogs raced past him and stood snarling under one of the neem trees lining the road. He turned the glowing side of the ring he wore on his left index finger to the inside, toward his palm, afraid its flashiness would provoke them. Squawking birds rose into the smog, leaving a trail of dead leaves that drifted to the ground. A monkey gawped at him through the foliage, startling him and then vanishing quickly.

He kept an eye on the dogs, attempting to judge the sharpness of their teeth against the thickness of the fabric of his jeans. A car passed. The dogs chased its wheels and, luckily for him, didn't return to tear him apart.

The birds flew back to their nests. He couldn't tell the time, but the day seemed to have vanished, quickly and silently like Bahadur. Omvir wondered where Bahadur was now. For months they had joked about escaping to a city where their fathers couldn't find them. A new beginning, in Mumbai, a city where two more boys on the street wouldn't make a ripple in the crowd, and the air tasted of salt from the sea, and where even children selling electric mosquito swatters at traffic junctions could press their noses against car windows and spot actors inside, Hrithik himself one day perhaps. Why hadn't Bahadur asked him to go along?

Something terrible must have happened at Bahadur's home. Omvir had to admit that his own father, though prone to dejection and whimpering at night and waking up his baby brother and in turn exhausting his mother, didn't have any of Drunkard Laloo's vices. His father didn't raise his hand against them or waste his earnings on drink. He was on his feet from dawn till late in the night, and he never complained about the cinders that left burns on his arms, or the ash that singed his brows, or the smog and the cold and the dust storms that lanced his nose and throat and ears a thousand times each day.

But his father also encouraged him to miss school so that his press-wallah trade wouldn't suffer, adopting a high-pitched pleading tone whenever Omvir said he was worried about exams or being struck off the school roll. "I'm doing this for you," his father would say, pointing to his stall which, like its owner, appeared to be on the verge of collapse. He didn't have the heart to tell his father that he had no interest in being a press-wallah. He was going to be a dancer so famous that people would recognize him on the street.

Omvir spread his hands out into the air. He wanted to imitate the steps he had seen in songs played on TV—Hrithik jumping into the air with his legs and arms extended or spinning on the floor upside down, balanced only on his head—but these were still beyond him. For now, he moved to the beats of a song only he could hear, letting its rhythm fizz through his entire body. His arms stiffened and relaxed as if pulled by invisible puppet strings. He pushed his chest backward and forward, pressed down on his heels and popped his knees so that his legs fluttered like washing in the breeze. A sense that he was someone else who was lighter and freer and happier swept through him.

"Are you having fits?" a watchman shouted from behind a gate, interrupting his dance. Omvir waved off the man's question. He was now in a posh neighborhood. Elevated side roads led to high-rises that were taller and shinier than Maple Towers, with worthier names too, Sunset Boulevard and Palm Springs and Golden Gate. Farther down this road, his father must be waiting for him, warming his hands against the orange glow of the charcoal in his iron, wondering what on earth was taking Omvir so long.

There were no street lights on the main road. The hi-fi people had no use for those; they drove up and down in cars with headlights and smog lights. They didn't walk except for exercise, and only in the well-lit gardens inside their gated complexes.

Looking up at the hi-fi flats, imagining the ease of lives conducted in such brightness, he was late to notice the dogs watching him with their mouths wide open, tongues sticking out, breaths loud and swift. One of them barked, then the others joined in. Omvir found himself running.

His slippers whacked the ground. Stones cut into his feet. His bedsheet-cape, heavy around his neck, slowed him down. The dogs gnashed their teeth. He was running in the wrong direction, away from his father's stall. The cape grew heavier. He wanted to loosen it, let the sheet fall to the ground, let it trip a dog or two. But his father would be mad, mad that he was late, mad that he had thoughtlessly lost a bedsheet, mad that he would need expensive rabies shots.

The dogs were gaining on him now. He felt one of them pounce, ripping through the air toward him, drool spattering on the back of his neck. If he were a superhero, like Hrithik in the **Krrish** films, he would have leaped into the sky and grabbed the wing of an airplane, and his sleek black cape would have soared into the air behind him. But his feet were still on earth, and his lungs were running out of air, and his eyes were blurring.

Yellow headlights cut through the smog, and a silver SUV stopped in front of him. The driver honked. The dogs barked angrily at the unexpected disruption. The vehicle's back door flung open, and it stayed open, like an outstretched arm waiting to pluck him off the ground and out of harm's way. His heart pounded as if it would burst from the exertion, and his mouth was so dry thorns seemed to be sprouting out of his tongue but, because he wasn't his father, in that moment he also felt hope.

PARI AND I DON'T SAY IT
ALOUD BUT—

—we have never gone farther than our school by ourselves. At least Pari has been to the city. Her dada who lives across the river took her once. She says she doesn't remember anything because it happened when she was two years old, and the Purple Line wasn't even running then.

We stop at a cycle-rickshaw stand by the highway. The drivers are waiting for customers, sitting in their passenger seats, chatting with each other, smoking beedis, and drinking chai from roadside tea shops. Pari takes out Bahadur's photo from her backpack. She asks the drivers if any of them ferried the boy in the photo to the metro station.

"Let's do this tomorrow," I tell Pari.

But she doesn't listen and asks idling autorickshaw drivers too about Bahadur. No one has seen him. Her questioning makes us so late, we have to hire a cycle-rickshaw to the metro station because walking will take us twice as long. Ma says rickshaws are for people with money, and it's a good thing our legs can do the job of wheels. I worry she'll see me from her hi-fi madam's flat but then I remember what she told me once: from up there, even a giant will look as small as an ant.

Our cycle-rickshaw rattles past men peeling potatoes and dicing onions and tomatoes outside roadside stalls. Cars with bumper stickers that say strange things like DON'T GET TOO CLOSE, I'M BRUCE LEE and PROUD HINDU ON BOARD honk and screech and brake at a junction where the lights flash red, orange and green at the same time. A dwarf who can travel for free on the metro because he's not over three feet tall begs in the middle of the road, standing on his toes to knock on car windows.

The road is full of craters like the moon, and I have to clutch the sides of the rickshaw so that I won't fall.

"How are there accidents when the traffic is so slow?" Pari says, looking at an overturned Honda City in the middle of the divider. The rickshaw's wheels trundle over a dead crow flattened against the tar.

At the end of the ride, Pari asks me to pay because she has just enough money to buy tickets for herself. She must have guessed I have more money than I let on. Ma's rupees look at me accusingly as I extend them toward the rickshaw-wallah. They disappear into his pocket. Forty rupees gone, just like that.

We have to climb a flight of stairs to reach the metro station. I keep my eyes and ears open so that I can catch all the sights and sounds I have never seen or heard before. At the top of the stairs, I point out hi-fi buildings to Pari.

"All this land, na," I say, "it was once empty." That's something Papa told me. He said the land was at first full of boulders, which farmers pounded with tractors to grow mustard. But after working hard for years, they sold their land to suit-boot builders from the city, and now the farmers sit at home, boredom curling out of their mouths and noses in clouds of hookah smoke.

"How do we buy tickets?" Pari asks. She doesn't care about farmers.

The counters are shut and boards pressed up against the glass say CLOSED. The ticket-vending machines, taller and wider than us, look like complex puzzles that even Pari can't figure out. She asks a man in a striped red-and-black shirt for help and he takes our money but asks us many questions: **Don't you have school? Why are you alone?**

Where are you going? Do you know how dangerous the city is? What if someone snatches your
money? What if someone snatches you?

It's good that Pari is with me because she comes
up with lies at the same speed with which the man
asks us questions.

"We're visiting our grandmother," Pari says, "and
she'll send her boy to pick us up at the station."

Only rich people hire **boys** to run their houses
but Pari makes the grandmother sound so real
that I can smell her old-woman smells, see her
papery skin and the talcum powder dusted into
the folds on her face and neck. The man is finally
convinced. He presses a few keys. A map of stations appears on the screen and he asks us where
we want to get down. Then he presses even more
keys. The machine slurps our money and spits out
plastic coins that the man says are like tickets. He
tells us to listen to the announcements so that we
will know where to get off.

"Be alert," he says before he leaves.

I'm very alert. I look around the station, wishing
I could tell which parts Papa worked on. Maybe
his fingerprints are hidden under the paint, stamped
in cement. The noise of the road outside streams
into the station but the walls hush them. It's like
we are in a foreign country. Even the smog looks
tame from here.

Pari grabs my sleeve and says, "Why do you

keep staring at things like a dhakkan? That too when we have no time to waste. Focus."

We copy what the people in front of us are doing and place our tokens against short, pillar-like machines that let us through. Our bags are X-rayed, then we pass a metal-detector gate that won't stop beeping. A policewoman checks ladies behind a curtain and a policeman frisks gents at the gate. "What's in there?" a cop asks a man, tapping a wallet sticking out of the pocket of his jeans-pant. But they let us go without troubling us because they know children can't be terrorists carrying bombs.

To get to the platform, we can take either a moving staircase or a regular one. An old woman wearing a red sari and many gold bangles stops in front of the moving staircase and says, **no, this is beyond me, I can't**, but her husband, whose back is even more stooped than hers, takes her hand and pulls her onto the stairs. Then they slide on up, happy like baby birds who have just learned to fly.

Pari and I get on the moving staircase too.

"You can hold my hand if you want," she says.

"No way," I say, and pretend to throw up.

A train glides into the platform and we run into it through the nearest door. Inside, the floor is as neat as Ma likes it. Everyone in the train is doing something on their mobile phones: talking, taking photos, listening to music, and watching videos of films or prayers like the Gayatri Mantra, their lips moving in sync with the words flashing on the screen. A man makes announcements in Hindi from speakers tacked somewhere up in the ceiling, and a woman translates what he says into English.

Pari and I stare out of the glass panels on the train's doors, smeared with people's handprints. The train goes underground for a little while and we can't see anything but then it comes up for air. We pass hi-fi buildings, gone before we can look into their windows, a clock tower, an amusement park with giant roller coasters that I have heard about, and the tops of trees going grey in the smog. Three streaks of green zoom close to the train and disappear. "Parakeets," Pari tells me. I feel like I'm in a dream.

This ride is the best. It's worth a hundred slaps from Ma and Papa. Maybe not a hundred. More like ten or five.

From the chatter in the compartment, I know the trains are late because of the smog, but I can't tell how late. The announcer-man and the translator-woman don't talk about the delays, but instead keep listing dos and don'ts like:

- see if there are suspicious objects nearby before sitting down. A toy, a thermos or a briefcase could be a bomb;
- don't eat, drink or smoke in the train;
- don't play music loudly in the train;

- cooperate with the staff during security checks;
- give the disabled, pregnant women or senior citizens your seat;
- don't obstruct the doors;
- don't travel ticketless.

Then they say that the doors will open on the left at the next station. A group of women in glittering salwar-kameezes, their faces decorated as if they are going to a wedding, get up from their seats and gather near the door. Their perfumes sweeten the air.

"Her stomach is too much sticking out," one says. "But she's doing hot yoga and all," another woman says. "She skips also," a third woman says. "No one can do that much skipping," a fourth woman says. "It's not enough to lose weight."

The train stops at the station, the doors magic themselves open and the women get down, taking their perfume scents with them. Pari and I claim their seats. Around us several phone conversations are happening at the same time. I catch a few words of each.

In fifteen minutes. It will take five minutes? Please change your attitude. Hello. Hello. Hello. Seriously, I'm telling you. Cut ho gaya. No, no, arrey, what are you saying? Hello?

The train slips underground again.

———

We get off at a metro station that looks like a well-lit tunnel. Announcements and voices echo around us. We watch people walking past, their trousers flapping and their shoes clicking on the floor. I tug at the hem of a man's kurta and ask, "Which way to the railway station?" and he laughs. "Where do you think you are right now?" he says.

"The main railway station," Pari snaps at him. "Not metro."

The man directs us to a moving staircase. I wonder how far below we are from the ground. Pari holds my hand.

"Your fingers are like ice lollies," I say.

Pari lets go.

We come out into the smog that has wiggled into every corner of the city and coats our tongues with ash. We have to ask strangers for directions again. The railway station is across the road, a man tells us, and he asks us to take an overpass that lies beyond a police post and an autorickshaw-taxi stand. His voice is deep like a villain's because he's wearing a black mask with white skulls to stop his nose from breathing the bad air. The masks in the city are hi-fi, pink with black buttons, red and green with mesh strips, and white with yellow snouts and straps. They make people look like giant, two-legged insects.

"The government schools here in the city, na, they're very good," Pari says when we are on the overpass. "Their students score better marks than private-school students who pay thousands and thousands of rupees as fees."

I hope we won't see a single school. If we do, Pari will insist on going inside.

We climb down the overpass, dodging the men and women who shoulder us, their bodies twisted by heavy bags. The main railway station is to our left. It's huge; as big as the malls I have seen from outside, and it's crowded too. I wonder why all these people are not at work and, if they don't work, how they have the money to take trains. Ma says the same thing about those who go to malls between Mondays and Fridays.

We walk around the station, looking for Bahadur and Omvir below boards announcing the times trains will arrive and leave. There's a Faiz-shaped space between me and Pari. Had he been with us, he would have seen djinns in the dogs lying around the station. He says djinns often shapeshift into dogs and snakes and birds.

I spot CCTV cameras poking their noses into everyone's business from the ceiling, but I don't look at them for too long in case the policemen watching me on the screen at the other end think I'm a suspicious character. There are policemen here at the station too, hovering near the many entrances, checking the bags of passengers.

"We can ask the police if they have seen Bahadur or Omvir," I say.

"They'll want to know what you're doing so far away from home and arrest you," Pari says.

Her plan seems to be to keep walking, which is a stupid plan. We study the faces of the men and women at the station, sitting on their suitcases or sleeping on towels spread out on the floor, their belongings tied up in large plastic or cloth bags by their heads or feet. There are a million people here and it will take us months to ask everyone about Bahadur and Omvir. But the police can slow down or speed up the footage from the CCTV cameras that are all around us, and zoom in on Bahadur or Omvir easily.

I see a run-down, double-storeyed building that's separate from the station, but within the same compound. A board hanging to its side says:

CHILDREN'S TRUST

Children First and Foremost
Of the Children, By the Children,
For the Children

"We should go there," I tell Pari.

"It sounds like a zoo with different kinds of children."

"Children are children," I say, but I'm not that sure. Faiz will be sorry he didn't come with us if it's an actual children's zoo.

We head past a mock train engine, a little girl

guarding a row of bags, a red-shirted porter balancing three suitcases on his head, and a man who barks into a mobile that he holds near his mouth and not his ear. Loud voices push themselves out of the speakers hidden around the railway station, warning people about bomb threats.

Then we are at the building. It has a locked door with a sign that says Reservation Counter. Next to the door is a puddle where two mynahs wash their faces like I do: in and out of the water in seconds. We climb up a mossy external staircase to a terrace that surrounds a large room with huge windows. I can hear murmurs but I can't see anyone.

A man with hair combed over his forehead comes out of the room and asks, "Are you lost? Where are you from?"

"We're looking for two boys from our basti," Pari says, showing him Bahadur's photo. "This is one of them. His brother-sister think he ran away from home to take a train to Mumbai."

"Could even be Manali," I say.

"The other boy must have joined him here yesterday. Or today," Pari says.

"You ran away too?" the man asks. He doesn't even look at the photo.

"Of course not," Pari says.

"We want to find our friends. We think they're at the station," I say. It's hard to get a word in when I have a blabbermouth for an assistant.

"Achha-achha, I thought you were runaways," he says. "Where are your parents? Why aren't you at school?"

"Our parents are at work. We don't have school today. The government has declared a holiday. Because of the smog," Pari says.

"Did they now?"

"Yes, this morning," Pari says. "You can ask someone if you don't believe us."

I don't think the man will check but he takes out his mobile, swipes his fingers up and down the screen and exclaims, "You're right. It's a holiday."

"We told you," I say. "You didn't believe us."

"And I'm sorry I didn't believe you," he tells me with a smile. "I work here, for the Children's Trust. Our center helps children like you who come to the city for whatever reason. Children who aren't with their parents. Children who may be in danger. That's why, when I saw you, I thought you were lost."

I didn't know this was a job; hanging around a railway station to help children. It's an odd job. If Faiz were here, he would have asked how much it pays.

"This city isn't safe," the man says. "All kinds of terrible people live here. I can't even begin to tell you—"

"We have heard about child snatchers," Pari says.

"I have seen them too," I say. "On **Police Patrol**."
Pari rolls her eyes.

"It's much much worse," the man says. "Things are so bad they can't even show it on TV. I'll tell you because you shouldn't have come here without your parents. I'll tell you so you won't do this again. Do you know there are people who'll make you their slaves? You'll be locked up in a bathroom and let out only to clean the house. Or you'll be taken across the border to Nepal and forced to make bricks in kilns where you won't be able to breathe. Or you'll be sold to criminal gangs that force children to snatch mobiles and wallets. Take it from me, I have seen the worst of life. This is why children should never travel unaccompanied. This is why I'm giving you a lecture. What you're doing, it's irresponsible. It's downright dangerous."

"Have you seen this boy?" Pari asks, her voice as cool as her ice-hands, holding up Bahadur's photo. "Was he here? Have you seen his friend?"

"The police should be doing this, not you," the man says.

"The police don't care about us because we're poor," I say.

The lecture-man clicks his tongue like a lizard but he takes the photo from Pari's hands and studies it.

"How old is he?" he asks.

"Nine," Pari says. "Ten maybe."

"I can't say I have seen him. Was this what he was wearing when he left home?"

"He was wearing our school uniform. Same as what he's wearing now," Pari says, jabbing my sweater.

Pari's uniform is the same colors as mine but instead of trousers she wears a skirt and long socks. When we reach Standard Six, her uniform will be a salwar-kameez like Runu-Didi's. Boys' uniforms are always the same, so Ma will make me put on these trousers even when I'm tall enough to pluck jamuns from trees.

"I haven't seen any children in uniform here other than you," the man says. "If they were waiting for a train on a platform, alone, a chai-wallah or a porter would have alerted us." He returns Bahadur's photo to Pari. "Truth be told, thousands of children come here daily, and we don't get to talk to every one of them. We try, of course. But the numbers, the logistics of it, it's a nightmare."

Faiz would say this man is ekdum-useless.

"Since you have come all this way, let's go inside and ask the children here. Maybe one of them saw your friends."

Pari and I look at each other because we don't know this man and maybe this room on the terrace is a trap.

"We have classes here for children to attend if they want. But sometimes we don't teach them anything and instead they watch TV."

This sounds like the kind of school I want to go to but it's also impossible that this is a real school.

"It's a place where street children can feel safe for a few hours," the man says. "If they like it, they can move into one of our shelters, or they can go home. We help them do whatever they want."

"We'll talk to them," Pari says.

Inside the room, just as the man said, a small TV is attached to the wall, but it's switched off now. Below it, children—some my age, some older, some younger—sit on bedsheets spread like mats on the floor. They look up when they see us and one of them says, "Tourist? One dollar please." But they realize quickly that we look like them, so their eyes go back to their teacher. There are only two girls in the classroom.

"These children are looking for their friends who are missing," the lecture-man says. He turns to us and says, "Show them the photo." Then he tells the teacher, "Take a break." The teacher sighs, removes his glasses and rubs his eyes.

Pari and I sit cross-legged on the floor and introduce ourselves. Pari talks to the two girls. Talking to the boys becomes my job. There are fifteen or twenty of them, so it's not easy. Bahadur's photo passes from one hand to another.

"Good photo," a boy says, but he hasn't seen Bahadur before.

"Where are you from?" I ask the boy sitting closest to me.

"Bihar," he says.

"How did you get here?"

"Train, how else? Think I have enough money to buy an airplane ticket?"

"Why?" I say though he's too rude. He looks a little like Faiz and has a scar on his face that's much fresher than Faiz's, running down from the tip of his left ear to the corner of his mouth. "Why did you come here?" I ask again.

He touches the scar and says, "Baba." His answer takes away all my words. I have no more questions. Our investigation is a waste. I spent Ma's money for nothing.

"Talk to Guru and see," a girl tells Pari just as we are about to leave. "He'll be standing near the main ticket-reservation counter with his boys. He knows everything that happens around here. He sees us even if we can't see him. He's like God."

THE CROWD AT THE RAILWAY
STATION LOOKS BIGGER—

—when we go back there from the Children's Trust. A busy train must be stopping here soon, or one such train has just arrived. I wonder why some trains are crowded and others aren't. It must be because the packed trains go to cities where millions work and the empty ones go to places like Nana-Nani's village where there are more buffaloes than people and hardly anyone has TV.

Near the ticket counters, Pari and I can't find Guru and his boys but that's because we can't see much; only the bodies of people, thin, plump, straight like rulers or bent like sickles.

"I'm beginning to think I was right about Quarter," I tell Pari. "Maybe he's snatching children and forcing them to steal things, like that lecture-man said. It must be a new gang that he has started."

Pari opens her mouth to speak, but just then, a hand grips my shoulder tight. It's a woman with two thin gold chains around her neck and gold hoop earrings dangling from her ears.

"You lost, boy?" she asks. "Come, I'll take you to your parents."

"We're fine," Pari says. "Our friends will be here in a minute."

The woman smiles. Her teeth and gums are stained blood-red with paan.

"You look hungry, beta," the woman says and pinches my cheeks with her sharp nails. "You too," she tells Pari. She removes a pouch tucked into the waistband of her sari and opens its strings. I have heard of thieves who carry vials of dizzy-making perfume in their pockets to spritz on people before stealing their wallets. This woman is up to no good. I move to the side and push Pari away from her too.

"Here," the woman says, taking an orange sweet wrapped in cellophane out of her pouch. It's crinkled like a real orange segment and dusted white with sugar.

"We don't want it," Pari says.

"No need to fight," the woman says. "There's one for you too."

"Don't touch the sweets," a voice hisses at us and, the next second, the voice is by our side, scolding the woman. "Auntie-ji, isn't it time for you to retire? Isn't it time to go to Varanasi and take a dip in the Ganga? Shouldn't you be uttering Lord Ram's name day and night?"

The woman spits to the side in disgust, releasing a thin line of pink-colored saliva, but she walks away from us.

"You should know better than to take sweets from strangers," says the voice, which belongs to a boy who has two other boys standing behind him, one on each side, as if they are his bodyguards. "It's the oldest trick in the world."

"We told her we didn't want it," Pari says. "We aren't stupid."

The boy smiles as if he's impressed with her for talking back. He has a narrow face, copper-colored hair, and the grey-green eyes of a cat. A black muffler with red stripes is wrapped around his neck. Tied around his wrist is a gauze strip brown with dirt and dried blood.

"Are you Guru?" I ask. "A girl at the Children's Trust told us to speak to you."

"You have run away from home, haven't you?"

he asks us like everyone else. I'm getting tired of these questions.

"No, we haven't," Pari says.

"That woman you were talking to, she works for a trafficker. You know what a trafficker is?" Cat-Eyes asks.

"They turn children into bricks," I say, which isn't what I meant to say at all.

Cat-Eyes laughs but it's a quiet, short laugh. "Her sweets put you to sleep and then her boss carries you away and sells you as a slave. You were lucky we came here when we did."

"If you know that woman is bad, why haven't you told the police about her?" Pari asks. "Why isn't she in jail? She must be giving the sweets to someone else right now."

"The police can only arrest her if they catch her doing something wrong," Cat-Eyes explains to Pari patiently, the same way Pari explains things to me. Even his tone is the same as hers; tinged black with irritation but also smooth and vain. "They can't put her in jail just because she has orange sweets in her bag. She's clever, that woman. Sly also. She'll never get arrested because she knows how to disappear before anyone realizes she has snatched a child."

"How do we know you aren't working for her?" I ask.

"You're smart kids," Cat-Eyes says. "What are

you doing in a big railway station like this without your parents?"

"We came here to take our friends back to our basti," Pari says. "They might be here."

"Guru is the right person to ask," one of the bodyguard-boys says. "This is his area."

"You're Guru?" Pari asks Cat-Eyes. He nods. She gives him Bahadur's photo. "Seen this boy before? He would have been wearing the same uniform we're wearing."

Guru stares at Bahadur's photo for a long time, biting the white skin flaking from his dry lips.

He and his sidekicks look much older than us, fourteen or sixteen or maybe even seventeen, it's impossible to guess. Their faces are burnt crisp by years of outside, their chins are bristly, and mustaches sprout above the corners of their lips like patchy thickets.

"Is this your brother?" Guru asks.

"Bahadur is our classmate," Pari says. "CLASS-MATE." She has to make her mouth a loudspeaker because the queues at the ticket counters are long and noisy, and people are fumbling and swearing at each other to get to the front. The air smells of sweaty feet and smoke. Our school queues are less rowdy and we behave much better and we aren't even half as old as these people.

Guru makes us move away from the counters and asks, "When did your classmate disappear?"

"Last week," Pari says.

"From where did he disappear?"

"The school," I say. "No, Bhoot Bazaar."

"It's a market near our basti," Pari says. "Bahadur disappeared and then a friend of his disappeared too. Omvir. Just yesterday. The two of them might have been planning to run off to Mumbai or Manali."

Guru looks at the photo again and returns it to Pari. "We haven't seen him," he says. "Or any other children in your uniform. We're certain. But we can ask the railway police to take a look at the CCTV footage. They might catch something we missed. Have you talked to them?"

"Pari didn't want to," I say.

"That's smart," Guru says. "They can be mean to strangers. But we know one of them well. He was like us, then the Children's Trust took him in. He lived in one of their shelters for years before he became a cop."

We walk with Guru to the station entrance where we saw the policemen before. On the way, he tells Pari that she must be a good person; no one else would travel this far to look for missing friends. He even carries her backpack for her. My bag is growing heavier and heavier as if the air is stuffing books inside it.

Guru asks us to wait and talks to one of the constables who is inspecting a bundle carried by a woman dressed in a burqa.

"Why does this Guru refer to himself as **we**?" I ask Pari. "Does he think he's a king?"

"You're just angry he didn't offer to carry your school bag," Pari says.

The constable Guru is speaking to twists around to look at us. He's young, maybe only a year or two older than Guru. After he lets the Muslim woman go, he says something to another policeman, gesturing with his hands that he'll be back in five minutes.

"Look, I can't check a week's worth of CCTV images just because your friends are missing," he tells us straight away. "File a complaint with your police station. They'll ask us for the footage, and we'll share it with them. That's how it's done."

"Our basti-police refuse to help us," Pari says.

"They threaten us with bulldozers," I say.

"Rules are rules," the constable says.

"Bhaiyya, there must be something that you can do to help these children who have traveled from afar," Guru says.

The policeman looks at Guru sadly. Then he says, "Well, the truth is"—he lowers his eyes and voice—"the CCTV cameras at the station haven't been working for a month. We have put in a request to the maintenance department, but well, you know how it goes."

I don't know how it goes but I don't dare ask the policeman to explain.

"Can't be helped," Guru says. "It's not your fault."

"It's top secret," the policeman says. "If you tell anyone else, if one of those people on the nine o'clock news hears of it, I'll lose my job."

"We won't tell," Guru says.

"We won't tell either," Pari says.

After the policeman leaves, I say, "We should go home now."

"Be careful while moving around your basti," Guru tells Pari. His thick eyebrows knit together, and his eyes shimmer grey, shimmer green. "There could be a kidnapper in your midst. You have parents to take care of you, so you have no idea about the bad things people can do. We know because we live on the street."

"Haan, to do everything on your own, it must be very tough," Pari says. This is what she does in the classroom too; she listens to teachers goggle-eyed, agrees with everything they say, and answers their questions just as they finish asking them so that she'll be their favorite.

"Do you want to know how we survive?" Guru asks. "It's a secret we don't share with anyone, but we can see you're good people going through a bad time, and we want to help."

"Bahadur's ma is going through a bad time," I say. "Omvir's papa too. Not us."

"Guru tells good stories," Lackey No. 1 says.

"Very good stories," Lackey No. 2 says.

"Jai, we don't have to leave right now," Pari says. "The last Purple Line train is at 11:30 p.m. It's only afternoon now. We've plenty of time."

It's just like Pari to know everything, even the metro timetable.

"We can't get home that late," I say.

"This won't take long," Guru says. "And how can we let you leave without having chai in our house?"

"There's no chai," Lackey No. 1 says, looking worried.

"We have Parle-G though," Lackey No. 2 says.

I don't think we should trust them, but Pari is already walking with Guru and telling him about Bhoot Bazaar and inviting him to visit. He's her best friend now. Guru's lackeys hook their thumbs in their pockets and hop behind him like the kangaroos I have seen on TV, switching their guard positions from the right to the left or the left to the right. I should be happy I'm seeing new places but there's something niggling at my chest, a worm crawling through my insides. Maybe I'm worried about spending Ma's money. Maybe I'm worried the orange-sweets woman is following me. I turn around and confirm that she isn't.

We raise our hands so that the vehicles on the road won't run us over as we cross. Angry honks bash into my ears. Autorickshaws slow down near white people wearing mesh masks, with backpacks as tall as them looming over their shoulders. The auto-drivers shout at the tourists, "You going where? I take you. I, I." Some men run behind the foreigners shouting, "Taj, madam? We have a good deal for you. Very good deal."

The other side of the road is full of hotels with neon signs flashing **HOTEL ROYAL PINK** and **INCREDIBLE !NDIA** in the smog. Guru and his chelas flit through a tangled lane dark as night. Shops push their wares into our path: ribbons of paan packets and potato chips, nankhatai, kebabs and pink teddy bears with **I Love You** and **Just for You** embroidered on their chests.

Guru hares into a narrow lane between two multistoreyed buildings, where someone has stuck tiles with godly photos on both sides to stop people from peeing on the walls. There's a brown Jesus, a Sikh guru, a Muslim pir, Durga-Mata sitting on a tiger, and Lord Shiva. At the end of the lane is a clearing.

"This is where we live," Guru says. "Our house. Welcome."

I look around. There's no house, no roofs or brick walls, only flattened cardboard boxes piled next to punctured car tires under a banyan tree with upside-down roots. A clothesline has been strung between two of the roots, and on it hang five cream shirts, their collars rust-colored with stains. The banyan tree's leaves shudder in the smog. Guru's lackeys spread out cardboard sheets on the ground and ask us to sit. Lackey No. 1 climbs up the tree and, from a hollow, retrieves a sack that he brings down.

Pari points to a barber standing under the sprawling banyan tree, shaving a customer's soapy-foamy chin. Behind him is a tall table on which he has arranged a mirror and tubes and bottles and brushes and combs. The customer is holding the arms of his chair tight as if he's frightened the barber will slice his neck.

Lackey No. 2 takes out an open packet of Parle-G biscuits from the sack that No. 1 holds. "Have one," he says as if it's a dare.

"I'm not hungry," Pari says, which must be the biggest lie she has ever told. I say no too, but not because I think the biscuits are made with sleep-pills. They are speckled black with mold.

"We tell stories here at night," Guru says. "Children come from all over to listen to us."

"There's no place where they can watch TV?" I ask.

Pari elbows me in the ribs.

"Guru loves telling stories," Lackey No. 1 says. "He talks to himself sometimes, or crows and cats and trees, if there isn't anyone around to listen to him. The children always give him something though, when he finishes a story."

Lackey No. 2 squints at us as if to check we have understood what he's saying. Then he rubs his thumb against his index finger to clear any doubt we may have. I can't believe it. He's asking us to pay for a story we don't even want to hear. He's worse than the corrupt senior constable who came to our basti. Everyone's mad after money.

"Just give us however much you think is right," Guru says.

I wonder what will happen if we don't pay. We could run to the railway station by ourselves; it took us less than ten minutes to get here. Guru can't do anything to us now, when the barber and his customer are around.

"We only have enough cash to get home," Pari says in a small voice. I guess he isn't her best friend anymore.

"Five rupees you can't spare?" Lackey No. 1 asks.

"Never mind," Guru says. He sniffs the gauze around his wrist as if it's a string of jasmine. "We brought you here so you could learn about Mental. There'll be someone like him in your basti too. You need to find that spirit and ask him to help you."

Guru sits cross-legged in front of us on a cardboard sheet, hands on his knees, palms facing down as if he's doing one of Runu-Didi's yoga poses.

"Even a few years ago, you could have visited

the place where Mental used to live, but now it's been turned into a hair salon," Lackey No. 1 says.

"What sort of name is Mental?" I ask. Faiz would have wanted to know the answer too.

"When Mental was alive," Guru says, "he was a boss-man with eighteen or twenty children working for him, and—"

TWO

THIS STORY WILL SAVE
YOUR LIFE

We call her Junction-ki-Rani but when she was a mother—

What do you mean when she was a mother? You don't stop being a mother just because your children are dead.

Now look at what you have done. You have given away the ending of the story.

How is that the ending? Don't get mad at me, baba. Just start from the beginning.

Where else will I begin? Maybe you should tell the story. You seem to have become an expert on all these things.

Arrey, meri jaan, don't be angry. I won't

interrupt you again. We're waiting. We want to hear you speak. Only you.

We call her Junction-ki-Rani but when she was a mother—that doesn't sound right.

Jaan, you have never told the story this way before. But then you have never told it without a glass of something strong and dark to slicken your throat first.

Let me try once more.

They say her real name was Mamta, but we only knew her as Junction-ki-Rani. She stood at highway junctions like a scarecrow someone had uprooted from a paddy field and planted under a traffic signal for a laugh. Her thin arms stretched wide like Jatayu's wings, and curses funnelled out of her mouth like cyclones to shatter windshields.

Cyclones! I was there, right behind your wheelchair, and I didn't see any cyclones, but you tell it so well, I want to believe you.

Shut up.

The first time we saw Junction-ki-Rani, we thought she had discovered a new way of begging, and we were envious. People pressed buttons to open the windows of their cars, took her photo on their phones, and laughed and ducked when she sent arcs of spit hailing toward them as if their faces were gutters. But they looked at her.

It was a miracle.

You see, no one has the time anymore to glance

at us beggars, to feel pity for our faces mangled by time and hunger, for our bandaged legs that end at our knees, for the snot-nosed babies we hold in our hands like bouquets of flowers. The two of us, we plead with people for money through a loudspeaker, no less—here, see, it's attached to my wheelchair—but no matter how loudly we ask, sometimes it can seem as if the whole world has gone deaf.

We do desperate things to catch people's eyes. We sneak through traffic to thump on bonnets; we push our faces into the cool windows of cars as if they're made of water, our tears streaking the glass, hoping a child watching a cartoon on a gadget will look up and exclaim, "Mummy, see that man. Let's buy him ice cream."

We told you, we're desperate.

In the olden days beggars went from door to door, rattled a bolt on the gate, and said, "Ma, is there anything you can spare today?" and people gave them dry rotis left over from the previous night's dinner or an old kurta they were about to use as a rag to wipe the kitchen counter, or coins if their son had scored high marks in exams or if a wealthy groom had been found for their daughter. But now, those with enough money to feed us live in gated communities, behind walls twice our height, with signs that say BEWARE OF BIG DOGS or DON'T EVEN THINK OF PARKING HERE or NO PARKING ELSE TIRES WILL BE DEFLATED. Their mansions are guarded by sentries who sit on plastic chairs outside the gates in winter afternoons so that the sun will thread its warmth through their bones.

Is this a lesson about beggars? What about Junction-ki-Rani?

You're interrupting. Again.

A thousand apologies.

We thought Junction-ki-Rani was a beggar like us until someone told us otherwise. She stood tall in a green sari with white stripes, and we watched its edges unravel over time, and its colors darken from lashings of exhaust fumes. Her hair was in part as white as the light of gods, and in part as black as shadow. She spoke clearly and loudly, drawing out each of her swear words so that there was an eerie pause between sister and fucker or son and dog—the truth is that the terms she used were much more salty, but it would be inappropriate to repeat them here, and indeed unnecessary.

But they're funny.

Not now.

Please, continue. Ignore this idiot's ramblings.

Junction-ki-Rani didn't care about etiquette, and sometimes lifted up her sari and underskirt and pulled down her underwear and did her business right on the road, and those offended called the police. She was arrested and released, who knows how often? Perhaps the moon or the stars or the kites in the sky kept count.

Each time she came out of prison, she occupied a different junction. Coins collected at her feet, tossed toward her by those who mistook her curses for blessings, or understood them for what they were and pitied her, having recognized her from the time they had seen her on the TV news. But she didn't touch the money. She never bought food or a glass of tea. People claimed she ate stray dogs and cats and goats that wandered too far from their homes; they said she stuck out her tongue and lapped water from rainbow-colored, petrol-scented puddles. None of that worried us. We were like egrets picking off ticks from the backs of cows. We took her coins and argued about how to apportion them between us. We didn't care about her.

Not until she died.

Now you have given away the ending, fool.

But jaan, that's not the ending either.

Someone told us—

—was it the rickshaw-puller or the peanut vendor?

Will you be quiet, please?

We never met Junction-ki-Rani in the places we hid when the Anti-Begging Task Force tried to catch us, or at the shelters where we queued on nights the winter-cold snapped our bones, or in the long lines for the free food rich people distributed on Ram Navami or Janmashtami. But we heard all these stories about her: she once worked as a cook in eight or ten houses; she lost her husband to alcohol; her son shipped himself as cargo to Dubai from a port in Mumbai on the day he turned eighteen and ended up in Nigeria as a corpse. They say Junction-ki-Rani safety-pinned all her hopes on her daughter who studied engineering in the day and gave tuition in the evening, but four men snatched the girl one night as she walked back home. The men returned her to the exact spot from where they grabbed her, but only after tearing her apart such that she couldn't be mended.

Junction-ki-Rani lit her daughter's funeral pyre because there was no one else—certainly no man—to pick up a burning log and free the daughter's soul. Afterward she rummaged through hot embers with her bare hands to gather ashes and shards of her dead daughter's warm bones. She carried them in a pot to Varanasi to scatter in the holy Ganga.

For a long time, she believed the police would find the men who attacked her daughter. Newspapers interviewed her, and she appeared on TV to talk about her daughter the engineer-to-be-who-would-now-never-be, but the newspapers were discarded, eaten by cows or swept away by brooms. A bomb blast that killed and maimed a hundred displaced her daughter's face from the screen. When she spoke to them, the police wondered if her daughter had loose morals; everyone knew only a certain kind of woman was found alone in the street after a certain hour.

Junction-ki-Rani returned to her cooking job in the eight or ten houses where she had always worked, and the madams said **how unfortunate such things keep happening to you** in their different languages, Bengali or Punjabi or Hindi or Marathi, and then they asked her to deseed chillies because baba or nana had developed acidity in the brief while she had been absent. **Acidity so bad we thought he was having a heart attack**. But everything Junction-ki-Rani cooked tasted of her daughter's ashes. No matter how much she scrubbed, her fingers smelled of smoke and fire and burnt flesh. The madams let her go.

That was when she started standing at junctions, swearing at passersby. In every man's face she saw the face of her daughter's killer.

We got rich because of her anger.

No one got rich. We were beggars then and we are beggars now.

Junction-ki-Rani lived for a year after her daughter's death, or maybe it was two years. When you live like us without a house, with nothing to mark the passage of time except the weather, and the weather is mostly the same year after year, maybe a little too hot or too cold, it's hard for us to tell. We don't even know when we were born.

The police sent a van to collect Junction-ki-Rani's corpse. We heard that they cut her up like her daughter at a mortuary and burnt her at a crematorium by the river. They did that much for her; watched the wood crackle and pop as flames licked that poor woman clean. We thought she had finally found peace.

We can see, this is hard for you to hear. This is not the kind of story parents tell their children as they fall asleep. But it's good that you're hearing it. You should know what our world is really like.

If you have finished with that lecture—

—of course, my apologies again.

For a few months after her death, we didn't hear much about Junction-ki-Rani, and then we were always hearing about her.

By the traffic junction she frequented the most was a tomb with a dome made scaly by rain and fumes and pigeon shit; its grounds thrived with thorny shrubs whose names no one knew. People say when she was alive, Junction-ki-Rani used to go to the tomb in between cursing the men on the highway, to rest when her buckling legs couldn't hold her up anymore.

After her death, lovers from other parts of the city who used to disappear into this tomb for whole afternoons didn't stay half as long. Something gritty in the air, the men said. Voices called out to them.

Smells brought to mind the times they had sinned, perfume bottles broken in anger, the asafoetida in overturned dishes of masoor dal, the turmeric in the warm milk their wives gave them on nights they felt the beginnings of a cold or a fever—and here they were, with women who weren't their wives. The air had a strange energy to it as in the second before a closed-up fist makes contact with a cheek.

Their suspicions were confirmed one November evening when darkness descended quickly, as it does every winter. The sky was black that day, though still golden orange in the west where the memory of the last rays of the sun lingered. Inside homes, fathers pleated their legs in front of the television, glasses of whisky or tea raised to their lips, and mothers sliced enough okra for dinner and the next day's lunch.

At a traffic junction, a group of young men slowed down as they drove past a girl, asked her if she wanted a lift, and didn't leave when she said no. The girl clutched her handbag close to her chest, called a friend on her mobile and said, "Nothing, yaar, just some men, doing bak-bak, so I called." Maybe the friend stayed on the phone. Maybe the friend said, "I'll send the police" and she disconnected to call the toll-free Woman-in-Distress Helpline numbers the police advertises in newspapers, and no one answered.

The girl's dupatta trailed the ground. She didn't lift it up because what if a tiny movement of her wrist, a flash of the bare skin of her hand, made the men pounce?

Maybe she could smell the aftershave on the man closest to her, see the strands of his hair carefully arranged with thick gel so that the breeze wouldn't dishevel his style. Maybe she thought of the exams she hadn't yet written, the boy she hadn't yet married, the flat that wasn't yet in her name, and the children she would never have.

Maybe she remembered Junction-ki-Rani and wondered if her mother too would take to standing in scalding sunshine and winter rain. Who would look after her younger brother and sister, and who would remind her father to take his blood-pressure medications on time?

She heard it then, a slap that held in its five fingers the force of thunder. The man with the waxy hair screamed. His cheek reddened. The car's wipers flailed over the windshield. A dent shaped like a giant hand appeared on the roof. The driver pressed the accelerator, but the car didn't move ahead; its wheels spun and spun as if the vehicle was stuck in mud.

The men were repeatedly slapped and punched. Invisible fingers strangled their throats. Blood sputtered out of their mouths, and tears and snot trickled down their faces.

Sorry, they cried to the girl. **Make this stop. Please, we're sorry.**

The wheels moved forward. The girl, still shuddering, watched the car's tail lights disappear. Then she ran home.

Afterward, when she had grasped the enormity of what had happened to her, she told her friends about how Junction-ki-Rani saved her. Her friends told others and some of them talked about it in front of a shopkeeper who told a chai-wallah and he told someone we know.

Junction-ki-Rani should be worshipped like a goddess, like Durga Mata, but almost everybody is scared of her. On some nights, you can hear her cry, and on some afternoons, when the sun rinses the tomb's walls at a certain angle, you can see the tracks left by her tears. Very few people visit the tomb or only those boys who want to take photos of themselves posing in the backyard to impress their friends.

But, once in a while, a girl somewhere in the city, maybe she lives across the river, maybe she lives in a basti near here, will feel the fear that every girl in this country knows as she walks alone on a deserted road. It may be from the full-throated roar of bike engines behind her, or the sight of a hairy hand thrusting out of a jeep window to pull her inside, or the stink of a man's sweat. She will remember Junction-ki-Rani, and the rani's spirit will arrive to protect her. The man will be taught a lesson.

Junction-ki-Rani is not a story. She lives—

—**you mean her spirit lives.**

She lives because she's still looking for her daughter's killers. And if she could, she would tell every woman, every girl, in the city: **Don't be afraid. Think of me and I'll be there with you.**

We hope that you'll never need to call her, but—God forbid—if such a moment arrives, we can promise you that she'll help.

This story is a talisman. Hold it close to your hearts.

Wasn't that a good story? You liked it, didn't you, even if it was a bit too violent at times. Now, our throats are parched from speaking for so long. How about buying us a glass of chai, with malai on top perhaps? And a plate of samosas? The samosas of Bhoot Bazaar are famous even in the city. We will share. We don't mind, do we, jaan?

THREE WEEKS AGO I WAS
ONLY A SCHOOLKID BUT—

—now I'm a detective and also a tea-shop boy. I'm busy-busy but Faiz says he works a lot more than I do. That's because my job at Duttaram's tea shop is only on Sundays like today. It's still hard work. It takes ages to clean just one of Duttaram's pans. Their bottoms are sticky with burnt tea and spices and sugar. I have to scrub and scrub, and my fingertips turn blue from the icy water and my legs hurt from squatting to wash vessels.

Faiz has told me my muscles will get used to it. Today is only my second Sunday working at the tea shop. Faiz also says I shouldn't whine about a bit of hurt because I'm a thief and thieves deserve to be punished. I can't tell him to shut up because he got Duttaram to hire me. He has sworn on his abbu not to tell Pari or anyone else about me stealing from Ma's Parachute tub, or my new job. His abbu has been dead for a long time but Faiz is still afraid of him, so I know my secret is safe.

I finish scrubbing a pan, but Duttaram gestures I shouldn't get up, and hands me a dirty tea strainer and glasses to wash. His shop is only a table on wheels in an alley in Bhoot Bazaar, but his tea has a scent so strong it calls out to the tailor who stitches blouses for the headmaster's wife, the shoppers haggling over the price of fenugreek leaves, and the butchers at the other end of the bazaar who always have blood spatters on their eyelids and pink animal flesh under their nails.

If Pari were to see me now, she would say this is why India will never be world class like America or England. In those countries, it's illegal to make children work. It's illegal here also, but everyone breaks the rules. Sometimes Pari threatens to report the men who employ Faiz to the police, but she won't actually do that because it would make Faiz ekdum-angry.

I'm happy I have this job. I returned to the Parachute tub the 200 rupees I didn't spend the day Pari and I traveled on the Purple Line. It was the best day, we had a proper adventure, but if I don't earn 200 rupees quickly, Ma will find out I took her

what-if money. I calculated that I'll make that money by working at the tea shop for five Sundays, but last Sunday, my first day of work ever, Duttaram paid me twenty rupees instead of the forty he promised. He said I broke too many glasses. I think he's just a cheapskate.

Still, being a tea-shop boy is excellent cover for a detective. My ears can listen to gossip and collect evidence. After people buy a glass of tea, they stand around complaining about what's wrong with the world. Sometimes they grumble about Bahadur's ma who keeps pestering the police, the police who in turn have put up our hafta by ten rupees per house, and Omvir's papa, who cries all the time. Everyone's more upset about the hafta than the missing boys. Ma says ten rupees extra is a good price for peace of mind, but I don't think her mind is at peace. She has removed the rolling pin and the roti board from our bundle by the door, but the rest of our good things are still packed up.

"Chhote, how much time will you take?" Duttaram asks and tries to smack my head, but I duck, so his hand only hits the smoggy air.

My cleaning is not as good as Runu-Didi's cleaning, but Duttaram's customers don't care if there's a sooty fingerprint on the side of a glass the way Ma would.

After I finish washing, I serve tea and nankha-tais. I'm cold, so I could do with a glass of chai too, but Duttaram offers me nothing. Hot tea splashes on my wrists as I run around. A brown dog with a black nose tries to trip me and grins like he has done something funny. Then he hides under a samosa cart nearby.

Someone asks me if I'm Runu-Didi's brother. I don't see faces anymore, just dust-coated, paint-coated, cement-coated hands into which I press chai glasses. I have to look up to see who's talking. It's the spotty boy who follows Runu-Didi every-where.

"Your sister, the star athlete," he says. He isn't making fun of her; his tone is awestruck, like Ma's when she talks to gods.

"I don't know what you're on about," I say firmly. Even if Ma were to see me, I'll pretend I'm someone else.

The afternoon rush starts. It's mostly beggars who find Duttaram's tea to be loads cheaper than the roti-subzi that people with money buy for lunch. I ask them about gangs that kidnap children and train them to steal mobiles and wallets.

"Boys your age watch too many Hindi films," says a beggar with hair standing up like the points of a star, and brown teeth that curve sideways and backward like Buffalo-Baba's horns. "Go, get me some more chai instead of wasting my time."

I work and work. I grow tired, I sulk, but no one notices my sulking. I should be playing chor-police or cricket or hopscotch right now. I wish I had never stolen Ma's money. I want to pretend I didn't, but each time I remember the Parachute tub, sweat dampens my armpits and muddles my eyes.

Faiz turns up at the tea shop in the evening with a bandaged thumb and a mask around his face made of a rag. "I was chopping ginger, but the knife was too sharp," he explains like he doesn't want to explain at all, and sits down next to me as I wash glasses.

"Waiters have to chop things too?" I ask.

"The cook fell ill. All of us had to help in the kitchen."

Today Faiz worked at the dhaba by the highway, where truck drivers stop for lunch and dinner. He's always collecting wounds and scars like tips at the places he works. No one tipped me today. You don't get tips at a tea shop.

"I'm thinking of recruiting that dog for our detective mission," I tell Faiz, pointing at the dog under the samosa cart. "A dog can help us find Bahadur and Omvir's gone-cold trails."

Faiz pulls his mask down so that it hangs around his neck like a scarf.

"Dogs are stupid," he says. "They run toward dog-catchers as if the men are carrying shammi kebabs for them."

"Dogs can flare their nostrils and pick up the stink of a bad man's feet or the coconut oil in his hair from all the other thousand-million smells in the world," I say. "Your nose can't do that."

"Is this a playground or your place of work?" Duttaram asks me, which isn't fair. My hands are washing the glasses even as I'm talking. "Take this to those people over there," he says, gesturing first at a wire rack full of chai glasses and then a group of men standing around an empty pushcart.

"I'll do that," Faiz says.

"Fine," Duttaram says.

Faiz hands the glasses to the men prattling on about a beautiful woman who arrives in a fragrant cloud of ittar at the tea shop every morning as soon as it opens. They use words that Ma would say aren't fit for child-ears.

"Duttaram, you have started hiring children to cut costs?" asks a tall, hatta-katta man with a chest that looks wider than the door of our house. He's probably an egg-and-ghee-eating wrestler who goes to an akhara every morning, and he may also be the kind of man who calls the police about child labor.

The wrestler-type fellow eyes me as he accepts the glass of chai Duttaram reluctantly thrusts in his direction. His sweater sleeve rides up. A gold watch circles his hairy wrist. I can't tell if it's real gold or fake. On the inner side of his wrist where the hair is less and the skin is so fair it's almost white are red lines tinted pus-yellow at the edges, probably made when a mosquito bit him in his sleep and he tried to scratch the itchiness away.

"Everything okay?" he asks me. "This man isn't giving you trouble, is he?"

"He's my boss," I say. "A good one."

"You should be studying. Or playing."

"I do that too."

"You go to school?"

"Of course."

"You do your homework every day? Or do you stay out until it's night, playing cricket?"

This man isn't my headmaster that he should ask me such questions. I shake my head. Maybe I mean yes. Maybe I mean no. Let him guess.

"You'll eat a chocolate?" the man says, kindly, sliding his gold-watch hand into his trouser pocket.

"No, saab," I say. We shouldn't take sweets from strangers. Guru taught me that at the city railway station.

"Suit yourself," the man says.

"Jai, you work at my tea shop," Duttaram says when the wrestler saunters over to the group of men discussing the ittar-lady. "Does that make my tea stall yours?"

"What are you saying, malik?"

"Exactly. This fellow, he does some work for the owner of a hi-fi flat, and he thinks that makes him hi-fi too."

"What work?" I ask. I don't know any men from our basti who clean and cook for hi-fi people.

"Who knows," Duttaram says.

"Which building?" Faiz asks. He puts the empty wire rack on Duttaram's table.

"Golden Gate. People say the flats in those buildings are so big they take up an entire floor."

I make my eyes wide and look at Faiz. Ma never tells me these most-amazing facts about hi-fi life. She only bak-baks about her bad boss-lady.

————

In less than an hour, Duttaram gives me twenty rupees and tells me to beat it. Faiz doesn't let me protest and drags me off.

"Stop breaking his glasses when you're washing them, and he'll pay you properly," Faiz says.

I broke one glass. That can't cost twenty rupees.

I stole a nankhatai from a plate though. I make sure Duttaram isn't watching me, then drop a few crumbs for the dog under the samosa cart.

"Here, boy, here," I say to him. He has watery eyes that look like they are lined with kajal, and a tail curved like a C. Patches of fur are missing from his coat, and his ribs stick out, but he smiles at me and gobbles up the food in seconds.

I leave a trail of nankhatai crumbs on the ground

and the dog follows me, his tongue mopping up the food at my feet.

"What if that dog is a bad djinn?" Faiz asks.

No way this dog is a bad anything; he's too nice.

"I'm taking the dog to Omvir's house," I say. "Will you go get Pari and meet me there?"

"I'm not your assistant. Don't tell me what to do."

"Please, yaar, please." I beg with my hands folded as if in prayer.

"Fine," Faiz says, but he doesn't look pleased about it. He sets off on a run.

I decide I'll call the dog Samosa because he lives under a samosa cart and smells excellent like samosa too.

Samosa and I have a long chat. I bring him up to date on our detectiving. We haven't done much because we have to go to school and we have homework and our parents don't like us being out after dark. We did follow Quarter twice to the theka, but he didn't do anything suspicious, just drank daru. Unlike the other drunkards there, he became quieter and quieter with every sip.

"This is why I need your help," I tell Samosa. "Your nose can find out where Omvir and Bahadur went."

I wonder if their smells are still left in our basti or if new smells have pushed them out.

Samosa wags his tail. He'll be a much better

assistant to me than Pari. Samosa and I will have our own secret signal as soon as I think of one.

———

Omvir's ma is sitting on the doorstep with her boxer-baby on her lap, singing a song to him. Her right hand pats his tummy. I ask if I can have something that belongs to Omvir, she says **shoo-shoo-shoo**. "Don't bring that dirty dog anywhere near my child," she says.

I think she's always-angry because she has an angry baby. Samosa isn't dirty.

Omvir's bad-dancer brother isn't around. He must be helping his press-wallah papa like Omvir used to. A neighbor-nani sitting with her feet stretched out on a charpai calls me over.

"You're worried about your friend," she says in a voice that's cracking, maybe from oldness.

"We say prayers for Omvir and also Bahadur at assembly every morning," I say.

Samosa sniffs the legs of the charpai on which the nani is sitting. A hen clucks and hurries away from him.

"You must have heard," the nani says, "Omvir's father has stopped working. He's going from alley to alley with Omvir's photo, dragging his other son along. He isn't bringing home any money. What will they eat? How can they eat? She is"—the nani nods at Omvir's ma—"talking about going to work herself, but who'll look after her baby? Does she expect me to do it, at my age?" The nani's voice rises with each question.

Omvir's ma is talking in baby language to her boxer-baby, whose fists are now yanking her hair. The nani complains some more about Omvir's papa. "Kept borrowing money," she says. "There are thugs at their door every morning asking for it back, and still he doesn't go to work."

It's a sad story, but I only half-listen. I wonder what's taking Faiz and Pari so long.

"The press-wallah always believed something terrible would happen to him," the nani says. "He thought he would lose his job, that his wife and children would starve, and now it's all coming true."

"Where's the dog?" I hear Pari's voice asking.

"Look," I say, pointing to Samosa's black nose peeping out from under the charpai.

Faiz has brought Pari here just like I asked him, but she has a book in her hand, which even for a show-off like her is too much. She wants everyone to know that she's the only one in our basti who has got a green card from the reading center, which the center didis give those who have read over a hundred books. Faiz and I have zero cards because we have read zero books.

"All very well that we're sharing our food with

her," the nani continues, "but how long can we do it?"

"You'll not stop talking until I go mad," Omvir's ma screams at the nani from her doorstep. Boxer-baby pummels her face. "You think I can't hear you? Don't go around behaving like you're starving to death because you gave us two rotis last night."

"This is how people repay you for your kindness these days," the nani says, the folds of her chin quivering.

"What did your two rotis cost? Two rupees?" Omvir's ma asks.

I get up, tiptoe toward Pari and Faiz, and we slowly walk away from the two women. Their shouting is bringing people out of their houses. I worry Samosa will run away, but he stays by my side.

"You made them fight," Faiz says.

"Samosa is going to track Bahadur and Omvir," I say.

"Samosa?" Pari asks.

"My dog."

"Dogs should have proper dog-names like Moti or Heera," Pari says.

"A dog doesn't care what you call it," Faiz says.

We reach Bahadur's house. Only his little sister Barkha is there. She's washing clothes in a plastic basin full of soapy water.

"Will you give me one of Bahadur's shirts?" I

ask. "If there's one that you haven't washed yet, that will be better." It sounds disgusting when I say it out loud.

Barkha splashes the water around. I stand back a little.

"Samosa has to get Bahadur's scent first," I explain to Pari.

Pari opens her book, brings out the photo of Bahadur that his ma had given us, and shows it to the girl. "I'm going to put it back, in the cupboard where your ma kept it before, okay?" she says.

Barkha nods and gets up, wiping her hands against the boys' jeans-pant that she's wearing.

Pari pads into the house, places her book on the bed, squeak-opens the cupboard and puts Bahadur's photo inside. Then she points at Bahadur's school bag, propped up against their fancy fridge. "I lent your brother a book," she tells Barkha. "I need to see if it's in there." She takes out one of Bahadur's notebooks and hands it to me. Bahadur's round words float above black lines. I let Samosa have a good snuffle.

"What are you doing?" the girl asks.

"You want your brother to come back, right? Don't you feel like seeing him?" Pari says.

Tears dribble down the girl's cheeks.

"Arrey, don't cry, don't, no," Pari says.

I hand the notebook to Faiz, who leaves it on the doorstep.

"Where's Bahadur?" I ask Samosa. "Come on, find him, you can do it."

Samosa barks, turns around and runs. I dash after him, my feet lifting up into the air as I jump over bricks and pots and pans, and piles of ash from the rubbish that people burnt last night for warmth, I don't know how fast I'm going, I may be faster than Runu-Didi even, there's the cold wind pulling my cheeks back, zipping up my skin too tight, and there isn't enough air in my lungs and my eyes are watering and then Samosa ducks into a narrow lane between houses and I have to slow down.

Faiz is huffing behind me. I wave at him and shout, "Keep up." Pari must have stayed behind to comfort Barkha.

I turn to the side and inch through the lane. The walls are swirly with moss and dirt. I stumble out of the path and so does Faiz. We sit down on the ground with our mouths open so that our breaths can catch up with us.

Samosa appears in front of us. He's panting too.

"Was Bahadur here?" I ask. He barks. I think he's saying yes. Faiz dabs his forehead with the rag around his neck.

We are at the very edge of our basti, facing the rubbish ground that's much bigger than our school playground. Right in front of me, a man washes his backside with water from a mug. Pigs dive into the grey-black rubbish, their pink-white bellies splotched with dirt. Cows with dried dung on their backsides chew rotting vegetables, blinking their eyes to bat away flies. Dogs nose through the filth for bones, and boys and girls collect cans and glass. Smoke rises from the smelliest piles that people have set on fire to make them stink less.

The scavenger children remind me of Mental's boys, who also picked up plastic bottles, but from railway tracks. Pari says Mental is just a story made up by Guru. I can't argue with her. The green card from the reading center makes her the story-expert.

I stand up to get a good look at the rubbish ground and feel sad for the kikar trees and the thorny shrubs that were living here long before people started dumping their trash around them. Some of the trees are still alive but their leaves are black with soot, and the wind has bandaged their branches with Maggi wrappers and plastic bags.

Beyond the rubbish ground is the wall, and beyond the wall, hi-fi buildings disappear into the smog. The hi-fi people are trying to get rid of the rubbish ground, Ma says. The prices of their flats are going down because of the stench. Ma says the municipality was supposed to clear the rubbish ground years and years ago when the hi-fi buildings went up, before I was even born, but they didn't. The government ignores us always but sometimes they ignore the hi-fi types too. The world is strange.

"Boys," a man smoking a beedi and sorting

heaps of trash into glass bottles and plastic bottles calls us over. He must be a scrap-dealer. Many kabadi-wallahs live near the rubbish ground, and towers of plastic and cardboard grow tall outside their houses. A black parrot with open wings is tattooed to the man's forearm; it looks like it will fly away into the sky any moment.

"They'll have to stick three needles as long as palm trees into your stomach if that dog bites you," he says, pointing the red tip of his beedi at Samosa.

Samosa will never bite me because he likes me. Also, Samosa doesn't have rabies. He's not a mad dog.

"Want a puff?" the man asks, holding his beedi toward us.

"Ammi will beat me if I smoke," Faiz says.

"The missing boys, Bahadur and Omvir, ever seen them here?" I ask.

The man scratches his feathery beard. "Kids around here disappear all the time," he says. "One day they'll have too much glue and decide to try their luck somewhere else. Another day they'll get hit by a rubbish truck and end up in a hospital. Some other morning, they'll be picked up by the police and sent to a juvenile home. We don't make a fuss about anybody vanishing."

"We aren't making a fuss," I say. "We're looking for our friends."

Children with heavy sacks slung over their

shoulders slop-slop through the rubbish toward him. On his head one boy carries a sack so huge it covers his face.

"Good catch today, haan?" the man asks him.

"Haan badshah," the boy says.

A few stray dogs have followed the children. Samosa darts off toward his four-legged friends.

"Samosa, come back," I call after him, but he doesn't.

The scrap-dealer stubs out his beedi. A scavenger girl opens her sack that's splitting at the sides and takes out a broken toy helicopter. "I got this today, Bottle-Badshah," she tells the man.

Bottle-Badshah is an excellent name. I should have thought of a fancy name like that for Samosa.

Right now Samosa is sniffing another dog's backside, I can't even look.

The other children open their sacks, to show the badshah what they found. They don't answer my questions about Bahadur and Omvir.

Bottle-Badshah returns the helicopter to the scavenger girl. "You need a toy too," he says.

She grins. I guess Bottle-Badshah is a good boss-man like Mental.

Faiz asks the girl if she has seen anyone wandering in the dark, trying to catch children. I think he means djinns.

"We sleep in the open," the girl tells Faiz, "because we don't have parents or homes. There's always some idiot trying to snatch us, but we fight them off."

She must be lying; she's so small, she wouldn't scare an ant.

The light has swerved quickly from yellow to brown to black. Evening noises drift out of houses, TVs shouting and women coughing as wood fires scratch their throats. Ma will be home soon.

"Why do you think Samosa brought us here?" I ask Faiz.

"Because he's stupid?"

I call Samosa. His nose is now poking through the rubbish.

"Leave it, yaar," Faiz says. "That dog must be hungry."

I don't tell Faiz that Samosa just ate an entire nankhatai that would have made my belly happy and quiet.

The scavenger girl runs ahead of us, making **chop-chop** noises as she pilots her helicopter with her left hand, her now-empty sack swinging in her right hand. Faiz and I run behind her. At first we are her passengers, but then we spread out our hands so that it looks like we are flying too. We go high up into the sky, above the hi-fi buildings and the smog, and we **honk-honk** so that we won't crash into each other.

Flying is the best feeling ever.

RUNU-DIDI AND I ARE DOING
OUR HOMEWORK—

—when Shanti-Chachi taps on our door and gestures with her eyes and eyebrows that Ma and Papa should step outside. Chachi warns us with the strict expression on her face that we shouldn't get up, but she also gives us a smile that seems painted-on like a clown's. She makes her face work too hard. Then the grown-ups huddle outside, whispering with their hands over their mouths.

Maybe Bahadur and Omvir are back. It's been two days since Faiz and I followed Samosa to the rubbish ground and found nothing. So far, my whole detective mission has been a big failure. I have no clues, and my only suspect, Quarter, hasn't done anything that can be considered suspicious. If my story were to come on TV, newsreaders would say **Missing-Children Probe at Dead End, Child-Detective Admits**.

Outside, Papa tries to speak softly like Ma and chachi but doesn't have much luck with it. Runu-Didi and I hear him say a bad word: **randi**. Didi shakes her head disapprovingly. At my school, randi is the worst type of swear word for a girl; it means she's like the women in the kothas of Bhoot Bazaar.

I have never been to the kotha-alley but I have seen brothel-ladies around the bazaar, buying chow mein and chaat, their faces so thick with makeup that even their sweat lines look like scars. They make kissy noises at young men. "Oye chikna," they chirp, "come here and show us what you're hiding in those trousers of yours."

Once I asked Ma about kothas and she said the women there have no shame. She made me God-promise I wouldn't go to the bad parts of the bazaar, and I don't, but only because there are loads of other places to explore.

Runu-Didi gets up to stir the dal on the stove. I wish we had some meat to put in the dal. Meat gives you muscles. When I'm grown up and rich, Samosa and I will eat mutton for breakfast, lunch and dinner, and we'll solve cases that baffle the police because our brains will be twice as smart. I wonder what Samosa is having for dinner tonight.

Ma comes back inside. She sits down next to Runu-Didi, picks up a small ball of atta, and flattens it into a roti. Didi tucks the edge of Ma's sari into her underskirt because it's too close to the stove's flame.

"What happened, Ma?" Didi asks.

I notice only then that Ma's eyes are full of tears. Maybe she knows about the money I stole from her Parachute tub. I want to throw up and also do No. 2.

I crawl toward Ma. "What's it?" I ask.

"You," Ma says, grabbing my wrist too-tight. "When will you stop wandering here and there? People will think there's no one to take care of you."

A chachi from Ma's basti-ladies' network must have seen me at Duttaram's tea shop and told Ma. I try to free my hand. She lets me go and slaps her forehead. "Hey Bhagwan, why are you testing us like this?" she says.

I keep quiet because she's talking to God and not me and God has better things to do than answer her questions.

"Ma, tell us what's wrong," Runu-Didi says.

"Aanchal," Ma says, "Aanchal is missing."

"Who's that?" I ask but I have already guessed

that Aanchal is a brothel-lady. That must be what Shanti-Chachi just told Ma and Papa.

"Aanchal left her home on Saturday and hasn't come back yet," Ma says. "Three nights—tonight it will be four—she hasn't been home."

Runu-Didi removes the dal from the fire.

"You don't talk to boys, do you?" Ma asks Didi, who looks too confused to say anything.

"This Aanchal, she has a boyfriend," Ma says, and then she snaps at me. "Jai, go outside."

"I have homework," I say, but I get up. Papa and Ma keep sending me and Didi away for secret reasons. It's all right in summer but it's just mean to do that to your children in the rains or on freezy nights like tonight.

The talk outside is very grown up. Ma wouldn't have wanted me to hear it; serves her right for kicking me out.

"Her boyfriend is as old as her grandfather," a chachi says. "But worse, he's Muslim."

"She told her mother she was going to a movie with a friend. How was that poor woman to know her daughter was running around with a Muslim instead?" a second chachi says.

"Who knows how many boyfriends a girl like that has?" a third chachi says.

Brothel-ladies must be brothel-ladies because they have many boyfriends.

"Muslims kidnap our girls and force them to

convert to Islam. Love-jihad they're doing," a chacha says. "After bombs, this is how they terrorize us."

These chachas and chachis wouldn't have said such things had our Muslim neighbors like Fatima-ben been around.

Shanti-Chachi's husband warns Papa that girls can't be trusted. "They tell you one thing, they do something else. You should be stricter with Runu," he says. "She goes here and there for running races, doesn't she?"

"Didi only cares about winning inter-district," I say. "She'll marry her medal. Papa won't have to pay a dowry for her."

"Who told you to come out?" Papa asks.

"Your wife doesn't want to see my face," I say.

Papa sighs, then prods me back inside where Runu-Didi has put our books away so that we can have dinner. I wonder who Aanchal's Muslim grandpa-boyfriend is. There are loads of old Muslim men in our basti, but the only one I know is the TV-repair chacha. He can't be Aanchal's boyfriend, can he?

Ma angrily slops dal onto everyone's plates. She scowls at Runu-Didi like Didi has secret Muslim boyfriends.

"Papa," I say, "Ma is doing drama-baazi again."

Ma's ladle smacks my plate, telling me to shut up.

By the next afternoon, Pari, Faiz and I know loads about Aanchal, from the words grown-ups let out of their mouths when they forgot we were around, and the stories Faiz's brothers told him after he gave them his share of subzi at dinner. News about Aanchal came to us; we didn't have to take the Purple Line to learn about her. Hardly anyone knows Bahadur and Omvir but Aanchal is a world-famous lady in Bhoot Bazaar.

During the midday meal break, we stand in the school playground, keeping an eye on Quarter whose eyes are on the girls around him. Our class-mates play games that look like fun, but we can't join in because Pari and I have a case to solve.

Pari writes a missing-person report for Aanchal based on the instructions I give her. Our final report is as good as any I have seen on **Police Patrol**. It says:

NAME: AANCHAL
FATHER NAME: KUMAR
AGE: 19–22
IDENTITY MARKS: FEMALE PERSON
WITH WHEAT COLOR, FACE TYPE
ROUND, BUILD THIN, HEIGHT 5' 5"
(5' 3" OR 5' 4") WEARING YELLOW
KURTA
LAST SEEN: BHOOT BAZAAR

I pass Pari's notebook to Faiz, who squints at the report and says, "When did Aanchal become nineteen? People say she's twenty-three or twenty-four."

"It looks professional," I say.

"How is this going to help you find Aanchal?" he asks.

Faiz can't admit we're good at anything. But it's also true that I don't know how this missing-person report will be useful.

"Let's make a list of suspects," Pari says, and snatches her notebook back from Faiz.

"He is No. 1," I say, pointing my eyes at Quarter.

"Some women at the toilet complex were blaming Aanchal's papa," Pari says. "He was driving an auto before and now he can't because he has TB or cancer or something. Aanchal has to do all kinds of things for money, like work at a kotha."

Pari tap-taps her pen against her notebook, like she's sounding out the thoughts in her head through a secret code.

"Faiz, will you find out more about the TV-repair chacha?" I ask.

"More what?"

"Like, did he know Aanchal?"

"You think the chacha is Aanchal's Muslim boyfriend, haan? I knew it. You Hindus will accuse a Muslim of anything."

"The chacha is a suspect because Bahadur worked for him, and he was probably the last person to see Bahadur," Pari says. "There's no other reason Jai is saying that, right, Jai?"

"Right." I hadn't even thought of that.

"Faiz, you'll see the chacha at the mosque. Your kirana-malik might know him," Pari says. "Shopkeepers in Bhoot Bazaar know each other."

"You can ask questions even when you're working," I say. I almost add that's what I do on Sundays at Duttaram's tea shop, but I remember just in the nick of time that Pari doesn't know my secret.

"Jai and me," Pari says, "we'll ask the kotha-ladies about Aanchal."

"We can take Samosa with us," I say.

"There's no time," she says. "And that dog, it will just bark and annoy people."

———

"Arrey, why are you slow like Yakub-Chacha's langda horse?" Pari shouts though I am only two feet behind her. My school bag knocks against my legs as I sprint, and it hurts. I wonder if I really want to solve the mystery of the missing children-brothel-lady. It would be nice to take a break to play or watch afternoon-TV, which is boring TV, but at least I don't have to share the remote. This time of the day, Ma and Papa are working and Runu-Didi is training.

"You're distracted so easily," Pari says. "No focus. It's ekdum-true, what Kirpal-Sir says about you. You get bad marks because you look at a question and then you see a fly or a pigeon or a spider and you forget you're sitting for an exam."

I don't say anything because I have to save my breath for running. No detective on earth must have had to run as much as me. At least I am dressed for it. Byomkesh Bakshi fights crime wearing a white dhoti, and dhotis are the worst because they can slip off easily, leaving you in your chaddi in the middle of a bazaar. Everyone will laugh at you then, even the criminal you're chasing. My trousers may be short and old, but I don't have to worry they'll bunch up around my feet if I ever get into a fist fight with bad people.

The kotha-alley is narrow, with tumbledown buildings on both sides. On the ground floors are shops that sell tarpaulin and paint and pipes and toilet seats. A muscly man flexes his biceps on a signboard, holding a PVC pipe the same way singers hold guitars on TV. Floating out of his mouth is a bubble that says STRONG!!! Another sign says HARDWARE in big letters and PAINTER, CARPENTER, PLUMBER ALSO AVAILABLE HERE in small letters. The shops are so boring, even flies haven't bothered to visit. Above the shops are windows where brothel-ladies hang out, clapping their hands and whistling at passersby. Pari giggles. I think she's brave for giggling but then I see her face and I realize she's laughing because she's nervous. It happens to some people. Runu-Didi smiles like an idiot when Papa scolds her.

Though it's cold and smoggy, the brothel-ladies wear blouses and underskirts, no saris. Their lips are redder than blood and their necks are shiny with golden or silvery jewelry.

"Aanchal works here or what?" Pari looks up and asks a woman who's hanging clothes to dry on washing lines strung below the open shutters. Pari has cupped her palms around her mouth so that her shout will go straight up to the woman without splashing into the ears of shopkeepers. The woman peers down, half of her dangling over the window-sill, and says, "Who's asking?"

Pari looks at me. The woman will laugh at us if we say we are detectives.

"What business do you have here?" a shiny man wearing rings on all his fingers asks us. He's filling a clay cup with water, from a dispenser placed on a low stool in front of a shop counter.

"We have business," Pari says.

Someone pinches my cheeks. It's a woman carrying a cloth bag stuffed with vegetables. Her hands are goose-bumped because she's wearing a sleeveless shirt.

"You're too young to be here," she says. "Does your mother work in a kotha?"

"Basanti, don't use up your charms this early in the day," the man tells her. "I promise I'll send you someone special."

The woman smiles at us and waves goodbye. Her gold-colored chappals slap-slap against the pavement.

"You were asking about the girl who's missing," the man says to Pari. "I heard you. How do you know Aanchal?"

"She gave us tuitions," Pari says.

That's a bad lie. Why would a brothel-lady teach us Maths or EVS or Social Science?

"The Aanchal I have heard about doesn't teach children," the man says. He sips from his cup and gargles, but swallows the water instead of spitting it out.

"Where's the reading center?" Pari asks him.

"You know where it is," I say.

"There's a reading center in a kotha here, isn't there?" Pari says, shoving me aside.

The man extends his neck, splashes water on his closed eyes from the clay cup, then wipes the water with his knuckles.

"Two shops to the left," he says. "Take the stairs

to the first floor. I don't know if anyone will be there now. They usually shut by late afternoon."

"We'll check," Pari says. "Do you know a boy named Quarter? He's the pradhan's son."

"You ask a lot of questions," the man says.

"Have you seen him?"

"Which kotha does he work at? What number?"

"He doesn't work in a kotha."

"I don't ask the men who come here for their names. I help them, and they give me money. That's all."

I hurry away from the man, who is thickening the air around him with his sliminess. Luckily, this time, Pari comes with me.

"Isn't your reading center near Faiz's mosque?" I ask. "How did it get here?"

"Must have walked," Pari says. "Or did it take an e-rick?"

Her face is full of knowing. She looks exactly like this when she writes her answers noisily during an exam. If I as much as glance at her, she hides her answer-paper with her hands because she's afraid I'll copy her brilliant words.

We stop at the building where the shiny-slimy man said the reading center is. A staircase with cracked steps twists up into the musty-dark.

"The center here is for the children of brothel-ladies. The didis at my center work here on some days," Pari says. "I have heard them talk about it."

"This is the kind of thing an assistant should know," I say. "Good job."

Pari swats my arm.

We go up the stairs. The green walls on either side are crusted and brown in parts from old paan stains. Out of the corner of my left eye, I see a drawing of a boy-part that's pointed like a gun at a woman's mouth. Someone has tried to scribble over the boy-part to hide it, but they haven't done a good job. I don't laugh. Pari won't like it.

We enter a room where the walls have wonky paintings of orange lions and green camels and blue coconut trees that look like they were made by small children, maybe the ones who are sitting on the floor right now, drawing and reading.

"Pari, what are you doing here?" a woman screeches.

"Didi, why, I came to see you," Pari says. "They said you would be here."

"Asha told you to come here?"

"No, I asked around and someone said you were at this center today. This place is nice, didi. Better than what we have."

I lean against a fluffy lion-tail. Pari hasn't pinned up the front of her hair, so it's falling over her forehead. I can't tell if her eyes are full of shame from lying so much and so fast.

"This," says the didi, who wears a blue jeans-pant and a red sweater, "is no place for children." But right away she knows she has said a silly thing because two of the little girls sitting on the floor look up at her. Their faces say: **why are we here then?**

"Outside," the didi tells Pari with a sharp nod of the head. That includes me too. We obediently follow her to the landing, which is already narrow but made narrower by a shelf lined with empty plastic bottles, rope, and paint buckets with lids. Cobwebs drape the ceiling.

"Do your parents know you're here?" the didi asks.

This is the biggest problem with being a child detective. I bet no one ever asks Byomkesh Bakshi or Sherlock-Watson about their parents.

"Accha, didi, you heard about Aanchal?" Pari asks. "You know her, don't you?"

"I heard she's missing."

"Remember I told you about Bahadur and Omvir," Pari says. "Our friends who have disappeared. Like Aanchal."

"I'm sure Aanchal had nothing to do with your friends," the didi says. "Maybe Aanchal mixed with the wrong crowd, maybe she was at the wrong place at the wrong time. Like you two." She grabs Pari by the shoulders and shakes her. "What do you think you're doing, wandering around a place like this that your parents must have told you to avoid?"

"When did you see Aanchal last?" Pari asks as if the didi isn't frothing at the mouth. "Did she come here the night she disappeared? She was supposed to be with a friend but she wasn't."

"Aanchal didn't work in a kotha," the didi says, and she lowers her eyes as if she wants to cry. "She visited our center—the center from where you borrow books, Pari, not this one. She asked for books she could read to improve her English. That's the only time I met her."

"She wasn't a brothel-lady?" I ask and Pari pinches my arm so hard it hurts even though her nails have to get past my sweater and shirt to reach my skin.

The didi looks at me as if she wouldn't mind pinching me either and says, "Who is this?"

"He's an idiot," Pari says.

"Don't come here again, all right?" the didi says, breaking a splinter of wood sticking out of the shelf. "Go home now."

We say okay-tata-bye and run down the stairs, not touching the sides even when our feet are about to slip. Outside, the lane is filling with men arriving in cycle-rickshaws and bikes and scooters.

"Should we find out if the TV-repair chacha came here?" I ask.

"That didi doesn't lie," Pari says. "If she says Aanchal didn't work in a kotha, it means Aanchal isn't a brothel-lady."

"Then what is she?" I ask.

"We'll talk to her neighbors. They'll know."

That's a good idea. I wish I had thought of it.

"Chutiye, don't even try to take my photo," a brothel-lady shouts at a boy holding a phone in the direction of her window. A slipper lands on his head. He throws it back. Men in autos put their heads out and whistle.

Pari holds my elbow. Trying to make our way out of the crowd is like trying to swim with heavy weights tied to my legs. It's been ages since I swam. In Nana-Nani's village there are ponds for us to swim in, but we have to share them with buffaloes.

———

At home, I change out of my uniform, sit down on the floor with my Hindi textbook, and underline the words of a poem that I have to learn by heart for tomorrow's class. The poem wants to know why the moon is sliced in half on some days and why it's a circle on other days. The worst thing about the poem is that it doesn't answer its own question.

Runu-Didi pushes the door wide open and steps inside. Her sweater is bundled in her hands, her hair is damp, and yellow sweat stains hoop the armpits of her shirt. She kicks me out so that she can change, then leaves to gossip with her basti-friends. Didi studies even less than I do.

"He can't stop looking at you," I hear one of the

girls tell Didi. She must be talking about the spotty boy or Quarter whose eyes follow any girl passing by; I have seen him watch Runu-Didi too.

Ma and Papa come home, and our house starts smelling of the leftover bhindi bhaji Ma has brought with her from the hi-fi flat. I can't wait to eat it. I sniff the plastic packet in which it came. Ma clouts me on the back of my head.

"I'll grow up stupid if you keep hitting me there," I say.

"Jai," Didi calls from outside, "your friend is here."

I run out, wondering what big lie Pari told her ma to get permission to leave her house at night. But it isn't Pari. It's Faiz and his elder brother Tariq-Bhai.

"You finished work early," I tell Faiz.

"He does what he feels like," Faiz says of the kirana shop owner. "Closes at nine one night, twelve another night."

Now that I have a job, I know we servants have to adjust our watches according to our master's clocks.

Tariq-Bhai grins at me. He has got dimples like Shah Rukh Khan and he's dressed smart like a superstar too in a full-sleeved grey shirt, and black trousers held up with a thick belt.

"Theek-thaak?" he asks.

"Yes, bhai," I say. "All fine."

"We were having dinner when Faiz insisted he had to speak to you," Tariq-Bhai says. "I thought I'll come with him for a walk. It's time you got your own mobiles, don't you think? Then you can talk to each other whenever you want, midnight too, no worries. I'll get you a connection at a good price, Jai. Special rate. With my employee discount, it will be cheap."

"Bhai, no need to be a salesman here. Jai doesn't even have five rupees. You won't make any commission through him."

Tariq-Bhai laughs.

"Ma won't buy me a mobile," I say.

"She will one day," says Tariq-Bhai. "And that day you must remember me."

"Can I talk now?" Faiz asks, and Tariq-Bhai says **sorry, sorry**, and wanders down the lane, away from us. Tariq-Bhai doesn't treat Faiz like he's a fool, the way Runu-Didi treats me.

"I met the TV-repair chacha today," Faiz says.

"At the mosque?"

"Arrey, you know I was working today. But after the malik shut the kirana store, I went to the TV-repair shop, I talked to the chacha. I told him I'm in Bahadur's class. He said just last week he found an elephant toy that Bahadur had hidden behind an old TV. Also an envelope with cash."

"An elephant toy?"

"It was blue and orange, he said. I know,

ekdum-stupid. But listen, the TV-repair chacha thinks the envelope has all the money he ever paid Bahadur. Bahadur must have hidden it there. If he had taken it home, Drunkard Laloo would have found it, and that cash would have turned to daru in two minutes. That might still happen. The chacha said he gave everything to Bahadur's ma."

"If Bahadur ran away like we thought, he would have taken that money with him."

"That's what the TV-repair chacha said. Unless Bahadur forgot about it."

"Who forgets about money?" I ask.

"Nobody," Faiz says. "Not even crorepatis."

We both stand around in thinking silence for a while, a silence filled with basti noises, husband-wife arguing, TV blaring and baby wailing.

Then someone screams. My knees knock together. But it's just Tariq-Bhai playing night-cricket with two boys down the lane. They have textbooks for bats and a small plastic ball. Faiz leaves me to take up the wicketkeeper's position. Tariq-Bhai spins the ball. It's a googly. The edge of the batsman's book touches the ball, which bounces straight into Faiz's hands.

"Out," Faiz shouts. He and Tariq-Bhai high-five each other, their smiles so big I can see their teeth glinting even in the jittery light of the bulbs hanging outside houses.

Runu-Didi never plays cricket with me. Sometimes she challenges me to a running race, but it's no fun playing a game that I'm hundred-percent pakka I'll lose.

"Jai, join us," Tariq-Bhai says.

"Jai, dinner is ready. Ma wants you inside," Runu-Didi says.

Didi is the ruiner of my happiness.

THE BASTI IS LOSING
ITS SHAPE—

—in the smog when we get out of school the next day. Shadows sprawl across the roofs of houses where punctured cycle tires, bricks and broken pipes weigh down tarpaulin sheets. I should be lying under a blanket on Ma-Papa's bed, watching TV. Instead I'm doing detective work in the cold. I want to give up, but I can't say that to Pari. She's treating this mystery the same way she treats an impossible-to-solve Maths problem, making a million notes and wasting the ink of a thousand pens. I can't let her beat me.

We walk toward Aanchal's house. Faiz found out where she lives from shopkeepers.

"When will we work on our presentations?" Pari grumbles. Kirpal-Sir has asked us to collect pictures of winter vegetables and fruit for homework, but no one's going to do it because we don't have newspapers or magazines in our houses.

"If you want to study, go home and study," Faiz says. "But you won't do that, will you? You like playing detective."

"We aren't playing," Pari says. "This is serious. Lives are in danger."

"You can't save people from bad djinns," Faiz says. "Only exorcists can do that."

"We can be exorcists too," I say.

Faiz throws punches at me with his eyes. "You have to recite verses from the Quran to fight djinns. If even one thing goes wrong, the djinn will kill you. That's why only trained people do it."

"Baba Bengali might have training," I say.

"Hindu babas don't know the Quran or anything about djinns."

Pari grits her teeth. Our djinn-talk annoys her.

The houses in the alley where Aanchal lives are pucca houses made of brick. Some are ground plus one. They must have their own toilets at the back too.

We stop next to a woman sitting on a brick, washing vessels, and ask her where Aanchal's house is. The woman points to it with a soapy finger. A bearded goat bleats at us from the doorstep.

Pari picks up wilted leaves from the ground and feeds the goat. The bell around the goat's neck rings each time it chews, which is too many times. A boy who must be our age, wearing a red-and-white checked shirt that's thick like a sweater, comes to the door and pushes the goat outside with his knees. His face has the roundness of someone who eats too much.

"What do you want?" he asks. A truck horn blares loudly on the highway.

"Aanchal," Pari says.

"She isn't here. Who are you?"

"We were wondering if Aanchal knew our friends, Bahadur and Omvir. They have also disappeared," Pari says.

"We heard about them after they went missing."

"Ajay, who are you talking to?" a woman barks from deep inside the house.

"Nobody," the boy says. "Some children asking about Aanchal-Didi."

"Send them away," the woman shouts. It must be Aanchal's ma.

Faiz tut-tuts under his breath.

"We'll go," Pari tells the boy. "But can you help us please? We're desperate to find our friends. The police have done nothing."

Pari isn't letting me ask about Aanchal's old man-friend.

"The police aren't helping us either," the boy

says. He gestures that we should shift away from the door.

"Just today a policewoman told Papa, **why are you crying, your daughter has run off with her mullah-boyfriend.** But my didi didn't have a boy-friend. The day she disappeared, she went for English lessons like she does four times a week."

"Isn't your didi a—" I say but Pari cuts me off with, "Your didi goes to college?"

"She failed her tenth-standard exams this June," Ajay says. "She works at a beauty parlor, and she also goes to people's houses to do mehndi and face-bleaching and hair-dyeing and that type of thing, but really what she wants to do is join a call center. That's why she goes for English lessons."

I have too many questions I can't ask. First of all, why does a brothel-lady want to work in a call center? Second of all, how can Aanchal be twenty-three if she was only in the tenth standard this year?

"The police told Bahadur's ma that he ran away on his own. They said the same thing to Omvir's ma-papa too," Pari says. "It's good for them, right? They don't have to lift a finger. If anything happens to us, it's because we did it ourselves. If a TV goes missing from our homes, we stole it. If we get mur-dered, then we killed ourselves." Her hair rushes over her face as she furiously shakes her head while speaking.

Ajay hangs on to Pari's every word as if they are made of sugar or gold.

"How old is your didi?" I ask.

"Sixteen. Six years older than me."

Pari's police report got Aanchal's age wrong.

"People say such terrible things about Didi. She has never been to a kotha. Just because she's beautiful—"

"This place is so backward, I'm telling you," Pari says. "If the basti-people had their way, all the girls would stay at home and learn to cook and never go to school."

"Exactly," Ajay says.

I don't know how Pari does this; wherever she goes, she makes friends with everyone she meets, like Guru. She would probably be best friends with Mental too if she met his ghost.

"We haven't seen you around our school," Pari tells Ajay.

"My brother and I go to Model School," he says. "Aanchal-Didi went to a senior secondary near it."

"Isn't Model a private school?" Faiz asks, rubbing his nose with the back of his hand. "How does your father pay such high fees?"

"It's not by making my sister work in a kotha," Ajay says threateningly, his face inching closer to Faiz's.

"That's not what he meant," Pari says.

"Faiz asks everyone about money because he

doesn't have any," I say. It's the right thing to say. Ajay drops his tough-guy look.

"A rich man's jeep hit Ma, so he had to give her compensation," he says. "Ma also makes T-shirts from home for an import-export business. She gets good money. That's why we can go to private school. But I don't like it there. It's terrible."

"Really?" Pari asks. She looks shocked. Private school is Pari's idea of heaven.

"The rich kids call us names. Bhangi, kabadi-wallah. Rat-eater. Cow-killer. They tell us we stink. They tell us they'll kill us."

"What idiots," Pari says. "If it gets too much, you can always come to our school."

"Our school is terrible," Faiz says.

"And we have Quarter," I say. "A good school would have thrown out a goonda like him."

"Quarter the pradhan's son?" Ajay asks.

"Yes, him. Did your sister know Quarter?" Pari asks.

"I don't think so."

Pari looks at the goat that's bravely chewing a Kurkure wrapper as if it's only a leaf, and says, "Accha, why are the police saying your didi has a boyfriend?" She slips the question in as if she has just thought of it, but I know it's been waiting to cartwheel off the tip of her tongue from the second Ajay said **mullah-boyfriend**.

"Papa kept calling Didi's mobile, nonstop at

first. Each time, he got the same message, **the number you're trying to reach is currently unavailable**. But one time a man picked up the phone. He said **what do you want?** and then he hung up before Papa could answer. Papa told the police about it and they twisted his words and now they are saying Aanchal-Didi is with a man."

"Why would a man pick up her phone?" Pari asks.

"Maybe he stole it," Ajay says. "That's what Papa thinks."

"Did your didi lie about where she was going? The day she disappeared?" I ask.

Pari glares at me. She would have asked the same question, but nicely. I don't care. Ajay is talking anyway.

"That day Aanchal-Didi told us she was going to watch a movie with Naina after her English class. Naina is her friend from the beauty parlor. The first time Papa called Naina, she said Aanchal-Didi was with her. But then it got really late, and Papa called Naina again and only then Naina said, **I haven't seen her today at all. Aanchal asked me to tell you she was with me.** Papa went crazy after that. He has been going to hospitals to check if Didi was in an accident and is lying in casualty."

"Is anything missing from home," Faiz asks, "like your sister's clothes or your father's wallet or—"

"There's never any money in Papa's wallet, only Ma's." Ajay pushes the goat away from a soapy puddle that it's trying to lick. "Didi didn't take anything from home."

"Where does she study English?" Pari asks.

"Let's Talk in Angrezi. It's about twenty minutes by auto from here. Buses are there too, but I don't know which ones go to the institute."

"Is it any good?" Pari asks as if that matters to our detecting.

"Didi didn't say."

I know there's an important question I have to ask but it's not coming to me now.

"Did your didi know Hakim, the TV-repair man in Bhoot Bazaar?" Faiz remembers for me. "She didn't, right?"

He probably decided to come with us so that he could ask this one question.

"Why would she know a TV-repair guy?" Ajay says.

"Of course she wouldn't," Pari says. "Where's this parlor where your didi works?"

"Shine beauty parlor. Only for ladies and children."

I have seen it from the outside. It has black-tinted glass windows and doors decorated with photos of famous actresses.

"Ajay, get back here," says a woman with grey hair, standing at the door of their house, tapping the crutches in her hands against the floor. It must be his ma.

He runs off at once. What a baby.

"I have to go to work," Faiz says.

"Ask Tariq-Bhai if he wants to play cricket tonight," I shout after him.

———

The alley in front of Aanchal's house curves into the highway, and right at its entrance is a dhaba and an autorickshaw stand. A group of men lean against their bikes by the dhaba where puris puff up crisp and golden in hot oil. Tied to one of the four poles that holds up the dhaba's tin roof is a photo of Lord Ganpati in a fancy frame that has disco lights flickering blue, green and red.

We stop at the autorickshaw stand and ask the drivers how much it costs to go to Let's Talk, even though Pari and I don't have any money. Two hundred rupees, they say.

"You can travel hundreds of kilometers on the Purple Line for loads less than that," I say.

"Take the Purple Line then," an auto-driver says. "Oh wait, you can't, can you, because it doesn't go to Let's Talk."

Pari ignores his jibe and tells him about Bahadur and Omvir. She asks if they had seen Aanchal with the missing boys.

"Aanchal has no time for boys unless they're at least ten years older than your friend here," an auto-driver says, pointing at me.

"Did she take an auto last Saturday?" I ask.

"That was the day she vanished," Pari adds.

"She doesn't need an auto-woto. She's a princess with her own chariot," a driver says.

"With a bearded man as her charioteer," another says, laughing.

"The TV-repair chacha?" I ask. "Is his beard orange and white?"

"Mullah-type fellow, but young," the driver says.

Then they talk about Aanchal's papa as if we aren't standing there.

"I told him just last week to have a word with her."

"His daughter is making her own money. He doesn't provide for her. What does she care what he thinks?"

The other drivers make sympathetic clucking noises.

"Aanchal's papa still drives an auto?" Pari asks.

"He hasn't worked in years. Too ill," a driver says, shaking his head. "Poor man. There he is."

An auto has joined the others at the stand, and a man with straggly hair steps outside. He's wearing a full-sleeved cream shirt with black stains around the cuffs.

"No luck today?" someone asks as Aanchal's

papa pays the auto-driver, and he says, "She isn't in any hospital. I went to the city today to check."

"Have you talked to Aanchal's mullah-boyfriend?" I ask. "She could be with him."

A blanket of quiet falls on our group, turning up the whirring noises made by the vehicles on the highway. Then Aanchal's papa raises his hand and leaps toward me, his eyes almost bursting out of their sockets. I pull up the strap of my school bag, preparing to run. But a cough racks Aanchal's papa and he has to stop to take deep, loud breaths. I make my escape, Pari next to me.

"You fool," she hisses as she overtakes me.

———

Policemen have police stations and detectives have fancy theka-type places where they can sit and chat about their suspects. But Pari and I have to hold our meetings outside the toilet complex or at the school playground. Today, though, my house can serve as the office of my Jasoos Jai Agency, at least until Runu-Didi gets back from training. Pari and I are going to swap case notes about what Aanchal's brother Ajay just told us. I don't have actual notes. They are in my brain.

Pari asks if I have newspapers at home, which we can check for fruit-veg photos for her school presentation. I don't even bother answering.

Shanti-Chachi sits on the charpai outside her house, combing her hair. I can tell she dyed it today because it looks blacker than it did in the morning, and it's also blacker than Ma's not-dyed hair.

"You should have got home a lot earlier," chachi tells me.

"It's not that late," I say.

Inside my house, I tell Pari that we have to inter- view Naina, Aanchal's beauty-parlor friend, and keep under observation our three suspects: Quarter, the TV-repair chacha, and Aanchal's papa, a hot- tempered, shameless man who lives off his wife and daughter. Of course, djinns are still my main sus- pects, but I can't discuss them with Pari.

We talk about what Ajay told us.

"This case is tough," I say, "because we aren't one hundred percent sure there's a crime and a criminal. Aanchal could have run away. Bahadur and Omvir too."

"The man who answered Aanchal's mobile, he could be a criminal," Pari says.

"But what's he doing with Aanchal?"

"Don't you remember what the Children's Trust fellow told us?" Pari asks. "Haven't you seen it on **Police Patrol**? People use children and women for all kinds of bad things, not just cleaning toilets and begging."

I imagine someone making me clean our toilet complex and shudder.

Runu-Didi gets back from training. Pari asks her how it went.

"Didi goes to school only so that she can train," I say. "Not even for the midday meal. Definitely not for studying."

"Nobody asked you," Pari says.

Didi's clothes are dusty and bloodied where she fell down and stones grazed her skin, but she doesn't seem to be hurting. She says she's going to the toilet complex for a bucket-bath. She looks for coins to pay the caretaker, under the pillows on the bed, in the pockets of Papa's trousers hanging on nails, and on the clothesline inside our house. She doesn't touch the Parachute tub. Then she turns to me.

"Ma gives you extra money to pay for baths and I know you don't even wash your face," she says.

Pari looks embarrassed for me.

The water in the toilet complex is too-cold in winter, so sometimes I don't touch it and come out pretending to be clean. But I try to wash my face every day.

"How do you know what happens in the gents?" I ask Didi. "Do you peep inside because you want to see that spotty classmate of yours wearing only his chaddi?"

Pari pushes me and tells me to zip it as if Runu-Didi is **her** sister. Then she says, "Didi—Quarter and Aanchal, did they know each other?"

It's a stupid question but it stops Didi's eyes from burning me.

"Why do you ask?"

"Just."

"Quarter used to sing songs whenever he saw Aanchal. He gave her Valentine's Day cards all year round, like in June, or October."

"They were boyfriend-girlfriend?" I ask.

Didi looks at me with contempt, then she says, "She took his cards, she took everyone's cards. The girls at the water tap talk about it all the time. Quarter sang songs declaring his love for Aanchal, but for Quarter, that's nothing special. If we were to go by his songs, he's in love with every girl in the basti."

"And Aanchal? She liked Quarter?" Pari asks.

"Who knows?" Runu-Didi says. "She had many admirers. People say she liked the attention."

I don't know what any of this means. I can't ask either because right now Runu-Didi hates me for no reason.

AANCHAL

The girl sensed the skittering among the men gathered by the dhaba opposite Let's Talk in Angrezi. Their heads swivelled as her blue sandals squeaked against the tiled steps leading out of the institute, and their gazes tethered themselves to her, moving as quickly as she did. She pulled her yellow dupatta down to cover her arms. Only that morning, her mother had warned her against dressing for the boys in the Spoken English class. No good would ever come out of wearing a sleeveless suit in the cold weather, her mother had said, the crutches in her hands tut-tutting at the same pitch as her voice. She had insisted Aanchal wear at least a dupatta.

It didn't matter because yellow was Aanchal's color, even more so against the black winter air that stuck to her skin like wet tar. Besides, Aanchal was hardened to the cold, to the desire that ripped through the eyes of the young men who bribed the receptionist at Let's Talk to glimpse her timetable so that they could learn it by heart. Shirking jobs or studies, they showed up outside the institute at the exact hour her class got over, like now. The worst of them gestured at her crudely. Others whistled or surreptitiously raised their phones to click her photo. A few of them had her phone number too; the receptionist had taken offense when Aanchal suggested that at least certain details of her life be allowed to remain private. All day Aanchal's phone beeped with messages from these strange men: **hi! Hai!!! Can I make friendshp with u? how r u? u got my massge?** And those were just the decent ones.

She knew what they said about her in the basti and the alleys of Bhoot Bazaar. Men and women, the young and the old, even the wives who took many lovers because their husbands couldn't satisfy them or beat them too often, and the husbands who spent their earnings on hooch and mistresses, disassembled her character with the viciousness of starved dogs chancing upon a scrawny bird.

Let them have at it, these people who yearned for something more real and close at hand than the dramas they watched on television. Let them spin stories from a skirt that in their eyes was too short, or the bearded boy they had seen her with. **A Muslim, that too. Tauba tauba, now that's a girl who has no shame. Remember how young she was when she started?** They gossiped and returned to their homes pleased that their own children, while disappointing or ill-behaved or plain-faced, at least didn't embody utter moral failure like she did.

She made her way from the institute, seeing in the periphery of her vision the looming shape of a man following her. She refused to acknowledge his presence, but his steady footsteps caught up with her.

Remember me, he said. **Remember what we talked about.**

She did remember him, his face, the touch of menace in his voice. She quickened her pace, but not before she heard him say: **Don't be shy now, we know what you're like.**

A few months ago, his fingers had drummed against the glass windows at the beauty parlor where she worked, until she stepped out and asked him what the matter was. He outlined his proposition for her as if it were no more remarkable than deciding the length of fabric required to stitch a lehenga. She considered it; how could she not? She had heard of the fast money that college girls who worked as escorts made. That money would have got her out of the basti, away from a father who was always angry with her, and a mother who was perpetually puzzled by a daughter who was nothing like the rest of the family.

Perhaps this man was back because the pause between his question and her **no** had been too long.

Hello, madam, I'm talking to you, he said now.

Near her, schoolgirls haggled with bangle sellers. A hawker shook garlic heads in a bamboo basket, and their loose skins swirled up into the air like white butterflies. A young man balanced three empty metal bowls on an older man's head for a laugh. Everything around her was ordinary. Except for this man.

She hissed at him to leave her alone, or else she would call the police. The man moved closer. She waved at someone indistinct in the distance, forcing a cheerful smile onto her face before hurrying toward a huddle of construction workers around a dosa vendor. His stall stood in front of a building that changed its form each day, behind porous green sheets and scaffolding.

She approached the stall, a flush of shame spreading across her chest as if someone had spilled a hot cup of tea on her. In the basti, people said men chased her because of how she dressed or how she acted. She made it worse for herself by refusing to hold her books close to her dupatta-sheathed chest or by slouching in the manner of bashful girls who pretended they could avoid censure by shrinking closer to the ground.

She knew she had no reason to be embarrassed. But in moments like these, it seemed to her that perhaps those in the basti were right. Why did she think she was special? The chorus in her head was sometimes the same as the chorus in the alleys of the basti.

Sorry, excuse me, she said to the workers around the dosa stall. They parted at once, as if deferential to her clothes that were ironed and neat and still carried the scent of the perfume she had sprayed on herself that morning, and to her face, moisturized twice a day with Lakmé Absolute Skin Gloss Gel Crème. The men wore stringy clothes specked with paint and dirt and cement.

The dosa vendor and a child who was helping him spread the batter on a hot tava looked at her questioningly. Raising an index finger, she pointed to a construction worker's dosa plate and indicated she would like one too. The child spread the batter on the pan, expertly smoothing out lumps with the back of a ladle and crisping the dosa with dollops of oil. In spite of everything, the delicious smell of it made her mouth water. The construction workers watched her, but they did so with no sense of authority and mostly with an expression of surprise.

Her phone rang, and she was relieved when she saw Suraj's name flashing. She answered his call. It turned out that he had come to pick her up at Let's Talk, though they were supposed to meet at a mall only an hour later. She told him she was just ahead. He said he would find her. She fished out forty rupees from her handbag and gave it to the child, who was folding her dosa onto a plate. She asked him to give it to someone else; she had to go, she mimed with her hands and eyes. The child looked horrified at the idea of someone turning down food they had paid for.

When she came out of the crowd, she saw the man was still there. Then Suraj's old bike stopped next to her and the man retreated.

Below Suraj's helmet visor, she could see that his eyes were red. He worked all night and must have had only three or four hours' sleep. She sat behind him with her arms encircling his waist and her chin resting on his right shoulder. She didn't feel cold even when Suraj started the bike and the wind whisked her hair.

He took her to a mall and drove into its underground parking lot with its hi-fi parking charges. First they had to pass a boom-gate attendant who lived in her basti, and whose eyes blazed with recognition and judgment as they locked with hers, and a guard, also from the basti, whose job it was to inspect the underbellies of cars with a portable search mirror. The men took extra time to let them through.

Inside the mall, they went to a McDonald's where she bought Suraj an aloo-tikki burger though she had already spent beyond her budget for the day. They sat by huge glass windows that overlooked a bridge on which Purple Line trains drifted like white apparitions in the black smog. Suraj attempted to return his helmet-flattened hair to its original style but failed. They watched street urchins being shooed away by the security guards standing next to the metal detectors at the mall entrance. His arms pressed against hers. She could see the outline of his biceps under his tight sweater.

Suraj's fingers spelt out L-O-V-E on the side of her thigh. Her jeans were thick and snug, but the heat of his touch made her shift in her seat. He draped his left arm around the back of her chair. They took small bites of the burger so that the other would have more. He asked her about her lessons and suggested that she talk to him in English, but that only made her tongue-tied. He spoke to Americans all night at his call center. Her English-speaking skills, despite the classes she diligently attended, didn't go beyond **where do you work** and **how was your day**.

He asked her about her mother and father and brothers. She wondered what her parents would make of him, if they would worry that he was an upper-caste boy who would discard her when he tired of her, or if they would see the stillness in him that she admired most of all, the calmness in his voice that reflected a lack of expectation on his part. He wanted nothing from her, or only what she was willing to share. This was new to her. The boys and men whose messages rumbled her phone all day and night were clear about their intentions, their **wants**, though some of them attempted to couch these in flattering terms.

Even in her own house, unspoken demands seeped through the walls to enter her room where she sat with TOEFL textbooks. Her mother wanted her to pay her brothers' tuition fees and, some day in the future, marry well. Her brothers acted as if it was her responsibility, as the elder sister, to share with them the money she earned as a beautician. And her father? He lashed out at her when she didn't listen to him, calling her too-stupid-too-slow to pass the tenth standard exams. He always apologized quickly, weeping, choking back the phlegm that his cough brought to the corners of his mouth.

Suraj's phone rang. **Office,** he mouthed to her, and took the call. The image of the burly man who had followed her earlier came into her mind. She glanced around the McDonald's, fearful she would see him slurping a Strawberry Shake. But no, there were only office workers grabbing a bite, boys and girls her age, and indulgent mothers giving in to their child's burger cravings, nannies standing to the side holding Tupperware boxes crammed with home-cooked food in case munna-munni changed their minds about what they wanted.

Her mother must, at this very moment, be looking at her phone, wondering where her daughter was. Aanchal sent her a message saying she was still with Naina. **I'll be late, I'll let myself in.**

Suraj finished his call and asked her to eat the last of the burger. He showed her on his phone a rowhouse that had been put up for sale in a gated community a few kilometers away from the malls. Within its ivory-painted gates there was everything, swimming pools, gyms, gardens and supermarkets. Her phone beeped and she switched it off.

Suraj took her to the cinema on the top floor of the mall and paid for the tickets that were much more expensive than the burger and they watched an American film which he said would help them improve their English. The actors spoke so quickly their words sailed past her ears. There was much violence. She couldn't decipher the reason for the frequency with which characters appeared on the screen only to be knocked down by a fist or a bullet. But Suraj was engrossed and she pretended to enjoy it too.

After the movie they walked around the mall, finding spaces in the stairwells where they hoped CCTV cameras couldn't see them kiss. Suraj said he had to mend a rip in an expensive sweater bought at a sale from Gap, so they left the mall and drove to the part of Bhoot Bazaar where a slew of tailors sat in a row, measuring tapes wound around their necks like scarves, their feet at the ready on the pedals of their sewing machines, their signboards promising both sewing and dry-cleaning "without smell" in a matter of hours.

She was shivering in the cold by then. Suraj offered to lend her his jacket but she refused. While they waited for his sweater to be mended, they had masala chai and dal-chawal at a stall where everyone gawked at the two of them feeding each other without shame and maybe a bit of pride.

When his sweater was done, and it was time for him to start his shift, Suraj drove her to the turning off the highway; from there, she could walk to her house in under a minute. He looked exhausted but also sad to leave her company. He said he would wait until she reached her home and called him. She insisted it was unnecessary. Though the dhaba was closed, the autorickshaw stand still had two or three drivers sleeping in the passenger seats of their autos, their legs sticking out, feet encased in holey socks.

Suraj's phone rang again. He didn't answer it, but he took a laminated lanyard out of his pocket, hung it around his neck, and told her to call him as soon as she entered her room. In his voice were flecks of an American twang, as if he was already in his office.

As she walked home, a dog barked at her, but its heart was not in it. The air creaked as if made of wood. She turned around, hearing something, the dog's loud breaths, stones being crushed underfoot. A hand reached for her in the darkness and she jumped and said **Suraj,** but of course, he was on the road right now, probably going faster than the speed limit. **Be careful,** she told him in her head.

But then the same voice she recognized from before asked her to stop. She wondered if he had been stalking her all day.

Leave me alone, she screamed at him. **Do you want me to wake up the whole basti?**

He stood in front of her with his arms crossed against his chest, as if to tell her to try it. The shimmer of a golden sunbeam caught her eye as he moved, but then it was snapped up by the dark.

I'M WAITING
IN A TWISTY QUEUE—

—to use the toilet, waving at Faiz who's standing ahead of me with his brothers, when I spot Bahadur's ma in the ladies' line. There's an empty space of two feet in front of her and also behind her though all the other women and girls are jostling against each other.

She sees me and gives up her prime position to walk in my direction. Maybe she knows we went into her house without her permission and got Samosa to sniff Bahadur's notebook.

"You couldn't find my son, na?" Bahadur's ma says.

The constantly farting man ahead of me holds in his farts so that he can hear her clearly.

Bahadur's ma pats my head and my skull jumps under the touch of her fingers. "You did well," she says. "You and that little girl. Only the two of you wanted to help me."

"We put the photo back," I whisper.

"I saw."

"Chachi, do you want to stand here?" Runu-Didi calls out from her line, stepping back and making space for Bahadur's ma because her earlier spot, though marked with the mug she had brought with her, has been claimed by another woman. Bahadur's ma nods. She squeezes my shoulder and I avoid her eyes because she's making me feel guilty, like I was the one who stole Bahadur. Then she leaves.

"What did you do for her?" the farting-chacha asks.

"Nothing," I say.

The other chachas in my queue talk about how awful it is to have to go from morgue to morgue, to check if your child is lying underneath a white bedsheet. That's what all the parents of the missing have been doing. "There's no greater misfortune than to outlive your child," a chacha says.

I feel like crying. Two monkeys on the toilet-complex roof lean forward and bare their teeth at us. The smog is less today, so I can see them clearly.

———

I scold Faiz on our way to school. "You aren't doing any detective work," I say.

"When did that become my job?" Faiz asks.

"You aren't helping either," I say to Pari. "Nobody is. Even Samosa, all he does is eat."

"Just like you," Pari says.

Faiz laughs with his knuckles in his mouth.

"I asked you to keep an eye on the TV-repair chacha. Where are your case reports?" I bark at Faiz.

"Chacha is always at his shop, from nine in the morning till nine at night. He's not a criminal-type."

"You watched him yesterday?" I ask.

"Yes."

"But you said you were going to work," Pari says. "That's why you didn't come with us to talk to the auto-wallahs."

"Yes."

"So you didn't watch him?" I ask.

"Not yesterday."

"Will you watch him today?"

"Sure."

"It's Friday. Don't you have to go to the mosque?" Pari asks.

"True, I have to pray."

"Our case will never be solved at this rate," I say. I stamp my feet.

"Cool it," Pari says.

"Tariq-Bhai gave me a good idea yesterday that might help you," Faiz says.

I don't believe it. Faiz is trying to make me not-mad.

"Tariq-Bhai said every phone is given a special number called an IMEI number. And what happens is that even when you put in a new SIM card, the IMEI number stays the same. The police can track that number with the help of Airtel or Idea or BSNL or Vodafone."

"He's sure?" I ask, though I have seen the police track phones with IMEI numbers on TV. I just didn't remember it until now.

"Tariq-Bhai knows everything about mobiles," Faiz says. "He's smart. The only reason he's working in an Idea shop instead of doing an engineer job is because he had to drop out of school when our abbu died."

"The police need to find out what the special number for Aanchal's phone is," Pari says. "We know the kidnapper is using the phone. He answered when Aanchal's papa called."

"If it's a kidnapper," I say, "why hasn't he asked for a ransom?"

"We basti-people can't pay ransoms, everybody knows," Pari says. "Snatchers will make more money by selling the children they have snatched."

"Djinns don't need ransoms," Faiz says. "Or mobiles."

———

I became a detective not even a month ago, but I feel old and wise like a baba from the Himalayas as I push open the door of Shine beauty parlor after school that day.

The beautician tells Pari that yes, she's Naina. She looks only a little older than Runu-Didi, but she's fancy; her eyebrows are thin, high arches that make her look constantly surprised and her hair is soft and straight like it has been pressed with a charcoal-iron.

"You came here for a haircut?" Naina asks Pari while also brushing a white paste onto the cheeks of her only customer, a woman reclining on a black chair.

Pari touches her half-dome protectively. "Of course not," she says, insulted someone even dared to suggest such a thing.

I say, "We—"

"Don't talk," Naina says, but she's saying that to the woman on the chair. "Keep your eyes closed."

The customer-lady is getting bleached. Ma says Runu-Didi will need a hundred bleaches before someone will agree to marry her. Didi has ruined her color by running in the sun.

"If you feel like it's burning, tell me," Naina says to the customer-lady.

Faiz inspects the lotions and sprays on a counter, humming with happiness. My scolding has had zero effect; he's not doing any detectiving. Pari explains to Naina that we are looking for Bahadur and Omvir.

"I said Aanchal was with me when she wasn't, but so what?" Naina says to Pari. "Don't you lie to your parents? Do they know you are here now? And boy, you keep your dirty hands away from my products."

Faiz puts a can that he's been sniffing back on the counter, but slowly.

"Aanchal's father is strict, na?" Pari says.

"Did Aanchal have a bearded friend?" I ask. I know I have done the right thing by not saying Muslim-boyfriend.

"How is that any of your business?" Naina asks, applying the paste on the woman's forehead briskly.

"We want to find out if the person who took Aanchal also took our friends," Pari says.

Naina puts the brush down and wipes her hands with a light-green towel stained white in parts. "Aanchal's friend isn't a kidnapper," she says.

"Does he do TV repair?" I ask.

Naina's strange eyebrows arch even higher. "Stop this nonsense," she says, swatting at us with her towel. "Go now, I have to work."

"Who is Aanchal's friend then?" I ask.

Naina shakes her head. "What is this world coming to that little children think they can talk to me like this," she says.

I turn to Pari and raise my shoulders. Pari lowers hers. We have to leave now, I guess. But then Naina decides to speak: "Aanchal's friend isn't a Muslim. I don't know where people get such ideas from."

Faiz stops picking at the lotion that has clumped around the mouth of a bottle. Naina has his full attention now.

"Aanchal has known him for a while. He has a good job at a call center. And the night she disappeared too he was working. Call-center workers, they have to clock in and out with their ID cards, so that's not something you can lie about." Naina pats the customer on her shoulder though the customer is sitting still like a dead person with a dead-white face. "He's worried about Aanchal. He calls me every day to check if she's back."

"What's his name?" Pari asks. "Is he from our basti?"

"Aanchal doesn't like basti-boys," Naina says. "They trouble her all the time."

"Do you think Quarter took Aanchal then?" Pari asks. "The pradhan's son? He troubles her, we heard."

"Why would he snatch her? He hasn't tried anything like that until now."

"Is Aanchal's call-center friend old?" I ask. "In the basti they were saying she has an old-man-boyfriend."

"Where do people find the time to make up so many lies?" Naina asks. "Of course her friend isn't an old man."

"Naina-Naina, now it's burning," the customer lady says.

"We'll wash your face, and everything will look better than before," Naina says, helping the customer-lady up by holding her elbow. "Time for you to leave," Naina tells us.

"See, the TV-repair chacha is just that, a cha-cha," Faiz says when we are outside. "He's nobody's boyfriend."

"Even if he didn't know Aanchal, the chacha is still a suspect because of Bahadur," Pari says.

Faiz doesn't have the time to argue with us. He has to be at the kirana store and also the mosque. I shout "okay-tata-bye, loafer" as he leaves.

"Faiz found out about Bahadur's elephant and money," Pari says when Faiz is too far to hear her. "Not you."

———

Ajay and his brother are hanging freshly washed shirts on a clothesline nailed to the outside wall of their house when Pari and I get there.

"Your didi used to do this before?" Pari asks. She's barely hiding a smirk; she thinks the boys in our basti have an easy time because their parents force girls to do all the tough jobs. But her ma and papa don't even ask her to peel an onion.

"Heard anything about your friends?" Ajay asks.

Pari says no. Then she tells Ajay about IMEI numbers.

"Papa has already asked the police to track Didi's phone," Ajay says. "But they haven't done it."

"Your sister's mobile, you have a receipt from when she bought it?" Pari asks.

"She got it second-hand, I don't know from where. There's no receipt. Papa looked for its warranty papers to show the police, but he didn't find anything." Ajay wrings the water out of a shirt, badly, and gets his feet wet.

I wonder if Aanchal's boyfriend gave her the mobile. This part of our detectiving has turned out to be a failure like all parts of our detectiving.

"It's ekdum-stupid the police haven't already tracked Aanchal's mobile," Pari says as we haul our feet and our heavy bags home.

"I wish we had their technology," I say, but I don't even know how to use a computer.

"You think Byomkesh Bakshi was hi-tech?" Pari asks. "All he had was his brain."

Sadly, my brain isn't intelligent enough to tell

me where Aanchal is. I try to make my ears catch signals as I walk home, but I don't pick up anything more than the usual bazaar and basti sounds of arguing mouths and hissing cats and jibber-jabbering TVs.

DAYS PASS FAST AS HOURS AND—

—Aanchal doesn't come back and Bahadur and Omvir don't come back either, but on the TV news I spot a headline that says: **Dilli: Police Commissioner Reunited with His Cat!**

Papa sees it too. His face curdles like milk left out in summer, and his fingers harass the buttons on the remote. The volume goes up and down, the newspeople are replaced by singers and dancers and then cooks in other channels.

Even if our basti goes up in flames, we won't be on TV. Papa himself says so all the time, and he still gets mad about it.

I ask him if I can watch **Police Patrol**. He lets me even though it's an only-for-grown-ups episode about five children killed by their evil uncle who pretended to be their best friend.

One morning soon after that night, when November has rolled into December and even water smells of smoke and smog, Pari, Faiz and I see Aanchal's papa on our way to school. He's buying packets of milk and telling anyone who'll listen that the police are in the silk-lined pockets of rich murderers and kidnappers. "Laugh at me now," he says, "but you'll remember my words when other children go missing. And believe me they will."

A man howls as if he's shocked to hear that, but he's just getting his ears scraped out and oiled by an ear-cleaner with a brass ear-pick and several balls of fluffy cotton. We pass a bad-tempered Santa Claus with dirt streaks in his white beard, wearing a holey red suit, ordering around a group of workers making a snowman out of Styrofoam and cotton. People snap photos of the half-made snowman on their mobiles.

At assembly, the headmaster scolds boys caught making dirty drawings in the bathrooms. Then he talks about Bahadur and Omvir. It's almost six weeks since they have been seen, he says. He warns us against running away and also tells us about child-snatchers who carry sedative injections and sweets laced with drugs. "Don't go anywhere alone," he says.

I look at Faiz. He's alone at night in the bazaar. I should have remembered to worry about him.

In the classroom, as Kirpal-Sir asks us to list the names of state capitals, I tell Faiz not to stay out late.

"When did you become my abbu?" he asks.

"Fine, go get snatched then," I say, pushing his hand away from my side of the desk.

The spotty boy who is Runu-Didi's No. 1 fan bumps into me during the midday meal break.

"You must wait for your sister to finish training and take her home," he says, chucking black looks over the playground to where Quarter is holding his daily court under the neem tree. "She shouldn't be out by herself. Times are bad."

Everyone thinks Quarter is terrible and we still can't pin the kidnappings on him. Either he is too clever for a criminal or we are too stupid. Still, I'm not taking advice from a loser.

"The only person Didi has to be scared of is you," I tell the spotty boy and run away.

———

When the last bell rings, Kirpal-Sir shouts over our noise that we should remember to finish our projects and bring them to class on Monday. This project is to make greeting cards for New Year. It's the worst project I have ever heard of.

We dash out of the classroom, and then the school gate. It's a Friday and Faiz is making us hurry. On the road, there's a flurry of pushcarts and cycle-rickshaws and parents waiting to take their small children home. I can smell the roasted peanuts and the steaming sweet potato cubes dusted with masala and lime juice that hawkers sell from their carts and baskets.

A hand with a cluster of bangles clanking at the wrist pushes aside a woman wearing a burqa, and the voice that belongs to the hand shouts, "Pari, there you are."

It's Pari's ma. I have no idea what she's doing here; she has to work until much later.

"Ma, what happened?" Pari asks. "Is Papa all right?"

Pari's ma sobs. "Another child," she says and tightens her hold on Pari's wrist.

"Ma, it hurts," Pari says.

"Another child disappeared last night," Pari's ma says. "A small girl. Your neighbor-chachi called me on my phone as soon as she heard. People are looking for her everywhere. It's not safe for you to walk home alone."

"She's not alone," Faiz says. "We're here."

A cycle-rickshaw full of schoolchildren chugs past. Spicy smells of biryani and tandoori chicken waft by. It doesn't feel like something dreadful has happened. Everything around us is noisy and normal.

"Jai, where's your sister?" Pari's ma asks.

"She has training."

"Your ma said to get her too. I spoke to her on the phone."

The ladies-network in our basti is too strong. I run back to the playground. Runu-Didi is laughing with her teammates.

"Didi," I say, "somebody else has disappeared in our basti and Ma called Pari's ma and said we should all go home together. Pari's ma is waiting for us at the gate."

"I'm not coming," Didi says.

"Another child has disappeared?" Tara, her teammate, asks.

"Tara's ma is going to bring me home," Didi says.

"She isn't even—" Tara says but Didi shushes her. "Bye-bye," Didi says to me.

If she gets kidnapped, it will be her fault. I did my best. At the gate, I tell the lie Didi asked me to tell. Pari's ma says okay in between sniffles.

We walk home, in a row, ignoring the curses of rickshaw drivers who are angry we are blocking their way. Faiz leaves for the kirana store and doesn't let Pari's ma stop him. He tells her if he doesn't work, his family won't be able to eat, which is a half-lie. Pari's ma believes him.

The alleys are full of men and women pointing their fingers at the sky (**are the gods sleeping?**) or in the direction of the highway where the police station is (**when will those sons-of-donkeys wake up?**). "Let's gherao the superintendent of police, teach him a lesson," someone says. "I heard he's in Singapore," someone else says.

Pari's ma ushers us forward, not stopping to chit-chat, not letting us ask questions. When we reach her house, she says, "I have to leave Pari with the neighbor-chachi and go back to work."

I guess she doesn't care if I get kidnapped. But then I see that Shanti-Chachi is standing there, talking to Pari's neighbor-chachi. Ma must have told her to bring me home from Pari's house. Our basti has turned into a prison. Guards are watching us everywhere.

Shanti-Chachi asks me where Runu-Didi is. I repeat Didi's lie.

After chachi drops me home, I take my EVS textbook out of my satchel and stand on our door-step without changing out of my uniform. I listen to Shanti-Chachi talking to other chachis. I learn:

- the missing child's name is Chandni;
- she's five and doesn't go to school;
- Chandni's eldest sister is twelve and stays at home to look after her brothers and sisters;
- Chandni is the fourth of the five children in

their house. The youngest is Chandni's brother, who's only a nine-month-old baby;

■ that's four almost-children—Aanchal isn't a child because she's sixteen—who have disappeared from our basti. Who's taking them? Is it a criminal or do we have a hungry, bad djinn in our midst?

Pari would have written all this down in her notebook.

I don't know for how long I keep listening. Runu-Didi comes home, puts her bag down and squats by the barrel to wash her face. When she finishes, I shift to the side so that she can go inside.

"Why is the kidnapper stealing so many children?" I ask.

"Maybe he likes eating them," Runu-Didi says. She half-shuts the door so that she can change behind it. I can't see her, but she keeps talking. "There are people who like eating human flesh. The same way you like eating rasgullas and mutton."

"Liar."

"Where do you think the children who disappeared are right now?" Didi asks. "In someone's belly."

"A child won't fit in a man's tummy. And Aanchal? No way. A snatcher will sell the children he snatched for money, not eat them."

If djinns haven't caught them and locked them

up in dungeons, Omvir and Bahadur must be cleaning rich people's toilets right now. Or they must be carrying heavy bricks on their backs, and their eyes and faces must be reddened by brick-dust and tears.

Runu-Didi finishes changing and opens the door fully and goes out to talk to her basti-friends. I walk in and lie down on the bed with the textbook on my chest. I look at our roof, at the small wall-fan that we haven't used since Diwali, and the lizard sitting still next to it, pretending it's a part of the wall. I pray: **Please God, don't let me be kidnapped or murdered or djinned.**

I remember the railway-station boys and how Guru said gods are too busy to listen to everyone. I wish I could pray to Mental instead.

I think of every name I know, in case that's Mental's name. Abilash and Ahmed and Ankit, and Badal and Badri and Bhairav, Chand and Changez and Chetan, I'm finding it hard to think of names alphabetically, so I let them come to my head in whichever order they want, Sachin Tendulkar, Dilip Kumar, Mohammed Rafi, Mahatma Gandhi, Jawaharlal Nehru . . .

———

The sound of mustard seeds screaming in hot oil wakes me up. I must have fallen asleep chanting names. I hear Ma and Runu-Didi whispering about the missing girl.

"Runu, you have to be careful too," Ma says. "Whoever it is, they're not just kidnapping children. Aanchal is nineteen or twenty, don't forget that."

"She's sixteen," I say, sitting up.

"How long have you been awake?" Ma asks. She chucks onions into the pan and stirs, the ladle scraping against the sides.

"Ma, is it true that someone's snatching children to eat them?"

"Kya?"

"Because our flesh is sweet."

"Did you tell him this bakwas?" Ma asks Runu-Didi. She tries to hit Didi with her left hand, but she can't reach her.

"I didn't," Didi squeals.

"The truth of the matter is," Ma tells me, "Chandni was outside at night all by herself. She wanted to eat gulab-jamuns and her mother gave her money to buy them. Who does that in such a bad time? Shouldn't that woman have bought them herself?" Ma gathers ginger and garlic slivers and throws them into the pan, followed by a pinch of turmeric and coriander and cumin powder.

"Chandni's house is right next to the bazaar, is what people are saying," Didi says, wiping her hands against her kameez. "It's no different from me going to Shanti-Chachi's house."

"Can't be that close," Ma says.

"Maybe her ma was busy cooking, like you are."

"If Vishnu Bhagwan himself were to ask me to send you outside at night, I would refuse."

Papa comes in and looks at me with a serious expression.

"What's this I'm hearing?" he asks. "When we think you're studying, you're running around Bhoot Bazaar?"

Ma's ladle stops stirring.

"I'm here all the time," I say. "I'm here right now. Can't you see me?"

"Enough," Papa shouts in his loudest voice. "Do you think this is funny? We have never stopped you from doing whatever you want to do. Either of you." He looks at Runu-Didi. "But there's a limit to everything."

"Papa—"

"Runu, listen carefully. This applies to you too. From now on, no more running-jumping for you after school, understood?"

"But . . . my . . . inter-district . . . I . . ."

"Bring Jai back after school and sit in the house with him. Put him on a leash if you have to."

"Coach will kill me," Didi says.

"Is he coaching the Indian cricket team?" Papa asks. "He's just a useless fellow teaching PT."

"Inter-district is a big thing, Papa. Coach wants us to practice every day, even Sundays."

The onions are smelling burnt because Ma hasn't been paying any attention to the pan. I wonder how I'll go to Duttaram's tea stall day after tomorrow.

"Children are getting snatched only at night, Papa," I say. "Didi and I are always home before dark."

"Yes, that's true," Didi says, her eyes blazing with angry tears. "Papa—"

"I don't want to hear another word, Runu. And Jai, you'll get it good from me if I hear you're wandering around the bazaar on your own. Don't think I won't find out."

LIKE A LION IN A CAGE,
RUNU-DIDI—

—walks up and down our house on Sunday morning, her hair freshly washed and flying around her face like a mane. "Unbelievable," she says.

"Papa has gone mad," I say.

I'm late for work and Duttaram might have already given my job to someone else. I know Ma and Papa will beat me if they catch me breaking their no-wandering-around-Bhoot-Bazaar rule, but the beating will be loads worse if they find out the Parachute tub is half-empty and I'm the thief. I don't want to be a thief. I'm a detective. Jasoos Jai is a good guy.

"I can't miss training today," Didi says. "I had to leave early yesterday too. At this rate, Coach will pick that stupid Harini for my spot. She can't run half as fast as I can, but Coach is best friends with her father."

"Didi, why don't you go for training? I won't tell Ma-Papa."

"So you can run around the bazaar by yourself?"

"I just want to go to Pari's house. Pari and I will study together, I promise. We'll watch a little bit of TV, but we'll study too."

Didi thinks about it, still marching around, making the floor jump. "Those who got snatched were snatched at night," she says, which is what I had told Papa. "We'll be home before that."

I don't point out that she's copying my words. "Stupid Harini shouldn't get your spot," I say instead.

"But Pari's ma will call up our ma and tell her what we're doing."

"Pari's ma works on Sundays, just like our ma. And her papa, he goes across the river every Sunday to meet his ma and papa."

"They let Pari stay at home alone?"

"They take her to the reading center if it's open. But she'll be home today."

I'm not lying. Pari told me so.

Didi makes me sit on the doorstep so that she can change into her sports clothes. I'm allowed inside when she's dressed. She ties her hair in a ponytail with a white scrunchie, which Ma would have never allowed. If you tie your hair when it's damp, ugly, fruit-like things grow in it and you can't pluck them off or anything. You have to shave your head. That's what Ma says.

I'm already dressed in my usual cargo pants and two T-shirts. Now, over the shirts, I put on a red sweater. Then we make sure Shanti-Chachi and her husband aren't outside and run.

Luckily, Pari is sitting by her front door, studying.

"Can you make sure this idiot stays at home with you?" Didi asks Pari and, with her hand on the back of my neck, pushes me forward. "He's not supposed to go anywhere. Definitely not Bhoot Bazaar." Her voice sounds different; with me, Didi is shrieky, but with Pari she speaks politely, as if she's talking to a grown-up.

"God promise you won't do anything annoying, Jai," Pari says.

I touch the bottom of my nose with my upper lip so that I'll look like a pig. Then I say, "God promise." God knows I don't mean it.

Didi runs off.

"I need to go to the bazaar," I say.

"But you promised," Pari says, "just two seconds ago. Aren't you afraid God will punish you?"

"It's only to buy gulab-jamuns. God will understand."

"Where do you have the money to buy gulab-jamuns? Just sit here quietly."

I'm tired of people telling me what I can and can't do. "Faiz got me a job in Bhoot Bazaar," I blurt out.

"What?"

"I have to return the money Didi gave me to take the Purple Line."

"She wants it back?"

"She hasn't asked but I'm going to give it back. It will be a surprise. She doesn't know I work. You can't tell anyone."

"You're lying too much. About everything."

"Come see for yourself."

Pari waits until her neighbor-chachi's back is turned, and then we sprint toward Bhoot Bazaar. It's crowded like always. The biggest crowd is outside a shop that sells little Santas and teddy bears wearing round caps with ruffles around the edges.

Duttaram takes one look at me and says, "Where were you? Half-pay today. That's all you're going to get."

"It's wrong to hire children," Pari whispers to me.

"Just go," I say. She rolls her eyes at Samosa, who is licking his boy-parts under the samosa cart. He's doing that to embarrass me in front of Pari.

"Get back before your didi does," Pari says. She's a rule-stickler but she understands why rules have to be broken too.

Duttaram asks me to buy cinnamon from a stall nearby because his stock has run out. "This winter-cold is making everyone constipated," he says, "so they keep drinking tea for relief."

"Isabgol is better," I say.

"Don't go around telling people that," Duttaram warns.

I fetch him a bundle of cinnamon sticks. I listen to the basti-news that's always floating around the tea shop. Today's news is spiky with fear. People say they are worried about leaving their children alone. They blame the police who asked Chandni's parents for a bribe instead of filing a complaint. Some people want to organize a protest against the police, others say that can only end with machines crunching our houses. One man says the pradhan and his Hindu Samaj party are planning a demonstration. Only Hindu children are being taken; therefore, the snatchings must be the work of Muslims. Another man says Aanchal's boyfriend is a Hindu; that breaking news must have come from Naina, or her eavesdropping, bleach-whitened customer. It doesn't stop people from blaming Muslims though.

Most of Duttaram's customers are Hindus. They say Muslims have too many children and treat women badly. They say ultimately you can't trust people who write from the right to the left like Muslims do in their **demon** language.

No one says Chandni ran away; she's too small

to go anywhere by herself. This means there's a real snatcher in our basti, maybe more than one, and we don't even have a Mental to save us.

———

Sometime late in the afternoon, Duttaram hands me a kettle heavy with tea, a thick cloth wrapped around its handle, and glasses stacked on top of each other. He tells me to take it to the customers at a jewelry shop in the next alley; he gets many calls on his mobile with such requests for chai deliveries. I'm walking, thinking about how much better I have got at carrying tea without splashing, when I clap eyes on Runu-Didi and she sees me too before I can hide. Didi is taking a shortcut home through the bazaar. Just my luck.

She's so surprised she can't speak. Her eyes turn round like an owl's, her mouth opens and closes but no words come out, and even the sweat trickling down her face because she runs everywhere instead of walking seems to freeze for a moment. She steps closer, lifts my chin and inspects my face as if to confirm it's me, Jai. Then she looks at the kettle and the glasses in my hands.

"I work now, only on Sundays," I tell Didi quickly. "I'll give you half of what I make. You can buy the shoes you need for running and get rid of these." I point at her scuffed, black-and-white men's sports shoes that Ma bought for her, second-hand, from a hi-fi building watchman.

"What—"

"Can't talk. People are waiting for this chai."

"Jai, tell me what's going on."

"I'm working," I say, walking ahead.

"But why are you working? You don't even do anything at home."

"Pay me and I'll get up early and collect water for you."

"What do you need money for?"

I don't say anything because we are at the jewelry shop now. I distribute the tea glasses to the burqa-clad women sitting on floor cushions, pointing at the necklaces and bangles they want to try out. The owner must be hoping to make a big sale to these customers if he's paying for their tea.

"Five-star hotels don't serve tea of this quality," he tells the women.

Runu-Didi and I wait outside for them to finish.

"How long has this been going on?" Didi asks.

"Are you going to tell Ma-Papa about me?"

"Only if you tell them I'm still training."

I try to whistle so I'll sound cool, but only air comes out.

"It's dangerous to stay out after dark," Didi says. "Even an idiot like you knows that, right?"

"Duttaram sees a film every Sunday evening, so he shuts his tea shop by five latest. He watches even flop films. Last week he saw—"

"Just don't get snatched, okay?" Runu-Didi gives me a strange pat on the head. I pretend a ghost has touched me and shake all over. She mock-punches me in the face. Then she takes off running again, bumping into people. They curse her and ask if she thinks she's a hi-fi lady with an airplane to catch.

———

The next morning, I don't get a chance to tell Pari and Faiz about what I heard at the tea stall because Pari scolds us nonstop for keeping my job a secret from her.

"You two have formed a boys' club, haan?" she asks. "Fine, I don't need you. I'm going to be best friends with Tanvi from now on."

"Tanvi only cares about her watermelon backpack," Faiz says.

Pari gets angrier and walks ahead of us. I whisper to Faiz that she doesn't know I stole Ma's money.

"I guessed that," he says.

Pari doesn't talk to us at assembly, or after. Kirpal-Sir starts his Social Studies lesson, which is on cricket, but we know more about the game than he does. Then a strange sound rolls into the classroom.

"Bulldozers," somebody shouts.

"No," I shout back. I don't know what the sound is, but I don't want it to be bulldozers.

"Silence," Kirpal-Sir squeaks.

The sound becomes a roar. We dash out of the door and into the corridor. Kirpal-Sir doesn't try to stop anybody. Outside the school walls, the roars become angry words: **Give us our children back or else.** A voice we recognize shouts through a megaphone: **Don't forget, India belongs to us, India belongs to Hindus.** It's Quarter.

"They were talking about this demonstration at the tea shop," I tell Pari and Faiz. "But I didn't know it was today."

"Muslims took Bahadur and Omvir, and the other children also," Gaurav announces in the corridor. "The Hindu Samaj will stop them."

"Shouldn't they be marching against the police?" Faiz asks.

"They said it's against the police too," I say.

Kirpal-Sir chats with other teachers in the corridor. When the demonstration sounds drift away, he asks us to return to the classroom. We take ages to sit. One boy even blows bubbles, dipping a plastic ring into a small bottle of soapy liquid.

"Don't try to sneak outside during the break," sir tells us when we're done chasing the bubbles. "We'll be lucky if this doesn't turn into a riot."

"There'll be a riot?" Gaurav asks, and he can't keep the happiness out of his face.

"You don't start one now," Kirpal-Sir says.

"Riot, riot, riot," Gaurav chants, looking at Faiz. The red tikka on his forehead seems to be flaming.

"He can't do anything to you," I tell Faiz.

"Let him try," Faiz says.

The other Muslim students in our class squirm in their seats as if they have done something wrong.

"These people don't mean what they say," Pari tells Faiz. She doesn't look angry with us anymore.

Faiz flattens the pages of his notebook. His hands are trembling.

CHANDNI

Gods were good, demons were bad. Spinach was good, noodles were bad. Yesterday was good like gods and spinach, but today was bad like demons and noodles. Chandni could tell because all evening Nisha-Didi had stomped around the house instead of walking, and Didi had chopped the head of a cauliflower as if she was cutting down a tree, and she had rocked Baby too hard while putting him to sleep. Just now when Chandni tried to sit on her lap as she did every night, Nisha-Didi pushed her off and said, "Go do something else."

Chandni didn't know what **something else** was. Every night, after the too-noisy, too-small baby fell asleep, Didi asked their brothers to do their homework, switched on the TV with the sound sponge-soft, and watched a serial where a woman slept in a hospital room for weeks and didn't wake up even when her husband came to see her. First he went to see her every day and then he visited her hardly ever.

Nisha-Didi wouldn't put on **Chhota Bheem** or **Tom and Jerry**, even if Chandni begged **please-na-please-na-please-na**. But Didi tickled Chandni and pretended to eat Chandni's hands, whispering **tasty-so-tasty** until tears streamed down Chandni's cheeks from holding in the laughter to keep Baby from waking up and crying. Baby was always crying, sometimes even when he was drinking milk from under Ma's blouse, and then the milk got into his nose and he coughed and cried even more. Ma said Chandni had done that too when she was a baby, but Chandni liked grown-up things now, Kurkure and Kit Kat and aloo-tikki, and even the sight of Ma's milk wetting her blouse was **ewww**.

Now their house was quiet and all Chandni could hear was the scribble-scribble sound of her brothers' pencils on paper, and the low voices on the TV. Didi sat with the remote in one hand, turning the volume down when the men and women shouted on TV, and turning it up when they whispered. Then Baby started to wail. Chandni stuck her fingers in her ears. Baby's poo smell got into her nose. Baby's poo was stinky like old fish.

Didi took Baby outside to wash his dirty bum. Her brothers stopped studying and swiped the remote and changed the channels until cricket filled the TV screen. They pulled Chandni's hair and laughed when tears filled her eyes. She got up and went to the doorstep and watched Nisha-Didi hush Baby. Baby's mouth clung to Didi's sweater and made a circle of wet.

Chandni held out her hands, asking to hold Baby. Didi put Baby in her arms, but Baby kicked and tried to break the pretty pink plastic necklace that Chandni was wearing. Didi took him back and said **shush-shush, shush-shush.** Didi tried to put him down on the bed but he wanted Didi to hold him. He was cranky, so Didi was cranky too.

Her brothers talked about cricket. They spoke at the same time, two voices, same words. They were born a year apart but Ma said they behaved like twins. Didi snapped at them to be quiet. Her brothers told Didi to stop behaving like their boss-lady. Baby bawled. "Can we mute his sound the way we mute the TV?" the brothers asked. Didi muttered words Chandni couldn't understand. "Don't swear," the brothers said, pressing a button on the remote until the TV was louder than Baby.

"All of you will drive me mad," Didi shouted,

marching around the house, swinging Baby as if she wanted to chuck him out into the alley. Didi's feet clanged against a pot of yesterday's dal that she had reheated after adding water. The pot shook. The dal spilled onto the ground.

Chandni didn't like it when Didi was angry. It happened almost never. Every day, Didi washed their clothes, made their lunches and dinners, and threw stones at the dogs that came to take big bites out of their bums when they pulled down their pants or rolled up their skirts to pee or poo at the rubbish ground. Didi did all this without scowling or shouting.

Chandni knew a way to make tonight better. She stood on a footstool and reached behind a framed photo of Durga-Mata hanging by the door and found the rolled-up twenty-rupee note that Nana had given her for her birthday when he visited them. He had told her to keep the money a secret. Ma and Papa would only take it from her and use it for something good like buying vegetables. Nana wanted Chandni to spend it on something not-so-good like buddi ka baal. That name alone put a bubble of laughter in her tummy. A cloud of pink sugar spun around a stick looked nothing like old-lady hair.

Outside it was dark. Chandni slipped out and walked quickly. No one called her back. She hopped to the bazaar, where some shops were shut and some weren't. She wondered what time it was. No one had taught her to read a clock.

The candyfloss man was gone, and she felt a bit sad but then she saw a shop that sold gujiyas and gulab-jamuns was still open. She gave the sweets-shop man her twenty-rupee note and pointed at the gulab-jamuns drowning in a tray of sugary syrup, inside a glass case. The man scooped the gulab-jamuns into a plastic bag and leaned over the counter to drop it into her hands. He didn't give her back any of her money. But that was all right. The gulab-jamuns were going to do jantar mantar jadu mantar to Didi's bad mood. Just a small bite of the sweet and happiness would coat Didi's tongue and polish her eyes.

The lane was almost empty. The night made rattle-tattle sounds and clitter-clatter sounds and clip-clop sounds and stomping sounds. Some sounds could have been left over from the day, when too many people talked inside shops and all the voices didn't get a chance to be heard. Now they were coming out of cobwebbed ceilings and from behind doors and from under humming fridges and were as loud as they could be.

Chandni didn't like the sounds, which wriggled into her ears like worms and were also scratchy like blankets.

Then she had a good idea. She cluck-clucked like a hen and bow-wowed like a dog and meow-meowed like a cat so that the sounds chasing after her in the dark wouldn't know if she was a hen or a girl or a dog or a cat. This way the sounds would get confused and leave her alone. She skipped and jumped, her cat-tail puffing up, her chicken-beak pecking the ground, her dog-tongue licking the sticky syrup from the plastic bag splish-splashing onto her paws.

She was almost home.

THE HINDU SAMAJ
DEMONSTRATION IS LONG—

—gone but there are signs of it everywhere. Walking home from school, our shoes step on leaflets that hold the faces of the missing. I pick one up. The photo of Bahadur on the leaflet is the same as the one his ma had given us, but this poster is black and white, so you can't tell his shirt is red. Omvir's hair is neatly combed away from his forehead, and he's grinning into the camera. Aanchal is wearing a salwar-kameez with a dupatta over her head; she looks not at all like a brothel-lady. Chandni's face is small and grainy. Under the photos are the words: **Release Our Children Now.**

"Did they see a Muslim snatch a child that

they're going around doing"—Pari's fingers jab the leaflet I'm holding—"this nonsense?"

"Byomkesh Bakshi would have laughed at them," I say.

"We should go to Chandni's house," Pari says. "Maybe we'll see someone or something suspicious. We can't let the Samaj keep blaming good people for evil things."

She's trying to make Faiz feel better because his mood is off.

Pari asks a woman sitting on the roadside, surrounded by sacks full of spices, if she knows where Chandni's house is. The spice vendor points us to the left or the right, I'm not sure exactly, but Pari seems to have understood.

We go past the TV-repair chacha's shop, which is shut, just like every Muslim's shop in Bhoot Bazaar. If I were a Muslim, I wouldn't keep my shop open either while Quarter and his gang shouted threats outside.

"Faiz, why don't you go home?" Pari says, glancing at the padlocked shutters. "That might be safer."

"Will you just shut up?" Faiz says.

The alley ends in a clearing the size of three of our houses, bordered by piles of rubbish on one side that have been there for so long, everything has hardened like rocks. Goats try to find things to eat inside torn, ancient plastic bags. On the other side of the clearing is an electric transformer, a big, crinkled metal box that belongs to the electricity board, ringed by a tall iron fence. A severed Goddess Saraswati head with a jagged crack running across her shocked face lies in the weeds that thrive around the transformer. It's a terrible omen.

A white sign attached to the fence has red letters that say DANGER ELECTRICITY, with a skull below it; the skull has a huge mouth with crooked teeth. It's smiling, but it's an evil smile.

Strings of jasmine and marigold are tied to the fence railings. Maybe this place is a temple for the broken goddess. Ma drags me to the temples around Bhoot Bazaar during Diwali or Janmashtami but she has never brought me here. Our basti is quite big, and people say it has over 200 houses, so even Ma with her too-strong mobile-phone network doesn't know everyone and everything.

Two boys run into the clearing, screaming at each other. One hits the other with a stick, and the welts on the second boy's skin change color from white to red in seconds.

"You know where Chandni's house is?" Pari asks them. "Chandni, the missing girl?"

The boy with the stick points it in the direction of the houses that lie beyond the clearing. "Keep straight," he says. Then he goes back to hitting his friend.

We walk to the edge of the clearing, where the lane splits into two alleys, one heading straight toward where the boy said Chandni's house is, and the other turning right toward the highway.

"It seems like everything is happening around this transformer-temple," Pari says.

"What everything?" I ask.

"Bahadur was working at the TV-repair shop, which is close to this place. And Aanchal's and Chandni's houses are also near here."

"Omvir's house isn't," I remind her.

"Maybe he came here to talk to the TV-repair chacha, same as we did. This is a good place for a kidnapper to kidnap. It must be empty at night. It's almost empty now."

"Maybe," I say, but I say it sadly. I had all the clues and I didn't make the connection. Pari did, her brain knitting things together with the speed of light. Pari is Feluda and Byomkesh Bakshi and Sherlock. I'm only an assistant, Ajit or Topshe or Watson-type.

"Are you blaming the TV-repair chacha again?" Faiz asks. "How do you know it's a human kidnapper and not a bad djinn?"

"Maybe djinns hang out here the same way criminals like Quarter hang out at the theka," I say. "This must be their adda."

"Yes, the Shaitani Adda," Faiz says.

"Doesn't **shaitan** mean the devil?" I ask.

"Evil djinns are also called shaitan," Faiz says.

"Why don't you two start your own show called **Djinn Patrol** and save all this nonsense for it?" Pari asks.

"Loads of people will watch that show," I say.

Pari can't scold us more because we have reached Chandni's house. We can tell it's her house because there's a crowd outside it. I recognize a few faces: Quarter, the press-wallah, Aanchal's papa and Drunkard Laloo. Slouching at the doorstep of the house is a girl holding a baby. A woman leans into the shadows behind her, her face half-covered by a sari's pallu. That's Chandni's ma, I guess. The house doesn't have a door; a torn bedsheet hangs in its place.

Most men in the crowd wear saffron clothes. They must have been part of the Samaj demonstration. Only Quarter is wearing black, like always.

"I really don't think this place is safe for you," Pari tells Faiz.

"Quarter doesn't know he's Muslim. No one knows us," I say, but my stomach turns, and it's not from the stale rice and kadhi we had for the midday meal.

Faiz looks scared like a dog caught in a dog-catcher's net, but he says, "I'm not going anywhere."

He's proving a point to somebody, maybe even us.

A man wearing a saffron robe, with a rudraksha

bead necklace clattering on his chest, comes out of Chandni's house. It's a baba, I don't know which one. There are too many babas in Bhoot Bazaar.

I crane my neck to see clearly. The pradhan is here, just behind the baba. I haven't seen him in months. His black hair is glossy as if the sun is shining on it, even though today too the air is murky with smog. He's a thin, short man dressed in a white kurta-pajama and a hi-fi golden vest-jacket buttoned at the collar. A saffron scarf is loosely draped around his shoulders. He speaks to Quarter, who bends down so his papa can whisper straight into his ears. Someone tries to interrupt and the pradhan waves him off.

The baba sits down on a charpai. People clutch his feet, they touch the hem of his robe.

"You were so right, baba," a man says. He's kneeling, and his head is bowed, but I recognize him. I tell Pari that this is the wrestler-type fellow who told Duttaram children shouldn't work.

"Shh-hh, be quiet," a chacha hisses at me.

"So right," Wrestler-Man says to the baba. "Until your radiant presence shone light on the ugly truth of this basti, we didn't realize it was the Musalman-people who were causing us so much grief." He falls at the baba's feet. The baba lifts him up by his shoulders and thumps him on the back. Three hard knocks with his hand rolled into a fist, straight on the stones of Wrestler-Man's spine.

Wrestler-Man gets up to talk to the pradhan, who's still standing behind the baba with his hands clasped to the front. The pradhan usually ignores people like us, but he listens now with a serious look on his face. Wrestler-Man must be one of the pradhan's many informers in the basti. Ma says the pradhan pays his informers well; maybe that's how Wrestler-Man got the money to buy a gold watch.

It's Aanchal's papa's turn next. "Baba," he says. "Such a relief you're here with us. The second I saw you, my heart stopped aching. I know you'll bring my daughter back."

The baba combs his beard with his right hand. Ash gathers at the tips of his fingers as if by magic. He drops it onto Aanchal's papa's outstretched palms, then hugs and thumps him three times on the back. Aanchal's papa has a coughing fit. He's such a weak man, I don't think he could have done something to his daughter. He doesn't have the strength to lift even a small child like Chandni. I think we'll have to remove him from our suspect-list.

Drunkard Laloo gets up, and his slack arms swing like dead branches about to crash to the ground.

"Baba speaks the truth, no Muslim child has gone missing," he slurs, his words oily with hooch. "Stop the evil Muslims, baba, stop them."

I look at Faiz. He's acting like he doesn't care, but the scar near his left eye is twitching.

"She's only a child," a man standing next to Chandni's ma says from behind the baba. That could be her papa. His uncombed hair rises up like flames above his forehead. "Hindu-Muslim, what does she know?"

"Son, we understand," the pradhan says, turning around to look at him. "But do the bad people?"

A man hands the baba a glass of buttermilk, which he finishes in two quick gulps. Another man gives him a bowl of bhelpuri that he shovels into his mouth with a wooden ice-cream stick. I wonder if the baba is like Mental; maybe he can fix things, magic money like ash out of air and blankets out of smog.

"As I have informed Chandni's mother and father," the baba says, crunching the bhel and moving it from one inside-cheek to another, "they should do a special puja to seek God's blessings. You"—he points at Aanchal's papa and Drunkard Laloo and the press-wallah—"you can also help them."

The people sitting on the ground chant **Ram-Ram-Ram-Ram**. The baba keeps the bowl to the side and rewards each disciple with a thump on the back.

"That's how he blesses people," Pari whispers to me. "I have heard of this thumper-baba."

"Does he bless them or send them to the hospital?" I whisper back. Pari giggles.

"Children, come here!"

It's the baba. I don't know why or how he noticed us. Everyone else is looking at us too, and I wish they would stop and go back to whatever they were doing before.

"They're Bahadur's friends," Drunkard Laloo says.

Aanchal's papa watches me with narrowed eyes, but he doesn't try to hit me.

Forceful hands push us toward the baba, who kisses us on our foreheads with a mouth that's prickly with beard and mustache. He thumps us on the back, and the pain shoots up to my head but also down to my legs. He thumps Faiz too, which is good, because it means he can't tell Faiz is a Muslim.

I sneak a look at Quarter and Wrestler-Man, standing behind Thumper-Baba. Quarter smirks at me as I rub my sore back. Wrestler-Man is still whispering basti-secrets to the pradhan. He looks at us, but if he has recognized me from the tea shop, it doesn't show on his face.

Thumper-Baba's words walk with us as Pari drags me and Faiz away: "In this basti resides great evil that doesn't answer to our gods, and it's up to us to stop it before it does more harm . . ."

It's Christmas holidays now. We have more time to watch our suspects who aren't djinns. Pari had crossed out the TV-repair chacha from her list, but she has put him back on because his shop is close to the Shaitani Adda. Faiz says Pari and I should start wearing saffron because we are acting like members of the Hindu Samaj. Pari explains that if we catch the kidnapper, we will be helping everyone, Hindus and Muslims.

Stake-outs are excellent for child-detectives like us. I can take Samosa with me, when he isn't busy chasing his own tail and lapping dirty water from puddles.

Today we are near the TV-repair chacha's shop. Faiz has shirked work and come along with us because he's worried Pari and I will outright accuse the chacha of child-snatching, and then Quarter and the Hindu Samaj will set fire to chacha's beard or cut off his head with a sword. We have seen that happen to Muslims on the TV news. It's strange that Quarter, our main suspect, is acting like he wants to catch the kidnapper.

Right now we are hiding the fact that we are on a stake-out by pretend-playing with marbles that belong to Faiz's brothers. Samosa gets excited each time we flick marbles and barks too much.

"Why did you bring this idiot dog along?" Pari asks.

"He can track clues."

"Everyone's looking at us because of Pakoda," Pari says.

"You know that's not his name."

"Can you make Chow Mein shut up please?" she says.

Faiz scoops up the marbles and drops them in his pockets; maybe he's afraid Samosa will eat one.

I feed Samosa a bit of the rusk Ma gave me for breakfast. It's a good thing he loves rusk and I hate it. Ma thinks Runu-Didi and I sit at home all day, studying for our exams that will begin the day school reopens. But Didi leaves for training soon after finishing her chores. We don't ask each other questions. We are good at keeping our secrets.

The TV-repair chacha steps out of his shop with two of his customers and sees us. "You're playing here because you think Bahadur will come back to my shop first, haan?" he says. "You're such good children."

He asks us if we want tea, and we say no, but his words make us feel so bad, we call off our stake-out and go to the Shaitani Adda. We check for any clues the kidnapper or djinn might have left, but there's only the usual rubbish we see in every alley in our basti: toffee wrappers, chips packets, newspapers trodden into the ground by slippered feet, goat pellets, cow dung, a rat tail left over from a bird's meal. The broken Goddess Saraswati is still looking stunned in the weeds.

"We could tell grown-ups about this place," I say. "Maybe they can keep watch here, 24/7. Night too."

"When did you become so stupid?" Faiz shouts. The amulet that keeps him safe from bad djinns bounces around his throat. Samosa yelps. "You tell anybody anything about this place, people will hundred-percent blame the TV-repair chacha. They'll think he's the snatcher, same as you." Then he stomps off, the marbles rattling in his pockets.

"You shouldn't have upset him," Pari says.

"Me? You're the one who made the TV-repair chacha a suspect."

Samosa barks.

I can tell the Shaitani Adda is a bad place full of bad feelings because it makes even good friends fight.

CHRISTMAS DAY
IS ALSO THE DAY OF—

—the Hindu Samaj puja to ask our gods to vanquish the great evil in our basti. Even Ma has taken the morning off from work so that she can attend it.

I'm dressed in my usual clothes but Ma is wearing a gold-plated chain around her neck and she has lipsticked her mouth red. Runu-Didi has put on a blue salwar-kameez shimmering with sequins. Ma braids Didi's hair, and Didi keeps saying she isn't doing it right.

"When you were only a little smaller than Jai, you used to run behind me, begging me to tie your hair just like mine," Ma tells Didi. "You thought I looked beautiful."

"You're still beautiful," I say and Ma smiles. When she finishes with Didi's braid, she hands over bangles and a silvery chain for Didi to wear. Runu-Didi looks much older now, like she has secrets I can't guess.

The puja is being held near Aanchal's house, but closer to the highway, so that important Hindu Samaj people don't have to trudge through our basti's muck. I hope the men from the dhaba with the disco-light Ganpati and the auto-stand won't tell Ma they have seen me before.

A red canopy has blossomed like a gigantic red rose in front of the dhaba. Below it, brown rugs have been rolled out on the ground. In the middle of the rugs is a brick square piled with firewood.

The workers at the dhaba are making puris. This is the best bit of the puja: we are going to get free food at the end of it. I feel sorry for Pari and Faiz because they are missing out on a feast. Pari's ma has gone off to work, leaving Pari alone at home to study. Pari doesn't even mind because she likes studying.

The pandal is empty except for a few Hindu Samaj people dressed in their trademark saffron clothes. They wander around with their heads held high, pointing out to others the things that need fixing. Then I see a woman running toward us, her hair loose and wild, a blanket slipping down her shoulders, trailing behind her and gathering dust. She sits down at the very edge of the pandal, near its entrance from the direction of the highway. Her back rests against a pole that looks as if it could crash any moment. Ma and I go to her, but Runu-Didi stays behind so we won't lose our spots.

"What happened?" Ma asks the woman I recognize as Chandni's ma. Then Ma shouts at the men from the dhaba, "Get her some water. Hurry."

One of the dhaba-men brings Chandni's ma a steel glass, water filled to its brim. She drinks it quickly, looks at Ma, and says, "I went to the police station."

"Why?" Ma asks.

"I wanted them to attend the puja, so that they could hear the baba talk about Chandni. My daughter, who is missing."

Ma nods her head. "I heard."

"But those animals beat me here"—Chandni's ma touches her neck—"here"—she twists her left hand to touch her back, just below her blouse and above her sari skirt—"and here too." Now she touches her legs. "I asked them why they're not looking for my child, and they said, **We're your servants or what?** They asked me, **Why do you people pop out kids like rats when you can't take care of them? We'll be doing the world a favor if we wipe out your slum.**"

I think of the words RODENT BAIT STATION written on a metal box in our school playground, next to a paved area where the midday meal food is unloaded from vans.

"You take your grievances to baba," a man tells Chandni's ma. "He will help you. But now, in the name of Lord Hanuman, stop with all this rona-dona. We spent a lot of money to organize this event."

Chandni's ma smiles an embarrassed smile, draws in her sniffles, and smooths her hair with her bruised hands. The dhaba-wallah takes his steel glass back.

I don't know why the Hindu Samaj man said they spent a lot of money on the puja. The money came from us. Every Hindu gave what they could to the men from the Samaj who went around the basti with a bucket into which we dropped coins and rupees. The Samaj and their goondas are so scary, no one dared to say no to them.

"The police will change their tune," Ma tells Chandni's ma, "now that baba himself is on our side. A holy man like that wouldn't even have glanced at people of our caste before. Things are changing for the better. See, even the smog is less today."

People start arriving for the puja. They take off their chappals and shoes before they step inside the pandal. A Samaj man appoints three boys to watch over everyone's Poma and Adides and Nik shoes. Ma, Didi and I forgot to remove ours.

Thumper-Baba appears with the pradhan, Quarter and his gang-members, and Wrestler-Man. Maybe Wrestler-Man is not just the pradhan's informer, but also an important member of the Hindu Samaj. I edge closer to the pole so that the baba won't be able to hit my back.

"My dear child," the baba tells Chandni's ma, "you have had to endure so much. But worry no longer. I'll solve every one of your troubles."

Chandni's ma falls at his feet, wailing again because she's grateful or sad, I can't tell. The baba thump-thumps her back and then she can barely get up; this must be like a second police beating for her.

We leave our chappals with the watcher-boys, and Ma and I are allowed to accompany Chandni's ma. The baba, the pradhan, Quarter and Wrestler-Man sit right next to the fire. Our places are behind the baba, and our row soon turns into the sad row with all the parents of the missing children, Omvir's ma with her boxer-baby who's sleeping through the noise, his press-wallah papa and his bad-dancer brother, Bahadur's ma, Drunkard Laloo, Aanchal's papa and her brothers, Ajay and the other one whose name I don't know. Chandni's papa isn't around, probably because he's working. I smile at Ajay, but he turns his head away.

Ma calls Runu-Didi, but she refuses to join us.

She's sitting with her running-friend Tara and Tara's ma.

Someone lights the firewood, the puja begins with chants that I don't understand, and hot smoke burns our throats. Out of the corner of my eyes, I see Ma holding Chandni's ma's hand. I don't think Ma has seen Chandni's ma before today, or only at the toilet complex or in the queue for water, and now she's behaving like they are sisters. Ma's eyes are damp with tears as if her own child has gone missing. I'm right here and it's like she can't even see me.

———

After the puja, which is excellent because we get buttermilk with chopped coriander floating on top and as much aloo-puri as our tummies want, Ma lets Runu-Didi stay at home, but she leaves me at Pari's house. She thinks Pari can help me get good marks in the exams.

Ma would have taken me to work if she could, kept me under her nose and shouted at me to study all day, but she can't. Her hi-fi madam thinks basti-children are full of germs and TB and typhoid and smallpox, even though smallpox has been gone for ages.

I don't want to go to any building where they

think I have the pox. Papa says we should have self-respect even if others don't respect us. When he says **others,** he means hi-fi madams and also the guards at malls who are basti-people like us but won't let us in because we don't look rich.

"Will the puja work?" Pari asks Ma, standing at her doorstep and pulling down the hem of her blue frock, which looks like a hi-fi frock. Pari gets good clothes from her ma's hi-fi madam, who gives away shiny things when they lose even a bit of shine.

"Let's hope the gods have heard us," Ma says.

"You don't need a puja to talk to gods. They can hear even if you whisper," I say.

Ma taps me on the back of my head. It's a not-so-secret signal for me to shut up.

"Jai is wasting his entire holidays not studying," Ma complains to Pari as if Pari is my teacher. "Just see, if there's anything you can do to help him—"

"Of course, chachi," Pari says.

Ma looks pleased as she leaves.

I sit down on the floor next to Pari. She places one of her textbooks on my lap.

"Start studying EVS. When I finish Social Science, we'll exchange."

Pari reads for a bit. I watch black ants twisting along the floor and I confuse them by breaking their line with a corner of Pari's textbook.

"Police-police-police," a child screams. Someone

else is shouting **police** too. Pari and I leave our books and run to the door. Pari puts a hand out to stop me from going any farther.

"I promised your ma," she says.

"We have to find out what's happening," I tell her. "We're detectives." But I don't move. The good and bad thing about living in a basti is that news flies into your ears whether you want it to or not.

Pari and I listen carefully. We pick out the important-sounding words from the breathless clucks around us: police, arrest, snatch, children, baba, puja, success, TV-repair, Hakim. We put the words in an order that makes sense. The police have arrested the child-snatcher. Hakim, the harmless-looking TV-repair man? Not so harmless after all! The puja was an immediate success! The baba is truly God himself in human form! The canopy hasn't been pulled down and the rugs haven't been rolled up, but the gods have already blessed us.

"Is it true?" Pari asks one of her neighbor-chachis who's muttering **who would have thought** to anyone willing to listen to her.

"Baba was right," the chachi tells Pari. "It turned out to be the work of Muslims."

"Muslim who?"

"The police have arrested four of them. A mullah gang."

The chachi turns away from us and says the same thing to someone else.

Pari's right foot taps the floor. "Four Muslims, arrested on the same day a Samaji baba holds a puja? Doesn't it sound suspicious to you?"

"Faiz will be upset," I say.

I'm upset too; I wasn't the one who solved the case.

Pari and I sit down on the doorstep. I see Faiz walking toward us. I wave at him and move my backside so that there's space for him to sit. He slumps down next to me and says, "They took him." He doesn't look sad, just stunned, like somebody knocked him on the head and stars are still flashing in front of his eyes.

"We heard," Pari says.

"They took Tariq-Bhai," Faiz says. "They say he has Aanchal's phone. Just because he works in a phone shop."

"No," I say. "The police arrested the TV-repair chacha."

"Tariq-Bhai too," Faiz says.

Something tightens in my chest. I must have breathed in too much smog, so I cough to let it out.

Faiz scratches his stomach, then wipes his nose against his sleeve.

"Did he have Aanchal's phone?" Pari asks.

"Of course not." Faiz's nose turns an angry-red.

"I was just asking," Pari says.

"The police checked our house," Faiz says.

"Without a warrant?" I ask.

"They looked under the bed, even opened our flour tins. Said **when we find Aanchal's HTC phone, we'll—**"

"That's an expensive phone," I say. "You can only make calls on Ma's phone, but on Shanti-Chachi's mobile, you can—"

"Shut up, Jai," Pari says, widening her eyes at me.

"You must be happy," Faiz says. "You wanted the TV-repair chacha to be arrested."

"Maybe you should go to the police station," Pari tells Faiz. "Tariq-Bhai will need your help."

"Ammi is there with Wajid-Bhai. They told me and Farzana-Baji to wait at home, but I couldn't sit doing nothing."

"Look," Pari says. "You mustn't worry."

"It's very worrying," I say.

"Who else did the police arrest?" Pari asks.

"Two of Tariq-Bhai's friends from the mosque. Nobody you know."

I wonder if Tariq-Bhai could be a snatcher but it's impossible. I have known Tariq-Bhai my whole life. He never once tried to snatch me.

"A bad djinn has cursed us," Faiz says. "It's watching us cry and it's feeling happy, it's dancing." He pushes his tongue out against the insides of his cheeks and rolls it around as if that will stop the tears from falling out of his eyes.

"Let's go to the police station," I say.

"I promised my ma and your ma we will stay here," Pari says.

"You don't have to come," I say.

"Ya Allah," Faiz says, hitting his forehead with the side of his right hand and then hitting it again.

"Don't do that," Pari says, her voice cracking as if she's about to cry too. Then she pulls the door to her house shut and shuffles her feet into her chappals. "We'll all go."

———

At the highway we find out from autorickshaw-wallahs and vendors where the police station is. None of us have been there before. We fast-walk, Pari holding Faiz's hand, which is embarrassing.

Outside the police station are huddles of women in black abayas and men wearing skullcaps. Some of the women wail and beat their chests. The men whisper about the "evidence" the police might plant in their homes to make it appear that those arrested are really criminals. **We have to guard our homes**, they tell each other, **but we also have to be here**. I wonder which family belongs to the TV-repair chacha, but I can't tell and we don't have the time to talk to them.

The police station looks like a house. Its windows rattle, and brown, damp patches billow on the yellow walls though it hasn't rained in ages. When we step inside, the room is so dark, it takes a few seconds for my eyes to see what's around me. My heart races like it does before I have to show Ma my exam marks.

The air in the room is heavy with murmurs and ringing phones, landlines and mobiles both. My legs bend like grass in the wind or maybe that's just how it feels to me. I shuffle closer to Pari and Faiz.

The policemen's desks are cluttered with bulky computers and dusty stacks of files tied with string. In one corner of the room, to our right, are Faiz's ammi and Wajid-Bhai, sitting in front of the junior constable who had come to our basti with the senior to take Bahadur's ma's chain.

"Your people are here to protest against us, that's all very well," the junior tells them now, his voice loud and his face puffed up with importance. "But first, look at the state of this place. We aren't in one of those cyber-police stations you have seen on the news. We don't even have an air-cooler here. No drinking water. Out of our own pockets we have to spend money to buy twenty-liter Aquafina bottles. Everyone who works at this station has got malaria or dengue at least once. Think we have it easy?"

"No one thinks so," Wajid-Bhai says.

"If your brother isn't a criminal, the magistrate will let him out and you can take him home," the junior tells Wajid-Bhai.

"Please, I beg of you, this old woman is falling at your feet, don't keep my son tied to a bench," Faiz's ammi sobs. "Let him sit. He won't run away, I promise you in the name of Allah."

We look around to see where Tariq-Bhai is. The room we are in is like a corridor, with a door leading to a second room from where we can hear groans; that must be the lock-up. Faiz runs toward it and we dash behind him. A policeman sitting behind a wonky desk with newspaper strips folded under two of its legs gets up and scrambles toward us, shouting, "Stop-STOP." We don't stop.

The TV-repair chacha is chained to a chair. Two men stand in a corner, their hands and legs tied with rope. Tariq-Bhai is sitting on the floor, his head on his knees, hands cuffed behind him and chained to the leg of a bench. Faiz hugs him for a second before the policeman pulls him away.

"Get out," the policeman tells us. "You want to be arrested too?" He grabs Faiz by the collar and drags him out of the room.

We run behind them, Pari shouting, "Don't do that. Don't do anything to him. I'll complain to the commissioner. It's wrong, how you have chained our brother like an animal. This will come on TV, and you won't have a job tomorrow."

The policeman lets go of Faiz and turns to Pari. "If it comes on TV, maybe we will get a real lock-up," he says, arranging the surprised features on his face so that he looks superior to us. "Make sure you tell the TV-wallahs we don't have an inverter either, and so, when the current goes off, it stays gone for eight hours or more. Tell them we have rats in our quarters too, okay? Don't forget."

Wajid-Bhai hurries to our side. He straightens Faiz's sweater where the policeman's clutch has bunched it up. "What are you doing here? I told you to stay at home," Wajid-Bhai says. But he lets us stand with him while he talks to the junior constable some more.

Faiz's ammi hugs Faiz and cries. "You saw what they have done to your brother," she says.

Wajid-Bhai tells the policeman he's going to hire a lawyer.

"Try it," the junior sniggers.

"Take Faiz home," his ammi says, pushing him toward us and then wiping her cheeks. "Farzana must be wondering where he is."

"How will we pay the lawyer's fees?" Faiz asks when we are outside. "It must cost thousands of rupees."

"We'll figure something out," Pari says.

IT'S THE LAST DAY
OF THE YEAR—

—and it's dark now, but Papa and Ma aren't home yet. I'm sitting by our front door, my eyes following a bear-shaped balloon a boy flies into the smog. He must have snatched it from the decorations for New Year in Bhoot Bazaar.

Ma is late because her hi-fi madam is throwing a party that will begin at night and go on till morning. We never have parties for New Year in our basti, though some people burst crackers. I don't think anyone will do that this year though. Our whole basti is having a mood-off because too many bad things have happened. The missing are still missing, Tariq-Bhai is in prison, and Faiz is selling roses by the highway for extra cash.

Runu-Didi brings a pot of cooked rice outside to drain the water, one of Papa's old shirts twisted around the pot's mouth to keep the heat from burning her fingers. I stand up so that the water won't splash onto my legs. Didi does all the cooking and shopping these days, sometimes with her basti-friends, sometimes with the neighbor-chachis. She has to walk up and down the same alleys ten-twenty times a day, collecting water, going to the toilet complex, buying vegetables, buying rice. She says I don't help at all, but I do.

Something shifts the smoky air around us, a flurry of noises, footsteps pounding the ground. It goosepimples my skin, dries my mouth. A group of men zigzag through the alley, stopping to talk to grown-ups.

Shanti-Chachi comes out of her home. "Stay right there, you two," she says.

Didi takes the pot back in but returns to my side, Papa's old shirt still in her hands. She twists it tightly around her fingers. The men talk to the women in the alley, who scoop up their children and run into their houses. Windows are pulled shut, doors closed. Shanti-Chachi listens to the men with her hands on both cheeks. The bear balloon, now abandoned, brushes against the edge of a tin roof and bursts. It sounds like a gunshot on TV.

Shanti-Chachi clutches her heart. "What was that?" she asks. She sees the dying bear but doesn't look comforted. She walks over to me and Didi, puts her hand on our shoulders and steers us inside. She shuts the door even though the smoke from the kitchen-fire hasn't left our house.

"What have you made for dinner, Runu?" she asks.

"Just rice. We'll have it with dal."

"What did those men want?" I ask.

"I'll wait with you two until your mother gets home," Shanti-Chachi says. "It's past dinner-time and her hi-fi madam is still making her work. So heartless that woman is."

Runu-Didi switches on the TV. The newsreaders are sad that people can't celebrate New Year's outside because **the winter smog has other plans.**

Shanti-Chachi's husband knocks on the door to give chachi her mobile. "It won't stop ringing," he says. He nods at us and leaves. Chachi walks around the house with the phone pressed against her ear, not saying anything except **haan-haan** and **wohi toh.** She opens tins and checks what's inside them. She even inspects the Parachute tub. If Ma had told her the tub holds our **what-if** fund, chachi would have guessed a little money is missing because she's smart like that.

"Someone disappeared?" Runu-Didi asks when chachi finishes another phone call.

"You should tell your ma to put a clove or two into the chili-powder tin," chachi says. "That will stop the powder from getting spoiled."

The door opens. It's Papa. He's home early and he smells a bit like Drunkard Laloo. Papa never smells like that; only once or twice a year maybe. Nodding at Shanti-Chachi, he says, "Came home as soon as I heard. It was good of your husband to call me and Madhu to tell us they are"—he looks at Didi and me—"fine."

"Shocking," chachi says, "what's happening. I don't know how you can stand it."

"Stand what?" I ask.

"Two more children are missing," Papa says. "Musalman children. Brother-sister. Went out to buy milk earlier this evening and haven't got back yet. Almost the same age as you two."

Farzana-Baji is loads older than Faiz, so he hasn't been snatched.

"Jai, what this means is that the kidnapper is still out there," Papa says. "Do you know why I'm telling you this?"

I hate it when grown-ups talk to me like that.

"Will Tariq-Bhai be released now?" I ask. "He couldn't have kidnapped from jail."

"Who knows anything," Shanti-Chachi says.

"Did the Muslim children disappear near the transformer?" I ask. "It's also a temple and it's close to Chandni's house."

"How do you know where her house is?" Papa asks.

"We saw the transformer when we went for Thumper-Baba's big puja. That place is like a man-hole into which children keep falling tak-tak-tak. Shaitan djinns live there. We call it the Shaitani Adda."

"Who's we?" Runu-Didi asks.

"Pari and Faiz and me."

"Jai," Papa says, "this is not a game. When will you understand that?"

———

That night I dream of child-legs and child-hands hanging out of bloody mouths and then I hear fighting voices. I think it's part of my bad dream, but when I open my eyes it's morning and Ma and Papa are arguing outside about who should stay back to look after us.

Runu-Didi is sitting on the bed, her hands propping up her chin, her face scrubbed. She and Ma must have already fetched water.

"Look at how they're being raised," Papa says. "A girl who runs around like a boy, and a boy who wanders around the bazaar like a beggar. It's a wonder they haven't been kidnapped yet."

"What are you saying?" Ma yells. "Is that what you wish on your own children?"

"That's not what I meant," Papa says.

We hear shuffling feet and I lie down quickly and pull the blanket over my head.

"I know you're awake, Jai," Ma says. "Get up, come on. I'm taking you to the toilet complex today. Runu, roll up the mat, boil water for drinking, cut some onions."

Didi glares at me as if I'm the one forcing her to do chores.

Ma doesn't even let me brush my teeth properly. In the toilet queues, I see Pari with her ma and Faiz with Wajid-Bhai. Ma drags me toward Pari's ma; she wants to check if Pari's ma is planning to stay at home today.

"Are you trying to sneak them into our queue?" the woman behind Pari asks, waggling her fingers at us.

"We don't need your spot," I say.

"The police arrested Tariq-Bhai and the TV repair-chacha for nothing," Pari tells me.

"Musalman-people can't be trusted," says the nosey woman.

"Don't you know that Muslim children have also disappeared?" Pari asks, her right hand on her right hip. Then she turns to me and whispers, "You heard, the brother and sister who disappeared also lived near the Shaitani Adda."

"Faiz is right. It's the work of a bad djinn," I say.

"Nonsense," Pari says.

Faiz is watching us from his queue. I hardly see him anymore because he works all the time, to help his ammi pay the bills Tariq-Bhai used to pay. I shoot him with a finger gun.

"Yes, they should really be shot," the woman behind us says. "All this is their fault." She points at Faiz's ammi, standing ahead in the ladies' queue with Farzana-Baji. Both of them are wearing black abayas. "This basti has become a den of criminals. The government will kick us out any day now."

"It's **your** fault," someone shouts at her. "Two of our own have gone. You think my brother did that from jail?"

It's Wajid-Bhai.

"Who knows what you people are capable of?" the woman says. Monkeys chitter-chatter on the toilet roof. "Maybe you snatched your own so that we'll stop blaming you."

Ma's phone rings. "Haan, madam," she says. "Haan, you're right. No madam. Yes madam. This one time only . . ."

"Why doesn't your brother just tell the police where he has hidden our children?" a man roars at Wajid-Bhai.

"Don't talk to these Musalman-people," the woman who started the fight says, pushing her pallu closer toward her neck. I can see her belly button. It's turned down like a sad mouth. "They shout **Allah-Allah** over their loudspeakers day and night and none of us can sleep."

"In Lord Krishna's name, please stop. You're frightening the children," Pari's ma tells the woman.

"If your child goes missing, you'll sing a different tune," the woman says, pointing a long, black fingernail toward Pari's face, making Pari snap her head back.

"I can find a hundred people to do your job, like-that-like-that," Ma's hi-fi madam screeches so loudly on the phone we can all hear her. The madam has switched to English, which Ma says is something she does when her anger is extra-hot.

The monkeys on the toilet roof growl. Faiz's ammi clutches Farzana-Baji's shoulder as if her legs have turned rubbery and she's about to faint. "Ammi, Ammi," Farzana-Baji shouts, panic rounding her eyes, the loose folds of her abaya turning and spinning with her every time she moves.

"I remember I owe you money," Ma tells her hi-fi madam. "It was very good of you not to cut it from this month's salary."

Men with their mufflers tied around their faces lunge toward Faiz and his brothers. Mugs and buckets clank and clash. Faiz screams and closes his eyes and puts his hands over his ears.

"Madhu, chalo, let's get away from here," Pari's ma says.

The hi-fi madam's anger keeps spewing out of Ma's phone. Pari runs toward Faiz, and Wajid-Bhai punches a man taunting him. A scuffle breaks out, and Faiz clings to Pari. Someone shouts that they'll grind every single Muslim into the ground like so many cockroaches. Faiz's ammi and Farzana-Baji hobble toward Wajid-Bhai and Faiz.

"They're children," Faiz's ammi tells the angry men. "Let them be."

"Stop this," Pari's ma blubbers. "We don't want a riot in our basti."

Clever men use the melee to scramble over others so that they can get to the toilets without paying the fees. The caretaker runs after them. The woman behind us smiles and her face brightens like she has managed to do a big poo after ages. Faiz and his ammi and his brothers and sister flee the toilet complex, Pari holding Faiz's hand, and Pari's ma shouting **Pari, wait, wait.**

"If this is how the new year starts, imagine how it will end," someone says.

I had even forgotten it was New Year.

———

Ma decides she has to go to work after her hi-fi madam's phone call. "All that TV you watch," she tells me, "it isn't free."

She's scared of her hi-fi madam; she can't

admit it, so she's trying to make me feel guilty instead.

After she leaves, Runu-Didi starts washing clothes. I helpfully point out the dirt-smudges she's missing.

"That's it, enough," she says, splish-splashing me with soapy water.

Didi hangs the washed clothes to dry, then she ignores her other chores to gossip with her basti-friends. She doesn't have training today because it's New Year, when even her strict coach loosens his iron-hold on his athletes.

I calculate how many more Sundays I have to work to make up the 200 rupees I took from Ma's Parachute tub:

- I slogged at the tea shop for seven Sundays;
- Duttaram paid me half of what he promised on five Sundays, and my real salary of forty rupees twice;
- how long before I hit my target?

This is tough like a real Maths problem. I add and multiply and subtract and then I have the answer. Next Sunday, even if Duttaram pays me only twenty rupees, I'll have 200 rupees altogether.

I hear angry noises and look up. In the alley, a Hindu woman with sindoor on her forehead shakes a slotted ladle at a Muslim vendor wearing a skullcap. "What does the front of my house look like to you? A garage?" she screeches. He hurries his pushcart, bright and beautiful with oranges, away from her door.

"Child-killer," a boy shouts as the orange-seller's cart squawks through the alley.

Runu-Didi gestures that I should go inside the house. "Something terrible is about to happen, I can feel it," she says.

She doesn't look scared; she never does. Even now she speaks coolly, as if she's just warning me it might rain, and I should carry an umbrella.

I don't feel like gathering clues about the missing Muslim children. I will learn everything about them and I still won't find them. I just know it.

I pretend to study, I think about Pari and Faiz, I wonder if Faiz's ammi is at the police station asking for Tariq-Bhai to be released. Then it's time for lunch. Didi lets me watch afternoon-TV. I play cricket in our alley with a few neighbor-boys who are older than me. I doze off for a bit and soon it's evening and Ma and Papa come back home. Papa and I watch a 20/20 game, which Papa likes much better than one-dayers and Tests because they're short.

Today is how every day used to be before Bahadur and others disappeared, when I wasn't a detective or a tea-shop boy. It's a good day, the very best. Being a detective is too-tough. Maybe I don't want to be one after all. Maybe Jasoos Jai can retire un-hurt, okay-tata-bye. I don't know what I will be when I grow up. Sometimes when Ma sees the marks I get, she says Pari will be an IAS officer, a district collector or something, and I will be her peon.

———

Late that night I wake up hearing knocks on doors and wails and howls. Papa gets out of bed and fumbles in the darkness until he finds the light switch. The yellow bulb is angry we have woken it up, and it hisses and crackles.

"JCBs have come?" I ask.

"Is it an earthquake?" Runu-Didi asks.

"Outside," Papa shouts.

Ma picks up the Parachute tub. She ties it to the pallu of her sari. She bends down and looks at our precious-things bundle by the door. It's been waiting for this exact moment for almost two months, but Ma doesn't cart it out.

We scuttle into the alley. Our neighbors dash out of their houses too, some carrying torches. The lights catch the startled eyes of goats and dogs.

"Wait right here," Ma says, pushing me close to Runu-Didi.

"Maybe your djinn has snatched again," Didi says.

I look up and down the alley, imagining a djinn swooshing through the air toward us, and I half-hope, because I'm standing next to Runu-Didi, and because Didi is bigger and taller than me, that it will take her instead of me. **Please please please.**

PAPA AND SHANTI-CHACHI GO TOWARD THE SCREAMS—

—to find out if we should run away from the basti or hide in our homes. Shanti-Chachi's husband talks to Ma, nervously scratching his man-parts when Ma's head is turned.

Runu-Didi and I wait on our doorstep, a single blanket pulled up over our heads, prickling our skin. "Sit still," Didi says each time I stretch my legs to stop them from falling asleep.

I wonder what the gods want from us. Maybe a bigger hafta like our basti police. Maybe a grander puja than Thumper-Baba's. Maybe it was grand enough and the gods just don't care about us. Maybe maybe maybe. I'm sick of maybes.

"There they are," Didi says and stands up. Her side of the blanket falls to the ground. I try to fold the blanket so that Ma won't be angry with us for dirtying it, but it's heavy and spiky and it feels like I'm trying to smush a thorny kikar tree and my fingers hurt. It makes me sad that I'm too small to do even such a stupid thing. Tears burn my eyes.

"Don't cry," Runu-Didi says. "Nothing's going to happen to you."

"I'm not crying."

Didi takes the blanket from my hands, and her training must have made her strong because she forces it to behave and folds it neatly in seconds.

Papa picks me up. I'm not such a small child that I should be carried around, but I press my face against his neck. I can hear his breathing. It's loud and panting, like Samosa's. Torch beams swing around the alley, lighting one half of a satellite dish, a quarter of a washing line on which someone has hung their clothes to dry, pigeons waking up on rooftops and fluttering their wings.

"Fatima's buffalo," Shanti-Chachi says, her voice cracking like glass, "it's dead. Beheaded."

I look up. When butchers like Afsal-Chacha kill animals, it's only to eat them. Nobody would want to eat Buffalo-Baba. Even a useless man like Drunkard Laloo considers him God.

Shanti-Chachi has slipped her hand into the

crook of her husband's elbow. Runu-Didi draws half-circles on the ground with her right foot.

"Someone left the buffalo's head on Fatima's doorstep," Papa says.

"Fatima can't stop crying," Shanti-Chachi says. "She loved that buffalo like a child. It gave her nothing, not even enough dung for a day's fuel. Still she spent so much money feeding it."

Papa puts me down, and I run into our house. I slide under Ma-Papa's bed. I'm brave in the day, but my braveness doesn't like to come out at night. It's sleeping, I think.

"Jai, what are you doing?" Ma asks. She has followed me into the house.

I must look ekdum-stupid. Only half of me fits under the bed because of the bags and sacks she has stored in her cave. Ma kneels down. "Come out, sona," she says. She calls me sona only when she loves me more than anyone else in the whole world. Ma removes the Parachute tub from the pallu of her sari, and she wipes the dust from under the bed off my face with the sari's edge. I wriggle out so that she can clean me properly. Ma returns the Parachute tub to the shelf. Papa and Didi come inside.

"Did a djinn eat Buffalo-Baba?" I ask.

"There are no djinns, Jai," Papa says. "It's the work of goondas. The buffalo's head was cut neatly with a sword. There are bloody tracks going up and down Fatima-ben's alley."

Djinns don't need weapons. They can behead people just by thinking about it.

"The Hindu Samaj boys must have killed Buffalo-Baba because he's Fatima-ben's," Runu-Didi says. "To teach Muslims a lesson."

"We worship cows," Ma says. "Our people would never do such a horrible thing."

"Everyone knows the Samaj boys have swords," Didi says. "They bring them out during riots. We saw it on the news, haan, Papa?"

"I'm going back to Fatima's," Papa says. "The poor woman is so shocked."

"Don't do that," Ma pleads. "Don't go out—who knows what horrible thing will happen next?"

But Papa has already put on his outside sweater and a monkey cap. "At least take a muffler," Ma says. "It's very cold outside."

"Madhu, meri jaan, will you leave the worrying to me for once?"

Runu-Didi looks embarrassed like she always does when Papa calls Ma his life or his liver or his heartbeat. But it makes me feel safe.

Ma puts a muffler around Papa's neck as if it's a garland and she's marrying him again.

I can't believe Buffalo-Baba is gone. He never hurt anybody, not even the flies that went buzzing round and round his eyes for hours until they got tired and dropped dead right between his horns.

———

We lie down to sleep and the next thing I know, it's time to wake up and Ma and Papa are arguing about who should go to work. Last night Ma was worried about Papa, and now she sounds like she wants to push him into a djinn's mouth. They do this each time something awful happens, though they know they can't watch us every day. They are fooling themselves, but not me. I sit on my mat with the cold clawing my throat. I'm pakka Papa is going to get his way again, but Ma wins the argument to everyone's surprise, even Ma's, it sounds like.

"Don't you dare complain if I lose my job," Papa says as he click-clicks his fingers at me, telling me to get up. "I don't even know how we're going to eat this month. Looks like we'll have to use your emergency money." Papa walks to the kitchen shelf and grabs the Parachute tub. My stomach twists into a ball. Ma snatches the tub from Papa and puts it back on the shelf.

"This isn't the time for jokes," Ma says.

"Who says I was joking?" Papa says.

"It's just for today and tomorrow," Ma says. "Shanti said she can watch the children on Sunday, and Monday they'll be back at school."

Runu-Didi and Ma go to fetch water. Papa says he'll take me to the toilet complex.

"Buffalo-Baba?" I ask when we are outside.

"It's all cleared out," Papa says.

"Fatima-ben took it?" I ask.

"A butcher from Bhoot Bazaar."

"Afsal-Chacha?"

"Who's that? Have you been talking to strangers in the bazaar again? Didn't I tell you not to do that? Bhoot Bazaar isn't a playground for children."

"I don't play," I say.

We pass a dog that looks like Samosa. I hope Samosa is all right. I hope he stays away from djinns and people with swords.

We are cursed, just like Faiz said, poor Faiz who is now a hawker-boy. Ma says Faiz's ammi is disappearing inside her abaya. She's worried about what her eldest son is eating in prison: rice cooked with cockroaches, tea stirred with fallen-off lizard tails, water seasoned with rat droppings.

"Will we go hungry this month?" I ask Papa.

"Don't worry about it."

"But you'll go to work tomorrow?"

Papa shrugs. Ma or Papa will have to open the Parachute tub soon if they keep taking chuttis like this.

I'm so close to the finish line. All I need is twenty rupees.

"Papa—"

"Look, Jai, we'll be fine. You aren't going to starve."

———

When we are having our rusk-breakfast, Pari's ma brings Pari to our house for safekeeping. Ma must have told Pari's ma to do that over the phone. She didn't even think to tell me first.

Pari doesn't want rusk because she has had breakfast already, probably Maggi noodles, which she'll eat five times a day if she can.

"You aren't studying or what?" she asks.

"Listen to her, Jai," Papa says.

Papa walks with Ma and Pari's ma to the end of the lane. He comes back and chats with our neighbors. Then he asks Runu-Didi what she's making for lunch though we only ever have rice and dal. He switches on the TV, sits on the bed and shakes his legs. He keeps changing channels. He hums a tune. He combs his hair, using a steel tin on a shelf for a mirror. He sings. Usually by the time he gets home he's so tired, he just lies on the bed and watches TV. If he decides to sing, it's never more than one song. Now he can't stop singing.

"Papa, we're studying," I say.

"Of course," he says. He turns down the volume of the TV as if that's the problem.

Pari and I sit on the doorstep. I interrupt her studying to tell her we can't be detectives anymore. "What all can we track? We don't even know the Muslim children's names."

"Kabir and Khadifa," Pari says. "They're nine and eleven. They don't go to our school, but to some free school near our basti. Their mother is about to have another baby."

"You're making this up," I say.

"I heard it in the ladies' queue."

A frown pulls down the corners of her mouth and draws lines between her eyebrows. "What's he doing here?" she asks.

It's Quarter with his gang-members and a few men from the Hindu Samaj. They talk to the people in our alley. When they reach my house, Pari and I stand up.

Quarter smells a bit like daru, but he looks fresher and cleaner. I squint at him to understand why and I realize it's because he has shaved off his almost-mustache and not-quite-beard.

Papa and Runu-Didi come to the door.

"This is the pradhan's son," Pari tells Papa. We still don't know Quarter's real name.

"Has someone else disappeared?" Papa asks hurriedly.

"We're trying to find out who's causing all this trouble in the basti," Quarter says, looking at Runu-Didi. "Is there anything you can tell us? Have you seen any Muslim acting suspiciously?"

Papa pulls Didi back and stands in front of her.

"You shouldn't be trying to sow divisions in this community," Papa says, which sounds like something a good newsperson would say on TV.

Quarter unrolls and then rolls up the sleeves of

his black shirt. His hair is slicked back with oil or something more expensive like Brylcreem, which the TV ads say is a cream for **men and not boys**.

I wonder if Quarter killed Buffalo-Baba with a sword he hides in his hi-fi home. I look at his black canvas shoes to see if there are splashes of blood, but there's only mud. Then I remember he hires others to do his dirty work for him.

Quarter tilts his head at an angle from where he can still see Runu-Didi, maybe.

"Don't you have something on the stove to watch?" Papa asks Didi. She goes to the kitchen corner. Then Papa talks to Quarter, forcefully, his hands clasped behind his back. "Things are getting worse every day. Your father should be doing more for us. He should be asking the police to find the kidnappers. He should be telling Hindus and Muslims to stop fighting."

I watch Quarter's face closely though I have given up detectiving; I can't help it. With the TV-repair chacha in jail, Quarter is back to being a prime suspect. He scratches his chin with the tip of his thumb. Papa's words scatter onto the ground, for hens to peck and goats to chew, because Quarter's ears are shut and they can't get in.

SHANTI-CHACHI IS OUR
BOSS-LADY FOR SUNDAY BUT—

—she's a terrible boss-lady. She keeps darting back
to her home because she's cooking for once, and
she's worried she'll burn the food. She can't ask us
to study at her house; it's filled with ointment-tubes
from factories. Her husband works as a sweeper for
the municipality, which is an excellent government
job, but he also has a second job screwing caps onto
tubes from home. One day I ran in and my feet
squashed a tube or maybe ten tubes, so children
are banned from her house.

"Study, study," Shanti-Chachi says, appearing
at our door before hurrying back to her house to
confirm her lunch is still tasty.

Runu-Didi puts on her shoes.

"Where are you going?" I ask.

"Coach restarted training on Friday. Tara told him about Buffalo-Baba's murder, so Coach agreed to give me a couple of days off. But I miss today too, that's it, I'll be out of the team."

"If both of us aren't here the whole day, Shanti-Chachi will know."

"You're still doing that tea-stall thing?"

"You're still doing that training thing?"

"Wait here," Didi says. She picks up her sweater and runs off, leaving the door half-shut, and me inside. She must have gone to the toilet complex. I wait one-two-three-four-hundred minutes but there's no sign of her. I can see from Ma's tardy alarm clock tick-tocking on the shelf that I'm extra-late for work. I can't believe Runu-Didi tricked me like this.

Shanti-Chachi's anklets are returning to our house. I leap out of the bed and stand in front of our half-shut door so she can't see inside.

"Runu-Didi has women-troubles," I say. "Her stomach hurts." Ma told me that once when she asked me not to disturb Didi.

"Oh-o," chachi says. "Let me see."

"She's sleeping now. She took a Crocin."

"If she needs anything—"

"She'll ask you."

"You must be bored, just sitting here like this."

"I'm studying."

Shanti-Chachi's face clouds with doubt but she leaves. When I hear her ladle stirring a pot, I pull our door almost-shut and sprint toward Bhoot Bazaar.

"Lo, he has arrived, ladies and gentlemen, the maharaja of Bhoot Bazaar has finally decided to grace us with his presence," Duttaram says the second he lays his eyes on me.

"They cut a buffalo in half in my alley," I say. "There's a big crowd there. I couldn't get out for hours."

"Sad business that," Duttaram says, but he doesn't look sad. He gestures with the kettle spout that I should serve his waiting customers. I don't spill a drop. I'm an expert tea boy now.

———

It's not even afternoon and I see two of my neighbor-chachis at Duttaram's tea stall. "Chokra, you're in big trouble," says the chachi who lives next door to Shanti-Chachi. "We have been looking for you and your sister everywhere."

Duttaram twists my ears when the chachis tell him they were worried I had got snatched.

"Where's your sister?" a neighbor-chachi asks.

"What do I know?" I say.

This is the worst kind of bad luck. If I had been caught after five in the evening, I would have made the last twenty rupees I needed.

"Let's go," the chachi says. "Poor Shanti must have had a thousand heart attacks by now."

Duttaram takes twenty rupees out of his shirt pocket and places it on my palm which is wet and dirty. "Give it to your parents," he says.

I push the note down into my pocket. I got caught but my bad luck is less bad than I thought.

Shanti-Chachi shouts when she sees me, then hugs me so tight, I worry my bones will snap. "Why did you lie to me, Jai? Where's your sister?" she asks.

"Runu-Didi went to school to talk to her coach. She'll be back before Ma gets home."

"Your ma is coming home right now. I called her, I had to. Wait, let me call her again and tell her not to worry." Chachi almost drops her mobile, then steadies her hands. Though the rotis her husband makes are glossy with ghee and though he always adds a scoop of butter to his dal, chachi is thin like Ma, and now she looks even thinner. She tells Ma I'm safe and that Runu-Didi is with me. Clumps of pink nail polish are stuck to the bottoms of chachi's nails, which are turmeric-yellow at the top like her fingertips. I can see the white strands in her hair where the dye is fading quickly.

"Your ma says she's going back to work because her hi-fi madam is having a party later today," Shanti-Chachi says. "I told her Runu is with you because I didn't want to worry her anymore. She's safe, isn't she, your didi? You weren't lying again, were you?"

"She's at school."

"We have to go and get her."

"She's with her coach, chachi. They're training."

"I don't care if she's with the prime minister himself. I'm bringing her back."

"Can I change? Someone spilled tea on me at the stall."

"Be quick."

I run inside, open the Parachute tub, and fold into it the twenty rupees Duttaram gave me. Ma can kill me today and I won't die a criminal.

———

Shanti-Chachi asks me loads of questions on the way to school. Why did I tell her Runu-Didi had women-troubles? Did I even know what women-troubles were? What was I doing in Bhoot Bazaar? Wasn't I afraid of kidnappers? When did a little boy like me become such a shameless liar?

In a small voice, I tell her I work on Sundays, but Ma and Papa don't know that. I tell her about Runu-Didi and her inter-district contest.

"Didi's going to get a big pot of money if she wins and she'll give everything to Ma and Papa. That's why I'm working too. We're just trying to help."

"That's all well and good," chachi says impatiently, "but if you two get snatched, then what happens, haan? You have the best mother and father in our whole basti. You just don't know how good you have it."

"I know it too."

"What if Runu is not there?" chachi asks when we are close to the school. "Your mother will kill me. I'll have to kill myself."

The school gate is half-open today. Didi's No. 1 fan, the spotty boy, is peeping through the gate.

"Move," chachi barks at the boy, and he leaps aside, looking ashamed, like we caught him stealing.

Runu-Didi is standing on a fading track drawn with chalk powder on the ground, her left hand outstretched to grab the baton from her teammate. She has told me that the baton-exchange shouldn't take more than two seconds. Fumbling or letting the baton fall can get you kicked out of the team.

Didi starts to jog as her teammate comes closer, she grabs the baton even before the teammate has finished shouting "stick" and then she races, her ponytail flying behind her, her arms swinging, her legs kicking up into the air as if they weigh nothing. She's the last runner in her relay team because she's the fastest.

"Runu, come here right now," Shanti-Chachi yells.

Didi keeps running, like she'll never stop. Chachi

calls her name again, **what do you think you're doing, Runu?** she shouts. Didi reaches the finish line, hands the baton to her coach, says something that makes him look angrier than ever. Then she jogs toward us.

———

When Ma gets home late in the evening, she doesn't say a word to me or Runu-Didi. I watch her face closely, but she isn't noisy like she usually is when she gets mad. She tastes the dal Didi made and adds some salt and garam masala to it. She rubs her lower back, just above her underskirt, where she's always saying it hurts. I try to give her an old tub of Tiger Balm and she pretends she can't see me though I move my hand to wherever her eyes go. I put the balm back on the shelf. Runu-Didi stares at Papa's belt hanging from a nail that's been hammered into the wall so hard, there's a starburst of cracks around it. Papa has never used the belt on us.

Finally, Papa gets home. Ma and Shanti-Chachi and Shanti-Chachi's husband push us out of the door and give Papa a high-level briefing inside. Runu-Didi and I sit on the doorstep, shivering.

Tomorrow is exam day. Exams seem unreal, like they belong to another world. In our world we are doing daily battle with djinns and kidnappers and buffalo-killers and we don't know when we will vanish.

The grown-ups are whispering, but I can hear Papa's shock that comes out in gasps.

Shanti-Chachi opens the door and calls us inside. Then she and her husband leave.

"Jai, you thought we wouldn't have enough money to pay for food unless you worked?" Papa asks.

"I won't do it again," I say.

"Are we starving you here?"

"I just . . . I thought I could give Faiz some money because his brother is in jail and the lawyer charges a lot." It's a good lie and it makes sense to me but not to Papa.

"And this Faiz, he takes your money?"

"I haven't . . . Duttaram hasn't paid me anything. Maybe if I had worked until the end of the month."

"And you, Runu," Ma is speaking now, "I asked you to watch your brother. Instead you ran off to school? Running around all the time in the smog because you like your coach, haan? Think I don't know what's going on in that mind of yours?"

"The coach?" Runu-Didi asks.

She looks at me, eyebrows raised, as if asking me to explain Ma's thinking to her. I tuck my chin into my chest. I can't explain anything.

"Your coach is your hero, isn't he?" Ma asks.

"You'll risk being snatched if it means you'll get to see him."

Didi's coach doesn't look like a hero at all.

"No one will snatch me when I'm going to buy vegetables for dinner," Didi says, flapping her arms around, hitting my face by mistake, and still not stopping. "Nothing will happen to me when I stand in the queue for water by the tap or for rice at the ration shop. But the second I do something that I want to do, that's when I'll get kidnapped. Is that what you're saying?"

"Watch your mouth," Ma tells Didi.

"You have a little brother to care for," Papa says.

"If you two couldn't look after Jai, why did you have him?" Didi asks.

Papa moves in a flash and slaps Runu-Didi on her left cheek. Her small hoop earring falls down. Papa is shaking. His eyes are round, and he looks at his hand as if he can't believe what it has just done. Ma starts to cry. Papa has never hit Didi before; he has never hit me either. Ma clouts us all the time, but never Papa.

Ma bends down and picks up the earring. She tries to put it back but Didi pushes her away and climbs onto the bed and sits in the corner where I do my headstands. Papa seizes a blanket and marches out.

"Won't you have dinner?" Ma asks after him.

Papa raises his right hand to say no without looking back.

I sit on the bed, away from Runu-Didi, squishing the battered mattress with my knuckles. I guess Didi won't be able to go to the inter-district championships. I bet she's feeling a lot sadder about that than Papa hitting her.

KABIR AND KHADIFA

It felt like she had been waiting in the alley for hours. Behind her, the curtains that marked the entrance to the video-gaming parlor twitched, letting out ribbons of light that unfurled toward her feet. Night had swooped down without her noticing and erased the rooftops of Bhoot Bazaar.

Khadifa imagined stomping into the parlor and hauling her brother out, but her sense of propriety stopped her. Basti-girls didn't go inside such places, not even those girls brave enough to wear short skirts and talk back to their parents. She was doing the responsible thing by trying to stop the boys staggering into the parlor, but they were too distracted to listen to her.

"Please, my brother is there, inside," she said to yet another boy whose bristly mustache and grownup smell of cigarette smoke she registered now, in alarm. "His name is Kabir, he's small, just nine. Ask him to come out, please. Tell him his sister is waiting."

The boy's expression didn't change. She moved to the side to let him pass, and touched her hijab, feeling self-conscious. Shame burnt her cheeks even in this chill.

She jammed her knuckles into the crooks of her elbows, a familiar anger surging through her. Ammi had sent Kabir out to buy a packet of milk in the evening, and then Khadifa to bring him back when he didn't return a couple of hours later. No matter that Khadifa had friends to talk to, and sewing work to complete. Each time Kabir misbehaved, it fell on Khadifa to set things right. How was that fair?

Ammi didn't care about fairness. All she seemed to think about these days was the new baby growing in her belly. The sweetness with which Ammi spoke to it late at night and early in the morning, cooing in a voice heavy with sleep that she couldn't wait to meet **him**—and why wouldn't this baby too be another boy like her parents wanted?—set

Khadifa's teeth on edge. The new baby brother would probably be a rogue too, just like Kabir. All of Khadifa's time would go in chasing after these brats; she wouldn't have a minute to try on a new nail polish or a hairband at a friend's house.

Ammi and Abbu didn't know it yet, but Kabir had been missing classes at their school that wasn't really a school but a center run by an NGO where students aged two and sixteen were packed into the same classroom. He skipped the Friday afternoon sermons and prayers at the mosque, and nicked rupees from Abbu's wallet, careful to steal only a note or two each time so as not to attract Abbu's attention. The money Kabir made by running errands for the shopkeepers of Bhoot Bazaar wasn't enough to buy him the number of hours he needed at the gaming parlor. He would have pinched coins from Khadifa too—she saved more than half of the money she earned by sewing—but she knew to watch out for him; tripped him before he got anywhere near her savings.

Their parents were lenient with Kabir, maybe because he was a boy, but once they found out about his stealing, and his absences at the mosque and the school, they would pack him off to the village where their grandparents lived, and no doubt assign Khadifa the position of his minder. They thought her reliable enough to care for him

on her own. Khadifa supposed she could view that
as a compliment, but Ya Allah, this wasn't the kind
of praise she needed to hear.

Ammi missed her childhood home, three hours
away from the basti by bus. She spoke often of the
sweetness of the fruit and the freshness of the air she
had given up for this city where she couldn't even
breathe. But for Khadifa, that village was a different
world, another country altogether. Evenings there
were spent in the quiet-black punctuated only by the
sound of buffaloes flicking their tails and mosquitoes humming, because the mullah had banned TV
and radio and perhaps even talking. Her grandparents nodded their heads when the mullah said girls
should be married off before they turned too old,
and his too-old was thirteen or fourteen.

Kabir would lose nothing if they moved to the
village, and Khadifa would lose everything.

It made her mad, how he took things for granted.
She had friends whose older brothers played in these
parlors, and from whom she had first learned about
Kabir's secret thrills; she could plead with these
boys, through her friends, to give Kabir a fright.
Rough him up even. He deserved it, Allah was her
witness.

She kicked up some dust, drawing the wrathful
eyes of passersby, then pressed herself against the
parlor wall, hoping the smog swirling around
her would hide her. The curtain that covered the

entrance to the parlor lifted. Kabir stumbled out, blinking, his eyes slow to adjust to the sickly light of the alley. Then he saw her and smiled sheepishly.

"Where's the milk?" she snapped. "Where's the money?"

His fingers checked his pockets as if there was still a chance that his addled brain hadn't spent it on games. She marched him to a stall that sold milk and curd. All the way there she chided him for his selfishness.

"The Hindus are after our lives, they're calling us terrorist-pigs and child-snatchers and child-killers," she said, "but you, you can't think of anything other than those stupid games, can you?"

Kabir's heart ached when his sister said that, mostly because it was true. At first, his gaming had been for **timepass**, but now he craved the highs of a gunfight the same way the glue addicts he saw in choky alleys seemed to pine for Eraz-ex. He had forgotten to offer namaz that day and on several other days, the muezzin's call unable to jolt his conscience inside the parlor, where the only thing louder than gunfire was the stream of ridiculous abuse that poured out of the mouths of gamers. **A thousand dicks in your ass, brother,** or **you're in this world only because of a torn condom.**

He knew he was too young to be in that room with its scratchy screens and unpliable joysticks, lit only by a tube light and aired by a ceiling fan whose blades were encased in black dust. But outside the gaming parlor he was a nobody; inside, he was good at fighting and part of something bigger than the basti and the bazaar.

"I won't do it again," he said now, unsure if he meant it.

"You won't," Khadifa said. "I'll see to it, I promise you that."

He braced for more of her anger, but she was quiet. She looked tired. He watched her purchase a packet of milk with money she must have earned herself and felt ashamed. He didn't know how to tell her he was sorry.

A crowd had gathered in the alley outside. At its heart were two beggars, one in a wheelchair that had a loudspeaker attached to it, and the other his friend who ferried him around. They were telling a group of children returning from a cricket or a football game a story, bickering with each other about how it should be told. His sister, enthralled, stopped to watch them, shoving the little boy next to her so that she could get a better view.

It was already dark, and they were late, but Kabir didn't say that to her. The beggars talked about Junction-ki-Rani, a woman ghost that saved girls in trouble.

Even while watching TV, Kabir had found his mind drifting toward **Call of Duty 2**, but

Junction-ki-Rani was such a brutal story, it made him forget for a few minutes the recoil of the MP40 with which he mowed down his attackers, and the blood-red spatters that subsequently leaked into his vision.

This story is a talisman, the beggar in the wheelchair said. **I hold it close to your hearts.**

His sister nudged him and said it was time to leave. The streets were beginning to empty.

They hurried home. Kabir's thoughts quickly drifted back to the gaming parlor, where today he had fought Nazis in Russia. Images from the game flashed in front of him: a long and cold winter, snow smoothening into ice, him hiding behind a pillar, throwing a grenade, the smog a smokescreen saving him from enemy bullets. He tripped over something and ended up in a heap on the ground, his two worlds merging together in the pain that washed over him from his feet to his skull.

His plastic sunglasses that had a black frame and yellow arms, carefully tucked into the collar of his sweater, crunched under him. Still lying down, he lifted his chest high enough to check if they were broken. Only a few scratches. He would wear them again tomorrow, sun or no sun, because it made him feel hip as he walked into the parlor. But he wasn't going to the parlor again, was he?

Khadifa waited for him to get up, watching the

smog blot out lamps and houses, feeling an unexpected burst of tenderness. Kabir was only a child
still, living in a grown-up's world. It was exhausting, even for her.

"Okay?" she asked.

He gave her a thumbs-up.

"Do you think Ammi will make us move?" Kabir
asked once upright. "To another basti? Because here
the Hindus"—he paused—"are after our lives?"

"The police have taken the Muslims they wanted,"
Khadifa said. "The Hindus must be happy. They'll
leave us alone." She hoped this was true. She had
never met the Muslim men the police had arrested,
and she was glad for it.

She didn't want to move from the basti. All her
friends were here, girls who called her when their
parents were out working so that they could hold
pretend hi-fi parties, who lent her their clothes and
jewelry, and who gossiped about the scandalous
love affairs that grown-ups considered their secrets.
These girls were the ones who had taught her to
sew sequins onto shirts sent in bulk from factories,
and to save a few sequins for herself so that her
headscarves could sparkle.

The idea of leaving it all behind, being forced to
get married, these thoughts brought her to the edge
of a tantrum again; she wanted to scream, break
the red glass bangles on her wrists by slamming her
hands against walls. But something in her stopped

her from acting out. Maybe Ammi and Abbu were right; she was a responsible child.

Kabir waited for his sister to say something but she didn't. He wished he wasn't such a disappointment to her. He decided he would henceforth spend his time only at some place good and wholesome, like the gym in Bhoot Bazaar whose posters promised to turn **lambs into lions**. Kabir saw his chest growing broad and muscly like a Hindi film hero's. He imagined his heavy footsteps echoing through these alleys, the shopkeepers he worked for quaking as he walked by. The thumping footsteps seemed to be real, and he turned around to see what looked like a hulking form wrapped in a black blanket, but how could he be sure this form was real? Half of his mind was still in 1942.

Khadifa looked at her brother and, from the glazed expression on his face, could tell he was dreaming again.

"There are no secrets in this basti," Khadifa said. "Abbu is going to find out soon how much money you steal from him to waste on video games. He'll kick you out. You'll have to live on the streets, and sniff glue to fall asleep on cold nights like these."

Then she saw something move. A gleam of a golden coin in the dark. She glanced at Kabir and knew he had seen it too. They should have been home by now. They had heard the stories of the children who had been snatched.

From the corner of her eye, she saw the flash of a silvery needle, the flutter of a square of cloth that reeked of something sweet, the smell so strong it cut through the smoky air to reach her nose. She heard the clinking of bangles that weren't on her wrists. The packet of milk in her hand felt damp and slushy.

"If you're scared, you can call Junction-ki-Rani," Kabir said, seeing his sister shiver. "She protects girls."

"Hindu ghosts won't have anything to do with us," Khadifa said, grabbing his hand and running. "And what about you? Who will protect you?"

THREE

THIS STORY WILL SAVE YOUR LIFE

We believe djinns moved into this palace around the time our last kings died, their hearts broken by the crooked victories of white men who claimed to be our rulers. No one knows where the djinns came from, if Allah-Ta'ala sent them, or if they were summoned here by the feverish utterances of the devout. They have been here for so long, they must have watched the walls of this palace crumble, the pillars soften with moss and creepers, and pythons slither over cracked stones like dreams wavering in the light of dawn. Every year they must feel the wind trembling the champa trees in the garden, shearing flowers as fragrant as vials of attar.

We can't see djinns unless they take the form of a black dog or a cat or a snake. But we feel their presence the moment we step into these palace grounds, in the rustle that tickles the backs of our necks like the branch of a shrub, in the breeze billowing our shirts, and in the lightness we feel in our hearts as we pray. We can see you are frightened, but **listen, listen,** we have been caretakers of this djinn-palace for years, and we can assure you, they have never harmed anyone. Yes, there are bad djinns and trickster djinns and infidel djinns who want to possess your soul, but the ones who live here, the djinns who read the letters that believers have written to them, they are the good djinns Allah-Ta'ala shaped out of smokeless fire to serve us. They are saints.

Look now at the crowd thronging these grounds, flinging cubes of meat up into the sky for kites to catch, leaving foil bowls of milk for dogs on the odd chance that one of the kites or the dogs is a djinn in another form. These believers are from all faiths. It's not just us Muslims, Faiz—you said that's your name, right?—Faiz, see, here there are Hindus and Sikhs and Christians and maybe even Buddhists. They come here clutching the letters they have written to the djinns, and they will paste their petitions on the powdery walls. At night, when the gates are locked, and the ash-tips of joss sticks collapse to the ground, the djinns will read the letters scented with incense and flowers. They read fast, not like us. If they find your wish genuine, they will grant your request.

As caretakers of the djinns' home, we have seen that happen many times. But don't take our word for it. Over there by the champa tree, you will notice a grey-haired man barking orders at four boys carrying cauldrons of biryani. For years his daughter had a constant cough that no medicine could cure. He took her to government hospitals, to private hospitals that looked like five-star hotels, to a god-woman who lived in a hut by the Arabian Sea, and to a baba's ashram high in the Himalayas. She was X-rayed and CT-scanned and MRI-ed. She wore rings with blue gems and green gems and purple gems for good health. Nothing helped. Then someone told them about this place and the father came here with a letter for the djinn-saints. He would have done anything for his daughter by then, pulled out all his teeth and tied them up in a satin cloth like pearls if that was what the djinns wanted.

His letter to the djinns was brief. Some people write pages listing their grievances, and they attach copies of birth certificates and marriage certificates and sales deeds of houses that are being divided, unequally and disagreeably, between brothers and sisters and uncles and aunts. The father, however, just wrote: **Please take pity on us and cure my daughter of her cough**. He showed the letter to us, that's how we know. He pinned a photo of his daughter from **before** to his letter, **before** the cough made a rattling skeleton out of her.

And now, see for yourself. The daughter is the girl in the green salwar-kameez standing by the champa. Her hair is covered fully with a scarf so as not to tempt the djinns—even the good djinns have a weakness for beautiful girls, we will be honest with you—but doesn't she look well? There's color in her cheeks, strength in her bones, not a bend in her spine, and her cough is gone. She's getting married next month. The father is thanking the djinns by feeding biryani to visitors.

You have done the right thing by coming here. Now you must go inside, join your ammi and your brother. It's darker there, certainly. The curls of smoke from joss sticks and candles have stained the walls black. We won't lie, you will encounter fearful sights: a woman shivering, madness spouting from her lips, brought here by her husband who hopes our good djinns will expel the bad djinn that resides in her; a young man bashing his forehead against the wall until blood furrows his skin; and bats that hang upside down from collapsed roofs, their screeches a chorus to the frantic prayers of the distraught.

But **listen, listen,** our djinn-saints are powerful. Your ammi's letter will tell the djinns what your family wants: good marks for you in your next exam, a suitable bride for your brother, the safe return of a missing cousin or a friend. Perhaps— and we are not saying this is the case with you—you hope to secure justice for your father or someone in your family who has been unfairly targeted by the police or the court. Don't look so surprised. It happens to us Muslims more often than you can imagine. But whatever bad air hovers around you, trust us, the djinns will make it vanish.

We will tell you a secret: by the smoothest roads in this country, lined by amaltas and jamun trees, live politicians who became Union ministers only because they called us Muslims foreigners. They holler during rallies that Hindustan is only for Hindus, and that people like you and me should go to Pakistan. But even they come here to pray. They send their henchmen at dawn, when these ruins are almost empty, to clear the grounds of people so that no one can take a photo of them bowing before our djinns. They also stop the Archeological Survey from locking us out because they trust our djinns as much as we do. These politicians have rotten tongues and wicked hearts, but the djinns don't turn them away. Everyone is equal here.

Talk to any of the visitors. You will learn that they are here because they have lost something. Sometimes they have lost hope itself and it's here, in these ruins that frighten you so much, that they will find a reason to live.

Dear boy, listen to us for your own good. Take off your slippers, wash your feet, and step inside. The djinns are waiting.

SCHOOL IN THE NEW YEAR
IS THE—

—same as school in the old year but also worse because of exams. After the last bell rings, Pari and I stand in the corridor, Pari biting her nails and then adding up numbers with her fingers because she thinks she has got one answer wrong in the Maths test. I must have got one-two-three-ten-all answers wrong, but I don't care. I tell Pari about Papa slapping Runu-Didi and she clenches and unclenches her hand and says, "Five times, five times you have told me about this today."

"I didn't too," I say. Pari didn't even let me talk this morning because she wanted to revise in her head. I wish Faiz was here because Faiz is good at listening. But Faiz is at a traffic junction, selling roses or phone covers or toys we don't get to have ourselves, but we are too old for toys anyway. He's missing exams, and afterward he'll miss many days of school, maybe even a whole year if Tariq-Bhai isn't released soon.

Runu-Didi comes out into the corridor.

"We're ready," I say when she stops near us. Didi, Pari and I are supposed to go home together.

"Don't wait for me," Didi says. "I have to talk to Coach."

"Will he be angry you have to miss inter-district?" Pari asks.

Didi's hard eyes tell me off for being a blabbermouth. Then she says, "He'll have to make a change at the last minute. What do you think?"

Didi's ears look bare without her earrings. I put my hand out to pat her forearm.

"Chi," Didi says. "Why is your hand so sticky?"

"Better not to ask," Pari says.

"Pari scratches her backside. Not me."

"Stay away," Didi says.

"Go pick the ticks off your coach-boyfriend's balls. That's what you do best anyway," I find myself saying.

Pari gasps and covers her mouth with both her hands. I march toward the school gate, and Pari comes running after me. At the gate, I turn my head to look at Runu-Didi. She's still standing in the corridor outside our classrooms, leaning against a pillar. Her fan, the spotty boy, stands on the other side of the pillar, smiling a wide smile into what must be the camera of his mobile. He runs his tongue, slowly, over his teeth. Didi is looking at the part of the playground where the coach is about to start his training session for girls, so she may not have noticed her fan.

No one talked about Kabir and Khadifa today; maybe because they aren't from our school. Even the headmaster didn't name them at assembly, but he did warn us to be on our guard at all times.

———

"Runu-Didi told me to come home by myself," I say when Ma gets back. "She's still at school. Her coach must be making her train extra."

Didi and I are fighting, so we don't have to keep each other's secrets. That's the rule. Didi will understand.

Ma sighs and sits on the bed. I look at the alarm clock. It's six, which means it's six-fifteen or six-thirty. Didi's training should be over by now. I guess she's staying out just to spite Ma and Papa. It's a stupid thing to do.

"Runu must be angry," Ma says. She closes her eyes and starts to pray, **Lord, let my daughter be safe.** She says it nine times and opens her eyes.

"Parents shouldn't hit children," I say. "We aren't in ancient times like when you were a child."

Ma goes out to talk to Shanti-Chachi. I put on another sweater over my first sweater. Ma comes back and tells me she and chachi's husband are going to the school to speak to Coach.

"I'll go with you."

"Jai, I can't do this today."

Ma leaves. I say sorry to Runu-Didi in my head. I ask her to come back. I promise her I'll never bother her. Shanti-Chachi sits with me and rubs my back and tells me to breathe slowly.

"Where's your ma, Jai?" I hear Papa ask. "Shanti, what's going on?"

I pray hard. I hear Runu-Didi's voice. She's home! I look around. She isn't here. My ears tricked me.

"What do you mean Madhu is looking for her?" Papa shouts. "Where is Runu?"

When he raises his voice in anger, he seems much bigger. I want to curl up like a millipede or go into my shell like a turtle and never come out.

"What exactly did Runu say to you?"

Papa is talking to me. I tell him everything, but I also don't tell him everything, like how I said **your coach-boyfriend's balls** to her.

"Runu wanted to talk to the coach?" Papa asks, grabbing me by the collar. "How long do you think talking takes? You couldn't wait for her?"

"Don't shout at Jai," Shanti-Chachi says. "He's just a child."

"Didi isn't snatched," I say as Papa's grip loosens. "Coach must have convinced her to stay on the team."

Papa takes out his mobile and calls someone.

"I'll go to the school right now," I say. "I'll bring Runu-Didi back."

"Shanti, can you watch him?" Papa asks, his phone pressed to his left ear.

"Of course," chachi says.

"Haan, Madhu," Papa says into the phone as he runs out of the house.

I squeeze into the headstand corner of Ma's and Papa's bed and try to think like a detective, but I can't think at all because of the noise around me. Neighbors keep wandering in to ask Shanti-Chachi and me if we have heard anything. They knock against Ma's precious-things bundle and scatter our textbooks and clothes. They ask each other if a Muslim has taken Runu to avenge Buffalo-Baba's beheading. At first they speak in lowered voices so I won't hear them, but soon they forget about me in their excitement and their voices shoot up into the sky. Shanti-Chachi tells them not to speculate until we know more. When they don't listen, she threatens to cut out their poisonous tongues.

I pinch my arms so that I'll wake up from this bad dream, but I'm already awake. I ask myself the questions Pari and I asked Bahadur's brother and sister. I decide Runu-Didi is hiding because Papa beat her, though it was just one slap and hardly matters.

Shanti-Chachi checks with Runu-Didi's basti-friends if they know where Didi is. They don't. "She was fine this morning at the water tap," one of them says. "She didn't look upset."

A chachi asks me if Didi could have gone to a mall, or the cinema, but Didi doesn't have the money to watch a movie and we never go to malls and mall security guards won't let us in anyway. Shanti-Chachi calls Ma on her mobile. Ma says Didi isn't at school, and she and Papa are now going to the homes of Didi's relay teammates.

I try to think of where Didi might be. I would have hidden behind a pushcart in Bhoot Bazaar or in the kirana shop where Faiz works. But Runu-Didi can't hide in those places because she's a girl, and also, she doesn't know any shopkeepers and they will just tell her to go home.

———

All night people search for Runu-Didi. She can't be found. I believe it and I don't believe it. Ma and Papa return home, Ma's hair sticking to her cheeks, Papa's eyes redder and bulging. I ask them if I can go out to look for Didi. My secret plan is to find Samosa and let him track Didi. Ma says I'm not to move.

I have been in this night before. This is the night Bahadur went missing, and also the night Omvir and Aanchal and Chandni and Kabir and Khadifa disappeared.

Pari and her ma turn up. Pari sits with me on the bed and Pari's ma cries even more than my ma. Faiz visits with his ammi. "What are these mullah-types doing here?" a chachi asks, jutting her chin at Faiz's ammi.

I'm floating above everyone, watching them cry, watching them trade gossip. Some people are here only to feast on our tears and words. They'll carry our stories in their lips that stick out like beaks and feed them to their husbands or friends who aren't here. "Beat Runu like she was two, he did," I hear a woman say. "Shanti told me. You can't raise your hand to your daughter after a certain age."

"Don't listen to them," Pari says.

"Don't you have to study?" I ask.

"These exams don't matter. They can't fail us until we're in Standard Nine."

"I'm not sitting for the exams either," Faiz says. "No big deal."

Pari's ma cries some more.

Papa goes with a few men to search around the rubbish ground, the bazaar, and hospitals.

This isn't happening. This is happening. God is

twisting a screwdriver under my skin, not stopping for a break.

People talk about Runu-Didi. **She was such a good girl**, they say. **Did all the chores around the house, no complaints. Talked to everyone politely, even when there was a scuffle at the water tap. That running business, she would have outgrown it in a year or two, and then she would have made a perfect wife, a perfect mother.**

I don't know the person they are talking about.

"My daughter isn't dead that you should speak of her like this," Ma says, sweat beading her forehead. Everyone hushes.

Forty-eight hours. When children disappear, if you can't find them in the first forty-eight hours, then they are more likely to be dead. I'm not sure if it's twenty-four hours or forty-eight hours. Either way Runu-Didi isn't dead now.

"Do you remember this boy with loads of pimples?" I ask Pari. "Runu-Didi's classmate who follows Didi around like he's her dog or something?"

"I know that guy," Faiz says. "Ekdum-waste."

"He was standing next to her when we last saw her," I say. "Pari, you remember?"

"I'll tell someone," Pari says. "We will find him."

When I look at her, I can't tell if Pari is upset or sad because she's talking in the same manner as she always does. Her voice is not-high-not-low. It makes me feel I shouldn't worry too much. I keep looking at her so that the screwdriver will come out of my chest, but she and her sobbing ma have to leave my side so that Pari can tell the right people to look for the spotty boy, and everything hurts even more than before.

"Jai, see, a man gave me this today," Faiz says. It's a crumpled green note that Faiz straightens between his hands. "American dollar," he says.

"Is this the time for that?" his ammi asks.

Faiz puts the money back in his pocket. His nose is leaking.

If Didi had an amulet like Faiz does, would she have been home by now?

Someone leads Ma and me out of the house because the visitors are taking our air and neither of us can breathe. We sit down on the charpai outside Shanti-Chachi's house. Tears run down Ma's face and she doesn't wipe them away.

I want to tell Ma that it's my fault Runu-Didi is gone. I said a terrible thing to Didi, but worse, just the other night, I wished for a bad djinn to take her. I invited the djinn into our home.

Ma's eyes loop me like a red-ink pen around a wrong answer. I bet she wishes I had disappeared instead of Runu-Didi. I don't win any medals. I don't get good marks in exams. I don't help her with the chores around the house. I have never once carried water home from the tap. I deserve to be snatched. The smog twists around my ears, whispering the same thing. **Should have been you-you-you**.

Ma locks her palms in her lap. I see burn marks on her skin, and knife-nicks. She works too much, too fast, here at home and the hi-fi madam's flat. Only Runu-Didi helped her, never me.

I hear Pari's voice. She is cutting a path with her swinging hands through the crowd around us. "Move, move," she yells at our neighbors until she reaches the charpai.

"Your papa has gone to the Shaitani Adda," she says. "He's talking to Runu-Didi's classmates. Even that spotty boy he will talk to, okay?"

Faiz joins us.

"Jai, you have to be strong for your ma," Pari says.

"Let him cry a bit if he wants," Faiz says.

I don't want to cry but I can't turn off my tears either. There's a blob of something salty in my mouth and I swallow it because I can't spit it out. I see Ma watching me with an odd expression, tears wetting her chin and neck. **Why are you crying?** her face asks me. **You never cared for your didi. You were always fighting with her.**

———

Around midnight, the crowd thins. Pari has to go because she has to write the exam tomorrow-**today**, and Faiz has to leave because he has to work. Pari grips my hands tight, and even her usual ice-hands are warm from having been around so many people for so long.

"It's my fault," I whisper to her. "I wanted the djinn to take Runu-Didi and not me."

"Don't talk nonsense," she says, but she says it softly. "You're not the snatcher. It's a bad person from our basti."

"Djinns don't listen to you or anybody else," Faiz says. "They do what they feel like."

Soon it's just me and Bahadur's ma and my ma. Bahadur's ma leads us inside, and she sits in a corner, coughing and catching Ma's eyes once in a while and weeping. She tells my ma about the morning she caught Bahadur sneaking the kitchen knife into his school bag. When she asked him what he meant to do with it, he told her: **I'm taking it so that Papa can't stab you.**

"That's how much he worried about me," Bahadur's ma says. "And what did I do for him?"

Soon she leaves too. The smog creeps in through the half-open door, dimming our already-dim bulb.

———

Papa comes home alone, shaking his head. "She isn't there," he tells Ma and Ma bursts into louder tears and Papa cries too and they seem like small babies.

"Did you go to the Shaitani Adda?" I ask Papa. "Did you talk to that boy who's always around Runu-Didi? Did you see her school bag anywhere?" I'm asking these questions like a detective, and they sound stupid in my ears and it feels like I'm talking about a stranger, not my sister.

"That boy said something odd," Papa says, but he's telling Ma and not me. "He said, after Runu talked to the coach, she went and stood near the place Jai calls the Shaitani Adda. As if she wanted to be snatched. That area is empty even in the daytime. The boy said"—Papa's sobs shake his shoulders and rattle his chest—"Runu pushed him away. Shoved him so hard he fell down. He went home after that."

"Did he really go home?" I ask.

"The people who live near his house saw him. He helps their children with their homework, and he helped them tonight too."

"Why would Runu do something like that?" Ma asks.

"It's my fault," Papa says, clutching his hair violently as if he wants to pull every strand out. "This is all my fault."

IN THE MORNING
WE GO TO THE—

—police station where Faiz's ammi and Wajid-Bhai are already standing near the senior constable's desk. Wajid-Bhai slouches as he demands justice, the words slipping out of his mouth easily. He must have been saying the same thing to the policemen for ten-twelve days now. Faiz's ammi clutches a file that she sometimes holds out toward the policeman who pretends he can't see it.

I glance at the white cloth bag that Papa is carrying. Inside it, Ma has put her Parachute tub. I wish I had worked for more days, filled the tub with more rupees. Ma hasn't even opened it to check how much money it holds.

The bag also has a photo of Runu-Didi. I didn't have to tell Ma and Papa that you need a photo to investigate a missing-child case. They knew it already. In the photo, Didi is receiving a certificate for winning a race. She and the person awarding her the certificate are half-turned toward the camera, and Didi is smiling like she would rather not smile. A medal hangs around her neck on an orange ribbon.

We don't have proper photos of Runu-Didi taken in a studio, like the ones of Bahadur and Chandni, and no family photos either with all of us standing in front of the folds of a painted curtain pretending to be the Taj.

A woman wearing a green sari with the pallu wrapped over her head, both hands guarding the baby in her belly, stops in front of Ma. "My children are also missing," she says. "Kabir and Khadifa."

"You spoke to the police?" Papa asks.

The man with the pregnant woman, who must be Kabir-Khadifa's abbu, whispers, "We have to keep bothering them until they do something."

They ask us to go with them to the junior constable, who is nodding sympathetically as he listens to a man dressed as if he works in a fancy office. A bus driver has dented the man's car worth thirty-two lakh rupees. The policeman hisses when he hears the price as if hot water has burnt his hands.

"It's not me you need to convince about your

son's innocence," the senior constable says across the room to Faiz's ammi and Wajid-Bhai. "Speak to your lawyer. The magistrate has given us permission to hold him for another fifteen days, and only the magistrate can tell us to free him."

At least they know where Tariq-Bhai is, even if it's a terrible place like jail. I would rather Runu-Didi was in jail than a snatcher's car or a brick kiln or a djinn's belly.

The senior constable calls us over. He asks Wajid-Bhai and Faiz's ammi to leave. Faiz's ammi pats Ma's hand as she passes us.

Ma and Papa, and Kabir-Khadifa's abbu and ammi, start talking at the same time. "Slow down," the senior says. Ma's mobile rings and, in the two seconds it takes her to cut the call, the senior scolds her, "Do you think I'm running a bazaar here that you can walk up and down, taking your time, deciding what to buy?"

"It's my boss-lady," Ma says. "She must be wondering why I haven't turned up."

Papa gives the senior constable Runu-Didi's photo and says she's the best athlete in her school, maybe even the whole state. He says she'll compete in the National and Commonwealth games when she's older. When I tell Runu-Didi that Papa praised her, she'll laugh and say, **who ever knew he had even one good word to say about me.** Then I realize I may never hear her speak again;

those who went missing haven't come back. My eyes sting as if someone has rubbed chili paste into them. My chest hurts.

"I have seen you before," the senior says, waving a file at me. "You ran away from school one day because you were bored."

Ma and Papa glower at me.

I can't see Bahadur's ma's gold chain around the senior's neck. Maybe he sold it and split the money with the junior. "Are you going to put Runu-Didi's photo on the Internet to send to other police stations?" I ask.

"What do we have here, Byomkesh Bakshi in disguise?"

The senior laughs as if he has cracked the best joke. I bite the inside of my cheeks like Faiz does so I won't cry.

Papa takes the Parachute tub out of the bag and puts it on the constable's desk. "We can get more," he says.

"You think I need hair oil?" the senior asks, but he picks up the tub, opens the lid, and sees what's inside. Kabir-Khadifa's abbu-ammi look sadder. Maybe they don't have any money to give the policeman.

The senior returns Didi's photo to Papa.

"Internet?" I say.

"Not working now," he says.

Ma and Papa plead with him. **Come back in two**

days, he says finally, shaking his head and jiggling his legs as if we are the ones being unreasonable.

Outside the police station, I tell Papa, "We don't have a second Parachute tub to pay him again."

"At least he listened to you," Kabir-Khadifa's abbu says. "He told us he'll have our basti demolished because it's causing nothing but trouble for him."

Ma looks at the sky, like she's hoping God will come out of heaven and give us an answer, but the smog keeps its coat zipped up and doesn't let out even a sliver of light.

———

Papa and Ma decide they have to check the hospitals Papa couldn't check last night. I think they mean the Casualty sections but maybe they also mean morgues, and they don't want to say morgues in front of me.

Ma's hi-fi madam calls her on her mobile again. This time, Ma takes the call. She explains why she can't be at work today. The hi-fi madam is not on speaker, but we can still hear her. **When will you come? Tomorrow? Day after? Should I find a new bai to do your job? Your daughter must have run off with a boy. I heard it's happening a lot in your area.**

Ma says nothing, just snaps the threads that are

hanging loose at the end of her pallu. Finally, she says, "Two days, madam. That's all I'm asking for. Please forgive me for giving you so much trouble."

After she hangs up, Papa says he and Kabir-Khadifa's abbu will go to the hospitals. Ma and Kabir-Khadifa's ammi will go home with me.

"I'm not scared of morgues," I say. I have seen morgues on **Police Patrol**; they are ice-cold metal freezers that maybe smell of Lizol.

The grown-ups look startled as if I have said a word that no one should say aloud because it brings bad luck.

"Why don't you help your ma look for Runu around the bazaar?" Papa tells me.

Papa and Kabir-Khadifa's abbu hire an auto-rickshaw to take them to the hospitals. Ma and Kabir-Khadifa's ammi and me, we go toward Bhoot Bazaar. Vehicles zoom past us but they don't sound loud anymore. A glass wall has come up between me and the world.

———

Ma and I walk the length of every lane in Bhoot Bazaar, asking about Runu-Didi. We describe her again and again.

"She's twelve," Ma says.

"Thirteen in three months," I say. My birthday is a month after Didi's.

"Hair tied in a ponytail, with a white band," Ma says.

"Grey and brown salwar-kameez," I say. "The government school uniform."

"This height," Ma says, pointing at her shoulders.

"She was wearing black-and-white shoes," I say. "She was carrying a school bag, brown color."

We have no luck, but this is better than sitting at home. Ma keeps calling Papa, and she lets out a big sigh of relief each time he tells her **nothing, nothing**. I pray to God, to Mental, to the ghosts who hover above Bhoot Bazaar and whose names I don't know. I don't want Runu-Didi to be in a morgue. **Please please please.**

We go into the theka lane. The anda-wallah is taking a delivery of eggs stacked in plastic trays and tied to the pillion of a bike, from a man who hasn't removed his helmet. Quarter and his gang-members are making fun of a drunkard half-asleep on the ground. Their feet prod the drunk's ribs. Quarter never sits for his exams, so today is the same as any other day for him.

Ma asks Quarter too about Runu-Didi. I don't think Ma knows who he is, but Quarter knows who Ma is talking about. His mouth widens, he snaps his fingers at his lackeys, he takes out a mobile from the back pocket of his black jeans-pant and scrolls up and down. If he snatched Runu-Didi, he's hiding it well; he looks extremely surprised.

"She's the one who's always running, yes?" he says, his eyes on his mobile.

Ma nods, maybe shocked that Runu-Didi is famous.

Quarter asks us to wait and walks around making calls on his mobile. He orders his gang to **search for Runu, everywhere**. He introduces himself to Ma as the pradhan's son.

"My father is concerned about the goings-on in your basti," he says. "He's doing all he can to help."

"Can't your father talk to the police?" Ma asks.

"He will," Quarter says. "You go home now. We'll bring you news."

———

I tell Ma about Samosa and how he can track scents. Ma hardly listens, just says **don't go near stray dogs, they have rabies**. We pass Duttaram's tea stall, and I explain to him that Runu-Didi is missing.

"What's happening in this world?" he says. "Who's doing this to our children?"

His children are at school, and safe, and not even in our basti.

He asks Ma if she would like some tea, **no need to pay me**, but she says no.

Samosa comes out of his home under the push-cart, shakes off the shreds of blackening coriander that the samosa vendor has chucked on his patchy fur for a laugh, and sniffs around my legs. Samosa can find Runu-Didi by smelling me; we are brother and sister.

"Where is she?" I ask Samosa, pushing him forward.

"Jai, come here," Ma says.

Samosa runs back to his home. He can't find Runu-Didi through me. I stink too much.

———

We search and search for Runu-Didi, around the bazaar and the rubbish ground where we ask scavenger children and Bottle-Badshah about Didi. I try to think of who could have taken her. It's not the TV-repair chacha because he's in jail, not the spotty boy, and not Quarter either because he didn't know Didi had been snatched. That leaves djinns and criminals I don't know.

Ma's tears slash lines into her cheeks and around her lips that seem to be turning blue. She leans on me when we finally walk home, and her weight makes me tilt to one side. Our neighbors stare.

At home, Ma takes out Runu-Didi's framed certificate from our precious-things bundle by the door, and unwraps the dupattas bound around it. "Remember the day Runu won this?" she asks.

I don't remember. Ma hardly ever comes to our school, so I don't think she has seen Didi run.

"One of her teammates dropped the baton that day," Ma says, "but Runu was so fast, her team still won."

Someone knocks on the door. It's Fatima-ben. She forces Ma to accept a tiffin box filled with something. "Roti and subzi, it's no feast," she says. She talks about Buffalo-Baba. "My heart has been burning since I found him . . . in that state," she says. "Who would do something so cruel, and why, I can't even imagine. It's not the same as what you're going through, of course . . ."

When she leaves, Ma puts the tiffin box on the kitchen shelf.

Shanti-Chachi also brings us food, wrapped in foil. "Puris, your favorite, Jai," she says.

I put her food on top of Fatima-ben's tiffin box.

Ma and Shanti-Chachi go outside to discuss something grown up.

I look at Runu-Didi's books stacked by the wall. Her clothes hang from nails. Her track-pants for yoga class lie on a footstool, waiting for Friday when the class will take place.

I can smell Runu-Didi on her clothes and her pillow that has acquired a dip in the middle from the weight of her head. If I stare at it long enough, the snatcher or the bad djinn who has caught Didi will let her go. I stare and stare. My eyes hurt, but I don't look away.

RUNU

When the school bell rang, everyone hurried out of the classroom, but she stood behind her desk, taking her time with her textbooks, uncreasing dog-ears, and arranging the folds of her dupatta so they formed a crisp V on her chest. She could feel the tautness of the starch in her uniform, carefully soaked for hours in rice water, then rinsed and pinned to a clothesline where it dried, slowly, collecting every smell in the alley: spices, smog, goat shit, kerosene, smoke from woodfires and beedis. What even was the point of washing, her ma liked to say. By the time Runu finished her training in the evening, the uniform was damp and sticky with sweat anyway.

Ma couldn't understand why Runu put in so much effort for a mere few hours in which her clothes looked as if they had been ironed by a press-wallah. Ma couldn't understand anything about her. No one did.

Runu stood now in the empty classroom, its walls darkened by cobwebs and inky fingers, the blackboard cracked at the edges and whitened by years of chalk. Curls of smog crept in like unruly tendrils through windows that wouldn't shut fully. She saw for herself a life that would be a series of misunderstandings, and hated herself—and the world—for it.

She touched her cheek where the previous night her father had slapped her. She could still hear the sound of it, his hand swinging backward and then slicing through the air toward her as she stood unable to move. That moment of humiliation had thankfully left no mark on her skin, but part of her also wanted her face to be disfigured so that even strangers could tell a man needn't be soused up to the eyeballs like Drunkard Laloo to be a bad father.

Her resolve grew firmer. She wasn't going home (not today, not ever). She would never wear earrings again (not today, not ever).

Textbooks in her bag, she walked outside, into the corridor where her brother was gleefully narrating the events of last night—**and then he slapped Runu-Didi**—to his friend Pari, who was a hundred times smarter than him and made sure he knew it too. Runu told him not to wait for her, and the donkey spat out a swear more colorful than usual.

Since he had been born, she had considered Jai with a blend of loathing and admiration; it seemed to her that he had a way of softening the imperfections of life with his daydreams and the self-confidence that the world granted boys (which, in girls, was considered a character flaw or evidence of a dismal upbringing). At least tonight she wouldn't have to sleep next to the smells he carried on him, sometimes the butcher shop in Bhoot Bazaar, sometimes tea and cardamom, and always in winter the filth of days that accumulated on him from his refusal to wash himself with cold water.

Runu leaned against a pillar in the corridor and watched her brother leave. On the other side of the pillar stood a boy from her class. Pravin turned up wherever she went, the school ground where she trained, the ration shop from where she procured sugar and kerosene, and the basti water tap, where she and her mother left their pots to hold their positions in the queue as they talked to friends. At least he didn't try to talk to her.

She felt separate from the world. It wasn't a new feeling; it had been there for a while. While other girls her age smiled at their distorted reflections in glass windows, her own body had become so strange to her that she could barely glance at it as she poured a mug of cold water over herself in one of the dark washrooms at the toilet complex. Her friends considered the sprouting of breasts and the wearing of bras exotic, but to her, the arrival of periods and the accompanying cramps only signalled the end of even more freedoms. The months her mother couldn't afford to buy pads, she had to use folded cloth from which it was impossible to scrub out the stench of blood.

These days she had to worry about bloodstains on her clothes, and the boys (even the boys who trained with Coach in the mornings) leering at her as she ran. Coach was always chasing them off, but the boys managed to scale a wall or a tree to take videos of her and the other girls with their phones, zooming in on their breasts, which were (truth be told) barely there. The videos were then shared across school, and the boys ranked the girls according to their physical attributes and scrawled their ratings (**Five-star! Three-star! One-star!**) on bathroom walls for everyone to see.

Runu lifted her bag strap where it was cutting into her shoulder. She never showed that she cared about the boys' rankings, but they preyed on her mind sometimes. Why was she three stars and not four like Jhanvi or even five like Mitali? Why was

Tara a two when she looked like she could be Miss Universe? On the days they scribbled the latest rankings, the boys approached her and Tara, as if they thought the odds of the girls agreeing to an outing were the highest on the days their confidence was the lowest. Pravin's devotion to her, strangely enough, remained unwavering in the face of such graffiti.

Runu had no dreams of falling in love, not with Pravin, not with the seniors who styled themselves after film heroes; and certainly not with Quarter the gangster, whose eyes stalked any girl in his vicinity. She didn't want romance. All she cared about was getting onto a podium and lowering her head to receive a gold medal. (National? State? District? **Something**.) But right now, she was a not-good-enough daughter to her parents and, someday, she would be a not-good-enough wife to a strange man. Without a place on the school's athletics team, this was who she was now and who she could be in the future, though **future** itself seemed like a mere possibility, a slit in the smog that suggested sunshine but not really.

"Isn't it training time for girls now?" Pravin asked, having walked around the pillar to speak to her at last. He pointed his nose toward a corner of the playground where Coach was smoothing the ground with the tips of his scuffed canvas shoes. She practiced in this playground dotted with penguin bins and see-saws and slides, and she was still faster than most students who went to private schools. Her speed made her special. Without it, she would be nothing, an unperson. The thought felt to her like a hand parting her ribs. Her chest ached wildly, her head throbbed.

"You aren't feeling well?" Pravin asked, his voice frail, as if he couldn't believe he was talking to her.

She pressed her back against the pillar, watched the other girls in the team—Harini would never be as fast as her—nodding to Coach's instructions. Runu drew a sharp breath. The image in front of her curved and collapsed in on itself. Pravin put his hand on her shoulder, above her bag's strap.

"Runu, Runu."

His voice shook off the sleepiness that warped her vision. She shrugged off his hand, twisting her mouth. "Don't touch me," she said.

"You almost fainted," he said, the pustules on his face turning redder.

"Leave me alone," she said and sprinted to the playground.

Coach nodded at her and said, "Knew you couldn't keep away."

"I'm not here," she said, and just saying that made her want to cry.

"I don't like anybody watching my team train," Coach said, his voice as stern as always. "If you aren't joining them"—he swept his hand toward the other girls—"then please leave."

Her teammates, panting, puffing, looked at her with consternation when she half-lifted her hand in a gesture that she hoped combined hello and goodbye. They were her tribe (even Harini), these meticulous girls who were also her rivals, who ran because they wanted sports scholarships to study, or hoped to secure a government job through the sports quota when they finished college. She considered them with envy. She thought of the times they had traveled for inter-school competitions and shared good secrets and bad secrets and shameful secrets and she didn't know what she would do without them without hope without dreams.

The sky hung low, cropping the school roof. She walked out of the playground and into the alley. Empty wrappers and foil bowls rustled and winked brightly on the ground. The alley was deserted. The vendors had moved their carts to wherever their customers were. She felt alone in a way that frightened her, and not because of the bad djinns her brother worried about, or the men who took one too many sips of desi daru and attempted to pinch every passing woman's bottom. Who was she if not an athlete?

She wondered if her parents would allow her to resume training when the snatchings ended. "Jai needs someone to teach him Maths," she imagined her father saying. "Water has to be fetched every evening," her mother would say. It was as if she existed solely to care for her brother, and the house. Afterward, she would similarly look after her husband, her hands smelling of cow-dung cakes. Her own dreams were inconsequential. It seemed to her that no one could see the ambition that thrummed in her; no one imagined her **becoming** someone.

When she reached Bhoot Bazaar, she stood for a moment to tug at her ponytail and tighten it. On the paan-spattered walls around her were advertisements for computer classes, banking and insurance exams, tuitions, and appeals for votes from politicians. She withered under the lecherous stares of the men who sold carrots and radishes and capsicums. She wished she were a boy because boys could sit on culverts and smoke beedis without anybody stopping them.

She went into a fabric shop and the shop-girl considered her suspiciously as she browsed. Runu asked the girl to pull out a blouse-piece as blue as the sea (she had seen the sea often enough on TV) from a shelf behind the counter. The shop-girl hesitated, her eyes asking what someone wearing a shoddy uniform was going to do with the shiny material. Runu made up a story about a wedding she had to attend, thinking all the while of her teammates running, and she missed the taste of dust in her mouth and the grit in her eyes and the pounding of her heart, and this picture of her running interrupted her story of a fake wedding such that the shop-girl said, "The bride ran away? But what of the wedding?"

She must have said something aloud, unaware, as if talking in her sleep. Embarrassed, Runu felt the blouse-material between her fingers and said, "This isn't right."

She turned on her heels and ran out of the shop and the bazaar until she reached the highway. Her shoulders and her school bag smacked against strange men and women. Then she collided with a toddler who toppled sideways to the ground and bawled, though he appeared unhurt. His mother swung her shopping bag toward Runu, missing her by a millimeter. The gust of violence propelled Runu forward. But where was she going? Who knew who cared not her.

She walked along the highway, smelling the corncobs that vendors were roasting on charcoal, watching bhelpuri-sellers balance their almost-empty baskets on their heads and fold their wicker stands, a hard day's work done at last. The stone slabs on the pavement see-sawed with every footstep. People hissed at her for being in their way. She was directionless, and they read it in her stride. They had dinners to prepare, Purple Line trains to catch, children whose homework needed supervising. When the crowd dwindled for a moment, she saw a young man who stood proprietarily next to a steel box on wheels that said:

FILTERED WATER
FRESHEST! PUREST! CLEANEST!
2 RUPEES PER GLASS ONLY

He gaped at her as if she were mad, which all things considered, she might be. Traffic rushed by on the highway like streaks of light. Her mother must be home and already beside herself with worry. Runu could hear Jai's voice suggesting daft ideas stolen from **Police Patrol** to find her. Her parents would probably listen to him. Jai wasn't Runu. Jai wasn't a girl. She turned her hands and looked at the calluses ringing her fingers, these timestamps of every bucket of water she had carried, every brinjal she had sliced, every shirt she had washed. There were black ribbons on her hands where flames had singed her when she cooked. These were the lifelines pitted into her palms, the ones that sealed her destiny.

The water-vendor approached her hesitantly. On the highway, a bus rolled past, the driver keeping his hand pressed on the horn, the honk like an endless scream.

"Are you lost?" the vendor asked. "What are you doing here?"

"What's it to you?" she said, but only in her head. She turned and walked away from him, remembering this was why she had started running, and running fast; she didn't want people asking her why she was blowing her nose or eating gol-gappas or watching the rain tumbling from the sky. No part of her life was hers, no corner of the world either. On the running track was the only place where she felt alone even if a hundred eyes were watching; there, it was just her and the sound of her shoes thudding against the earth.

"Runu?" said a voice that cracked with hesitation. Then Pravin stepped forward with his hands in his pockets. "I heard children have been going missing from this very spot," he said. "You should go home."

She looked around and realized, from the electric transformer safeguarded by an iron fence, that she was in the Shaitani Adda of Jai's stories. Something had brought her here, anger or sorrow or an emotion she couldn't name.

"Runu, chalo," Pravin said.

"Try Clearasil," she said, gently. "Maybe it will help."

"You're only a three," he said, and it took her a minute to figure out what he was talking about.

"Three is much higher than minus hundred,

which is where you are," she said. She was surprised, and grateful, that her brain had come up with a retort.

He looked as if he might cry, but then he left.

The Shaitani Adda was now empty. The pulse in her temples quickened. Even if djinns weren't real, the disappearances had indeed taken place. She didn't want to be a number, a totem for the Hindu Samaj. She had dreams (still). In a year or two, she would figure out a way to escape from home, but for now she would have to make do with the stale air of their one-room house.

A man's voice spiralled out of the blackness toward her: "What are you doing here?"

"Do you know what they say about girls who stay out at this hour?" a woman asked.

No place could be quiet for long in this basti (she should have known).

PAPA SAYS WE ARE GOING
ON A PATROL—

—as soon as the smog lets a bit of morning light into our basti.

"We should have kept watch at your Shaitani Adda," he tells me, "when the children started disappearing. It was careless of us, not to do even that much."

I stay quiet. It's not yet forty-eight hours since the spotty boy saw Runu-Didi; that will be tonight. We have a whole day to find Didi.

When our patrol starts, our group is just Papa, Ma, Kabir-Khadifa's abbu, Shanti-Chachi and me; soon others join, men who don't have to work in the day, grandpas and grandmas, and a few women holding small children wrapped snugly in shawls and dupattas. No one calls Kabir-Khadifa's abbu a terrorist; maybe we Hindus don't hate Muslims anymore.

Papa knocks on every door, pulls back every curtain, asks, **where is my daughter? Have you seen her? Look at this photo, look carefully, look closely.** If Ma knows the woman of the house, she says, **you have seen Runu at the water tap, remember?**

The parents of all the other missing children join us, except for Omvir's ma and Kabir-Khadifa's ammi and Chandni's ma and papa. Even Drunkard Laloo is here. Maybe there are fifty people in our patrol group now, or seventy.

We knock on more doors. A woman Ma knows from the water tap tells her, "You're so unlucky. What a horrible thing to happen." She looks gratefully at her baby who is safe in her hands.

Another woman says Ma should have been stricter with Didi. "All that running business, I told you it wasn't going to end well. Daughters should never be allowed out on their own."

Ma's face contorts in pain, as if someone has stabbed her.

News of our patrol spreads across our basti and Bhoot Bazaar. Quarter turns up with his gang. His eyes dart around, and his legs and hands shudder as if he's nervous. Maybe he's worried about Runu-Didi. Maybe he knows something he can't tell us.

If Quarter is the child-snatcher, he shouldn't have been here. Or he's here so that we won't suspect him. Which one is it? Pari would know the correct answer. But Pari is writing the EVS exam right now.

"My father is going to speak to a minister in the city," Quarter tells Papa now. "He will insist that special police be sent here."

"Are we fools to believe such lies?" someone in the crowd says.

"Who said that?" Quarter shouts, but no one admits to asking the question.

"Does your father even live here anymore?" Papa asks Quarter.

"Let's focus on finding your daughter first," Quarter says.

He forces his way into people's houses as if he will find Runu-Didi tied up inside. No one protests, not even an old woman who is changing out of her clothes when Quarter kicks open a door. She quickly wraps a sheet around herself.

I see older sisters taking care of little babies, families that are still whole, nobody missing, not even a pet goat or a kitten.

We go around Bhoot Bazaar. Our throats run dry. Someone offers us water. Someone else offers us tea. Bahadur's ma stays close to my ma, but she tiptoes around her as if she's afraid she'll step on Ma's sadness, which must be the same size and shape as Bahadur's ma's sadness, only a lot fresher.

"The rubbish ground," someone shouts.

I run and so does Ma and Papa and everyone else. I stumble and fall.

Ma's hands help me up. "Maybe they have found Runu," she says. "Maybe she was hiding when we went there yesterday."

Her eyes are bright like a crazy person's, her hair has come undone, and white spit-marks have crusted around her lips. I want to believe her, but I can't. Nothing good is ever found at the rubbish ground.

———

"Send the women and children back," a man's voice roars at our patrol. I can't see him because I'm too short.

"Who are you to tell us what to do?" a woman roars back.

There's a gash in my palm from when I fell down. It stings and throbs. Clothes hanging from washing lines flap against the faces of grown-ups. There's pushing and shoving and cursing. Elbows punch my face. I scream but no one hears it, the scream is quiet.

"We deserve to know what's happening to our children," a woman shouts. "We gave birth to them, not you."

The crowd sweeps forward, carries us forward too. It's like the wind, and Ma and Papa and I are kites with broken strings, going where it takes us. A hundred people might be around me, maybe two hundred. The air, stinking of rot and shit and burning rubber and batteries, shudders with our fear and anger.

We enter the lane that faces the rubbish ground. There's more space here and the crowd spreads out and I can finally see what's happening. Quarter, Aanchal's papa, the press-wallah, and Kabir-Khadifa's papa are standing near Bottle-Badshah and the ragpicker children. I grab Papa's hand and we join them.

"Go on, tell them, don't be afraid," Bottle-Badshah says to a snotty boy my age, wearing a yellow glass-bead chain around his neck and holding a muddy-brown sack tight in his hand. I don't think Ma and I talked to him yesterday.

"My kids are always on the hunt," Bottle-Badshah says, looking at Quarter as if he knows Quarter is the most important person here. "Whoever gets the best stuff makes the most money."

I wonder what the children found. I want to know. I don't want to know.

A girl with a red headband keeping her hair out

of her face pushes the bead-necklace boy. "Talk," she says. He doesn't.

I recognize her; she's the girl who was flying the broken helicopter when I came here with Faiz. She doesn't seem to remember me.

"Arrey, just now," the helicopter-girl says, "we saw a man go deep into the rubbish with something hidden under his blanket. Nobody goes that far to do No. 2."

I look around. Everywhere there are small fires and smoke and pigs and dogs.

"After the man left, we went to check—we didn't go close at first, in case he had really done No. 2. Then we saw a plant this high"—she brings her hand down to her waist—"and it had a white rag tied to it. The rag wasn't dirty. Everything is dirty here, even us, look at us." She shows us her sooty hands.

"I was the one who found it," the bead-necklace boy finally speaks. "I pulled up the plant and checked underneath. I thought the man had hidden something that cost a lot of money. Something he had stolen that he didn't want his wife or mummy to see. And it was this—" He looks at the sack he's holding.

Bottle-Badshah takes it from him and brings out a blue plastic box spattered with mud and filth. The box is the length of his forearm and less than a foot wide. He opens the lid, but it's above my head. Aanchal's papa gasps. Omvir's papa screams. Kabir-Khadifa's father cries.

"Is that . . . ?" Papa asks.

Bottle-Badshah looks at me and brings the box down so that I can see. "Is this hairband . . . is this your didi's?" he asks.

Inside there's loads of stuff, a plastic ring that glows white, bead necklaces, black-and-yellow folded sunglasses, red bangles, anklets made of a silvery material that has turned black in parts, a headband with a red, papery rose to its side, an HTC phone and, underneath it, a white scrunchie. It could be didi's but it could be someone else's too.

"Jai?" Papa says, his voice stretched thin as if he is begging.

"The phone is Aanchal's," I say. "The glow-ring is Omvir's."

Aanchal's papa picks up the mobile, turns it around. "It's Aanchal's," he says.

"The sunglasses are my son's," Kabir-Khadifa's abbu says. "And the red bangles could be Khadifa's, I'm not sure."

"All of you came here searching for your children," Bottle-Badshah says and pauses as if he's giving a speech. I wish he would hurry. "You told me what they were wearing." He looks at Aanchal's papa. "I remember you telling me about your daughter's HTC phone. You asked me to call you if I saw something like that being sold second-hand in the bazaar. And little boy"—he looks at me now—"when you and your mother were here yesterday, she told me about your sister's hairband. As soon as the children brought this box to me, and I saw what was inside, I knew something was wrong."

"The man who buried it, where is he?" Papa asks.

"The children didn't follow that man, regrettably, because it took them some time to find this box. By the time they brought it to me, he was gone."

"Big he was," the bead-necklace boy says. "Like a tree."

"Very tall," Helicopter-Girl agrees. "Looked like a fighter."

My breath gets stuck in my throat. "Was he wearing a gold watch?" I manage to ask.

"Don't know," a scavenger boy says. He's drinking from a crushed-up mango-juice box. I want to kick it out of his hands.

"Hatta-katta he was," someone else says. Then I'm sure.

I turn to look at Quarter. He knows Wrestler-Man. But I can't ask him anything because he has moved away and is speaking into his mobile, hand over his mouth. He doesn't want us to hear what he's saying.

Bahadur's ma and Drunkard Laloo and my ma jostle through the crowd to reach us.

"What's it, what's it?" Ma asks.

"It's a box with a few things that appear to belong to the missing children," Bottle-Badshah explains.

Ma picks up the scrunchie.

"Put it back," I tell her. "It's evidence."

"This is not your stupid show," Ma screams at me. "What's wrong with you? I cannot bear to listen to you for a second more."

Ma knows it's my fault Didi has disappeared. Hot tears spring out of my eyes. Papa pulls me close.

"Bahadur?" Bahadur's ma asks. Bottle-Badshah gives her the box and she roots through it and says, "But there's nothing of his here."

"Something might have fallen out when the children were playing with it," Bottle-Badshah says. "They didn't mean to—they're only children. They didn't know what this was."

The bead-necklace boy touches his necklace proprietarily.

"Where did you find this?" Bahadur's ma asks the scavenger-children. "Take me there."

Two of the children start walking through the rubbish. Bahadur's ma lifts up the hem of her sari and follows them. Drunkard Laloo goes with her, but he collapses into the rubbish and she has to pull him up. This will take forever. We don't have time. We have to find Wrestler-Man. He has Runu-Didi.

"Papa," I say, "I have seen that man at Duttaram's tea shop." I look at Ma. She is getting ready to scream at me again, so I cut my words short. "I think he lives near the Shaitani Adda. We should go there."

It's only a guess but that's where the snatchings took place, so his house must be there.

"My children will go with you," Bottle-Badshah says. "They'll recognize him if they see him, won't you?"

The children nod, but their faces don't look so sure.

———

Quarter tells us he has called the police. They will bring JCBs so that they can move things around in the rubbish ground and check it properly. But JCBs are for destroying our homes, not for finding Runu-Didi. She isn't in the rubbish.

"The kidnapper is from your party," I tell Quarter before Ma can stop me. "You know him. He looks like a wrestler."

"I doubt it," Quarter says, and he says it calmly, but his fists are clenched, and his knuckles have turned white.

"He works at Golden Gate, but he lives in our basti," I say. "He was at Thumper-Baba's puja. I saw him talk to your father."

"Lots of people talk to my father," Quarter says.

"We'll check around the adda, okay, Jai?" Papa says, almost as if he feels sorry for me.

"I'll wait here for the police," Bottle-Badshah says.

I look at the box in his hands. There are too many fingerprints on it now, and the kidnapper's might have been wiped out.

"Shouldn't you stay here?" Papa asks Quarter as he follows us with his gang-members. "The police don't listen to us, but they'll listen to you."

Quarter waves his mobile in Papa's face. "They'll let me know when they get here. It will take them some time, especially as they have to call for JCBs." With a hooked index finger, he beckons me. "What is this kidnapper's name?" he asks.

"Don't know," I say.

I think he'll punch me, but he lets me go back to Papa and Ma.

———

The people who live near the adda say there's only one hatta-katta man in this neighborhood, and they show us his house. We knock on his door. A bicycle, black and speckled with mud, leans against the wall by a row of empty jerrycans. Wrestler-Man comes out, looking cross.

"It's him," I whisper to Papa.

"It was him," the bead-necklace boy confirms with a vehement shake of his head.

"Arrest him," Helicopter-Girl shouts. Then she looks at me sadly.

Quarter and his gang grab Wrestler-Man by the collar. He's so strong that he shrugs, and they fall aside in a heap.

"What do you want with my husband?" screams a woman who rushes out of the house to Wrestler-Man's side. Her sari is askew, and her bangles smash against each other as she clutches the sleeve of his shirt.

There are enough people in our patrol to form a cordon around Wrestler-Man. He can't fight everybody off. Papa and me and Ma scramble into his house. Runu-Didi has to be inside.

The house is one room, just like ours, and Didi isn't there. Ma stifles a cry and hobbles back outside.

Someone switches on the light. I look under the charpai, I drag out the vessels stacked there. Quarter's gang-members open flour tins and empty their contents. Lids spin and clank; shelves nailed to the wall crash; voices circle me like trails of smoke. I slip on the sugar and salt on the floor, but I still crawl around, searching every inch for clues. Was Runu-Didi here? I can't tell. Papa and someone else, it's the press-wallah, they rummage through the clothes in the house, both washed and unwashed. Other people want to come in, but it's too crowded inside the house. Aanchal's papa asks some of us to leave so that he can look for his daughter's belongings. I go out, Papa holding my hand.

The air is heavy like sludge with the weight of shouts and curses and swears. Quarter's gang-members tie Wrestler-Man's hands with a rope. His gold watch is on his wrist, and it's broken. There's a flurry of movement, hands curling into fists, muscles flexing, legs and hands slamming through the air to hit him. The sound of the thwacking is the same as the sound of bloody cleavers hacking meat at Afsal-Chacha's shop in Bhoot Bazaar. My heart pumps blood into my ears too-fast.

Wrestler-Man's wife screams and wails. A woman puts a hand around the wife's throat and tells her to shut up **or else**. The bicycle I had seen earlier lies on the ground, its frame crushed, the tires slashed. I remember the scratch marks I had spotted on Wrestler-Man's wrist at Duttaram's tea shop. Had these been made by Bahadur and Omvir while trying to claw out of his grip? All of him has been cut up by people now, and one dotted red line on his skin looks like the other.

Four policemen, including the senior and junior constables I have seen many times, turn up. Quarter takes them aside and talks to them. The senior constable doesn't even look at Bahadur's ma though he took her gold chain.

The arrival of the police doesn't soften the sharpness of the anger in the alley. Wrestler-Man crumples under the kicks and punches that don't ease up. Everything unfolds in slow motion. The smog dips and rises; the light turns blue and grey; a man scratches his armpits; voices whip through the air asking **could the children be . . . no, not dead!** The buzzing in my ears grows louder. Blood spills from Wrestler-Man's broken lips, but he doesn't say a word. "Where are the children?" each man hitting him asks. A thousand questions, and he stays silent through them all.

I go near Quarter. He's telling the constables that Wrestler-Man's name is Varun. He has been seen at a few Hindu Samaj events, but he doesn't know Varun and neither does his father. The constables ask the scavenger children a few questions: **who saw Varun bury the box, what is in it, where is it.** They don't write anything down in a notebook like Pari does.

"Where is Runu-Didi?" I scream. The words taste like rust in my mouth. I don't understand what is happening. I can't think like a detective because I'm not one. The constables look at me and look away.

The pradhan arrives in a cycle-rickshaw. The policemen stand around him in a half-circle. He puts his hands together, he says **thank you for coming.**

"I can't believe someone who worships our baba can be a criminal," the pradhan says. "When Eshwar called me and told me about it, I was heartbroken."

I don't know who Eshwar is and then I realize it's Quarter.

The pradhan approaches my ma and Bahadur's ma, who stand up. Aanchal's papa and the press-wallah stagger out of Varun's house empty-handed.

"He's your friend," I say, and push aside grown-up legs so that the pradhan can see me. "Wrestler-Man Varun. I have seen you talk to him. Ask him where he has locked up my didi."

"Eshwar said Varun has done some work for the Samaj," the pradhan says, addressing the crowd and not me. "But the Samaj has so many members, and I speak to so many people, I'm afraid I do not personally know this fellow." He doesn't even glance at Varun. "Be assured we will get to the bottom of this. You have my word."

"But where's my daughter?" Ma asks.

"My son?" Bahadur's ma asks.

"Why were their things in a box?" I ask.

"All in good time," the pradhan says.

"You're waiting for all of us to die?" Ma asks, her words soft and clear. "Will that be a good time for you to do something?"

———

The police put handcuffs on Varun and his wife and say they are taking the two of them to the rubbish ground.

"He'll show us what else he has hidden there," a policeman explains to us. "Since the children aren't in his house, and since he seems to have collected souvenirs from every child he snatched, there's only one logical explanation as to what he was doing with them."

"What do they think they'll find there?" the press-wallah asks my papa as we follow the police procession. "Our children aren't there."

He knows what they are looking for; we all do. We can hear the questions the police are asking Varun and his wife.

"Did you cut them to pieces and throw them in the rubbish?"

"Leave them to be eaten by dogs and pigs?"

"Tell me, you motherfucker. I'll make you talk."

People spill out of their shops to watch us. "What is happening here?" they ask. The Muslim shopkeepers wrangle their skullcaps into little balls in their hands and turn away from us.

"Runu-Didi is alive," I tell Papa.

Varun must have hidden Didi somewhere, maybe an abandoned factory or a godown. A trafficker would sell those he snatched, not kill them. Who has Varun sold Didi to? Or is Varun a djinn that has taken the form of a human?

Papa scrambles ahead and grasps Varun's elbow. "My daughter, Runu, where is she?"

Blood trickles down Varun's bruised face and onto his sweater. He eyes Papa with his swollen eyes and smirks.

At the rubbish ground the policemen question Bottle-Badshah and the scavenger children again. The blue plastic box is now in the hands of the police; none of them are wearing gloves.

"Why does your husband have this?" a policewoman asks Varun's wife.

We don't have anything to do with it, she says.

"Where have you buried them?" another policeman asks.

Nowhere, we don't know anything, she says.

The pradhan steers clear of the rubbish that he seems afraid will stain his kurta-pajama. He makes calls on his mobile, one after the other. Quarter ferries messages from him to the policemen and back.

I don't understand why they are wasting their time like this. My head feels like it will burst. I speak to a scavenger boy passing by. "Are the missing children lying in the rubbish?" I ask.

"Wouldn't we have told someone if they were?" he says.

A police jeep trundles down to the rubbish

ground, its engine sputtering. Behind it is a yellow JCB excavator and a police van with wire meshes that keep its windows safe. More policemen and policewomen than I have ever seen before step out of the vehicles and stomp through the rubbish. The letters P and O are missing from the jeep's side, so it reads LICE.

"Call Chandni's father," a man shouts at another man. "He must be at work. He said to call him if we got any news."

"You do it," the second man says. "I don't have his number."

The police form a cordon in the part of the rubbish ground where the scavenger children discovered the box. Varun and his wife are moved to its center. The excavator lurches toward the cordon, its track wheels flattening the rubbish, its long claw dangling in front.

Men and women from our basti walk behind the excavator. Policemen snap their fingers and cluck their tongues, and order everyone to turn back.

An old woman flings a handful of blackening vegetable peelings at a constable whose shirt has no arrow-badges. Soon others pelt the policemen with whatever their hands can gather from the ground, pebbles, stones, plastic wrappers, balled-up newspapers, shreds of clothes, Tetra Paks.

"Traitors," they yell. "Child-killers. Murderers."

A stone hits the senior constable's knee and he hops around on one leg. I want his leg to be broken.

"Stop, stop," Quarter pleads with everybody. "They're here to do a job. Let them do it."

The senior constable limps through the trash toward the jeep.

"We will leave if you do it again. We will take the JCB with us," he shouts.

That stops the stone-pelting. Two scavenger girls share a muddy carrot, giggling after each bite. The sound of the JCB scatters pigs. Bottle-Badshah walks up and down, surveying his kingdom, telling his children not to scavenge in front of the police. "You'll end up in a juvenile home," he warns.

———

We wait and wait and wait, me and Papa and Ma. We take turns to cry. I cry first and then Ma and then Papa.

"My boys and girls are the real heroes," Bottle-Badshah tells a man who was in our patrol. "If not for them, that criminal would never have been caught. I'm telling everyone because by tomorrow my children will be forgotten, and the Hindu Samaj will take credit for everything."

The badshah sees me between Ma and Papa, and his ashy hand reaches forward to tousle my hair. I shrink into Ma's sari, and the buttoned sweater she's wearing on top of it.

"Don't worry, daughter," Bottle-Badshah says to Ma. "The police are asking the right questions. Finally."

A policewoman dressed in a khaki shirt and trousers, holding a baton in one hand and a cap in another, comes over to talk to Ma about Runu-Didi.

"You wouldn't even file a complaint," Ma says. "That's why people are so angry."

"I'm from a chowki," the policewoman says. "It's under the big police station but we can't tell the people there what to do."

The policewoman pats Ma's elbow. They both look uncomfortable.

An hour or so passes, I don't know for sure. The JCB keeps shifting the trash from one side to another. They haven't found anything. This is good news or bad news, I can't tell which. The waiting people whose families are whole and who have got nobody missing chat around us, pretending to be detectives. **Why did Varun do it when did he do it how did he do it**. It's like a game for them, a guessing game.

I can't listen to these people anymore. Ma can't stand it either. She gets up and races toward Varun. I run after Ma and so does Papa.

Runu-Didi would have been four times as fast as us.

The waste around us hisses and sputters as we run, it bites our feet, it tries to pull us down. Two cows stumble away from us.

We reach the cordon.

"Ask that man to tell me where my daughter is," Ma shouts.

The policewoman who said she was from a chowki stands in front of Ma, her palm an inch short of Ma's face. "Have patience," she says. She doesn't let Ma move forward.

Dogs bark excitedly. Samosa isn't here, he must be under the samosa cart near Duttaram's tea shop. Varun sways as if he's drunk, dark blood thickening around a cut on his eyebrow. His wife cries.

The JCB's claw turns the waste again. A black plastic bag comes up.

"What's that?" a voice shouts from near my ma. It's Aanchal's papa.

A policeman picks up the dirty bag with his bare hands, unties it and holds it upside down. Out falls a bunch of old Hindi film VCDs.

"What did you do to my Aanchal, you animal?" Aanchal's papa screams.

Varun's eyes are half-shut. His chin drops down to his chest. A policeman prods him with a baton. He stands straight.

———

It's late afternoon now, not yet forty-eight hours.
Bottle-Badshah asks his scavenger children to spread
out sacks on the ground so that we can sit. I know
Runu-Didi isn't hidden here but Varun knows where
she is, and maybe if he stands here for long enough,
stones slicing his skin, the truth will rush out of his
mouth.

Chandni's ma and papa arrive. People circle
them like hawks.

The pradhan isn't here anymore. I didn't see
him leave. Quarter is in charge. His gang-members
bring him food in plastic packets from Bhoot
Bazaar.

Pari turns up at my side with her ma, who must
have left work early to bring Pari home from school.
Faiz isn't with her.

"We heard," Pari says. Her ma sobs.

I move to the side, making space for Pari on the
dirty-white sack. She sits with her shoulder pressed
to my shoulder, and she puts her hand into mine.

"How did your exam go?" I ask.

"Okay," she says.

I don't ask her if she thinks Varun is a djinn. I
know what she will say.

Drunkard Laloo presses one nostril with his
index finger and shoots snot out of the other. Ma
and Bahadur's ma talk, their heads down, cheeks
damp. Another jeep arrives with even more police.
Varun collapses to the ground. The policemen

wake him up with kicks and spit that waterfalls out of their mouths, which he can't wipe off because his hands are cuffed. "Don't, don't, forgive, forgive," his wife shouts.

Ma gets up and wanders by the rubbish like a ghost. A fish bone is stuck to the sole of her left slipper. Pari's ma walks with her, saying **Runu will come back, I know**. But she cries the entire time she speaks.

"I wish my ma would stop," Pari says.

The air turns colder. The smog licks us with its mangy-grey tongue as we rub our red eyes. What are the police hiding behind the cordon? Have they found bodies? Is Runu-Didi in a plastic bag? I can't think of it, I won't think of it. The JCB growls, it beeps and pings as it goes backward and forward, it sputters and coughs.

"Getting dark, haan," Drunkard Laloo says. This must be when he usually goes to the daru shop for his evening quota of hooch.

"Leave if you want," Bahadur's ma says. She sounds as disgusted as I feel.

Faiz and Wajid-Bhai arrive. They say they heard what happened from the basti-people and Bhoot Bazaar shopkeepers.

"Don't you have work?" I ask Faiz. I know he stacks shelves at the kirana store after a day of selling roses.

"Not tonight," he says. He sits on the very edge

of our sack, most of him on the filth-strewn ground. His hands are full of thorn-cuts, and his voice is hoarse, probably from breathing fumes on the highway.

"You didn't go to the police station?" Pari asks Wajid-Bhai. "They can't keep Tariq-Bhai in jail when that man"—she gestures toward the cordon—"has been caught. Red-handed."

"They say it will take time. But Tariq-Bhai will be released, I'm certain." Wajid-Bhai sounds excited though his face is trying to look normal. A sharp stone rolls down my throat.

The pradhan returns to the rubbish ground. He speaks to the police. Then he claps his hands so that we know he is about to give a speech.

"Varun and his wife will be taken to the police station now," he says. "They're refusing to talk, and the police haven't found anything else in the rubbish."

"Can't they get some battery lamps and continue this work over the night?" Chandni's papa asks.

"They'll come back tomorrow," the pradhan says. "You have already seen how tirelessly Eshwar—my son—has worked for you today. And I have done what I can too. Remember the puja I organized? Our prayers are slowly being answered."

"But our children," Kabir-Khadifa's abbu says. "My wife, she's about to have our baby, she can't take this much tension."

"What about Runu?" Papa asks.

"The police have to complete the formalities of filing a case against Varun and his wife," the pradhan says. "There are procedures to be followed. Leave them to do their job."

"If they had done their job, we wouldn't be here today," a man says.

"Let's not antagonize the police now," the pradhan says. "I'll personally go to the police station and check they're doing everything right."

"Duttaram had said the wrestler worked in a hi-fi building. Remember its name?" Faiz asks me.

"Golden Gate," I say.

"Maybe he has locked up Runu-Didi in that building," Faiz says.

"His boss-lady wouldn't let him do that," I say, but then I think of the bad boss-ladies I have seen on **Police Patrol**. I'm too stupid for forgetting something so important. How could I have forgotten? I must be going crazy. I can't think a single thought clearly.

I tell Papa and Ma about the hi-fi flat. Faiz says sometimes flats are empty for ages because hi-fi people live in foreign countries or in the city and visit only once in a while. Ma says this is true. Papa repeats everything to the pradhan and Quarter, who are preparing to leave. "We should go there," Papa says.

"We can't wait," Ma says. "My daughter could be there right now."

"Only very special people live in that building," the pradhan says, looking irritated. "They don't even know about this basti, I'm sure. It's not their fault their servant has been arrested."

"Surely you can ask the police to check," Papa says.

"Golden Gate is not a tea shop that you can drop in for a glass of chai whenever you feel like it," the pradhan says.

The police shove Varun and his wife into the back of the van. People shout abuses at him, call him sisterfucker and motherfucker.

When the police vehicles and the JCB drive away, the press-wallah says, "They didn't even tell us anything about our children."

"I'm going right now to the police station," the pradhan says. "I'll talk to them about this Golden Gate business. I'll call you." Quarter asks a lackey to take down everyone's mobile numbers. Then they leave.

It's almost forty-eight hours and we still don't know where Runu-Didi is.

THE RUBBISH IS A SEA OF—

—rustling black now except where charcoal fires smolder orange. Pari tugs my hand.

"We need answers," Kabir-Khadifa's abbu says. "We have to make the Golden Gate people open their gates."

"Let's show them what we are made of," Aanchal's papa says, thumping his chest.

"Off we go," Drunkard Laloo says, but he heads in the direction of the rubbish ground. Bahadur's ma runs after him and brings him back.

Our long procession sets off, passing Bottle-Badshah, now reclining on a charpai-throne in front of his house. "Be careful," he shouts after us.

Strangers join our group, drawn to us maybe because of the anger in our stride. Their day must have been ordinary and dull, like mine once used to be, and now they are eager to witness a fight so that they will have a story worth repeating at the tea shop tomorrow.

Past the rubbish ground are the first of the hi-fi buildings, and here the roads pick up width and smoothness. They are paved with asphalt and lined with neem and amaltas trees. Pari and Faiz stay close to me. I don't want them to see my sadness, but I'm also glad they are here.

A bunch of stray dogs bark as they chase their enemy dogs across the dark road. Samosa would never snarl at anyone like that.

We reach a sloping side road that leads up to Golden Gate. It's lined with street lamps and plants trapped in cages. The building is a jumble of cream and yellow, not gold. I imagine Runu-Didi with her face pressed against the window of a flat, her breath drawing a misty circle on the glass.

Papa and other men from our basti talk to the watchmen who have two offices by the entry and exit gates. CCTV cameras with their pointy noses snuffle around us. Hi-fi people go past boom barriers in their sleek cars and jeeps. Special Golden Gate stickers are stuck on their windshields so the watchmen can tell easily that they belong inside.

"How could anyone have smuggled Bahadur

and Aanchal and Runu-Didi through all this?" Pari asks. "They would have made some noise."

"If Varun had a car, he could have hidden them inside," Faiz says. "They aren't looking at the backseats"—he gestures at the watchmen—"if you live here, they know your face, they let you in. But how can Varun have a car?"

He can't. He only has a bicycle. Does this mean Runu-Didi isn't here?

Papa and others are still talking to the watchmen, their voices and hands rising up into the air. One of the watchmen says **this tamasha has been going on for too long, we're calling the police.**

"Call them," Aanchal's papa says. "You think we care?"

The sound of a siren forces us to turn around. For once, the police are everywhere today.

There's just enough space between the people in the crowd for me to see a policeman's shoes clack-clacking on the side road. The shoes are brown, not black like those of the constables, so this policeman is an inspector. A man standing on the balcony of a first-floor flat takes a video of us with his mobile phone.

The police inspector talks to the watchmen, then turns to us and says he has called the owner of the penthouse flat where Varun worked. "The owner isn't here right now, but we are checking everything, I assure you," he says. "But please, remember, these are all top people who live here. Let's keep the noise down to a minimum."

We wait, again. Pari finds out from someone that a penthouse flat means the topmost flat.

Keep my daughter safe, Ma prays next to me. She repeats the prayer nine times as she has been doing all day.

I look up. I imagine Runu-Didi flinging open a balcony window from the highest flat and jumping, all of us running to catch her before her head hits the ground.

Another police van arrives. Constables stroll around, leisurely, as if they are taking a walk in a park.

"What happened to that Varun fellow? His wife?" Pari stops one of them and asks.

"Lock-up," the constable answers. "They will never see the sky again."

"Who wants to see this sky?" his friend says and laughs. "It's full of poison. They are better off in jail, not breathing this air."

The crowd at Golden Gate gets bigger. I don't know where the people are coming from, if it's from our basti or elsewhere.

The watchmen let in a silver car that's as big as a jeep, but it stops just inside the gates. Pari, Faiz and I shove and make our way toward the barriers so that we can see what's happening. Ma, Pari's ma and Wajid-Bhai come with us.

A woman dressed in a white-and-gold salwar-kameez, silky black hair falling down her shoulders, wearing sandals with heels as long as pencils, steps out. In her left hand she clutches a black bag, and in her right a mobile phone. The inspector is allowed in to talk to her. I can't see the woman's face clearly. She waves her hands toward us, the basti-crowd, and keeps making and taking calls on her mobile.

It gets darker. The inspector finishes his conversation with the woman and comes out. Her car-jeep disappears behind the walls. A watchman offers the inspector a plastic chair, and the inspector stands on it as if it's a podium. Constables hold the chair's arms and back steady.

"The madam is horrified and saddened to hear of the tragedy that has unfolded in your slum settlement," the inspector says. "She's a very important person, a friend of our police commissioner." The inspector touches the upward-curving edges of his thick mustache with his thumb and index finger spread out. The chair wobbles, the constables grasp it tighter. "Such an upright citizen would have had nothing to do with the disappearances. However, as a courtesy to me, madam will take me to her flat, which she tells me, she bought only recently, for investment purposes. Madam doesn't stay here often because she has several properties. Madam's mistake was to hire the criminal who is currently in our custody. Please understand, his family has been working for madam's family for three generations. They're from the same native place. When madam was looking for a caretaker for this flat, someone suggested his name to her. Hiring him was her only mistake. She regrets it deeply. Now, madam is being generous enough to allow me inside without a warrant. We're going to check everything thoroughly. We request your cooperation. If we find something, we will let you know immediately."

The too-long speech has made everyone restless. Murmurs rustle through the crowd, spin and gather weight, turn into shouts.

"No," someone says, raising their fist.

"We have to see with our own eyes if that monster has tied up my daughter inside," Papa says. He's standing near the watchmen's office by the entry gate.

Aanchal's papa and the press-wallah and Drunkard Laloo and Kabir-Khadifa's abbu agree and, in voices as loud as Papa's, they ask to be let in. The constables help the inspector get down from the chair. He makes a call on his mobile. Then he announces that madam is a generous and kind woman, but she cannot have riff-raff rooting through her flat that costs five to ten crores. "Let us do our work," he says. "Please, just wait here."

"How many zeroes in ten crores?" Faiz asks Pari as the inspector and constables go inside the gates.

"Eight," she says. She doesn't have to count on her fingers.

The gash in my palm stings. I stand away from everyone, tears running down my cheeks. I feel all alone. Even Bahadur's brother and sister have each other.

"As expected, madam's house was empty," the inspector says when he comes out.

"Where's my Runu?" Ma shouts.

"Where's Chandni?" Chandni's ma asks.

Other people pick up her words and our words and throw them at the inspector: "Chandni-Runu, Aanchal-Omvir, Bahadur-Kabir-Khadifa, where are they, where are they?"

"They aren't here," the inspector says. "I suggest you disperse now, otherwise we'll be forced to take strict action."

"You have done nothing for us," Omvir's press-wallah papa shouts. "Nothing. You never looked for our children."

"None of this would have happened if you had listened," Aanchal's papa says.

"Listened," Drunkard Laloo repeats.

I hear something breaking. A stone has cracked the headlight of a police jeep. Who threw it? A twig zigzags through the air and my eyes follow it until it knocks the khaki cap off the police inspector's head. People throw whatever they can at the police, the watchmen, and into the balconies of the flats.

One stone hits a watchman's forehead and blood flows out like water from a wide-open tap. The other watchmen puff up their cheeks and blow into the whistles they wear around their necks. There's loads of pushing and elbowing and scrambling. Pari and I and Faiz are getting smushed like atta. Ma's hands grip my fingers tightly. I can't see Papa.

People kick down the cages around plants, break off branches and, shaking them like spears, approach the watchmen. The policemen swing their batons. We push past them and, because there are so many of us, they can't stop us. We jump over the barriers, we enter the watchmen's offices, we throw the gates open. We run in, Ma and Pari's ma and Pari and Faiz and Wajid-Bhai and me. I don't even know what we are going to do.

"Runu must be here," Ma says.

"We will turn their tower to dust," someone shouts.

I hear sirens, screams, batons smacking flesh, hands clapping, and people crying, pressing their mufflers or monkey caps or mask-kerchiefs against bleeding heads and arms and legs. Flocks of hi-fi people hop around their balconies, shooting us with their phones. Through the glass doors that lead into Golden Gate's entrance room, I see a group of women from our basti who must work in the building.

A golden light hangs from the ceiling, and two gold-and-white fans spin on either side of it. The floor is white and shiny like a mirror. Tall plants curl out of white pots in the corners, and their leaves are a rich shade of green I have never seen before, not even on the trees in Nana-Nani's or Dada-Dadi's village.

"Gita, Radha," Ma shouts.

"Meera," Chandni's ma hollers.

The basti-women who work at Golden Gate push open the glass doors that don't have a single smudge on them. They tell us many things at the same time:

"Something strange has been going on in the top-floor flat the past few months."

"Ever since that madam bought the flat. Six or seven months now."

"A guard said the top-floor flat gets deliveries even late at night. Past midnight even."

"Varun said it was new furniture, he said the owner was putting in shelves, counters in the kitchen. Who's going to check if that's true or not?"

"The watchmen are always gossiping about her. They say she takes a different man up to her flat each night. But it's hard to know for sure. We can't see their faces, even on CCTV. The men sit in the backseat when she drives her SUV past the boom barriers."

A wail begins from behind me. It's Bahadur's ma.

"We have to find out if our children are inside," a man says.

We run into the building. We are faster than the grown-ups, Pari, Faiz and I. We get into the lift. We have lost our mas and papas and Wajid-Bhai, but it doesn't matter because some people from our basti have also entered the lift with us. Faiz presses the button right at the top: 41. We go up, zooming-zooming, fast like rockets. My head feels light. I lean against the glimmering steel wall. I sniff the metal smells, like Samosa. My nose tries to track Didi.

The lift opens into a square room with marble floors and a door that's shiny and black. We ring the bell by the door, we knock and kick until our feet hurt, and the boss-lady, mobile pressed against her ear, opens it. We race past her. She can't stop us anyway; other basti-people are behind us and they corner her, push her against the wall.

A chachi snatches the boss-lady's phone and gives it to a chacha, who puts it in his jeans-pant pocket with a grin. Her phone keeps ringing.

The windows in the flat stretch all the way from the ceiling to the floor. Everything outside looks small from here, the malls and the roads and the white and red lights of cars and maybe even our basti, but I can't tell where our basti is. I can't see people. The Purple Line train dashing across a bridge is a toy train on a toy bridge.

Pari grabs my hand. "Don't just stand there," she says. "Focus."

We look around. Everything is in perfect order. Cushions sit up with their spines straight on cream sofas. Lights tucked into the ceiling shine like so many little suns, too bright to stare at. Fresh and fragrant yellow roses press against each other in black vases. Metal sculptures of birds and animals and gods sit still on the wooden shelves built into the walls. The rugs on the floor are soft like clouds.

"The police will put all of you in jail," the boss-lady threatens. Then I remember why I am here. I forgot. The strange thing is that other basti-people are behaving like me too. We are all open-mouthed. Our feet and hands move slowly in this room that's bigger than twenty of our houses put together. The hi-fi flat is doing black magic to us, it's stopping us from thinking; maybe this is how they trapped children.

"Runu-Didi?" I say. Then I say it louder, "Runu-Didi? Runu-Didi?"

Our handprints and fingerprints and footprints will destroy the evidence here, but what can we do? A man who says he has already inspected the whole flat shouts, "No children here." He must know a chant that protects him from black magic.

The boss-lady screams **security, security, anybody there, anybody?** Then she says, "I know your pradhan. You won't see your houses when you return tonight. I'll have that entire stinking slum of yours demolished."

"I'll check the kitchen," Pari says, which we can see from where we are standing. "Faiz, you check the bedroom, and Jai, take a look at any other room they have." We can't even guess how many rooms this flat has, or for what purposes.

Through a narrow corridor, I run into the **other room** that's a bedroom, with a big bed on which five people can sleep, and a wooden cupboard with four doors that takes up a whole wall. I check under the bed. The white bedsheet on it is crisp. The peacock-blue pillows have a new smell to them. I open the cupboard doors. Saris, salwar-kameezes, bedsheets, men's shirts and trousers are folded neatly on each shelf.

I go outside to the balcony that borders the bedroom. There's nothing there except for plants in blue pots, and two chairs on either side of a low table. The wind is louder here, and it's freezing-cold. My ears hurt. I shiver, I peer out into the smog, I shout **Runu-Didi, Runu-Didi** and, when there's no answer no matter how many times I call her name, I go back inside.

Behind a door in the bedroom, I find a hidden bathroom, with two washbasins and a tub and a shower too. The tiled floor is sparkly and dry; no one has used it.

Just as I turn to leave, two men from the basti thunder into the room. "Look at the fan, look at the split AC, look at this bedsheet—is it made of silk? How much do you think this bed costs? One lakh? Three lakhs?" the men ask each other. They flop down on the bed and say, **arrey-waah, how soft it is also.**

I hear Pari calling me and Faiz. Has the boss-lady caught her? I run outside, through the corridor where basti chachas and chachis have caused a traffic jam, and into the kitchen, where everything is painted blue-grey. People are opening cupboards and stealing spoons and masalas and even sugar cubes and salt containers. One man tucks a bottle of daru into the waistband of his trousers.

Pari is kneeling on the floor by a washbasin, her head bent over a bucket. Faiz is by her side.

"What is it?" he asks. "Are you okay?"

Pari shows us what the bucket holds: brushes, soap-water bubbling inside plastic bottles, sponges and rags. Underneath it all lie three dark-brown glass bottles with labels that are hard to read. It takes me ages to figure out that one says Chloroform LR. The labels on the smaller bottles say Midazolam Injection BP and Mezolam 10 mg. I don't know what that means.

"Why is this here?" Pari asks.

"What is it?" Faiz asks.

"The headmaster talked about syringes and sleep-making medicines, remember?" Pari says. "Maybe you weren't at school that day."

"Faiz was there," I say. "It was before Tariq-Bhai was arrested."

"Chloroform puts you to sleep," Pari says. "Even forever."

"Don't touch the bottles," I say. "Fingerprints. Evidence."

"Does this mean," Faiz asks, "that the boss-lady is a child-snatcher? Did she and Varun run a child-snatching business together? Was this their headquarters?"

"But," Pari says, "this woman is a friend of the pradhan and the police commissioner. Does that mean . . . what does it mean? They knew she was a criminal and did nothing?"

"Where has she kept Runu-Didi?" I ask.

"We'll find her," Pari says. "The boss-lady will have to tell the police the truth now."

"Take a video of this," Faiz tells a chacha who is picking up the knives in a drawer and examining them against the light, maybe to decide which one he should sneak out of the flat. "See, this bottle, it's a sleep-making medicine. That Varun must have used it to kidnap children and bring them here to his boss-lady."

The chacha puts the knife down and does what Faiz asks. Police constables run into the kitchen, batons held high, panting, shouting, **out, now, you monkeys**.

"We have proof that the madam of this flat, your commissioner's best friend, is guilty. She's a child-snatcher," Pari tells them.

"We have already taken videos of all this," Faiz says, "and we have sent it to a thousand people. You can't make it go away."

The policemen lower their batons. They ask the other people in the kitchen to file out. The chacha who took the video stays.

"Check these labels," Pari tells the policemen. "These drugs, they put people to sleep. Why does this woman have these in her flat? It's illegal. You have to arrest her."

The kitchen is silent except for something humming, maybe the fridge or a light. A policeman tries to touch the bucket but Pari stops him. "Where are your gloves?" she asks.

"That Varun must have hidden the bottles here. Do you think a boss-lady bothers with the rubbish under her kitchen sink?" a constable asks.

A scream is growing inside me and I feel like I will explode all over the ceiling. I stand up and move my hand to the kitchen counter where there is a black bowl filled with oranges. I push it to the edge as Pari talks to the policemen. Then I tip it over. The bowl shatters. The oranges roll around the floor, stopping at people's feet.

Papa and Ma and Pari's ma and Wajid-Bhai come into the kitchen.

"Pari," her ma cries. "I thought you had disappeared."

"Runu-Didi isn't here," I say to Ma and Papa.

In the living room, the inspector explains to the boss-lady that it is in her best interest to go with him to the police station. "I can't guarantee your safety here," he says. Then he orders us to leave or face arrest. "You can see there are no children here. Madam can't be held responsible for what that vile man did. But we're taking her in for questioning anyway."

Papa and Wajid-Bhai shepherd us out of the crowd with their spread-wide arms. We take the lift down, walk past the entrance strewn with glass, out of the gate and the broken boom barriers. TV vans are parked on one side of the road, behind police vehicles. A reporter stands with a mike under a street lamp that has come on. The cameraman tells her to move a little to the left.

"This is going to be on TV," Pari's ma says, sounding surprised. "Now the police will have to do something."

"It's too late," I say without meaning to, but after I say it, I know it's true.

ALL WINTER THE SMOG
HAS BEEN STEALING—

—the colors of our basti and now everything has turned grey-white, even the faces of Ma and Papa as a newswoman pushes a mike into their faces. I stand outside Shanti-Chachi's door, half-hiding behind chachi.

It's been three days since we found the sleep-making bottles in the boss-lady's Golden Gate flat. Our basti has become famous and also the opposite of famous. Every hour a new TV van pulls up at Bhoot Bazaar. Reporters who look only slightly older than Runu-Didi dash around with their camerapersons, talking to anyone who'll talk to them.

The journalist who is interviewing Ma and Papa

now is doing a story about the parents of missing children. She told us so. Papa holds in his hands the photo of Runu-Didi we showed the police. Ma presses the pallu of her sari against her mouth.

"We would like our daughter back please," Papa says, extending Didi's photo closer to the camera. His usually too-loud voice is so soft now, the microphone can barely catch it.

The reporter swishes her hair back. "Speak up," she mouths.

"Our daughter, please, give her back," Papa says. Then he and Ma stare into the camera in silence. The reporter makes a cut-throat hand gesture to the camerawoman.

Shanti-Chachi calls the reporter over. "Did the police tell you why they ignored our complaints for so long?" chachi asks. "Did they say why they didn't look for a single missing child for over two months?"

The cameraperson zooms in on Shanti-Chachi.

"Will the police let the owner of the flat go because she's rich?" chachi wants to know. "Where has she hidden our children?"

"Did you get that?" the reporter asks the camerawoman, who nods. She turns her back to chachi and says to the camera, "The residents of this blighted slum are accusing the police of negligence. Questions are being raised about the role of Ms. Yamini Mehra, the owner of the penthouse flat worth seven crores at Golden Gate. Ms. Mehra has asserted that she was unaware of her servant Varun Kumar's nefarious activities in the flat. Meanwhile rumors are spreading like wildfire about Varun Kumar's motives. Was he part of a child-trafficking ring or a kidney racket? What has he done with the children he snatched? Why did he collect souvenirs from his victims, which the police have pointed out, is the behavior of a serial killer?"

Ma crumples to the ground. The camerawoman bends down so that she can catch Ma's sadness for the news at nine. Shanti-Chachi runs to Ma's side and puts her hand on Ma's back before Papa can.

"How can you live with yourself?" Shanti-Chachi shouts at the camerawoman. "You want us to cry, pull our hair out, beat our chests. What will you get from it, a promotion, a big bonus next Diwali?"

The camerawoman stands up.

"Let's go to another house," the reporter tells her.

"Yes, leave, that will be very easy for you to do," chachi says. "We're the ones who have to be here, today and tomorrow and the day after that. This is our life you're talking about as if it's just some story. Do you even understand that?"

———

Runu-Didi's friends come to see us. They are here and Didi isn't and it seems wrong. Ma asks them to sit on the bed, then we fold ourselves into the corners of our house. The girls don't know what to say; we don't know what to tell them. Ma's alarm clock tick-tocks awkwardly, misshaping time between its slow hands. It feels like morning and night and yesterday and tomorrow and last week and next week all at once.

Papa asks Didi's friends if they had seen Varun Kumar hanging around the school. They say no. I saw him so many times and I talked to him too and I never thought he was the kidnapper.

Didi's coach visits us with Mitali and Tara and Harini and Jhanvi.

"Runu, she was the best of the lot," Coach says as if Didi is no longer alive. "Faster than anyone I have trained in my life."

"It's true," Tara says. "It will be tough for our team to win without her."

Nana and Nani call Ma on her mobile. "I told you that place wasn't safe," Nani says. "I told you to send the children to live with us."

Ma cuts the call.

Pari and Faiz turn up with Wajid-Bhai, who says the lawyer his ammi has hired is certain Tariq-Bhai will be released soon. "Things always turn out okay," he says.

"When will you be back at school?" Pari asks me. "After the exams will work best. I told Kirpal-Sir he can expect you then."

"Pari's ma is talking about moving to another basti," Faiz says.

"Shut up," Pari tells him. "Your ammi is the one who's planning to move."

"Move where?" I ask.

"Ammi thinks we should go to a place where there are more of us." Faiz scratches his scar. "More Muslims. Then the Hindu Samaj can't threaten us like they keep doing here."

———

When our house is empty, and it is dark outside, Ma serves Papa and me the roti and aloo Shanti-Chachi's husband made for us. We pretend to eat, moving food from one side of the plate to another. I no longer feel hungry, but I chew a piece of roti so that my stomach won't hurt at night like it has been hurting the past few nights.

Shanti-Chachi comes running to our door and asks Papa to switch on the TV news. Then she puts her hand around Ma's shoulder, as if preparing her for something terrible. A newsreader wearing a black jacket, her hair pulled back tight from her forehead, says that chilling details have just emerged in the **Slumdog Kidnapping** case.

"Varun Kumar has confessed that he lured victims with drug-laden sweets or rendered them unconscious with sedative injections, bottles of which were recovered from the flat where he was a caretaker. His wife, who cleaned and occasionally worked as a cook at the same flat, is thought to have been his accomplice. More shockingly, police sources say Varun Kumar has confessed to killing and dismembering the children he abducted. He carried their body parts in plastic bags tied to his bicycle and dumped them in rubbish grounds, drains around malls and the metro stations on the Purple Line. These abductions were not limited to the slum where he lived. He is thought to have preyed on street children too. The exact number of those missing is still unclear. Is it seven or seventy, we simply do not know. The police hope that the souvenirs he collected will help them identify his victims."

A policeman's face fills the screen, an assistant commissioner maybe. Mikes are held up toward his mouth by invisible hands.

"We have launched an extensive search for the recovery of the children's remains," he says.

I don't understand. Are they talking about Runu-Didi and Bahadur?

The newsreader returns. "It's learned that following complaints of negligence by the local police, the case is likely to be transferred to the CBI, which will look into the possibility that Varun Kumar was part of a wider trafficking ring that indulged in child pornography or organ trade."

Ma snatches the remote from Papa's hand.

"The posh penthouse flat costing eight crores is thought to have been the site of these brutal murders. The role of the owner of the flat, Yamini Mehra, a socialite often spotted at parties alongside politicians and top policemen"—the TV screen shows photos where the boss-lady is standing next to politicians and policemen dressed in a commissioner's or a DCP's or an ACP's uniform—"is as yet unclear."

"My child isn't dead," Ma says.

"Of course she isn't," Shanti-Chachi says.

Ma switches off the TV and throws the remote against the wall.

———

JCBs return to the rubbish ground the next day. They are looking for **remains**. I don't understand why the police think Varun killed the children he snatched. Even if he said so, he must be lying. He isn't a djinn to cut them up or eat them; if he were really a djinn, he would have disappeared instead of staying in jail.

Papa and I watch the machines. Papa convinced Ma to go to work, telling her she'll have a heart attack if she has to witness every plastic bag in the rubbish ground being opened. "Our daughter isn't here," he promises Ma. He calls her every half hour, or she calls him. "Nothing," he says each time. "I told you Runu isn't here."

The police have formed cordons around the sections of the rubbish ground that the JCBs are plowing. They don't let anyone in, not even the scavenger children and the people who want to do No. 1 and No. 2.

"If there were bodies in the rubbish, one of my children would have seen them by now," Bottle-Badshah tells anyone who will listen.

Aanchal's papa turns up to taunt the policemen. "You said my daughter ran off with a boy, haan, and see what's happened. Are you happy now?" he asks.

"Thumper-Baba didn't bring your daughter back," I tell him. "You thought he would." I don't care if it makes him angrier.

"I won't let that fake baba set foot in our basti again," he says. "I should have never listened to him or the pradhan."

Papa asks a cop we have never seen before if what we heard on TV is true. "They said he hid the children in drains, but the stench itself, people would have noticed?"

The policeman says they have already located a bag behind a mall that has a 4D cinema on the top floor, but it's too early to tell whose **remains** it holds. The bag was found in the exact place where

Varun Kumar told them it was, which means he's speaking the truth.

"And the state of our drains?" the policeman says. "All of them stink of death. Ever seen anybody clean one? Look at how our roads flood when there's even a single shower."

"Why would a man like Varun confess to the snatchings?" Papa asks.

"The investigating officers must have used truth serum on him," the policeman says. "One injection and you can't lie for hours. Two injections, and he won't be able to shut up until he tells us where every child is buried."

I saw something about that injection on the news or maybe it was on **Live Crime**, but I didn't think it was real.

"Is it true," Aanchal's papa asks now, "that the Mehra woman brought strange men into her flat late at night? I heard there are eighty flats in that building. Nobody in those eighty flats saw or heard anything?"

"The police need time to question all the residents and find out what they saw and what they didn't," the constable says. "Not just residents, but also maids, gardeners, sweepers, watchmen. Trust me, we're doing everything we can. We're checking their mobile-phone records, finding out who the madam and her manservant talked to."

"But what the TV is saying about Mehra's male friends, that they were surgeons brought in to harvest the children's kidneys, that just can't be true, can it?" Aanchal's papa persists.

"Who knows," the policeman says. "The rich think they can buy anything, even us."

"The problem," Aanchal's papa says, "is that policemen like you are suspicious of maids and carpenters and plumbers, but when you see a hi-fi madam or sir, you bow your head, you jump out of the way."

The policeman laughs but it's a bitter laugh.

"If you bring sniffer dogs," I tell him, "you can find the missing children faster."

He shakes his head as if he has had enough of us and starts to walk away. But then he stops. "The top brass believes this is a clear-cut case," he says. "There's enough evidence to prosecute those who have been arrested. Besides, a dog won't be able to track a single smell in a dump like this."

Nothing of note is found in the rubbish except for scraps of school uniform and cut-up children's shoes. The police seal these for testing in case they belong to the missing children; I wonder if Samosa brought me here because he knew what was buried in the trash. Maybe he can do things that police sniffer dogs can't.

In the evening, when the JCBs go quiet, Papa

takes me home and asks Shanti-Chachi to watch me. He says he'll be back soon.

Chachi sits right next to me, as if to make sure I won't go anywhere.

Where will I go now? I'm not a detective. If I had been one, I wouldn't have let anybody snatch Runu-Didi.

"Your didi is fine. I know it. I feel it," chachi tells me.

I know nothing. I feel nothing. Sometimes, like right now, everything inside me goes numb, even my brain.

———

Ma gets home early. Shanti-Chachi tells her she doesn't know where Papa is, and Ma says, "He called me." She has brought fresh vegetables and eggs from Bhoot Bazaar. Runu-Didi used to ask Ma for eggs when she first started training, but Ma told her we weren't crorepatis like the Ambanis to eat what we wanted. Now Didi isn't here but we have eggs. It makes me angry, but I don't say anything.

Without the TV that Ma won't let me watch, the silence in our house is too-loud. I rustle the pages of a textbook, I wonder why Pari and Faiz haven't come to see me. Pari's ma has told her she can only walk around the basti if she has a grown-up with her. Maybe Pari didn't find a grown-up today. Faiz must be working still. Ma's knife goes chop-chop-chop. Oil sizzles, cumin seeds sputter, onions turn brown. Our house smells like it did when Runu-Didi cooked.

I lie on my tummy, on the bed, not reading my book. I smell Drunkard Laloo and look up. It's Papa. He stumbles to the bed and sits down, almost on my hand. I pull it away in time. He asks me to move so that he can lie down.

"Look, I made all of Runu's favorites," Ma says. She hasn't even noticed that Papa is drunk. "Anda-bhurji, baingan-bharta and roti."

Ma gets up and stands at the door as if she expects Runu-Didi to run into the lane at any moment. I wait with Ma.

Papa falls asleep. The food goes cold.

TODAY IT'S EXACTLY A MONTH SINCE RUNU-DIDI—

—disappeared. Inside our house, Didi's clothes are still waiting for her on footstools; I put out her pillow at night when I sleep; and I never roll over to her side of our mat. But outside our house, the world is changing. Fatima-ben and other Muslims have moved to another basti across the river, where only Muslims live. Some Hindus call that place Chhota-Pakistan.

Faiz and his family are also moving there. Today is his last day in our basti. Right now, Pari and I are helping Wajid-Bhai and Faiz pack up. We came here straight after school. Faiz's ammi and his sister are already in Chhota-Pakistan with most of their stuff. Tariq-Bhai can't help with the move because he's still in jail. He's supposed to be released soon, maybe this week even, but we can't be sure. The police take ages to do anything.

By the time we are finished, Faiz's house looks big because all the things and people in it are gone. It smells of cobwebs abandoned by spiders and dust left to thicken behind cupboards. Pari and I carry the last of their belongings outside in plastic bags. We wait for a cycle-rickshaw that Wajid-Bhai has arranged.

Some of the neighbor-chachas and chachis and children come out into the alley to watch Faiz and Wajid-Bhai leave. I take off my sweater and tie it around my waist. If Runu-Didi were to return today, she would be shocked to see that the smog is almost gone. It's a lot warmer too, too warm for February.

Sometimes I forget Didi is gone. The police say that everyone missing is presumed dead, but Ma says Didi will come back **tomorrow**. She has been saying that for days. I don't believe her.

"I never returned the money I took from you," Pari tells Faiz. It sounds like she's saying she'll never see Faiz again.

"After you become a doctor, treat me for free," Faiz says. His face and hands and even his white scar have turned dark from selling roses on the highway. "If you see me at a junction when you are driving around in your big car, slow down and buy all my flowers so that I can chutti-maro for the day."

"You're seriously not thinking of being a rose-seller your whole life, are you?" Pari says. "You should join a school near your new basti."

I feel as if a hundred butterflies are fluttering inside my chest. What is a whole life? If you die when you're still a child, is your life whole or half or zero?

"Chi, what are you doing?" Pari says, pushing Faiz away when he drops snot on her while trying to give her a hug.

I hug Faiz. Then he goes across the alley to say okay-tata-bye to his neighbors.

"Faiz is very sad to leave you two," Wajid-Bhai says. "But it isn't safe for us here. Someone was saying again at the toilet complex yesterday that we Muslims kidnapped Kabir and Khadifa and killed Buffalo-Baba to put the blame on the Hindu Samaj. It's tough to listen to such things every day. Allah knows why they still blame us."

"They're mad," Pari says.

"And Tariq-Bhai, once you have been in jail, that's a stain that doesn't wash off. He'll have better luck finding a job among our people."

Pari nods.

"You'll be leaving soon too, right?" Wajid-Bhai asks her. "You'll be a star at your new school. I heard every student gets to use a computer there."

Pari looks at me because she knows I don't like hearing about it. "I won't be going anywhere until this school year is finished," she says. "It might not even happen."

The cycle-rickshaw arrives. Wajid-Bhai loads the last of the bags into it. The rickshaw-wallah's feet are lined with deep cracks and ash-colored patches of dead skin. The back of his neck glistens silver with sweat.

Faiz sprints back to our side. "I'll come to school one of these days," he says. "When you're having the midday meal. That way I'll get lunch too."

"They're going to cut your name from the roll," Pari says.

"They haven't struck off Bahadur yet, and he has been gone for three months," Faiz says. "It will be a year or two before they get to me."

"Let us know when Tariq-Bhai is released," Pari tells Wajid-Bhai. "You can call my ma. Faiz has her mobile number."

"Inshallah it will happen soon," Wajid-Bhai says.

"Tariq-Bhai won't touch his mobile after the police release him," Faiz tells Pari and me. "He'll never want anything to do with a mobile again, so his mobile will become mine, and then I'll call your ammi and"—his eyes shift from my face to Pari's—"your ammi."

"Poor Tariq-Bhai," Pari says. "If the police had tracked Aanchal's mobile, the way Tariq-Bhai told you, that Varun-monster would have been caught before—"

She coughs, because she knows better than to complete that sentence.

"The good djinns at the djinn-palace are watching out for Tariq-Bhai," Wajid-Bhai says. "Jai, tell your ma to pray there."

"That place isn't as scary as it looks from the outside," Faiz says, clasping his amulet.

He and Wajid-Bhai get on the cycle-rickshaw. "You'll go to the palace for sure?" Faiz asks me, leaning out of the passenger seat.

I wave goodbye.

The rickshaw-wallah presses the pedals but the rickshaw is heavy, and it takes him a while to get going. Pari and I and others in the alley watch the rickshaw barely move forward.

Someone says a Hindu family is going to buy Faiz's house. A family with four children and a ma and a papa and a dadi too. I don't think I'll be friends with any of them. They probably don't even know what Purple Lotus and Cream soap is.

———

I tell Pari I'm going to the rubbish ground. "Ma won't be home for another two hours," I say.

"I'll go with you," she says. Her ma isn't home either.

We don't stay out in the dark anymore. We don't want our parents to worry. They have stopped following us around though. Maybe because no one else has been snatched since Varun, his wife and boss-lady were arrested.

"Do you think the boss-lady is innocent?" I ask Pari though we have talked about it many times before. "Her lawyer has applied for bail."

"She won't get it," Pari says. "It's such a big case, it's going to come on **Police Patrol**."

I'll never watch **Police Patrol** again. When they act out real stories of people getting snatched or killed, it will feel as if someone is trying to strangle me, I just know it. A murder isn't a story for me anymore; it's not a mystery either.

"The basti-women who work in Golden Gate, they're saying now that politicians and police commissioners went into the boss-lady's flat at night," I say. "Those VIPs will get her out."

Many things about the case make no sense to me, which is why I have to keep asking Pari about it. Even the newspeople on the TV I'm not supposed to watch, but which I secretly watch before Ma gets home, are confused. The reporters say different things each day, and their guesses change like the price of the boss-lady's flat, which was four crores one day and twelve crores the next day and **costs next to nothing today after the** shocking revelations that have caused property prices at Golden Gate to plummet.

According to the same reporters, the boss-lady and her manservant were part of a trafficking ring, a kidney racket, and a child pornography racket, which is a kind of racket that involves making films with children. They say the manservant is a psychopath who abused and killed children; the manservant and his wife went rogue and killed the children who were meant to be trafficked; the boss-lady is innocent; the boss-lady is a **criminal mastermind who enjoyed the patronage of India's top politicians.**

The headlines on the TV news are horrible. Sometimes I see them when I'm trying to sleep, blinking under my eyelids like neon lights:

EXCLUSIVE! Inside the Penthouse of Horrors!

Slumdog Killer Reveals Gruesome Details of Murders

Owner of Luxury Flat Pleads Not Guilty

Behind a Golden Facade, a Shocking Story of a Kidney Racket

What Really Happened in Golden Gate. See it first here!

Confessions of the Man-Eater of Golden Gate!

"We might never find out what really happened in that flat because we have useless police," Pari tells me. "The only reason Varun Kumar got caught, it's because he's too stupid. If he hadn't snatched Kabir and Khadifa, the basti-people would have kept on blaming Muslims. There might have been riots also."

"He mustn't have realized they were Muslim," I say. "Doesn't Faiz look Hindu to you?"

"Why did that idiot have to move?" Pari says.

We reach the rubbish ground. The JCBs are long gone. A woman flings a bucket of vegetable peels and fish bones into the trash. We hear a shout. It's Aanchal's papa, who has been watching over the ground ever since the police found bits of Aanchal's bag and the clothes she was wearing on the day she vanished—the yellow kurta that Pari noted in her report—in the rubbish.

"You're dumping rubbish on my daughter's grave?" Aanchal's papa asks the woman.

"What do you want us to do?" the woman says. "You think we should keep this"—she swings her empty bucket toward the trash—"inside our house?"

"The CBI will arrest you when they come," Aanchal's papa says. "You're ruining evidence."

"You have lost your daughter, I understand, but all this screaming at us, that's not going to bring her back."

Pari and I see Bottle-Badshah talking to the scavenger children. We walk over to them, ask them how they are. The helicopter-girl who told us about Varun hiding the blue box in the trash, on the day he was caught, is with Bottle-Badshah, and today she's holding a stick-thin, pink doll that has golden hair and zero clothes.

Bottle-Badshah squeezes my shoulder. The parrot on his forearm gives me the side-eye. "Sometimes," he says, "when I see the news on TV, I can't even watch it, the kind of shocking, filthy things they say those monsters did to our children."

"We should be getting home," Pari cuts him short.

"Yes, of course," Bottle-Badshah says. Helicopter-Girl holds out her doll toward me, because she feels sorry for me maybe.

"He doesn't play with dolls," Pari says.

"It must be hard for you to understand what is happening," Bottle-Badshah tells me. "But whenever you think of your sister, my wish for you is that you won't think of the horrors she may have experienced in that flat. I'll pray that you'll remember her at her very best, doing what she enjoyed doing, even if it was just watching funny programs on TV."

"Runu-Didi didn't watch a lot of TV," I say.

"Believe me," the badshah says, "today or tomorrow, every one of us will lose someone close to us, someone we love. The lucky ones are those who can grow old pretending they have some control over their lives, but even they will realize at some point that everything is uncertain, bound to disappear forever. We are just specks of dust in this world, glimmering for a moment in the sunlight, and then disappearing into nothing. You have to learn to make your peace with that."

"I'll try," I say even though I have no idea what he means.

———

I follow Pari to her house. Her neighbor-chachis ask her about her new school. It's a private school across the river, near her dada-dadi's house, where she has got admission with a full scholarship, which means she doesn't have to pay fees. The private-school people felt bad for her after seeing our basti in the news. Pari tells the chachis that her ma and papa have to find jobs near the school before they can move.

Pasted on the water barrel of Pari's neighbor's house is a leaflet with the words **Release Our Children Now**. It's the old leaflet that the Hindu Samaj distributed after Chandni went missing. Someone has drawn a mustache on Bahadur's photo. The police dredged up his shoes from a drain near a mall. They told Bahadur's ma that they have also **recovered** his bones, but they need to do more DNA-testing to be hundred percent certain. The police haven't found anything of Runu-Didi's other than the scrunchie.

"Why don't you stay?" Pari asks me when I say I'm leaving. "Ma is going to make Maggi for dinner tonight."

"My ma won't like it if I'm not home by then."

I keep my head down as I fast-walk toward somewhere, not home, because I don't want to go home just yet. But no matter how quickly I walk, chachas and chachis pounce on me and ask me the questions they can't ask Ma and Papa. I should start running everywhere like Runu-Didi. Then these people won't be able to stop me.

"Heard anything about your sister?" a man blocking my way asks.

"Your sister who was snatched," a woman standing next to him explains as if I don't know.

"Have the police called your parents about her?" asks a girl with black dirt folded into the creases of her neck.

"They say they don't know how many children are missing," the woman tells the man, "seven, twenty, thirty, maybe a hundred, a thousand even."

"There aren't that many children in our basti," the man says.

"Arrey, they were kidnapping street children and those ragpicker children too."

"The police are still doing DNA tests," I say.

"How long will this testing take?" the girl asks.

"Months," I say. I have no idea. Maybe when the CBI come, they'll speed everything up. Maybe they won't. I think Pari is right, and we'll never find out what the monsters at Golden Gate did to Runu-Didi.

More jabbering chachas and chachis appear out of nowhere, trying to trip me with questions. I slip out of the crowd and run toward Bahadur's house. I like to spy on other families that are sad like ours because I want to find out if they are doing anything different to stop ghosts from clutching their bones.

Shanti-Chachi keeps telling me that I have to man up now and take care of Ma and Papa. I am worried about Ma. Every night as we eat, she stares at my face, maybe hoping to see Runu-Didi in me, and then she turns away disappointed, tears trickling down her cheeks. Ma has also become so thin and weak I'm afraid she'll fall down and die one of these days, and it will just be me and Papa, and Papa doesn't even talk much anymore. He comes home smelling of hooch and staggers into bed. He's becoming Drunkard Laloo 2.

Bahadur's house is lying locked but there are TV people in front of it, interviewing Quarter. He has traded his black clothes for a saffron shirt and khaki trousers.

"We were the only party to step in when the

local police refused to help," he says. "We are an integral part of this community."

I wonder if the pradhan and Quarter knew the truth about Varun; if the boss-lady gave the pradhan a cut for every child from the basti who vanished. I heard Shanti-Chachi's husband say that to a man in front of him at the toilet queue.

I think of throwing stones at Quarter, then I decide I don't want to make him angry. What if he kidnaps me? What will happen to Ma and Papa then? I walk toward Bhoot Bazaar instead. I'll say hello to Samosa and then I'll go home for sure.

———

Our house is full of bad dreams. Ma has them and I have them too. In my dreams Runu-Didi flies out of a balcony in the Golden Gate building, spreading out her giant wings. She's Jatayu from ancient times but she's also wounded and bleeding. Ma doesn't tell me what her dreams are. From the way she gets up screaming, I can tell they are dreadful.

I feel a shadow, cold and lonely, passing over me. I look up, afraid it's the bird, afraid it's Didi. But the sky is empty. Something brushes against my legs. It's Samosa. I kneel down to scratch his ears. His pink tongue flops out as if he's smiling.

I search my pockets for food but they are empty.

Samosa nuzzles up against my legs. He doesn't care that I have nothing to give him. He's my real friend. Faiz has left me and Pari is leaving me but Samosa will never leave me.

I go to Duttaram's. He doesn't talk to me because he's busy.

I tell Samosa to come with me and we walk toward my house. I'm going to ask Ma and Papa if Samosa can live with us because, first of all, Samosa is clever; second of all, Samosa is like a policeman but a good one; and third of all, Samosa won't let anyone snatch me. These are excellent reasons.

"Race you home," I tell Samosa.

He watches me, wagging his tail.

"We're going to see who runs the fastest. Theek-thaak?" I ask him. "On your marks, get set, GO!" Then I run as fast as I can. My heart feels like it's exploding, my tongue hangs out like Samosa's, but I only stop when I reach my doorstep. Then I breathe in and out with my hands on my knees.

I turn around to see where Samosa is. He's trotting toward me, panting and looking puzzled. "I won I won I won," I shout, scaring the chickens and goats near us. Samosa licks my hands. He's not a sore loser.

"I'm the fastest runner in the world," I say.

"What a joke," I hear Runu-Didi say.

"Shut up," I say and then I remember that though her voice is still in my head, she isn't around. I sit down on our doorstep. Samosa puts his head on my lap. His fur is soft and warm. The TV blares in Shanti-Chachi's house. "Should slums be demolished? Have your say. Send us your thoughts on . . ."

I gaze up at the sky. Today the smog is a curtain thin enough for me to spot the twinkle of a star behind it. I can't even remember when I last saw a star.

"Look," I say to Samosa. But it's already gone. Maybe it was never there. Maybe it was only a satellite or an airplane. Maybe it was Runu-Didi telling me I shouldn't worry because gods are real and are taking good care of her. She's watching over me the way Mental watches over his boys, I just know it.

Then I see the star again. I point it out to Samosa. I tell him it's a secret signal, from Runu-Didi to me. It's so powerful, it can fire past the thickets of clouds and smog and even the walls that Ma's gods have put up to separate one world from the next.

AFTERWORD

I worked as a reporter in India from 1997 to 2008 and, for many of these years, I wrote news stories and features on the subject of education. Each day I talked to school and college principals, teachers, government officials, and, most important, students. Growing up in a home where finances were tight, I had believed that I had limited opportunities to pursue what I wanted to do, but as a journalist I saw that even those limited avenues were closed to young people from the most impoverished of backgrounds. I interviewed children who worked as scavengers or begged at traffic junctions, who struggled to study at home because of their difficult domestic circumstances, and who had to drop out of school after being displaced by religious violence. But most of them didn't present themselves to me as victims; they were cheeky and funny and often impatient in the face of my questions. We as a society, and the governments we elected, had abandoned them, as my articles inevitably pointed out, but writing under the constraints of word counts and deadlines, I failed to communicate their humor, sarcasm, and energy.

Around the same time, I started learning about the widespread disappearances of children from poor families. As many as 180 children are said to go missing in India every day. These disappearances typically make the news only when a kidnapper is nabbed, or if there are graphic details surrounding the crime. Perhaps because of all the time I had spent interviewing children about their aspirations, my interest was naturally in their stories, but these were nowhere to be found. The media focused mostly on the perpetrators. Before I could investigate this further, a change in my circumstances resulted in my leaving India, the country where I was born and grew up.

The article that I hadn't been able to write, about the missing children and their families, stayed with me. In London, I enrolled in a creative writing course and, for my first submission, tried to write about them and failed. I worried about the ethical

questions having to do with the fictional represen-
tation of a marginalized, vulnerable group of people.
I didn't want to minimize the inequalities I had
witnessed around me, but a story about a horrific
tragedy risked becoming part of a stereotypical nar-
rative about poverty and India that equated people
with their problems.

In winter 2016, I finally went back to the story
that I had set aside years earlier. In part this was
because, with Brexit, the election of Donald
Trump, and the rise of the right wing in India
and other countries, there was the sense that the
world was closing in on those perceived to be
"outsiders" or "minorities," groups to which I now
belonged as an immigrant in Britain. I thought of
the children I used to interview, their determina-
tion to survive in a society that often willfully
neglected them, and I realized that the story had
to be told from their perspective. Nine-year-old
Jai became my way into this novel. In Jai and his
friends, I tried to capture the traits that my news
articles had ignored: the children's resilience,
cheerfulness, and swagger.

My own life changed unexpectedly just as I
started working on this novel. An uncle I had looked
up to all my life, the kindest of people, a doctor
who treated patients for free if they didn't have
money, died. My only sibling, six years younger
than I, was diagnosed with a Stage IV cancer.

Suddenly the questions that Jai and his friends were confronting, even if obliquely, became my own and those of my family. How does one live with uncertainty each day? How do you find hope when you are told there is none? And what about my nephew, only eight years old at the time? How does one explain mortality to a child? I found I couldn't discuss these questions with others, not even my closest friends; instead, I turned to the characters in this book, seeking answers in their actions.

While personal experiences informed this book as much as professional, I should underscore that this novel is **not** my story, and it was never meant to be. But, in writing it, I was conscious of the narratives we craft to make sense of sadness and chaos, as Jai and others do in this book, and all the ways in which such stories may comfort or even fail us. This awareness erased on the page the many years between me and my characters, but ultimately **Djinn Patrol on the Purple Line** is about the children, and them alone. I wrote this novel to challenge the notion that they could be reduced to statistics. I wrote this so that we are reminded of the faces behind the numbers.

A final comment. As I write this note, in September 2019, India is seeing a disturbing phenomenon wherein rumors and WhatsApp forwards about child-snatchers have caused mobs to lynch those accused, many of them innocent people from marginalized, poor communities, those perceived to be "outsiders" to the area, or those with disabilities. It comes in the wake of similar mob fury against minorities, particularly Muslims, and a growing atmosphere of distrust in the country. The contradiction inherent in this situation can't be ignored: Children continue to disappear in India daily, child trafficking remains a real problem that doesn't get much attention, and yet there are people quick to act as vigilantes on the basis of rumors and false news, perhaps driven by fears of the "other" stoked by those in power.

Hope comes in the form of charities that work with children from impoverished communities. Those interested in learning more about them can look up the following organizations: Pratham (prathamusa.org), Childline (childlineindia.org .in), Salaam Baalak Trust (salaambaalaktrust .com), HAQ: Centre for Child Rights (haqcrc .org), International Justice Mission (ijm.org/ india), Goranbose Gram Bikash Kendra (ggbk .in) and MV Foundation (mvfindia.in).

GLOSSARY

ABBU
father

ACCHA
"I see"; "okay"; "yes"

ADDA
a place where people gather for conversation

AKHARA
a place where wrestling is taught and practiced

AMMI
mother

GLOSSARY

ARREY
a catch-all term used to express a range of
emotions such as surprise, interest,
exasperation, or excitement; can also be used
to mean "hey"

BABA
holy; can also be a term of endearment

BADSHAH
monarch, king

BAJI
elder sister

BAKWAS
nonsense

BASTI
settlement

BEEDI
Indian cigarettes

BEN
sister; also used as a term of respect for a
woman; can indicate closeness

BETA
son

BHAI
brother; also used to address a man

BHAIYYA
brother

GLOSSARY

BHOOT
ghost

CHAAT
savory snacks

CHACHA
uncle; used here as a term of respect

CHACHI
aunt; used here as a term of respect

CHADDI
underwear

CHALO
"let's go"

CHARPAI
a bed made with rope strung across a
wooden frame

CHOKRA
boy

CHOR
robber; chor-police is a game children play

CHOWKI
a police station; in this context, a smaller
police station that operates under a bigger
one

CHUTTI
holiday, leave

GLOSSARY

DADA-DADI
paternal grandfather–paternal grandmother

DARU
alcohol

DHABA
modest restaurant that serve food, usually on
the roadside

DIDI
elder sister

DOST
friend

EKDUM
completely

GHERAO
a protest in which people surround a person
or a building; similar to picketing

GOONDA
thug

GULAB-JAMUN
a deep-fried sweet made with evaporated
milk or milk powder, served in a sugary
rosewater and/or cardamom-scented
syrup

HAAN
yes

GLOSSARY

HAFTA
protection money (literally, "week"; protection money was typically paid weekly)

HATTA-KATTA
robust, strong, sturdy

JANTAR MANTAR JADU MANTAR
phrase used by magicians in India, similar to "abracadabra"

JASOOS
spy, sleuth, detective

JCB
construction and manufacturing equipment, such as a backhoe

KABADI-WALLAH
scrap dealer, scrap collector

KIRANA
small grocery shop

KOTHA
brothel

KYA
what

MALIK
owner, master

MERI JAAN
"my life"; a term of endearment

GLOSSARY

MULLAH
Islamic cleric, leader of a mosque; used here to indicate a Muslim man

NA
"Right?" "Isn't it?"

NANA
maternal grandfather

NANI
maternal grandmother

PAKKA
certain

PALLU
the loose end of the sari, worn over the shoulder

PANDAL
tentlike structure

PRADHAN
chief, leader

PRESS-WALLAH
someone who irons clothes for a living

PUJA
prayer, or a prayer ritual performed to honor a deity and to seek blessings

PURI
deep-fried bread

GLOSSARY

RANDI
whore

RANI
queen

ROTI
round flatbread

SAAB
sir

SHAITAN
devil, evil spirit

SONA
gold, precious; in this context, a term of
endearment

THEEK-THAAK
"All fine? Everything all right?"

THEKA
liquor shop

YAAR
friend, pal, buddy

ACKNOWLEDGMENTS

While working as a journalist in India, I often visited bastis like Jai's, and I am deeply indebted to the residents who invited me into their homes and shared their stories with me. If not for their kindness and generosity, I wouldn't have been able to write this novel. I am also grateful for the insights I found in the following works: **The Illegal City: Space, Law and Gender in a Delhi Squatter Settlement** (Ashgate, Surrey, 2012) by Ayona Datta; **In the Public's Interest: Evictions, Citizenship and Inequality in Contemporary Delhi** (Orient Blackswan, New Delhi, 2016) by Gautam Bhan; and **Swept Off the Map: Surviving Eviction and Resettlement in**

ACKNOWLEDGMENTS

Delhi (Yoda Press, New Delhi, 2008) by Kalyani Menon-Sen and Gautam Bhan. A list of the books and articles that informed this novel is available on my website, deepa-anappara.com.

I count myself fortunate to be working with two brilliant and generous agents, Peter Straus and Matthew Turner, who have steered me through the publication process with wit and warmth. Special thanks to Matt for his editorial suggestions, his good humor, and his steadfast refusal to be fazed by the most neurotic of my questions. Thanks also to the foreign rights team at RCW, particularly Stephen Edwards, Laurence Laluyaux, Tristan Kendrick, and Katharina Volckmer, and to Gill Coleridge and everyone else at RCW.

I couldn't have asked for more enthusiastic and meticulous editors than Clara Farmer at Chatto & Windus and Caitlin McKenna at Random House. My thanks to them for taking Jai and his friends to their hearts, for their sensitivity, and for their incisive edits. My gratitude to everyone at Vintage, particularly Charlotte Humphery for her patience and support, Suzanne Dean, Lucie Cuthbertson-Twiggs, and Anna Redman Aylward. Thanks to David Milner for his copyedit and John Garrett for his proofread. Thanks also to Emma Caruso, Greg Mollica, Evan Camfield, Maria Braeckel, Melissa Sanford, Katie Tull, and everyone else at Random House, New York. I am particularly grateful to

ACKNOWLEDGMENTS

have had the support and encouragement of the late Susan Kamil.

My thanks to the team at Penguin Random House, India, particularly Manasi Subramaniam for her suggestions, and Gunjan Ahlawat.

My love and gratitude to the friends who have kept me sane during an impossibly difficult time: Roli Srivastava for her notes on this novel and the kindness she has shown me over two decades; Rineeta Naik for her insights, and for always offering me a roof over my head in Delhi; Taymour Soomro for his wisdom, his sharp critiques, and all the virtual-water-cooler chats; and Kristien Potgieter for her feedback and generosity. Immense thanks to Harriet Tyce for her support. Thanks also to Avani Shah and Rory Power.

At the University of East Anglia, I am grateful to Joe Dunthorne, Andrew Cowan, and my workshop groups for their feedback on the first chapters of this novel. My thanks also to Giles Foden.

While writing **Djinn Patrol on the Purple Line,** I received early encouragement from contests for first novels in progress. My thanks to the organizers, readers, and judges of the Bridport/Peggy Chapman-Andrews Award, the Lucy Cavendish College Fiction Prize, and the Deborah Rogers Foundation Writers Award.

Thanks to Euan Thorneycroft for his support. Special thanks to those who have been there

ACKNOWLEDGMENTS

from the beginning: Alison Burns, Emma Claire Sweeney, and Emily Pedder. Thanks also to Essex libraries and the British Library.

Thanks to my family. My thanks and love to Shailesh Nair, for his stories, support, and enthusiasm.

Finally, notwithstanding what's written above, I should add that I remain solely responsible for any imperfections in this novel.

ABOUT THE AUTHOR

DEEPA ANAPPARA grew up in Kerala, southern India, and worked as a journalist in cities including Mumbai and Delhi. Her reports on the impact of poverty and religious violence on the education of children won a Developing Asia Journalism Award, an Every Human Has Rights Media Award, and a Sanskriti-Prabha Dutt Fellowship in Journalism. A portion of her debut novel, **Djinn Patrol on the Purple Line,** won the Lucy Cavendish College Fiction Prize, the Deborah Rogers Foundation Writers Award, and the Bridport/Peggy Chapman-Andrews Award. She has an MA in creative writing from the University of East Anglia, Norwich, where she is currently studying for a PhD on a CHASE doctoral fellowship.

deepa-anappara.com
Instagram: @deepa.anappara